D1246779

By Joe Schreiber

Star Wars
Star Wars: Death Troopers
Star Wars: Red Harvest

Chasing the Dead
Eat the Dark
No Doors, No Windows
Au Revoir, Crazy European Chick
Perry's Killer Playlist
Lenny Cyrus, School Virus

STAR WARS®

MAUL
LOCKDOWN

STAR WARS®

MAUL.
LOCKDOWN

JOE SCHREIBER

Del Rey | New York

Published in the United States by Del Rey,
an imprint of Random House,
a division of Random House LLC,
a Penguin Random House Company, New York.

DEL REY and the HOUSE colophon are registered
trademarks of Random House LLC.

This book contains an excerpt from *Honor Among Thieves* by James S. A. Corey.
This excerpt has been set for this edition only
and may not reflect the final content of the forthcoming edition.

ISBN 978-0-345-50903-1
eBook ISBN 978-0-345-53566-5

Printed in the United States of America on acid-free paper

www.starwars.com

www.delreybooks.com

facebook.com/starwarsbooks

2 4 6 8 9 7 5 3 1

First Edition

Book design by Elizabeth A. D. Eno

To Christina. The one my heart loves.

ACKNOWLEDGMENTS

First and foremost, I'd like to extend many thanks to my editors Frank Parisi at Random House, and Jen Heddle and Leland Chee at Lucasfilm. Erich Schoeneweiss at Random House also injected the proceedings with his own inimitable enthusiasm and insight. I'm grateful to Keith Clayton, whose support goes back to the beginning. Thanks as always to my wonderful agent, Phyllis Westberg, for making it all come together.

For inspiration and support in the trenches, I would be remiss if I didn't mention my good friend Dom Benninger, who was always ready with insight and the excellently Photoshopped cover art when I needed it most (*Au Revoir, Crazy Bando Gora Chick!*). Thanks also to Michael Ludy, an old-school student of narrative structure and this bewildered storyteller's oldest friend. Vigilant readers will also find the influence of Geddy Lee, Neil Peart, and Alex Lifeson among these pages, three gentlemen whose music animates much of the action as I initially conceived it in my mind. And of course, to George Lucas, without whom all of this never would have existed in the first place.

Closer to home, it is my pleasure and honor to thank my family—my son, Jack; my daughter, Veda; and especially my wife, Christina, to whom this novel is dedicated, for their patience and love during the long road that *Maul* took over the past two years.

Finally and ultimately, to God my creator, the author of everything good and restorative in my life, I owe a debt that words alone will never be able to convey. In the end this book is a humble offering to Him, an attempt to say thank you through my work. May He guide all of us, our work and our hearts, in everything that we do.

THE STAR WARS NOVELS TIMELINE

 BEFORE THE REPUBLIC
37,000–25,000 YEARS BEFORE
STAR WARS: A New Hope

c. 25,793 *YEARS BEFORE STAR WARS: A New Hope*

Dawn of the Jedi: Into the Void

 OLD REPUBLIC
5000–67 YEARS BEFORE
STAR WARS: A New Hope

Lost Tribe of the Sith[†]
Precipice
Skyborn
Paragon
Savior
Purgatory
Sentinel

3954 *YEARS BEFORE STAR WARS: A New Hope*

The Old Republic: Revan

3650 *YEARS BEFORE STAR WARS: A New Hope*

The Old Republic: Deceived

Red Harvest

The Old Republic: Fatal Alliance

The Old Republic: Annihilation

Lost Tribe of the Sith[†]
Pantheon
Secrets

2975 *YEARS BEFORE STAR WARS: A New Hope*

Lost Tribe of the Sith[†]
Pandemonium

1032 *YEARS BEFORE STAR WARS: A New Hope*

Knight Errant

Darth Bane: Path of Destruction
Darth Bane: Rule of Two
Darth Bane: Dynasty of Evil

RISE OF THE EMPIRE
67–0 YEARS BEFORE
STAR WARS: A New Hope

67 *YEARS BEFORE STAR WARS: A New Hope*

Darth Plagueis

33 *YEARS BEFORE STAR WARS: A New Hope*

Darth Maul: Saboteur*
Cloak of Deception
Darth Maul: Shadow Hunter
Maul: Lockdown

32 *YEARS BEFORE STAR WARS: A New Hope*

STAR WARS: EPISODE I
THE PHANTOM MENACE

Rogue Planet
Outbound Flight
The Approaching Storm

22 *YEARS BEFORE STAR WARS: A New Hope*

STAR WARS: EPISODE II
ATTACK OF THE CLONES

22–19 *YEARS BEFORE STAR WARS: A New Hope*

The Clone Wars
The Clone Wars: Wild Space
The Clone Wars: No Prisoners

Clone Wars Gambit
Stealth
Siege

Republic Commando
Hard Contact
Triple Zero
True Colors
Order 66

Shatterpoint
The Cestus Deception
The Hive*
MedStar I: Battle Surgeons
MedStar II: Jedi Healer
Jedi Trial
Yoda: Dark Rendezvous
Labyrinth of Evil

*An eBook novella
† Lost Tribe of the Sith: The
   Collected Stories

THE STAR WARS NOVELS TIMELINE

The Black Fleet Crisis Trilogy
  Before the Storm
  Shield of Lies
  Tyrant's Test

The New Rebellion

The Corellian Trilogy
  Ambush at Corellia
  Assault at Selonia
  Showdown at Centerpoint

The Hand of Thrawn Duology
  Specter of the Past
  Vision of the Future

Scourge

Fool's Bargain*
Survivor's Quest

NEW JEDI ORDER
25–40 YEARS AFTER
STAR WARS: A New Hope

Boba Fett: A Practical Man*

The New Jedi Order
  Vector Prime
  Dark Tide I: Onslaught
  Dark Tide II: Ruin
  Agents of Chaos I: Hero's Trial
  Agents of Chaos II: Jedi Eclipse
  Balance Point
  Recovery*
  Edge of Victory I: Conquest
  Edge of Victory II: Rebirth
  Star by Star
  Dark Journey
  Enemy Lines I: Rebel Dream
  Enemy Lines II: Rebel Stand
  Traitor
  Destiny's Way
  Ylesia*
  Force Heretic I: Remnant
  Force Heretic II: Refugee
  Force Heretic III: Reunion
  The Final Prophecy
  The Unifying Force

35 *YEARS AFTER STAR WARS: A New Hope*

The Dark Nest Trilogy
  The Joiner King
  The Unseen Queen
  The Swarm War

LEGACY
40+ YEARS AFTER
STAR WARS: A New Hope

Legacy of the Force
  Betrayal
  Bloodlines
  Tempest
  Exile
  Sacrifice
  Inferno
  Fury
  Revelation
  Invincible

Crosscurrent
Riptide

Millennium Falcon

43 *YEARS AFTER STAR WARS: A New Hope*

Fate of the Jedi
  Outcast
  Omen
  Abyss
  Backlash
  Allies
  Vortex
  Conviction
  Ascension
  Apocalypse

X-Wing: Mercy Kill

45 *YEARS AFTER STAR WARS: A New Hope*

Crucible

*An eBook novella

DRAMATIS PERSONAE

Artagan Truax, *inmate (human male)*

Coyle, *inmate (Chadra-Fan, male)*

Dakarai Blirr, *Operations Officer (human male)*

Darth Maul, *inmate (Zabrak male)*

Darth Plagueis, *Sith Lord (Muun male)*

Darth Sidious, *Sith Lord (human male)*

Dragomir Chlorus, *Commissioner, Galactic Gaming Commission (human male)*

Eogan Truax, *inmate (human male)*

Jabba Desilijic Tiure, *crime lord (Hutt male)*

Komari Vosa, *leader, Bando Gora cult (female human)*

Sadiki Blirr, *Warden (human female)*

Strabo, *inmate, leader of Gravity Massive (Noghri male)*

Vesto Slipher, *field analyst, InterGalactic Banking Clan (Muun male)*

Vas Nailhead, *inmate, leader of Bone Kings (human male)*

Zero, *inmate (Twi'lek male)*

A long time ago in a galaxy far, far away. . . .

STAR WARS®

MAUL
LOCKDOWN

1

COG HIVE SEVEN

Wham!

The first punch came at Maul sideways, spinning his upper body around with the sheer force of the impact and driving him back a half step before he fully recovered his equilibrium. Somewhere under his feet, the alloy plates of the cell's floor seemed to shiver and quake, threatening to give way.

He spat out a tooth and wiped away the blood.

The creature in front of him was a walking trophy case of previous kills. Two and a half meters high, its massive shoulders and upper torso encased in jagged plates of primitive armor that clearly had once served as the jawbone and carapace of a much larger predator, it seemed to occupy an entire corner of the prison cell.

Maul stared at the thing. The gray slope of its face was a surgeon's nightmare of ritualistic scars, organic rings, loops, and fibrous hooks, with bluish sacks pulsating beneath its eyes, all of it siphoning down and inward toward a gaping, razor-toothed mouth. Even its arms seemed to have been plucked from two different organisms. The right hand was a blunt-knuckled fist, the left an elongated spider-fingered claw. Together they formed a mallet and blade, one made for pounding, the other for slashing. It was the right that had come careening out of nowhere just seconds before, slamming Maul backward and knocking out one of his teeth.

The thing reached down and picked up Maul's incisor from the floor of the cell. Straightening up, it shoved the tooth into an empty space in its own mouth, twisting it until it lodged in place. Then it grinned at Maul as if asking how he liked the sight of one of his teeth in its mouth—another trophy for its collection.

Maul gazed back at it.

And then the rage came.

And the rage was good.

The uniform they'd given him was a standard orange jumpsuit whose heavy fabric cut off movement in most directions. Maul heard its seams ripping as he sprang at his opponent, closing the half-meter gap between them in less than a second. The thing responded exactly as he'd hoped, lunging up eagerly to meet his advance. Its mismatched arms pinwheeled wildly before it, swinging and clawing through the stale gray air of the cell, its voice screeching at him in a guttural, choking language he'd never heard before.

Let those be your dying words, Maul thought. *Right here. Today.*

Close enough now that he could smell the corpse-stink pouring off it like rotten meat, he fell into a reflexive series of moves. Both hands shot out and grabbed the creature by its throat, hoisting it up over his head and squeezing until he felt the deep tendons of its neck beginning to give and weaken in his grip. There was a wet, muffled click from somewhere inside the thing's chest and a sudden glut of warm, thick, sticky fluid began spurting up from its throat.

Blood.

Jet black.

The sight of it gave Maul no satisfaction, only the vaguely annoying realization that it never should have taken him this long to turn the battle to his advantage. Still, ending his opponent's life quickly would restore a certain necessary balance to the encounter—if not honor, at least vindication. He tightened his grip, and the screaming sound got louder, becoming a broken, birdlike squawk. More blood leapt up, inky black and viscous, and started pouring from its mouth and eye sockets.

Enough.

Executing a perfectly balanced spin, Maul swung the creature around and slammed it to the floor with a sharp clang, connecting hard enough that he felt the steel plates reverberate under his feet. The thing's head drooped on its broken neck, lolling sideways to expose the throbbing vessels beneath its gray flesh.

Only now did Maul allow himself to exhale. As anticipated, he hadn't needed his lightsaber staff or the Force to dispatch this waste of flesh—not that either was really an option. Staring down into the thing's face, he raised his foot and planted his heel in the exposed throat, ready to pulverize the trachea, or whatever the thing used for an airway, with one decisive stomp. For an instant he met its sagging, inarticulate eyes.

Now, he instructed the thing, which seemed to be realizing that it was destined to finish out the final pathetic seconds of its life here in nameless obscurity. *Die.*

All at once, with blinding speed, the creature yanked loose and burst upright, reaching behind its back to produce what appeared to be a long bow staff. As the staff blurred toward him, Maul realized that the weapon, which he'd first taken to be a piece of wood or some kind of biomechanical hybrid, was actually a living organism—a serpent whose head lashed out at lightning velocity, latching onto his face, slashing at his eyes.

Maul recoiled, but it was too late. With a jolt, his vision was gone, burying him in instant darkness. This was the second time in as many seconds that the thing had caught him off guard, and now he knew why: the creature was somehow cut off from the Force, utterly detached from the deep field of heightened sensitivity from which he was constantly drawing information about his surroundings. The intuitive sensory abilities that he took for granted in any normal battle were simply not there.

An acidic heaviness took hold of his optic nerves like a slow drip, seeping in, sinking deep, and he realized that he could already feel the poison taking control, spreading out in concentric layers of numbness through the muscle and tissue of his face.

Now the thing's shrieking laughter was everywhere. Willful. Triumphant.

You must end this now.

Maul straightened. The voice in his head was his own, an austere evocation of his own training. But the cadence was unmistakably his Master's—an echo of pitiless instruction, hours, days, years of unyielding pain and discipline. Sidious was never far from him. The evocation of the Sith Lord's presence here snapped him back instantly into the moment with total clarity.

Reaching up through blindness, Maul took hold of the serpent, grappling with its fully extended length. Somewhere in the void he could feel the rippling leathery sinew of the staff looping around his neck, felt the hundreds of small muscles twisting and constricting over his windpipe, pinching off his airway like a living noose. The next few seconds would be crucial.

He flexed, bent his head, and jerked it forward, but the thing would not release. It kept encircling him, looping round and round, defying every attempt to take hold of it.

Maul willed himself to be absolutely still, a study in perfect rigidity, allowing the serpent, in its moment of fatal overconfidence, to draw tighter still, stretching itself until he sensed its head coming back around in front of him once more. Still he waited. Above it all he could smell his opponent's fetid stench, could feel the claws of his opponent raking his skin, twisting into his face, gouging for purchase. It shrieked at him, and this time the cry was pure victory, what might even have been laughter. Starved, insane. A warrior with nothing to lose.

You are no warrior, Maul thought. *You know nothing of the dark side.*

The moment had come. He grasped the head of the serpent-staff, seizing its blunt nose and fanged mouth. His fingers took hold of its distended upper part, twisting, wrenching, until he tore the serpent's head off its body with a moist and meaty pop.

The results were instantaneous. With a twitching galvanic shudder, the snake loosened and fell slack, the coils already beginning to slide from his neck, and Maul allowed himself a single, unobstructed breath before finishing his work here.

Somewhere in front of him, the attacker had already responded to the death of his weapon with a howl of cheated rage. Maul no longer heard it. Primal as it was, it was still only emotion, a cry of weakness no more instructive or relevant than the pain he'd willed away moments earlier. He had no more use for it now than he ever did.

He did, however, take advantage of his opponent's scream just long enough to reach into its open mouth, feeling the moist warmth of its breath on his hand as he retrieved his tooth, plucking it from the thing's gums. Holding the mouth agape, Maul crammed the serpent's severed head inside, then clamped the gray lips tight to keep the snake's head from falling out. He ripped three of the larger piercings from the thing's right arm and jammed them upward through the lips, bending them back into barbed hooks and fastening the mouth shut with the serpent's head still trapped inside. With his hands flattened against those lips, Maul could feel the head twitching around inside the mouth, sinking its fangs in reflexively, squirting out venom while his attacker jerked and spasmed and tried in vain to scream.

End it.

Still sightless, now holding his opponent at arm's length, Maul inclined his own head down. He thrust forward, driving his horns into the thing's sagging eyes, feeling them crushed to jelly against his scalp.

The spasms stopped, and Maul stepped back, releasing the body, allowing it to collapse at his feet.

He blinked and narrowed his own still-burning eyes, clutching his tooth in his hand. His vision was already starting to come back in murky shades of gunmetal gray and metallic blue. The process was infuriatingly slow, but it was happening. There was no reason not to assume that within a few hours, he would be fully recovered, and when—

The floor began to shake.

Maul whipped around, scanning the depths of his cell for the vibration's source. From all around him, a ratcheting cacophony had taken hold of the cell, the sound of massive chains being dragged through the sprockets and pulleys of some vast piece of clockwork. It filled the entire chamber, rising to a deafening roar. Everything around him had begun to shift and tilt. Maul reached out, fingertips confirming what he'd already begun to suspect.

The walls were closing in.

This was no illusion, no side effect of crippled vision. The cell itself was literally changing shape—the individual steel plates that formed the walls and floors and ceiling all overlapping and sliding together like great mechanical scales, curving inward as the slant of its floor became steeper, transforming into a kind of bowl, opening in the middle to create a funnel.

Reaching backward, Maul grabbed the handhold bolted into the bench behind him, clutching it for balance and holding on tight. All around him, the grating howl and shriek of metal got louder as a hole opened in the middle of the floor.

He furrowed his brow, squinting down into it. His vision had become clear enough now that he could make out the lifeless corpse of his former attacker, the thing in its broken and now utterly useless organic armor sliding downward toward the center of the cell. It sagged forward on a streaking smear of its own black blood, a slave to simple physics, its passage into oblivion followed in short order by the limp, decapitated body of the snake-staff.

Maul watched as warrior and staff both slipped through the hole and out of sight into a bath of darkness almost as deep as the one from which he himself had just emerged. For an instant—was it real?—he thought he saw something pale and eyeless reaching up to suck the bodies down.

The hole closed again and the floor shifted itself, smoothing out and becoming flat once more. The clanking and shaking stopped. The cell around him had resumed its previous rectilinear shape.

Somewhere in front of him, a panel of red lights blinked and went green.

He waited as the cell began to carry him upward.

2
SADIKI

Stepping inside her office, Warden Sadiki Blirr flicked her gaze up at the bank of holoscreens that ran the length of the wall like a jury of accusatory eyes. A few of the screens were dedicated surveillance feeds, displaying different areas of the prison—the mess hall, the medbay, the warren of concourses, tunnels, and catwalks that branched like spokes off the vast open gallery area where inmates milled about before and after matches.

The majority of the screens, however, represented incoming calls waiting for her, a queue of holonet conversations with bookies, bureaucrats, and the heads of various gambling combines, all no doubt in response to last night's bout.

"Good morning, Warden," the 3D-4 admin droid announced cheerily as Sadiki crossed the office. "And how are we feeling this morning?"

"Living the dream." She settled in behind the central console, where her morning coffee was already waiting. Leaning forward, she fingerprinted in the biometric code to bring up her morning schedule, watching the vivid swaths of data-wash scrolling over the tablets in front of her. "Pull up the holovid of last night's match, would you?"

"Of course," ThreeDee responded, and turned its head to the row of waiting calls. "However, as you can imagine, we already have several representatives from the casinos and the Gaming Commission who are extremely interested in—"

"They can wait."

"Perhaps I ought to remind you also of your morning meeting with—"

"Thanks for your input," Sadiki said, without glancing up. "Is the holovid ready?"

"Certainly," ThreeDee said crisply. "You wish for me to replay it from the beginning?"

"Would you mind terribly?"

"Not at all." The admin droid had been working with her for three years, and its sheer obliviousness to her sarcasm was one of its most endearing traits. It chirped and swiveled, and its dedicated holoprojector fluttered to life, already making subtle adjustments to amplitude and phase modulations to enhance the image. Behind her desk, Sadiki sat back, put her feet up, and took a sip of coffee as the entire wall of her office filled with the footage of last night's fight.

This would be the third time she'd watched it.

She made it a habit to view every match at least twice—once live, as it was happening, and then later, with a more analytical eye for the strengths and weaknesses of the individual fighters. What she'd discovered over hundreds of fights was that sometimes, upon repeated viewings, the fight itself would emerge like some third organism, something bigger than either of the combatants, a kind of composite presence knitted together of sweat, desperation, and perhaps unexpected elegance, with a personality all its own.

Last night's former champion had been a particularly monstrous species that the prison's most sophisticated recognition algorithm hadn't been able to identify. Two meters tall and crosshatched with ritualistic scars, brandishing some kind of living staff and little else, the inmate had arrived here on Cog Hive Seven six standard months earlier with a shipment of other convicts, two of whom it had already dispatched in transit. Since that time the thing had defied all attempts at classification. It had screeched and chattered a language none of them recognized, and systematically slaughtered everything pitted against it. Some of the guards thought it was female.

On the other side was the newly arrived inmate—a bald and muscular Zabrak, red-skinned, covered with black tattoos and a crown of ten vestigial horns. Even now, after repeated viewings, Sadiki couldn't take her eyes off him. In the final moments, when the challenger destroyed the serpent-staff, literally ripping off its head and feeding it to his opponent, she'd felt a dark tremor of excitement that she hadn't experienced in ages. It was, she supposed, the same primal fascination that kept the gamblers across the galaxy betting millions of credits as they gathered to watch live holofeeds of the contests.

When the fight was over, she froze the holo on the face of the new champion, his red skin and yellow eyes glaring back at her. Gazing at it, she took a thoughtful sip of her coffee.

"He took back his tooth," she said finally.

ThreeDee's head swiveled back toward her. "I beg your pardon?"

"Our new champion. Before he killed his opponent, he took back his tooth."

"Perhaps it is customary for his species to—"

"What's his name?" she asked. "The new inmate?"

"Prisoner 11240?" ThreeDee answered back. "I've already taken the liberty of uploading all relevant data onto your tablet."

Sadiki punched the numbers into the console in front of her, watching her new champion's file scroll across the screen. It read:

> Inmate 11240
> Date of Entry: 01102211224
> Name: Jagannath
> Species: Zabrak
> Gender: Male
> Height: 1.75 meters
> Mass: 80 kg
> Eyes: Yellow
> Skin: Red
> Prior Occupation: Mercenary
> Charged With: Murder

"That's it?" Sadiki stabbed the cursor down, but the screen was blank. "Where's the rest of it?"

"There is no more."

"Where did he come from? Can somebody at least tell me that?"

"He was apprehended on a routine sweep of the mining colonies on Subterrel, where local authorities identified him from an outstanding murder charge. Initial lab cultures and blood work are still pending." The droid clicked and whirred toward her, photoreceptors brightening. "So far he has eluded any more detailed classification. Would you like me to order a full psychiatric workup?"

Sadiki considered before shaking her head. "No. Not yet. For now let's see how long he lasts. He wouldn't be the first big noise to come through here and pull a quick fade."

"Of course," ThreeDee said. "If there's nothing else, I have Gaming Commissioner Chlorus for you. And Eamon Huang of the casino on Ando Prime. Whom would you like to speak to first?"

"Chlorus?" Sadiki found herself reaching up instinctively to check her reflection in the nearest screen, sweeping her fingers through her bangs. "Put him through."

"Very good."

The holovid switched over to a life-sized image of a silver-haired, distinguished-looking human in a double-faced worsted greatcoat that tapered smoothly down to his ankles. Dragomir Chlorus was at least sixty, but his olive-eyed, almost tropically tanned face appeared twenty years younger, even furrowed with the lines of impatience that he wore now.

"Commissioner," Sadiki said, raising her cup in mock salute. "You're looking dashing as always. One day you'll have to tell me your secret for never aging a day. Is it dietary?"

"Yes," Chlorus said dryly. "I've eliminated all gratuitous flattery from my diet." That famous scowl deepened, drawing deep brackets along either side of his mouth. "Now, I trust that takes care of the pleasantries between us?"

"Mm." Sadiki sipped coffee and nodded. "Apparently so."

"Good. You've kept me waiting quite long enough, Warden, and regardless of what you might have heard, the galaxy does not revolve around you."

"Sadly, no." Sadiki smiled, eyebrows raised. "But there was a time, wasn't there?"

Chlorus blinked. "I'm sure I don't know what you're talking about."

"Of course not," she said, still smiling. "Well, give me a moment to put on my penitent cap, and then you can tell me what I've done today to offend the delicate sensibilities of the Galactic Gaming Commission."

"This isn't an occasion for levity, Warden. Exactly what sort of operation are you running out there?"

Sadiki's eyebrows spiked. "My goodness, we are formal this morning." And then, folding her hands on her desk, "All right. Well, as you know, *Commissioner,* Cog Hive Seven embodies a profitable gaming industry while providing a valuable service to millions of—"

"I think we can bypass the investment propaganda. I want to know about that new inmate from last night's bout. And I want to know exactly how many credits you won when he tore his opponent apart."

"Me personally?"

"Don't play coy with me," Chlorus snapped. "You'll discover that I have neither the time nor the temperament for it."

"Oh dear. And I liked to think that I'd already discovered everything there was to know about you." Lowering her head, Sadiki flashed him her best innocent look. "I take it that your constituents weren't satisfied with the outcome of the match?"

"To say the least," Chlorus said. "And this morning you've got odds-makers and casinos from every Core planet yanking their hair out over this business. Frankly, I don't blame them. Your reigning champion, whatever that thing was, was favored by an outlandishly large advantage. He'd won six straight fights in a row. But that Zabrak beat him handily."

"He beat the odds," Sadiki said, and shrugged. "That's why they call it an upset."

"May I remind you," Chlorus said, "of how often that has happened recently in your facility?"

"Now hold on just a moment." Sadiki sat forward. "You're not implying that we enjoy an unfair advantage?"

"I never—"

"As you know, my brother and I determine the odds of every fight by a unique algorithm based on the fighting history, weight, criminal record, and all sorts of mitigating factors, the specifics of which are available to our millions of subscribers. Whether or not those individual elements add up a win, of course, is never a sure thing." She shrugged again. "Which is why it's considered gambling."

"Yet the house always wins."

"As do millions of others." She looked at him carefully. "It's a business, Commissioner."

"An insanely profitable one."

"Is that a question?"

Chlorus cleared his throat. "Since its inception," he said, "there's no question that Cog Hive Seven has enjoyed an unprecedented popularity among the gambling community—"

"Good of you to say so."

"But at this point I'd remind you to be aware of the fact that there are an increasing number of casino owners, galactic bankers, and . . ." Chlorus hesitated. "Particularly the small-time crime syndicates that control the gambling activity in the Outer Rim, all of whom have taken notice of how regularly you set the odds and then proceed to beat them."

"Which syndicates are we talking about, exactly?" Sadiki asked. "And isn't that sort of thing really outside your scope of influence?"

"You're not hearing me."

"Oh," Sadiki said, "I think I am. You're worried about the Commission saving face among its IBC cronies and upholding your personal reputation for being tough on corruption and organized crime. All of which I respect. But I hardly think you need to threaten me with fines—"

"Fines?" Chlorus leaned slightly forward, and his voice softened, becoming almost gentle. "Sadiki, I'm going to stop you right there. I know your proclivity for unorthodox behavior, but out of respect for our shared history, I want you to consider this a friendly warning." He paused, sighed like a man about to lift a particularly unwieldy weight, then gathered himself and continued. "If Cog Hive Seven is using insider information to place its own bets, then you of all people should know that the Gaming Commission is the last thing you need to worry about."

"Meaning what, exactly? I'll have a mob of Black Sun vigos showing up and throwing their weight around my prison?" She gave a throaty chuckle. "Respectfully, I'd like to see them try."

"Not necessarily Black Sun."

"Who, then?"

Chlorus cast an uneasy glance to the right, at something offscreen that she couldn't see. "I've said enough. Good-bye, Sadiki."

"Wait a second—"

But his face was gone. Chlorus had already cut off the transmission. Leaning back into her seat with a sigh, Sadiki reached for her coffee, only to find that it had gone cold.

"Lovely." She glanced around the office for her droid. "ThreeDee, can you please heat this up for me, and find out whom I'm supposed to placate next?"

"I think," a voice said from the doorway, "that should probably be me."

Sadiki glanced up at the tall, slender Muun who seemed to have materialized without warning in the office's open hatchway. She saw with a certain resigned dismay that he was dressed in signatory Palo fiduciary garb, a round-collared green tunic, formfitting trousers, and boots. The uniform told her all that she needed to know about who he was and, in all likelihood, why he'd come.

With a cool smile, she rose from behind her desk.

"I'm sorry, do we know each other?"

"Vesto Slipher," the Muun said. "InterGalactic Banking Clan. We've spoken before by holofeed, but I've never had the pleasure of a face-to-face encounter."

"Well." She allowed the smile to retract just slightly into the corners of her mouth. "Always a pleasure to host an unexpected visit from the IBC."

"Really?" Slipher's smile matched her own. "Your expression tells me otherwise."

"Oh, don't take it personally. It's been that kind of morning." Sadiki glanced at ThreeDee, then back at Slipher. "Are you on my schedule?"

"I tried to tell you—" the droid began to protest, but Slipher just smiled.

"My dear," the Muun said, with infinite civility, "I *am* your schedule."

3
HOT MESS

Maul moved across the prison mess hall like a predator recently released from its cage, passing sleekly through the mob, parting it with scarcely a glance. Some of the inmates took an uneasy step back to allow him to pass, while others simply froze in place. Heads swiveled to watch him as he went. The continuous ambient drone of voices dropped to whispers and the whispers lapsed into watchful, estimating silence as he made his way among them.

He walked to the last table and sat down.

On the other side of the table, two inmates who had been in the middle of an argument—one a pallid, frightened-looking human with a four-day stubble, the other a Gotal that appeared to be missing an eye—stopped talking, picked up their trays, and made a hasty departure.

Maul sat motionless, observing everything around him without giving any indication that he was doing so. Although his peripheral vision still hadn't fully recovered from last night's attack, he saw enough to realize that he had become the current object of everyone's attention. Even the guards up in the catwalks overhead seemed to have gone on high alert, each with one hand on their blasters, the other resting on the small flat consoles that they wore on their belts. From both inmates and guards, Maul could smell a certain unmistakable commingling of fear, desperation, and the grinding monotony of paranoia that emerged when living things were penned up together in close quarters for indefinite spans of time.

It disgusted him.

Yet, for the time being at least, it was home.

He had stepped aboard this floating sewer less than twenty-four standard hours earlier, and in that time he'd come to understand all that he needed to know about the place. The rest of his time inside, he knew, would simply be a question of patience, of accomplishing his mission here without being discovered for what he truly was.

Neither of these things would be difficult for him.

They were simply the mandates of his assignment, and as such, beyond all question.

His arrival on Cog Hive Seven had come courtesy of the only transport of the day, a nameless prison barge with a stripped-down interior that reeked of high-carbon anthracite and unwashed flesh. The cargo hold was stocked with thirty-seven other inmates whose presence Maul barely registered after gauging none of them worth a moment of his time. They were a foul-smelling, nit-infested lot comprising a dozen different species, some clearly deranged and muttering to themselves, others staring blankly through the vessel's only viewport as if something in the depthless black void might give perspective to their pointless and insubstantial lives.

Throughout it all, Maul had sat apart from his fellow inmates in absolute stillness. Some of them, apparently, couldn't wait to start fighting. As the trip wore on, boredom became restlessness, and scuffles had broken out as sidelong glances and petty grievances erupted into acts of seemingly unprovoked violence. Several hours into the journey, an overmuscled ectomorph with bulging crab-stalk eyes had leapt up and lunged at a Rodian who'd somehow managed to smuggle aboard a whip-band that he'd sharpened and apparently planned to use as a makeshift vibroblade. The fight hadn't lasted long, and only when the blade-bearer had accidentally bumped into him had Maul glanced up long enough to drive an elbow upward and shatter the Rodian's lower spine. The guards onboard hadn't even blinked as the Rodian pitched over sideways, wailing and paralyzed, to the deck, where he lay whimpering for the duration of the trip, gazing up through moist and pleading eyes.

It was the only time during the entire trip that Maul had moved.

When they'd finally docked, a retinue of fatigued-looking corrections officers had met them in the hangar, herding them down the berthing port with static pikes and go-sticks, running the biometric scans as the new inmates shambled forward, blinking, into the unfamiliar surroundings. Maul had seen more guards at this point in processing than anywhere else aboard the space station. At the end of the line, he stood motionless as a jumpy young CO whose ID badge read *Smight* swept a wand over him, scanning for infection and hidden weapons. There was no mistaking the tremor in the man's hand as he passed the wand in front of Maul's face.

"You know why you're here, maggot?" Smight had asked, struggling to hide the quaver in his voice behind a pitiful note of bravado.

Maul had said nothing.

"Twenty-two standard hours a day," Smight told him, "you're free to roam the gallery and mess hall. Twice a day, when you hear the clarion call go off, you return to your cell for matching." The guard swallowed, the bump in his throat bulging up and down. "Any attempt to escape results in immediate termination. Failure to report back to your cell for matching will be treated as an escape attempt and will result in immediate termination. You got that?"

Maul had just stared back at him, waiting for the guard to finish his business and back away. As he'd walked away, he heard the young CO find enough courage to snarl out one final declaration.

"You'll die in here, maggot. They all do."

Medbay had come next, an hour's worth of decontamination and tox screens, neuro readouts and electroencephalograms administered by uninterested droids. After a long round of ultrasonic full-body scans, a refurbished GH-7 surgical unit had inserted a long syringe into Maul's chest and then withdrawn it, only to plunge it back in again at a slightly different angle. A final scan had confirmed whatever the droid had done to him, and the CO at the far end of the concourse had waved him forward.

Afterward, two more officers armed with E-11 assault blasters had appeared and led him through a circuitous network of increasingly narrow concourses. The final walkway had led unceremoniously to his cell, a featureless, alloy-plated dome perhaps three meters in diameter. The carbon composite floor was the color of dirty slate. A single air vent whirred overhead. Stepping inside, Maul had sat hunched on the single, narrow bench, gazing at the only light source, an unremarkable panel of blinking yellow lights on the opposite wall.

"This is where you'll come for lockdown and matching," one of the guards had told him. He was a grizzled older man, a veteran whose ID badge identified him as Voystock. "You hear the clarion, wherever you are, you have five standard minutes to get back here before lockdown before you're terminated."

Maul looked at him coldly. "Terminated?"

"Yeah, I guess nobody told you." The guard nodded down at the flat gray control unit strapped to his hip. "We call this thing a dropbox. Wanna know why?"

Maul just gazed at him.

"Oh, you're a hard case, right?" Voystock snorted. "Yeah. They all start out that way. See, every inmate that comes through medbay gets a subatomic electrostatic detonator implanted in the walls of his heart. *Both* your hearts, since apparently you've got two of 'em. What that means is, I type in your prison number here, 11240"—he ran his fingers over the dropbox's keypad—"those charges go off. And that's when you drop. Permanently."

Maul said nothing.

"But hey," Voystock said with a crooked grin, "a tough guy like you shouldn't have any problems here." He reached up and patted Maul's cheek. "Have yourself a nice day, right?"

They left the hatch open behind them, but Maul had stayed in his cell, crouched motionless, allowing his new surroundings to creep in around him in the slow accretion of physical detail.

There were words scratched on the walls, graffiti in a dozen different languages, the usual cries of weakness—pleas for help, forgiveness, recognition, a quick death. The bench was equipped with handgrips, their surface worn smooth by hundreds of palms, as if the inmates who'd occupied this cell before him had all needed something to hold on to. Maul had dismissed this detail as irrelevant.

Until the clarion had sounded.

Then he had sat up, snapped into total alertness, as the panel of yellow lights in front of him stopped blinking and turned solid red. The signal keened for five minutes. From outside, Maul had heard voices along with the frantic scuffle and clang of footsteps on floorboards as inmates hurried back to their cells. As the alarms cut off, he heard the sounds of cells around him sealing shut.

The walls had started shaking. Complicated scraping noises came from somewhere deep inside the prison's infrastructure itself, gnashing together in complicated arrangements of pneumatics. Reconfiguration. Maul looked down. The floor beneath him had already begun to bow downward into a bowl shape as the dome became a perfect sphere.

And the cell had begun to turn.

Only then had the well-worn handgrips on the bench made sense. He'd taken hold of them for support, hanging on as his cell rotated completely upside down and backward again, then barrel-rolled sideways like a flight simulator with a broken oscillation throttle. Throughout it all, the metallic clacking and clanging continued as the various plates of his cell reshaped themselves around him.

When the rotation stopped, a recessed hatchway had hissed open into what appeared to be another empty cell, thick with shadow and little else. At first Maul had simply stood gazing into it. Then he'd taken a step inside. By the time he'd picked up the presence of another life-form behind him—the warrior with mismatched arms and the weird, living staff—the first blow had already come.

And now.

Sitting in the midst of the mess hall, feeling the eyes of the other prisoners upon him, sensing the slow accumulation of tension gathering around him like an electrically charged flow of ionized particles, Maul realized that the inmates of Cog Hive Seven, both individually and collectively, were already planning his demise.

Let them. It will only make your task easier.

From everything he'd gleaned so far, the prison was an open sewer, its circular layout fostering an illusory sense of false-bottomed freedom among the incarcerated. In actuality, the prisoners' ability to roam unimpeded between fights only heightened the steadily percolating sense of animosity among them, the willingness to rip one another to pieces at the slightest provocation.

Maul allowed his thoughts to cycle back to the electrostatic detonators that the droid had implanted in the chambers of both his hearts, tiny seeds of death that the population of Cog Hive Seven carried around with them every day. In the end, for all of these pathetic creatures, freedom was nothing but the promise of oblivion. No matter what they'd done to land themselves here—whatever they were running from or dreamed of or hoped to achieve—those detonators, mere microns in diameter, represented the totality of their lives, and the ease with which they could be taken away.

You are to locate Iram Radique, Sidious had told him back on Coruscant during their final moments together. And then, perhaps sensing the physical reaction that Maul himself had not quite been able to suppress, the Sith Lord had added, *It will not be as easy as it sounds.*

According to Sidious, Radique was a highly reclusive arms dealer, legendary throughout the galaxy, a ghost whose base of operations was located somewhere within Cog Hive Seven, although no one, even Sidious himself, could confirm this fact.

Radique's true identity was a closely guarded secret. As an alleged inmate in the prison, he operated exclusively behind a constantly shifting palimpsest of middlemen and fronts, guards and inmates and corrupt officials, both inside and outside its shifting walls. Those who served him, directly or indirectly, might not know whom they were working for, or if they did, they could never have identified his face.

You will not leave Cog Hive Seven, Sidious told him, *until you have identified Radique and met with him face-to-face to facilitate the business at hand. Is that understood?*

It was. Maul looked around the mess hall again at the hundreds of inmates who were now staring at him openly. At the next table, two human prisoners—they appeared to be father and son—were sitting close together, as if for mutual protection. The older one, a powerfully built, scarred-looking veteran of a thousand battles, was holding a piece of string with knots tied at carefully measured intervals, while the younger one looked on in mute fascination.

Three tables down, a group of inmates hunched over their trays, groping with utensils. When one of them lifted his head, Maul realized that the man's eyes were missing—as if they'd been gouged out of his skull. Had that happened in one of the matches? The man's hand found his fork and he began, tentatively, to scoop food into his mouth.

Across the room, another inmate, a Twi'lek, was glaring directly at Maul. Beside him, a Weequay with a sunbaked face like a desert cliff and a half dozen topknot braids stood expressionless. Watchful. Any of them could have been Radique, Maul thought, or none of them.

Maul scanned the rest of the mess hall, absorbing all of it in a single sweeping glance. There were a hundred alliances here, he sensed, gangs and crews and whole webs of social order whose complexity would require his close attention if he was going to find his way among them to complete the mission for which he'd been dispatched. And time was not something he had in unlimited quantities.

It was time to get to work.

Picking up his tray, he dumped the remains of his meal in the nearest waste bin and cut diagonally across the mess hall. There were groups of inmates clustered around the exit, and he turned left, following the wall to a hatchway in the corner, from which the smell of cheap prison food came wafting out, mixed with the stench of cleaning solution.

Exactly what he was looking for.

He slipped inside.

4

COYLE

The prison's kitchen was like every kitchen Maul had ever been in, frantic and noisy and breathless, clamoring with enough inmates and service droids that he could slip among them without attracting much notice. Every surface was cluttered with bulk food and utensils—massive blocks of half-thawed bantha patties dripped from the counter; enormous pots boiled on the stove. The sticky air reeked of cheap synthetic protein, gravy, and starch, all of it billowing in the steam of the massive industrial-sized dishwasher bolted to the floor in the corner, where endless rows of trays juddered through the scalding spray on an automated belt.

Maul approached the dishwasher, studied it for a moment, and then picked up a large, unused pressure cooker from the cabinet behind him. Next to it, he found a bottle of ammonia-based cleaning solution and silica bicarbonate, poured them in together, and sealed the pressure cooker, placing it onto the conveyer belt among the trays and sending the whole thing directly into the four-hundred-degree heat of the machine.

"Hey, buddy," one of the inmates said. "What's your business here?"

"Trouble." Maul turned around and stared at him. "You want some?"

The inmate went pale so quickly that his face almost seemed to disappear. "Hey, you're right," he said, hands raised, voice shaking. "I didn't see anything."

Maul waited as the inmate back away, then turned and walked out. Reentering the mess hall, he leaned against the wall and waited.

Ten seconds later, a loud metallic bang erupted from inside the kitchen, followed by shouts of surprise.

The noise had an immediate effect on the mess hall. Maul watched as two gangs of inmates jumped instinctively together in response to the sound, gathering on either side. In the middle of the room, the older human fighter he'd noticed earlier swung out one hand in a protective gesture around the boy. Three inmates sprang forward, seemingly out of nowhere, placing themselves in protective stances around the Twi'lek inmate whom Maul had seen studying him earlier.

In the midst of everything, only one inmate—a diminutive Chadra-Fan, his growth so stunted that he scarcely stood three feet tall—never even looked up. Throughout it all, he continued happily eating his lunch, picking out the small bones, humming to himself as if nothing had happened.

As order returned to the mess hall, Maul walked over to him and sat down directly across from him.

"Hello, brother." The Chadra-Fan glanced up, grinning, his large front incisors fully exposed, rodent-like ears twitching as his flat, slightly upturned nose wiggled as if trying to catch a better whiff of Maul. Or perhaps he was still sniffing his breakfast, the putty-colored block of gelatinous synthetic protein clutched in his free hand. Reaching into it, he pulled out a small, thin bone and held it up appreciatively. "The greatest treasures are found in the unlikeliest of places, don't you think?"

"Who are you?" Maul asked.

The Chadra-Fan responded with a humble nod. "Coyle's the name. But I'm just a microbe here, a nobody among nobodies, aren't I? You don't want to waste your time with me, brother."

Maul leaned forward to speak into his ear. "You're the only one who didn't jump when that explosion went off," he said. "Why?"

Coyle smiled shyly. "Noticed you slipping into the kitchen, didn't I? Already stirring the pot a little? Did you get the information that you were looking for?"

"Who's the Twi'lek?" Maul asked. "The one those other inmates moved in to protect?"

The Chadra-Fan ignored the question, sizing Maul up from across the table. "Big one, aren't you? A lot bigger than you looked on that holovid." He crammed the remains of his meal into his mouth, chewed for a moment, and then stopped, fishing out another bone and placing it on the growing collection in the corner of his tray.

"I'm looking for someone," Maul said.

"Aren't we all?" Coyle asked pleasantly enough, brushing the last of the crumbs from his whiskers. "Quite a brawl last night, wasn't it? Offed that ugly tosser in less than five standard minutes, didn't you? Brother needs some wicked fierce skills to fight like that, doesn't he, then? And we asks ourselves, who trains the wrecker to do his wrecking?"

"I'm looking for Iram Radique."

"Radique, then, is it?" Coyle narrowed his eyes and scratched the tuft of hair between his ears. "Nope, can't say I know that name, do I? Never heard of him, not around here, not likely, no sir."

Maul shifted his gaze across the mess hall to the two gangs that had come together when the explosion had gone off in the kitchen. In the ensuing moments they'd loosened up and spread out again slightly, but the social fabric was still clear enough. One crew had gathered in the far right corner, near the place where inmates had come spilling into the hall from the cafeteria line, maybe two dozen in all. This group was all human, their heads shaved, their ears and noses pierced with what looked like bits of bone. Maul could tell just from the way they were standing that they were holding something hidden in their uniforms, inside their sleeves, tucked up into their tunics. Something sharp and secret.

Across the room, a second group stood, a human and nonhuman mix with a vicious-looking Noghri positioned in front of them, clearly their leader. They'd all cut the right sleeves off their uniforms to expose a series of matching tattoos that spiraled from wrist to shoulder. At first glance they were a more random, ragtag group, and it made them look primitive and dangerous. Their gaze shifted from Maul to the other group and back to Maul again.

"What about them?" Maul asked.

"The two crews? Bone Kings and the Gravity Massive. Vas Nailhead runs the Kings"—he nodded at an enormous, thickly bearded human with sharpened incisors—"and the Gravity Massive answers to Strabo over there." He switched his attention to a hairless, gray-skinned Noghri on the opposite side, accompanied by an attentive Nelvaanian sidekick. "Me personally, I wouldn't go messing with none of them, brother. Don't know much besides killing, do they? And even that's a stretch for most of them, isn't it?"

"And the Twi'lek," Maul said. "What's his name?"

"Twi'lek?" Coyle blinked. "Got no name, doesn't he? Not one I've heard. We just call him Zero, doesn't we?"

"Zero?"

"As in Inmate Zero, on account of he's been here from the beginning."

"Why is he protected?"

Coyle gave him a shrug. "Zero's always been the one who can get things."

"What things?"

"He's the one with three I's."

Maul frowned. "Three eyes?"

"Items. Influence. Information." Another shrug from the Chadra-Fan, who was back to sorting through his collection of small bones. "Always been that way, hasn't it? Least since I've been here."

Maul turned to direct his stare at the place the Twi'lek had been standing when the explosion had gone off in the kitchen. Now he was gone, as if he'd simply vanished amid the rest of genpop.

"If I wanted to find him again, where would I look?"

"Who, Zero?" The Chadra-Fan considered. "Oh, I suppose he's been known to visit Ventilation Conduit 11-AZR, is maybe one place he's been known to entertain visitors, from time to time. Of course that's just hearsay, isn't it? Nothing guaranteed, is there?"

"Conduit 11-AZR," Maul repeated.

"That's right, but—"

Maul had already turned to walk away.

5
KNOCKOUT MOUSE

"That's him," Eogan whispered. "He's the one, isn't he?"

The man leaning against the wall next to him with his hands in his pockets didn't have to look up to know whom his son was referring to. Even if the boy hadn't been talking about the new champion all morning, ignoring his breakfast and then loitering shamelessly around the gallery in hopes of catching a glimpse of the red-skinned newcomer, it would have been obvious.

Upon reflection, it struck Artagan Truax that from the moment they'd come to Cog Hive Seven, his sixteen-year-old son's day-to-day existence here had always been focused on the prison's current champion, either fearing the day that he'd have to fight him or idolizing him from afar. Or perhaps both.

"Yes, that is the one," Artagan said, still not raising his eyes as the new inmate strode past them, twenty meters away. "As you well know."

"I hear he answers to Jagannath," Eogan said. "A mercenary and hired killer wanted in a dozen different systems. They say it means—"

"The Tooth," the man said with a nod, bemused at the boy's enthusiasm. "Yes, I have heard that as well."

"Do you think . . ." The question trailed off as Eogan struggled to phrase it in some way that sounded off-hand. "I mean, just supposing, if I had to—if it came down to it in a match, if I kept up my training . . . you think I could ever . . . ?"

Artagan didn't respond right away. He had never enjoyed withholding the truth from his son, and before the two of them had come here, he'd sworn an oath to always be absolutely honest with him—he owed the boy that much. After dragging Eogan from one end of the galaxy to the other, making him stand at the edge of the crowd watching as Artagan took punch after punch, night after night, in an endless series of pit fights and loading-bay brawls, the truth was the least he could offer.

Yet again, today, he found himself incapable of speaking it.

We fail ourselves again and again, he thought. *Every day—it's what we do.*

"You're almost ready," he said, reaching out to toss the boy's fine reddish brown hair. "Another month or two of training—heavy training, mind you, with no backing down when it becomes difficult—ought to do the trick."

Eogan's face lit up, and he turned to his father, hope shimmering in those pale green eyes. "Really?"

"No doubt in my mind," Artagan said, putting on what he hoped was a reassuring smile. Unable to sustain the artifice any longer, he turned his attention back to the throng of inmates all around them. "Go down and wait for me in the metal shop. You'll chase rats today."

"Yes, sir." Eogan smiled. "I'll meet you there." He turned and walked away, edging through the crowds of prisoners.

Artagan watched him go, the smile fading from his face.

No doubt in my mind, he'd said.

But there *were* doubts.

All kinds of them.

It had been almost a year since they'd first arrived here, father and son, scooped up alongside a handful of counterfeiters and low-level street enforcers and plunged unceremoniously into Cog Hive Seven's festering soup of sociopaths, killers, and thugs. But regardless of what the boy thought, it had not been an accident.

Such was the deal that Artagan Truax had made with the shadowy hand of the galaxy.

Since his arrival here, he had been matched a total of five times. He had triumphed in the first three of those matches, providing speedy, deliberate kills. Still strong and fast, with reflexes honed over three decades of fighting, he'd dispatched his opponents quickly, and even enjoyed a brief moment of celebrity among the population.

The fourth match, however—against a Kaleesh whose tusks were sharpened to surgical points—had not gone as well. Those tusks had gouged into his chest wall, puncturing his lung. Artagan had managed to snap one of them off and use it against the Kaleesh in a stroke of good luck. Once again he'd emerged battered but victorious.

And the fifth match—

The fifth match had nearly killed him.

He'd been pitted against a Klatooinian, and he'd known right away that he was in trouble. Two minutes in, the thing had smashed him in the temple so hard that Artagan had almost lost consciousness. The pain was worse than anything he'd ever experienced, and amid it all the beckoning promise of unconsciousness had been so seductive that Artagan had actually *wanted* to leap down into it, if only for a brief reprieve. Only the notion of leaving Eogan alone here, unprotected amid a sea of predators, had kept him from blacking out completely. Rallying, he had managed—barely—to hold on long enough to twist the Klatooinian's battle-axe away and bury the blade in his opponent's skull.

He had not been matched again.

But the damage was done. The Klatooinian's blow to his skull had capped off a career of closed-head injuries and concussions, and ever since then, Artagan suffered chronic migraines, nausea, and night sweats. His vision, once his greatest asset, so keen and clear that he'd been able to see an ambush reflected in his opponent's pupils, had gone foggy around the edges; sometimes he awoke to dazzling halos of opalescent light, auras that he'd come to associate with the onset of excruciating pain. He'd developed a slight tremor, and once, two months ago, he'd had a seizure, thankfully after Eogan had already fallen asleep. When the boy had rolled over in his bunk and muttered sleepily to his father, Artagan had assured him it was only a dream. After that he'd

smuggled a spoon out of the mess hall and slept with it clamped between his teeth, just in case it happened again, to keep him from biting
his tongue.

These days, whenever he was out among genpop, he kept his hands
tucked in the pockets of his prison uniform to hide the way they trembled. He hid that from the boy as well—although how successfully, he
didn't know. All the strength and poise and confidence that he'd brought
to the ring were gone. Some mornings he could barely see straight, let
alone fight. In his fifty-fifth year of life he'd become what the other inmates referred to as a knockout mouse, a former champion who'd hit
the ceiling of his abilities and was waiting for the inevitable final bout.

The one that would kill him.

"Heard you were looking for me."

Artagan half turned, hands still tucked in the front pockets of his
prison tunic, and saw the grizzled old guard, Voystock, standing just
behind the semiopaque mesh of wire and transparisteel, blaster in hand.
How long the CO had been standing there, Artagan didn't know. He
hadn't heard him approach over the noise of the gallery.

Leaning backward, careful to keep his eyes on the crowds of inmates
passing in front of him and not to move his lips, Artagan spoke just loud
enough to be heard. "Appreciate you coming."

"Skip it," Voystock said. "You got something for me or not?"

Artagan's right hand came out of his pocket to reveal a finger-thin
stretch of polymer filament string, carefully coiled. He slipped it through
the mesh, into the guard's waiting palm. Voystock took the string, shook
it out and stretched it out in front of him, scowling at it.

"What the kark is this?"

"The item that we spoke of earlier."

"You promised me thirty thousand credits," Voystock sneered. "Told
me you had an offworld private bank account with an untapped
balance—"

"Officer, look at what I gave you. What do you see?"

"A piece of string," Voystock said. "A lousy stretch of thread you pulled off your shirt cuff. And another maggot trying to weasel his way out of getting matched." He tossed the filament to the permacrete floor beneath his boots and was already turning around to disappear back to wherever he'd come from. "You waste my time like this again and you aren't gonna have to wait for your next bout to get your ticket punched. You understand what I'm telling you, you worthless puke?"

"Wait," Artagan said. His head was starting to ache in that old familiar place behind his left eye. "Just look at it. Please."

Something of the desperation in his voice must have given the guard pause, because Voystock stopped, leaning down to pick up the filament again and holding it up for a better look. The glow of recessed lighting shimmered off the array of tiny knots tied throughout the filament, whole clusters of them, none any bigger than the glint of light reflected in the guard's suspicious gaze.

When Artagan spoke again, his voice was quiet and patient.

"There are over six billion different knots in the galaxy, Officer Voystock. Each one reads like a specific deformation of a circle in three-dimensional space, as unique as individual letters in an alphabet."

Voystock grunted. "Is that supposed to mean anything me?"

"What you're holding in your hand is called a *khipu*," Artagan said, "also known as a talking knot. Any droid with the most basic analytical drive will be able to unravel each knot's linking integral. It shouldn't take more than thirty seconds. You'll end up with a twenty-one-digit number."

"What, like a code?"

Artagan nodded. "The first twelve digits of this *khipu* make up the ID reference for the orbital account off Muunilinst with a balance of thirty thousand credits. The last nine are the password to access all those funds." He flicked his eyes up at Voystock. "See for yourself."

"Knots." The guard snorted, but he slipped the filament into his own pocket. "You're as crazy as a mutant womp rat, old man, you know that?"

Artagan smiled thinly. "You wouldn't be the first to make that observation."

"Say you are telling the truth," Voystock said. "You want to tell me how a washed-up chunk of mynock dung like you gets his meat hooks on that kind of cash?"

"Winnings," Artagan said. "Saved up from fifteen years of fights."

"There's no way you could make that much in pit fights."

"I was saving for my retirement." Artagan cocked a bushy eyebrow at the gallery and its inhabitants. "I never thought I'd be spending it here."

"Retirement, huh?" This time Voystock actually chuckled. "You got a funny way of looking at things, old man, you know that?"

"Perhaps we both do."

"How do you figure?"

"We both spend our days walking around this floating slice of hell," Artagan said. "Just on different sides of the wire, that's all."

Voystock glared at him narrowly.

"Yeah, well, one big difference between us is, I'm not walking around with a bomb inside my heart," he said, reaching down to the flat-pack dropbox on his belt. "Six digits, and down you go permanently. Maybe you could use a reminder of that."

"Wait." Artagan looked at him, eyebrows raised. "If I've done something to offend you . . ."

"You know I don't even have to justify this to the warden?" A narrow, almost cunning look stole over Voystock's face, something that couldn't really be called a smile. "All I have to say is that the prisoner posed a threat. No board of inquiry, no paperwork. Shoot, I don't even have to report it. That's how disposable you are." He leaned in. "Where's your kid?"

"Now just wait a moment." A sudden bolt of panic shot across Artagan's face. "What are you doing?"

"Just a little demonstration." Voystock reached down to his dropbox and tapped a series of digits onto the console. "Your boy is Inmate 11033, right?"

"Please, don't—"

Voystock shrugged. "Too late."

He hit enter.

Artagan didn't move. Two meters off to his right, a Vulptereen inmate who'd been leaning with his back to the wall went suddenly rigid, and then his tusked face went abruptly slack. Knees buckling, he slid down against the wall and crumpled to a heap on the floor of the gallery.

For a moment, the other prisoners in the area gave the Vulptereen a sidelong glance, then went along with their business as a clanking, balky class-five Treadwell droid rolled over, hooked its manipulators to the corpse's ankles, and began to drag it away.

"Whoops." Voystock shrugged. "Must have typed the numbers in wrong." He flicked his eyes up at Artagan. "Next time I'll make sure I get 'em right." The CO returned his attention to the *khipu,* running his fingers over the cryptic arrangement of the knots. "This better be legit."

"It is." Artagan's skull was pounding so hard that his eyeballs felt like they were going to squeeze right out of their sockets, and more than anything he yearned for the silence and darkness of a quiet corner in his cell. But the canny part of him realized that any indication of weakness might ruin the faint flicker of trust between himself and the guard.

"If you're yanking me on this," Voystock said, "it's not going to end pretty for you or your boy. You see that now, don't you?"

Artagan just nodded. "Just take it."

The CO's eyes narrowed. "And in return, what? You want me to make sure you don't get matched again? Protect that youngling of yours?" He shook his head. "Word is you've been training him hard on your own, trying to teach him the Fifty-Two Fists, get him ready for his first match. You think he actually stands a chance in there?"

Artagan drew in a slow breath through his teeth. Releasing it seemed to cost him something deep and heartfelt that he would have preferred to keep to himself indefinitely.

"No," he admitted in a voice barely above a whisper. "The boy's not a fighter—a blind man could see that. He's fast enough, I suppose, and he's growing stronger every day . . . but he's no killer, and that's not something you can teach." It hurt to say these things out loud, all the terrible certainties that he'd mulled over in private, night after sleepless night, but it was also a relief to give them voice and hear them spoken aloud. "And I know there's nothing you can do to keep either of us from being matched again. That's well outside your scope of influence."

"So what then?" Voystock glared at him, visibly annoyed. "You can't honestly tell me that you're just handing over your life savings to me for no reason."

Artagan shook his head. "Not at all."

"Then what do you want?"

"I want something much bigger," Artagan said. "I want you to help us escape."

6

THE WHOLE THING RUNS ON BLOOD

Twenty minutes later Sadiki and Vesto Slipher were taking the turbolift down through the levels of Cog Hive Seven, the Muun standing quietly on his side of the lift with his hands folded together and the same slight, inscrutable smirk on his lips. Seeing it now, Sadiki found that she didn't like that smirk any more than she had twenty minutes earlier.

"Our loan payments are up to date," she told the Muun. "I really don't see why the IBC should have any reason to investigate our operations here."

"*Investigate* is perhaps too piquant a word," Slipher said, gazing placidly at the lift's readout. "You may consider this a routine audit, if you prefer."

"And is it standard protocol to dispatch top-level executives on routine audits?"

"Mm." The Muun beamed at her as if conceding some minor point. "I see. In fact, to be perfectly frank, Warden, Cog Hive Seven *is* something of a unique case in the IBC's Outer Rim portfolio. Of course, there's no question of your profitability or the ongoing security of our investment here."

"So if we're all so in love with each other," Sadiki asked, "why the sudden interest in our operation?"

"Oh," the Muun said, "I assure you, there's nothing new about our interest in Cog Hive Seven, Warden." The lift began to slow down. "If anything, the IBC has always been highly sensitive to the unique par-

ticulars of your rather spectacular success out here in the middle of nowhere." The smile returned, as pleasant as ever. "After all, what you're
doing here is another form of gambling. Yet unlike the casinos, podracing courses, and sabacc parlors that the IBC bankrolls, your operation
never seems to have a bad fiscal quarter—not once. To be perfectly
frank, we've begun wondering how you've managed a profit margin on
such a sustainable basis."

"You make that sound like it's a bad thing."

"Of course not." Something sharpened in the Muun's gaze. "But
wouldn't you agree that if something seems to good to be true, it probably is?"

"Too good to be true?" Sadiki cocked an eyebrow. "Well, in that
case, take a look."

The lift had stopped completely. As the doors opened, she gestured
for him to step out onto the open scaffolding and couldn't help feeling
a twinge of amusement as Slipher's eyes widened slightly, losing their
veneer of detachment.

Below them, a herd of inmates burst into the gallery, snarling and
jeering, shoving one another aside, feet clanging on the steel gallery
floor as they formed an open circle. In the middle of the circle, someone
was screaming.

"Ah," Sadiki said, "the morning festivities have already begun."

Directly underneath them, thirty yards down, three inmates, all of
them human, with shaved heads and thick beards, were holding a fourth
prisoner and beating him savagely with what looked like long shafts of
sharpened bone. When the victim fell to his knees, one of his assailants
hoisted him back up again while another plunged the sharpened bone
spear directly into his chest, shoving it through so far that it burst out
between the inmate's shoulder blades in a spray of blood and shattered
vertebrae.

"Oh," the Muun said thickly. "What . . . ?"

"Bone Kings," Sadiki said. "Along with the Gravity Massive, they're
one of the biggest gangs in the Hive." She shrugged. "Every so often,
tensions boil over."

The Muun considered this for a moment. "How can there be any allegiance within the gangs when one member might be matched against another at any given moment?"

"We screen for that," Sadiki said. "The algorithm factors in sociological variants as well as physical ones. Actually, we've discussed the idea of pitting entire crews against one another."

"Really?"

"Oh yes. The prospect of a crew-on-crew tag team brawl, for example, between certain members of the Kings and the Gravity Massive could be something that the gambling community has never seen before. It's already generated significant interest with some of the odds-makers."

"I can see why," the Muun said. He had to raise his voice to be heard: down below the impaled prisoner was somehow shrieking louder. His gurgling cries only brought laughter from the crowd, whose response in turn seemed to encourage the three Kings to greater frenzies of violence. Howling, they yanked their weapons loose and stabbed their victim again until he collapsed, sagging forward, his broken frame dangling on the end of the makeshift spear like a twisted puppet. A great cheer went up from the mob of prisoners, and then as suddenly as it had begun, the assault was over, the other inmates drifting away, leaving the three Bone Kings to bend over the mangled corpse of their victim.

"Now what are they doing?" Slipher managed.

"Deboning."

"I . . ." The Muun swallowed audibly. "I beg your pardon?"

"They rip the bones out," Sadiki told him. "Sharpen them on the walls, carry them around in their sleeves, that sort of thing."

"And you permit that as well?"

Sadiki shrugged. "Every standard week or so the guards will search the cells and confiscate whatever they find."

"I see." The Muun nodded. "I suppose it's all great theater."

"Oh no," Sadiki said, "it's not theater at all. That's one of the reasons that gamblers can't seem to get enough of what we do here. Face it, Mr. Slipher, in a galaxy where so much has become virtual or simulated, what we offer is as real as it gets. We've actually discussed the possibility of offering VIP packages to high rollers so that they could come and watch the fights in person."

"Here? To the prison itself?"

"We've had real interest from communities as far away as Coruscant."

"Well." The Muun was nonplused. "It seems that you're just a font of brilliant ideas, Warden."

"Not just me." Sadiki nodded modestly. "Although I do like to think of this place as a crucible from which true superiority emerges, and everyone profits. The Rattataki people have a particularly memorable way of putting it: *Chee moto, mando sangui.*"

"Meaning?"

" 'The whole thing runs on blood.' "

"A provocative sentiment," the Muun said, looking down again as the three inmates turned and fled with an armload of bloody bones, leaving the shapeless, scooped-out mass on the steel floor behind them. "They're amazingly fast, aren't they?"

The Muun shuddered. Although the catwalk where they were standing was enclosed in a thick layer of protective transparisteel, the overpowering smell of spilled blood, dirty fabric, and airborne bacteria hung permanently in the space around them.

"A little bit different from the sabacc parlors on Lamaredd, isn't it?" she said.

A new possibility seemed to have occurred to Slipher. "Can any of the inmates see us up here?"

Sadiki shook her head. "Not from this angle. We have guards stationed at various posts around the upper scaffolding, and cameras down below."

"And you just allow them to wander freely like that?"

"*Free* is hardly the word," Sadiki said, and checked the chrono display on her tablet. "They're always watching each other, and we're always watching them."

"So you've never had an escape?"

She cocked an eyebrow at him. "I thought we were discussing profit margins, Mr. Slipher."

"It's a valid question. These inmates of yours have nothing to do all day but study their surroundings and isolate any vulnerabilities in your security systems."

"We've implanted every inmate with—"

"I'm aware of the procedure," the Muun said dryly. "Still, it occurs to me . . ." His voice trailed off. "Never mind."

"What?"

"Well, you've given me an admirable demonstration of why your operation here continues to generate such fervent interest among gamblers and blood sport aficionados. But that's only part of it, isn't it?"

"I'm not sure that I follow."

"Oh, I think you do." His fingers knit themselves inward, pressing against his chest in thought. "In order for Cog Hive Seven to make the astronomical profit that it reports to my board of directors, you have to predict the winner of the bouts almost one hundred percent of the time." He turned to her. "I don't suppose you'd be interested in telling the IBC how exactly you do that?"

Sadiki glanced back at the lift.

"Come with me," she said.

7

GRAVITY MASSIVE

Maul watched the mess hall clearing out.

After the other inmates left, he had remained standing against the wall, observing the guards along the upper perimeter as they went about their patrols. He marked their passage along with the servo droids that circulated in and out of the hall along with the other inmates. At first nothing seemed to have changed. In the glare of the overhead lights he watched how the guards and the droids and the inmates all interacted, how they moved among one another, observing their patterns. There were places that they moved and stood and waited, and there were gaps—openings in the gallery that led back to the cells, vacancies where no light fell.

He's been known to visit Ventilation Conduit 11-AZR.

It smelled like a setup, pure and simple. Yet it might also be the opportunity that he'd been waiting for. Remembering what Coyle had said, Maul felt a sharp wedge of tension pressing low and tight beneath his sternum—a sense of urgency to go forward and assert himself among those who would try to cut him down, to betray him and undermine his mission here. It was what his Master would have wanted.

You'll go in as a criminal, Sidious had told him, *and live among those animals, within the confines of your new identity of a mercenary and assassin, relying only on your own wit and cunning—not only for the purposes of the mission, but for your very survival. You must assume that every inmate will be looking for an opportunity to stab you in the back at any moment.*

Straightening up, Maul took one more look at the mess hall until he found what he was looking for. In his mind, an idea had already begun to take shape. It was primitive, but it would work.

Off to his left, a crew of inmates that Coyle had identified as the Gravity Massive—perhaps six or seven in total, headed up by their Noghri and his Nelvaanian sidekick—had continued to loiter near the exit, all staring at him intensely. Maul stepped directly toward them. Drawing nearer, he saw all their exposed right arms beginning to tense and flex together, like the individual muscle fibers on a single organism. None of them took a step back.

"Are you Strabo?" Maul asked.

The Noghri didn't flinch. "Who's asking?"

"The Bone Kings." Maul glanced back at the other gang on the opposite side of the mess hall. "They want a meeting."

The inmate's eyes narrowed. "What?"

"That scum over there." Maul turned and shot a glance across the mess hall to where the Bone Kings were standing on their side, glaring at him more intensely than ever. "They told me to give you the message."

"What kind of meeting?"

"I don't know," Maul said, "and I don't care." He locked the Noghri in his glare, defying him to look away. "They said it's happening in Ventilation Conduit 11-AZR."

Turning, he walked away, not bothering to look back. By the time he got to the exit, an inmate from the Bone Kings crew, the bearded human that Coyle had identified as Nailhead, was blocking his way. The man was a monster in human form, scars rippling across his forehead, with a sharpened fragment of bone rammed through his nose. There was dried blood in his beard, and his teeth were crooked yellow pegs set at uneven intervals in his mouth.

"Hey, puke," he said.

Maul stared at him.

"I'm Vasco Nailhead. I run the Bone Kings." The man allowed a grin to flash across his face. "Suppose you tell me what you were saying to the Gravity Massive about us back there?"

"Ask them yourself," Maul said. He started to take a step, and the man's hand stopped him.

"I'm asking *you*." The man leaned in close enough that Maul could smell the blood in his beard. His breath reeked like an open grave. From the cuff of his shirtsleeve, something sharp and yellowish gray gleamed, just barely visible at throat level, ready to slash. "Now, I'm gonna ask again, real nice. What did you say? Was it about what we done to them this morning?"

"They want a meeting," Maul said.

"Is that right?" Nailhead licked his lips. "And just whereabouts did they say this little rendezvous was supposed to take place?"

"Ventilation Conduit 11-AZR." Maul leaned in close. "Oh, they told me one more thing."

"What's that?"

"They said get ready to bleed."

8
MUTE MATH

The turbolift opened onto absolute silence.

Stepping out, Sadiki led Vesto Slipher across the datacenter full of blinking consoles and cabinets of server racks whose sweeping ergonomic curvature filled the entire width of the viewport overlooking the prison's central docking station.

The entire room around them seemed to be holding its breath. Off to her right, Slipher opened his mouth to speak and then stopped, puzzled, when no sound came out. Sadiki tilted her chin up, indicating the crosshatched wedges of acoustical foam running perpendicular to one another, lining the walls and ceiling, absorbing every decibel of ambient noise.

The Muun nodded in understanding. For a moment they just stood there watching the young man at the console going about his work, streaming the previous night's data-flow, running diagnostics, making all the fine adjustments that constituted the fabric of his existence here.

At last Sadiki tapped a switch and the foam wedges changed angulation ever so slightly, the eerie silence draining away as the datacenter filled with the buzz and rumble of ambient sound. At once, the whole room seemed to exhale around them with an audible sigh of relief.

"Very impressive," Slipher said when his voice returned. "White noise generators, I presume?"

"Not entirely." Sadiki nodded. "There's a design component as well. The whole datacenter is an anechoic chamber."

"A soundproofed room?"

"Both inside and out," she said. "Do you know anything about tapered impedance?"

"I'm afraid it's rather outside my field."

Sadiki nodded at the walls. "Those foam wedges alternate at ninety degrees out of phase with each other. When they're properly aligned, the pyramidical absorbers simulate a continuous change in the dielectric constant." She shook her head. "It's all been designed to create what my brother calls an absolute free-field open space of infinite dimension. It literally swallows sound waves."

"Your brother . . ." The Muun glanced at the young man seated in front of the command suite. "He sounds highly intelligent."

"He is." She shuddered. "Personally, I find it all incredibly creepy."

"Ah." The Muun gave her his smirk again. "You prefer noise?"

Sadiki shrugged. "I prefer reality."

"In that, we find ourselves in agreement. Still . . ." The Muun regarded the room with new respect. "You know, for a moment I couldn't even hear my own heartbeat."

"I've never quite gotten used to it. Of course, I'm not the reason it's been installed here." Walking over to the young man in the gray tunic, Sadiki leaned down to brush her lips against his cheek. "Sleep all right?"

He turned and glanced up at her, an abstracted, childlike smile rising over his face, this silent twin, her own personal ghost, as if she'd only just now wakened him from a pleasant dream. Knowing that the smile wasn't for her didn't make it any less endearing; Sadiki understood that her brother's first and truest gratification in life had always come from his algorithm.

"May I introduce my brother Dakarai," Sadiki said. "Dakarai, this is Vesto Slipher from the IBC. He's come to check up on us and make sure we're not dipping into the till."

"Oh, now, really," Slipher said, "I'd hardly phrase it that way." He ventured nearer, approaching the cabinets of data storage and processing units. "So this is the famous Dakarai Blirr. I have heard so much about you, from many trusted sources." He extended his hand. "The pleasure's all mine."

Dakarai just gazed at the hand, his expression inscrutable, then turned instead and reached for the white ceramic coffee cup with the stylized CH7 logo emblazoned on the side.

"You'll have to excuse my brother." Sadiki watched as he lifted the cup with both hands like a child, bringing it up to his lips. "He hasn't spoken aloud to anyone in ten years."

"Really?" the Muun asked. "Not even you?"

"Not a word, I'm afraid," Sadiki said, gazing down at her brother with what might have been a hint of melancholy—real or artificial, even she wasn't sure. "At this point I don't think I would even recognize the sound of his voice."

Dakarai looked back up at her. Above the rim of the coffee cup, his programmer's eyes shimmered, pale blue and slightly watery, lit from deep within. In the ambient monitor glow Sadiki sometimes thought their irises appeared almost liquid-crystal gray, like beads of condensation, deeply set in the smooth, pale face whose high forehead and patrician nose were so strikingly an evocation of her own. Like her, he wore his jet-black hair just slightly shaggy, the chopped bangs tumbling over the brow in an errant simulation of serrated recklessness.

"Not a word in ten years," the Muun reflected, looking back at Dakarai as if seeing him in an entirely different light. "Is it a vow of some sort?"

"Nothing so monastic, I don't think," Sadiki said, running her fingers fondly through her brother's hair. "Dakarai's a connoisseur of soundlessness. The last time we spoke, he told me that he found the silence of the algorithmic certainty to be the closest thing to pure joy that he ever heard. Everything else, including his own voice, is just a distraction."

"I see."

"Math is music, he told me once, and it's perfect, so why should we think that we can somehow improve on it with our grunts and howls?"

"Math is music," the Muun reflected, visibly pleased with the phrase. "Again we find ourselves uncannily like-minded. And speaking of mathematics . . ." He turned back to the consoles. "I assume that this is where you run the software? The systems that arrange all the fights, correct?"

"That's right," Sadiki said. "Dakarai wrote all the code himself. After he finished upgrading the Ando Overland Podracing course for the Desilijic Clan five years ago, he got the idea to create a completely new piece of software—" Seeing Dakarai wince at her choice of words, she corrected herself. "Excuse me, an *algorithm,* that could analyze all the data from every potential contestant in a closed gladiatorial environment to create the closest and most exciting competitions in the history of galactic pit fighting."

"So," the Muun said, leaning in, "from this suite you can monitor—"

"Every aspect of every inmate's behavior," she said, "yes, that's correct. Everything from weight gain to heart rate to the constantly changing alliances among prisoners and gang allegiances that might factor into the outcome of a bout. The algorithm analyzes all of it and generates two sets of inmate numbers for two matches, every day."

"Two?"

"We're considering adding a third." Sadiki's eyes flicked back to the monitor screens again, scanning them more carefully. "Anything new to report?"

Dakarai paused, steepled his fingertips on either side of the bridge of his nose, and shook his head. Frowning a little, he tapped in another series of commands, waiting while the data washed up over the screen, and then squinted at what he saw there.

"What is it?" she asked him.

When Dakarai's frown didn't change, Vesto Slipher leaned in, glancing at one of the monitor screens on the far right of the console, where a Zabrak inmate with an array of horns on his head was moving away from the crowd in the gallery, cutting down one of the concourses into the shadows.

"If I'm not mistaken," the Muun said, "that's your new champion, is it not?"

"He did win last night, yes."

"Quite spectacularly, if I recall." Slipher turned to Sadiki. "Where is he going?"

"Wherever it is," Sadiki said, checking her chrono, and the most recent data that had just come streaming across Dakarai's inflow monitor, "he won't be there long."

"Why not?"

She cast him a wry half grin. "You're about to find out."

9

STRAPHANGER

Cutting sideways along the well-lit expanse of the prison's central gallery, Maul glanced up at the ventilation shafts that ran overhead, each one stenciled with call signs and architectural designations. A series of worn letters were faintly visible overhead: *VC 09-AMA*.

He kept walking, fingertips tracing the beads of condensation from the walls, feeling it growing colder to the touch. The ceiling was sloping downward, the walls closing in as he made his way forward. Air filtration systems, atmospheric reprocessing units with fans the size of starship turbines, roared out their incessant threnody overhead, but the noise wasn't enough to block out the sound of the prison's gallery behind him. In between slabs of machinery, black lenses gleamed, following his every step. When the walkway ended in a T, he turned right, passed by the first corridor, and checked the shaft above him: *VC 11-AAR*.

Closer, then.

The big fans had gone quieter, and now Maul could hear his own footsteps echoing down the passageway. He stopped and sniffed the air, smelling stale water and engine lubricant. The cameras would still be watching him here, of course. That didn't matter. If the prison administrative staff wanted to stop him, they could have shut down the concourse in front of him at any time.

He moved on, checking the ventilation markings every few meters now. When he reached 11-AZR, the walkway intersected with another passage. Maul stopped, turned right, and took three steps until he came across a series of curved steel rungs bolted into the wall, leading up to a maintenance hatch.

He froze.

Behind him, in the direction from which he'd come, something was coming, making a steady pounding noise. Maul held his breath and listened.

It sounded like wings.

Glancing up, he saw it coming, a black shape flying straight at him down the passageway. He ducked just in time, and it brushed past his face close enough that he felt the oily, musky-smelling slickness of its black feathers against his cheek. Pivoting in midair, the thing flapped its wings, settling itself on an electrical conduit, staring down at him with black, incurious eyes.

Maul looked up at it.

It was a clawbird, almost a half meter high, small for its breed. Maul had seen holos of them hunting womp rats on Wayland, with claws like vibroblades and a serrated beak that could rip through flesh like butter. But what was a mutated avian species from an Outer Rim planet doing in a prison?

Still staring at him, the clawbird opened its mouth and emitted a harsh, scolding caw. It sounded like laughter. The cry rattled down the length of the corridor. Maul scowled at the thing. It was making too much noise, and he couldn't hear anything else over the din.

"Get out of here," Maul told it. "Go."

The bird stayed and croaked louder than ever, as if determined to betray Maul's location to anyone in the area. Bending down, he found a loose metal bolt on the floor and pitched it at the bird, sending it upward with a startled croak. It flew away down the passage.

In the silence, Maul cocked his head, listening again. Now he could make out what he'd come to hear.

Footsteps.

Rapid but not panicked, coming faster now. Big, by the sound of it, but not clumsy or uncertain. Boots. Authoritative.

Maul climbed up the steel rungs toward the ceiling of the shaft. Bracing his feet against an overhanging electrical switchplate, he gripped the edge of the maintenance hatch and drew himself up until he disappeared into the shadows. He kept his body absolutely rigid, every muscle locked in place, staring straight down at the intersection of the two passageways below.

Directly below him, a figure emerged into view. The faint glow of equipment illuminated the helmet and face shield, the heavy broadcloth fabric of his uniform rustling as he approached.

A guard.

Maul found himself staring down at the top of the corrections officer's helmet. From here it was impossible to see his face. Not that it mattered.

"I know you're out there," the CO said, looking from side to side. His hand was resting on his belt, not on the blaster but on something else, a flat black console of the dropbox strapped to his hip, with a green-glowing display that Maul couldn't read from this angle. "Why you looking for Zero?"

Maul gripped the hatch in front of him more tightly, allowing himself one deep breath. A drop of moisture, ice cold and oily, fell from one of the overhead condenser units. It struck the top of his head, rolled down between his horns and off his scalp, and slithered down the side of his face to his chin.

"Zero already knows you're different," the CO was saying. "Heard you're an assassin. Saw you fight. You're not here by accident."

Maul held absolutely still.

"The way he sees it, there's only one reason that somebody like you would come out to the far corner of the galaxy and start asking for him," the guard continued. "You came here to kill him. Am I right?"

Maul waited. The CO had stopped looking from side to side now. His eyes were riveted to something straight ahead of him.

The droplet fell from Maul's chin and hit the guard's helmet with a soft but audible plop. The CO stiffened, tilted back his head, and looked straight up at Maul, the whites of his eyes reflecting yellowish red in the light spill.

"I thought so," he said. "You know what? I don't even need this blaster to take care of you." He indicated the dropbox strapped to his belt. "I got your numbers plugged in already, maggot. I touch this button, set off those bombs inside your chest, you're dead before you hit the floor."

"Where's Zero?" Maul asked.

"You're kidding, right?" His fingers flickered over the switches of the belt console, and Maul was almost positive that he hadn't yet heard the noises at the far end of the walkway, whispers and footsteps that had become steadily more audible over the past few seconds. "You actually think he'd let you get the drop on him like this?" Now the CO's entire demeanor had changed, developing an edge, losing whatever playfulness it might have had. "You never had a chance."

"I don't think so," Maul said.

The distant sounds were clearer now, the whispering no longer bothering to keep itself stealthy, the footsteps no longer muffled. Maul watched as the CO started to react, the man caught completely by surprise by what was happening, but it was already too late. A storm of stomping feet came thundering down through the passage, an avalanche of noise clanging off the metal and shaking the length of the corridor from end to end. From either side of the walkway below, the sudden roar of inmates' voices filled the closed space with howls and bellows of rage.

"What—?" The guard swiveled around, not sure where to look first.

They hit him from both sides at once. From where he was positioned overhead, Maul had a perfect view of the carnage below. A wall of bald human inmates burst forward, the Bone Kings barreling down one end of the walkway, while a second mass of bodies, the Gravity Massive, led by the Noghri Strabo, came stampeding from the opposite direction to meet their enemies head-on. The guard disappeared between them, immediately trampled underfoot.

Maul waited, timing his response to an internal clock whose nuances were a matter of pure reflex. The prisoners were already screaming. In the closed space above, he heard bones snap, the brittle crunch and crackle of cartilage being crushed, bodies flattened underfoot.

Now.

Hanging by his legs, extending both arms just above the battle, Maul thrust both hands down into the fray. He seized the guard by his helmet strap and yanked him upward, using his helmet like a battering ram to smash open the maintenance hatch and shove the man up inside. Alarms began to beep and wail from all sides.

Maul scrambled into the utility shaft alongside the guard, his hand locked around the CO's throat.

"Switch those off," he ordered.

"Can't," the guard panted. "It's not—"

Maul pushed the guard back toward the open hatchway. "Turn them off or I'll throw you down to them. They'll rip you to pieces in a heartbeat."

"I'm telling you, I can't! Alarms have to be deactivated by central control! I swear!"

Maul took hold of the man's right hand, pinning it down on the chain coupling where the hatch cover fit into its housing, and slammed the hatch down on it hard. The guard shrieked, his voice shattering as it reached the upper registers.

"Where's Zero?" Maul asked softly in his ear.

"I don't know!" The guard's face had gone terribly pale except for two bright spots of red high up in his cheeks. Tears of pain stood out in his eyes. "Nobody knows!"

"How can that be? There are cameras everywhere."

"Not on him! He comes and he goes! Even the guards don't see where or how he gets in and out!"

"Then why did the Chadra-Fan send me here?"

"I told you, Zero thought you were here to kill him!"

"You tell him that I'm looking for him," Maul said. "You tell him I want a real meeting, not a setup."

"He doesn't work that way!"

"Where's his cell?"

"It's on Level 8, Cell 22. Around the far corner—you have to look for it, but it's there, I swear. *Now please just let me go!*"

Maul decoupled the hatch and let it hiss open. The guard groaned, withdrawing his fractured arm with a shuddering whimper, cradling his hand and wrist like a small dead animal dangling limply from his sleeve.

Slowly he looked at Maul. Something savage had trickled into his eyes, filling them with rage.

"Inmate 11240," he said, resting his good hand on the activation stud for the dropbox. "You're as good as dead, maggot."

Maul studied him. "We'll see."

The CO hit the button.

And nothing happened.

10

SKIN IN THE GAME

"You spared him," Vesto Slipher said, careful to keep his tone casual. "Why?"

Neither of the Blirr siblings answered him. From behind the console, Dakarai inclined slightly forward in his chair, his right forefinger still pressed tightly to the remote deactivation switch for the guard's dropbox.

Sadiki leaned down over her brother's shoulder for a better view. All five of the screens closest to Dakarai's workspace had been redirected to display the maintenance shaft from different angles, providing multiple views of the Zabrak and the guard whose wrist he'd just shattered.

Dakarai tapped another button, keying in the initiation sequences.

"What's going on?" Slipher asked. "Is it—"

All at once, the very air around them took on a low and sonorous hum. A time code blipped into view in the corners of all the screens, counting down from five minutes. Slipher heard a burst of static, and a split second later, a clarion erupted out of the framework of the space station, filling what felt like the entire world with one long, oscillating blast.

Dakarai winced. The tremors grew more violent, rhythmic, throbbing like the adrenalized heart of some colossal creature shocked into life. Ripples appeared at the surface of his coffee cup, and he reached over to steady it without taking his eyes from the screens.

"What is all this?" Slipher asked. He'd already surmised exactly what was happening, but he'd long ago discovered the value of asking obvious questions at the right moment. He turned to Sadiki, speaking loudly to be heard over the alarms. "What's going on?"

"My brother's algorithm has selected the next two combatants." The warden smiled at one of the monitors. "We're matching them now."

"Inmate 11240," the Muun read as the profile appeared on-screen. "That's the Zabrak?"

"Jagannath," Sadiki said. "Right."

"And that's why . . . ?"

She nodded. "We'll only override a guard's authority to activate the electrostatic detonator if the inmate in question is already scheduled for a fight." She nodded at the bank of monitors. "In this case, 11240 has been selected again."

"Who are you pitting him against?"

"Wait and see," Sadiki said. "I wouldn't want to ruin the surprise."

Slipher glanced around at the other screens, where inmates throughout Cog Hive Seven were scurrying down the corridors and back to their cells for lockdown. The entire space station was shaking hard enough that he had to brace himself against the wall and wrap his thin, slender fingers around the buttress for support. He could feel the whirring and clicking of Cog Hive Seven's interior clockwork through the floor beneath his feet, reverberating up through his ankles and knees.

"Is it always this loud?" he shouted. "It feels like the whole space station is shaking."

"Only about eighty-five percent of it." Sadiki pointed to the space just above the monitors, where a high-resolution ray-tracing of the space station's layout was displaying the reconfiguration in real time.

Slipher gazed at the rendering in fascinated silence. Numbers had always been his language of choice, data patterns his poetry, but what was happening here was equally captivating—the ray-tracing showed entire wings and cellblocks changing position, pulling themselves around, reformatting the very architecture of the prison itself.

"And here's our new contender," Sadiki said, pointing at the monitor in front of her.

Slipher looked at what had appeared on the other monitor. "*That's what* 11240 is fighting?"

Sadiki nodded. "We've never matched it," she said. "A couple of freelance bounty hunters brought it in from an abandoned spaceport in the Anoat system, along the Ison trade corridor." She checked the screen. "We think it's been used in previous illegal gladiatorial fights. It's called—"

"I know what it is," the Muun said.

Sadiki glanced at him, clearly impressed. "You've seen the species before?"

"Not exactly," Slipher told her. "The IBC was briefly involved in arbitrating a former client's involvement in a black market fur-trading operation in the Outer Rim. Nothing we were personally involved in, of course, but apparently poachers and big-game hunters had been tracking those creatures for decades." He shook his head. "Mortality rate among the poachers was often worse than the creatures themselves. You're talking about a predator two and a half meters tall, sometimes weighing two hundred kilograms or more, with razor-sharp teeth and claws. They're singularly vicious creatures."

"So you don't like the odds?" Sadiki asked.

"That thing against the Zabrak?" the Muun blinked. "It hardly seems fair."

"You haven't seen 11240 in a fight."

"Respectfully, Warden, I don't believe that I have to."

"We'll see." Sadiki indicated the overhead consoles, where whole lists of newly formatted data were streaming live through the galaxy. "As always, bookmakers and casino bosses have the standard five-minute window to evaluate the odds. We'll see what they think of the match in the offworld gambling combines." She watched as the displays showed bets, millions of credits pouring in on either side. "Looks like most of them agree with your assessment."

"And you?" the Muun asked. "How will the esteemed facilitators of Cog Hive Seven be betting?"

"We bet what the algorithm tells us."

"Always?"

"Without fail."

"And the algorithm is never wrong?" Slipher asked.

Sadiki turned to Dakarai. Her brother tapped in a series of commands and waited for the system to generate its verdict.

"You're right," she said. "It's going to be no contest."

11

FROM THE LAND OF THE ICE AND SNOW

Maul got back to his cell with seconds to spare.

The hatch slammed shut behind him, its magbolts clamping tight with a vacuum-sealed thump. The panel of yellow lights had begun blinking red. All around him, the cell had already begun changing shape, the floor bowing below his feet, wall plates sliding together with a now familiar grinding of alloy against alloy, constricting upward to merge with the ceiling.

He breathed slowly, in and out, and took a moment to review what had just happened. None of it made sense. Not that he'd expected it to.

The ventilation duct ambush had worked as he'd expected—up to a point. He'd gone in fully anticipating a setup, and in this the guard had not disappointed him. A man like Iram Radique hadn't survived this long without amassing an army of foot soldiers and lookouts, both inmates and guards, to mislead those who came looking for him. Was Zero working for Radique? Could it be that simple?

And there was the more immediate question of why he hadn't been killed when the guard had activated the implanted charges in his heart. Had the dark side itself somehow intervened at the last second to save him?

The implications of this possibility made Maul catch his breath. For all Darth Sidious's talk of his role as his apprentice and eventual successor, Maul still felt precious little connection to the Sith grand plan for the galaxy and his place within it. At the Dark Lord's command, he'd spent years training on Orsis and then on Coruscant in the LiMerge Building, enduring years of privation and the harshest imaginable discipline while awaiting his Master's visits. And it was true—Sidious had spoken at length, intoxicatingly, about the dark side and its power, and more vaguely about the role Maul would play as he continued in his study of the Sith arts. In his most solitary moments, Maul had dared allow himself to hope for that moment when the Force would announce itself within him fully, intervening in a way that could not be mistaken for anything but sheer destiny.

Could this be that moment?

If that's true—

There was a sudden lurch and everything jerked forward on its axis. Maul seized the handgrips on either side of the bench, wedging himself in place, feeling hydrostatic pressure building in his face and neck as the entire chamber turned upside down, then tumbled sideways, pitching first to the left, then to the right. The cell spun, jerked left, barreled forward, jerked right again. Equilibrium abandoned him momentarily and he tightened his grip.

There was a sharp clank and the chamber jerked to a halt. Something hissed, a hydraulic hatchway on the other side of one of the walls, but the hatch in front of him remained sealed.

Then, through the wall, he heard it.

A low, bronchial growl.

Maul closed his eyes and listened. Whatever was on the other side of that hatch sounded bigger and hungrier than the creature he'd fought earlier. The growl had a sonorous, barrel-chested timbre that shook the air itself. He caught himself stretching out with his feelings and forced himself to withdraw, his Master's voice burning in his ears from their final meeting on Coruscant.

If at any point you reveal your true identity as a Sith Lord, Sidious had told him, *the entire mission will be worthless, do you understand? You must not ever use the Force, no matter what the circumstances, or all will be lost. Do you grasp the magnitude of responsibility with which you are being trusted?*

Maul did. All too well.

He continued to hold absolutely still, listening, attuned to this moment. When the growl came again, it had risen in volume and intensity and was now a thick snarl of fury. Metal chains clanked, rattling audibly, and something slammed against the wall with a sudden, deafening crash that shook the very bulkhead in front of him. There was another bellow, even louder than before, that he could feel in the hollow of his chest. The thing on the other side of the wall could smell him now, he was sure of it. It wouldn't be long now.

The blinking lights went solid red.

And the hatch opened.

Maul remained motionless for a long moment, looking at it.

The wampa was in chains, bolted to the floor of its cell with heavy Nylasteel manacles around its legs, wrists, and throat. It stood almost three meters tall, its thick fur matted with filth, grease, and blood. One of its horns had snapped off midshaft, creating a jagged ocher-colored dagger that curled only halfway around the right side of its head. Across its chest and abdomen, great swaths and patches of its white pelt had been ripped away to expose a puckered landscape of scar tissue—no doubt the results of previous battles. Its lips wrinkled back to reveal rows of razor-sharp teeth, and spittle flew as it unleashed a bellow of hungry, frustrated rage and jerked at its restraints.

Maul stood his ground. He gave himself a few seconds to evaluate the space where they would be fighting—the height of the ceiling, the diameter of the chamber—before turning back to stare the thing straight in its yellow, semi-sentient eyes.

Come, then.

As if hearing his thoughts, the wampa leaned down, gathering its strength, and at that moment the manacles fell away. Maul never heard them hit the floor.

The thing came at him.

Maul leapt upward, dodging the initial attack—but the creature's massive arm swung around as it passed, its claws raking his back, ripping through flesh to gouge deep into the muscle along his spine. Maul felt his breath sucked from his lungs. A cruel, hot spike—even now he refused to think of it as pain—took hold of that entire side of his body, settling deep inside his nerve endings. The sudden smell of his own blood, sharp and coppery, filled the cell.

Ducking low and then jumping for the ceiling, he felt hot liquid splashing down his leg, streaking the floor beneath his feet. He skidded, colliding with the wall in front of him. Was the cell actually *smaller* than it had been a moment ago? Had they already changed the shape of it around him?

Maul took a breath and centered himself. Things were happening too quickly. He needed to slow it down. But the wampa was already lunging again, its long, apelike arms swinging, claws carving shadow, smashing him back into the curved steel wall as its jaws snapped inches away from his face. Maul slid down through the pool of his own blood, rolled free, and sprang up behind the thing faster that it could turn. Cocking back one arm, he tensed his shoulder and snapped his elbow into the base of the creature's skull, putting every ounce of upper body strength into a blow that should have shattered its neck.

Nothing. It was like launching an elbow strike against solid stone covered with a layer of thick fur. Now the creature rounded on him again, arms upraised, towering to fill what felt like the entire cell. This time when it roared, the noise was more like a scream—a broken, phlegmy, bronchial shriek—as if the beast itself were somehow being tortured into attacking him. A flicker of realization passed through Maul's mind.

Something's wrong with it. It's not—

The wampa's claw shot forward, slashing diagonally across Maul's face.

The moment of clarity vanished in the hot rush of his own anger. Maul lowered his head, tightening up his core, hearing a new growl rising up—his own growl this time, emanating from the most deep and primal pit of his being. He opened himself to it, the deep venom of wrath taking control, fast and sleek and powerful. It would not be long now. Dismissing the bright slash of heat across his cheek and the bridge of his nose as he had dismissed the odd shimmer of insight that had immediately preceded it, he fell into a low crouch, letting the wampa come at him again.

Its next move would be its last.

Maul sprang straight upward into it, driving his horned head into the thing's lower jaw, pulverizing its mandible and slamming needle-sharp bone fragments into its cranial vault. Maul could actually feel the joints and fissures shattering inside the wampa's skull and knew intuitively that he'd dealt it a killing blow.

But when he looked up again, the thing was on its feet and advancing toward him, howling and keening, a blind colossus. The head-butt had left its face a caved-in mass of blood and exposed bone. Somewhere within the cauldron of his anger, Maul felt a wave of disbelief.

How was it still fighting?

In defiance of all logic, it launched itself at him, all claws and teeth, a mass of unwavering death. Planting his feet against the wall behind him, Maul grabbed the thing by its remaining horn and put every ounce of his strength into twisting its head to the side. He wrenched the thing's head away from him, and realized at the last second that he couldn't hold it back. Whatever was inside the wampa was far more durable than he'd initially expected.

The thing lunged again, sinking its teeth into Maul's shoulder, hitting crucial nerve bundles. All the strength disappeared from his hand and wrist, his body turning traitor at the worst possible moment. His arms fell slack and he stumbled backward, staring up at his adversary. Darkness like he'd never known before was swarming through his peripheral vision, thick and pulsating, tightening with every second. For the first time the impossible occurred to him—the prospect that he might actually lose.

He lifted his head, wiped the blood from his eyes.

Look at it, a voice spoke from deep inside him—not the voice of Sidious but an instinct of self-preservation that far predated his service to his Master. *Do you not see?*

Maul looked. Something *was* wrong with the wampa—something deeply, profoundly wrong that went beyond genetically predisposed violence and a history of predatory killing. And just that quickly, he knew how to end it.

Summoning whatever remained of his strength, Maul fired himself at the beast. Hooking his hands into claws, he plunged them through its fur, ripping into the soft tissue of its torso. The wampa screeched and wailed. Maul barely heard it. Shoving his hands deeper, he sank both arms in up to the elbow, beneath its rib cage and into its thoracic cavity, groping until he found what he was looking for—the slick, pulsating mass of its heart.

Maul grabbed it, laced his fingers together, and squeezed.

The wampa's heart burst between his fingers like a dense and fibrous flower. At once the thing tumbled backward with a kind of graceless, shambling sprawl, slumping against the wall with a low moan, as if released from bondage beyond any chains or shackles. It gave a final braying cough, shuddered once, and fell still.

Maul licked the blood from his teeth and spat. He stumbled back, tried to catch himself, and failed. Fatigue was already taking hold, a dense and miserable web that made the simplest motions difficult. The blood he'd lost was not so easily countered. The darkness was coming again, and this time he knew that he wouldn't be able to hold it off.

The last thing he saw was the cell around him shifting and beginning to rise.

Then blackness.

12

FACE TIME

The Twi'lek known as Zero stepped around the corner and into the mess hall. He emerged as he always did, without fanfare, always within a crowd of inmates large enough to mask his point of entry. As far as appearances went, his was a model of absolute subtlety: one moment he wasn't there, the next he was.

All around him, the hall was already getting busy. The dinner hour had just begun. Falling silently into line behind two prisoners who'd just picked up their trays, he edged closer to them.

"Any news?"

At the sound of his voice, the other two inmates turned and glanced back at him with a squint of recognition. "Hey, Z," one of them said, his mouth twisting into a gap-toothed grimace. "Where you been keeping yourself?"

"Here and there," the Twi'lek answered vaguely. "Who's asking?"

"Just curious, is all. We were all wondering what happened to you when that bomb went off."

The Twi'lek frowned and shook his head. "That was no bomb."

"No?"

"The kitchen staff found a pressure cooker full of chemicals lodged inside the dishwasher." He glanced at the line of inmates waiting to be served their evening meal. "Guess we'll all be eating off dirty trays for a while."

The second inmate blinked, processing the information. "Somebody sending a message? Creating a diversion, like?"

"I don't think so."

"What, then?"

Zero didn't answer, scanning the room in front of him. The inmate to his right, a convicted smuggler and three-time loser named Miggs, gave a shrug. "Yeah, well, whaddaya gonna do, am I right?"

With a distracted nod, Zero stepped forward. They carried their trays into the serving line, bypassing a half-dozen members of the Gravity Massive, their faces bruised and swollen. At least one of them was still actively bleeding through his makeshift bandages.

"You hear what happened to them?" Miggs asked.

"Run-in with the Bone Kings," Zero said. "Word is they hashed it out in the tunnels last night before the bout."

"Figures." Miggs held up his tray so that the service droid on the other side of the counter could slop a ladle of colorless protein gel into it. "Ugh, this stuff smells even worse than usual."

Behind him, Zero raised his own tray. With a click of recognition, the kitchen droid paused and then turned to lift the lid on a different serving tureen, extending tongs from its manipulators to serve Zero a steaming portion of succulent-smelling meat and fresh vegetables.

"Traladon steak, medium rare, with Ramorean caponata and a side of fresh sufar greens," it announced.

"Thank you." Zero nodded and took the tray, carrying it forward while the droid went back to the vat of gray, semi-liquefied gel for the next convict in line.

"You see that fight, by the way?" he asked.

"You kidding?" Miggs glanced at the con who had followed them into the main dining area, to their usual table at the far end of the room. "Halleck and I clocked the whole thing on holo from the gallery, watched it like eight times already, right?"

Sitting down, the inmate behind him, Halleck, bobbed his head up and down. "Squall of a thing, too. You shoulda clocked on it, Zero, for real."

"Is that so?" The Twi'lek cut off a thin slice of steak and sniffed it before putting in into his mouth. "What happened?"

"That red-skinned freak, the one they call the Tooth? What's his name, Jagannath?" Miggs shoveled in a bite of his own food and gulped it down, wiping the corner of his mouth with his shirt cuff. "They put him in there again, and the powers that be or whatever, they match him up against this crazy snow beast—"

"A wampa?" The Twi'lek cocked an eyebrow. "I wasn't aware that they actually still have one of them here."

"*Had* one," Miggs said grimly, picking up his fork again. "So anyway, it starts out pretty much exactly like you'd expect. This wampa's just pounding the unholy guts out of old Redskin—really making him work for his dinner, right? I mean, it's not even fair. We're all thinking Mr. Tooth is gonna lose a lot more than his tooth this time, you know what I'm saying?" Another bite, loaded in, chewed twice, and swallowed. "Then all of a sudden, just when you think it's over—*bam!*" Miggs slammed his fist on the table and paused for dramatic effect. "The Tooth, like, actually reaches in and tears open the thing's chest—"

"Is that so?"

"—and then he shoves his hand into the thing's stomach up to his elbows, grabs the thing's heart, and, like, crushes it in his bare hands."

"Mm." Zero took another bite of steak. "Impressive."

"I'm not even yanking you, man—they showed the whole thing. And then, boom, the wampa just kinda sags back and dies on the spot." Miggs shook his head again. "Totally nonlinear. Makes you think, though."

Zero stopped chewing. "Does it?"

"Yeah, I mean . . ." Miggs picked up his fork, nudged his food around the tray, and put it down again. "'Cause, I mean, when you cogitate on it—if they've got a wampa in here, then seriously . . . who knows what else they got locked up downside, you know?"

"Such as . . . ?"

"Well, I mean, like the Wolf Worm."

Zero gazed at him opaquely. "You really believe that?"

"Dunno, man. I heard rumors, is all. Way down inside the prison where nobody ever goes."

The Twi'lek was about to comment when he felt something bump against him hard enough to knock his tray sideways. He turned around and saw the inmates standing directly behind him.

Bone Kings. Four of them. Zero studied their faces, one by one.

"Nice meal, Ze-ro," the bald, bearded inmate in front said, drawing the name out with deliberate, singsong mockery while he eyed the half-finished steak and greens on Zero's plate. "You know, there something I've always been meaning to ask you. How come you always get to eat better than the rest of us?"

"I would think that would be abundantly obvious," Zero said. "I walk a higher path than you do."

"Is that so?"

"In almost every conceivable regard," Zero said, "yes."

A silence fell between them. He recognized the man in front of him as Vas Nailhead, boss of the Kings. Nailhead was a flesh-eater, known among the gladiatorial fighting circuit for devouring at least some part of every living thing he'd ever killed. Word was that he enjoyed a cult following and was one of the few inmates to receive fan mail, packages, even the occasional wedding proposal—although rumors circulated that he actually had a family and relatives back on Tepasi.

"Funny thing is . . ." Nailhead leered at him, spit bubbles clustered at the corners of his lips—he was literally foaming at the mouth. From inside the left sleeve of his uniform, a long hard shape protruded against the fabric, its sharpened tip just visible at the end of his sleeve. "I bet your blood comes spilling out just as easily as anybody else's here. What do you think?"

On either side of him, in his peripheral vision, Zero saw Miggs and Halleck rising gamely to their feet into a protective stance. He gestured for them to sit down.

"It's all right," he said quietly. "I'm sure that Mr. Nailhead was just getting ready to apologize for his unseemly behavior."

"Wrong again, Ze-ro." Without waiting for an answer, Nailhead reached down and grabbed Zero's collar, yanking him to his feet so abruptly that the Twi'lek's tray flipped over and went clattering to the floor, spilling the remains of his steak and greens across the tiles beneath their feet. The sharpened shaft of bone in Nailhead's sleeve had edged up so and was now pushing into the soft place beneath Zero's neck.

"See, we learned something new last night when we faced off against the Gravity Massive in the tunnels," Nailhead said. "Us and them. Worked it out together, you might say."

"Oh?" The Twi'lek's gaze remained absolutely steady. "And what might that be?"

"We don't need you nearly as much as you need us. Fact is, the only reason you run the place like this is because these maggots think you do. Once they stop thinking it, you stop running it."

"Fascinating," Zero said. "It's a miracle that none of you was hurt, thinking so hard."

Nailhead grunted. "Not half as fascinating as it's gonna be when we haul you off to the tunnels and rip out your throat."

"Is that what Delia would want?"

Nailhead stiffened. He pushed the sharpened bone slightly deeper into the soft tissue of Zero's throat, fixing him with his stare. "What did you just say?"

"Your sister," the Twi'lek answered. "She still sends you letters, doesn't she? Because she thinks about you. She remembers what life used to be like on Tepasi. After everything you've done, she hasn't stopped hoping you'll come back and be the boy that she remembers. The one who could always sing and make her laugh with every verse of 'Sweet Fronda Fane.' "

Nailhead drew in a shallow, audible breath and cocked his head ever so slightly. Behind the erumpent tangle of his beard, all the ferocity had drained from his expression, leaving his face strangely slack and vacant.

"How did you . . ." He swallowed and continued, his voice oddly hoarse. "How did you know about that?"

"I've been here a long time," Zero said. "You learn all sorts of things when you've been here as long as I have. A person of interest such as myself *hears* things. About your family and your sister in particular. And of course, I can always pass on messages in either direction."

Nailhead released him and took a step back. For an instant a spark of what could have been actual civility shimmered in the cloudy depths of his eyes—a distant clarity that reflected back on the man he might have been beneath years of suffocating depravity.

"Perhaps it's time you return to your friends, Mr. Nailhead." Zero spoke in the same gentle, patient tone with which he might suggest an evening stroll through the common area. "It sounds as if you still have some thinking to do."

Nailhead took another step away, his hands hanging limp at his sides. He said nothing, didn't even blink, just turned and began making his way back across the dining hall to where the other Bone Kings were waiting.

"Whoa," Miggs exhaled as he and Halleck watched Nailhead depart. "Zero, man, that was *crazy*, even for you. How did you—"

He looked back at the table and stopped.

Zero was already gone.

13

CAUTIONARY TALE

Maul was waiting just inside the cell when the Twi'lek came back from the mess hall, hiding in the shadows to the right of the hatchway. At the sound of approaching footsteps, he stepped into view.

For a moment Zero just stared at him. To his credit, he didn't bother trying to run. He didn't even look particularly surprised.

"Jagannath," he said. "You're looking surprisingly well, all things considered."

Maul said nothing. In the twelve hours since his last fight, he'd recovered almost completely from the wounds that the Wampa had inflicted on him. His face still bore the blood-encrusted slash marks from its claws, but he'd regained full use of his arm, and his strength actually seemed to have intensified in response to the attack, like an organism that had thrived from being pruned down close to the taproot.

"You know," Zero said, "I was wondering when we'd get a chance to meet."

"You didn't make it easy," Maul said. "Sending that guard to come after me in the tunnels."

"Well, of course, someone like me can't afford to cast too long a shadow. I'm sure you understand. In any case," Zero said, giving Maul a small smile, "you didn't seem to have any trouble handling yourself."

"I expected a setup," Maul said.

"In which case I'm glad that I didn't disappoint you. To what do I owe the pleasure?"

"I need something."

"A refreshing lack of pretense." The Twi'lek smiled again. "Please, sit down. Make yourself comfortable. Can I get you anything?"

Maul remained standing, allowing his silence to answer for him. In the hour that he'd spent waiting inside the cell, anticipating Zero's return, he'd searched it thoroughly. The investigation had proven highly fruitful. Although outwardly similar to every other cell in Cog Hive Seven, Zero's quarters had been customized with a thousand subtle luxuries that might escape casual observation. Beneath the bunk he'd discovered a small library, a secret storage chamber stocked with a private supply of food, drink, and utensils, and whole caches of electronic components in various states of assembly.

"Something to eat, perhaps?" Zero asked, reaching under the bed to pull out a narrow cabinet of prepared meals. "My own dinner was somewhat rudely interrupted, so I hope you'll forgive me if—"

"I want Iram Radique."

"I—" Zero stopped what he was doing and looked up, his expression unreadable. "I beg your pardon?"

"I know he's here. I seek an audience with him privately, as soon as possible. And you seem to be the one who can arrange such a thing."

The Twi'lek said nothing. Maul stood riveted to his gaze.

You must be relentless, Sidious had told him. *Use every means at your disposal to gather information. We have an extremely finite amount of time in which to arrange for the purchase of the nuclear device from Radique and its delivery into the hands of the Bando Gora. But throughout it all you must keep in mind that in Cog Hive Seven, the name of Iram Radique will always be spoken with dread.*

In this case, however, Zero surprised him. He looked at Maul blankly for a moment, his lips tightening, then twitching—and then burst out laughing, a spontaneous bray of amusement that seemed, for the moment at least, to cost him every ounce of his composure.

"I must apologize," the Twi'lek managed when he finally appeared to pull himself together. "You see, it's just . . . oh *my* . . ." Attempting to catch his breath, he wiped the tears from his eyes and looked up at

Maul. "Iram *Radique,* you say? You don't ask much, do you?" With another chuckle, he shook his head. "Tell me, is there anything else I can get for you in the meantime? Your own private starfighter, perhaps? An audience with the Galactic Senate? The lost moons of Yavin?"

Maul just stared at him, expressionless.

"Forgive me," Zero said. "It's not your fault. I can see that you've been misinformed about the scope of my abilities here. If you were looking to have a certain type of food smuggled in, or a more comfortable uniform, or even a particular pet, then yes, perhaps I could be of assistance, but . . ."

"I want Radique," Maul said. "I know he's here. And if anyone can find him, it's you."

The Twi'lek had settled himself completely now and stopped laughing. He lowered his weight down on his bunk, gazing up at Maul with his meal unopened on his lap.

"Let me tell you a story," he said. "If you'll indulge me." Without waiting for Maul's reply, Zero peeled back the synthetic wrap that covered some kind of glazed-looking reddish-pink fruit dish, waved it momentarily beneath his nose, and took a small nibble.

"About two years ago, another inmate arrived here—he, too, claimed to have come searching for Iram Radique. This misinformed soul, in fact, claimed not only that he'd met Radique before but that he'd actually saved Radique's life years ago, on the other side of the galaxy—and that Radique had somehow summoned him here to Cog Hive Seven to offer him a kind of protection as a way of thanking him." Zero took another bite of the fruit loaf, chewed, and swallowed. "Never mind the practical inconsistencies of this story. This new inmate insisted that Radique was locked up and hiding in here somewhere. No matter how many times he came to me for answers, insisting that I help him, he refused to accept the fact of the matter."

"Which is?" Maul asked.

Zero paused long enough to finish his bite and blotted his lips before looking back up at Maul with an expression of deeply earnest sincerity.

"*Iram Radique does not exist.* He's a cautionary tale, a myth—a bedtime story that small-time galactic gunrunners tell their kids at night. 'Don't get too big for your britches or Iram Radique will come and get you,' that sort of thing." Zero finished his snack, tossed the carton aside, and stood up in front of Maul, tilting his head so that he could meet Maul's gaze, even as he maintained a careful distance from him. "Hear me well, Jagannath. The so-called man that you seek is not here."

"What happened to the inmate?"

"I'm sorry?"

"The one who came here claiming to have saved Radique's life," Maul asked. "What happened to him?"

"Oh," Zero said vaguely, "he's still around somewhere. Eventually he gave up looking. Disabused of his delusions, I suppose. This place has a tendency to do that. You'll discover that for yourself . . . if you survive that long."

Maul said nothing.

"Now," the Twi'lek said, "since you've taken the trouble to come searching for me, I feel compelled to ask, is there anything else that you're looking for? Anything *real*?"

"Yes," Maul said.

"And what might that be?"

"I need a transmitter device. An undetectable means of long-range communication—any basic subspace image transmitter would suffice. I know you've got the necessary parts here in your cell."

"You . . ." For the first time, Zero looked nonplused. "You've discovered that, have you?"

"I need it as soon as possible," Maul told him.

"What you're asking for won't come cheaply," Zero said. "You must realize that the components that you saw all had to be smuggled in at great personal—"

"What do you want?" Maul interrupted.

"Well." The Twi'lek drew in a breath, letting it out slowly. "Since you asked, I do seem to be having some recent difficulty with the gangs. The Bone Kings and the Gravity Massive, they—"

"What else?"

"What *else?*" Zero blinked up at him, bemused. "I assure you, that's quite enough."

"Get the transmitter ready for me," Maul told him. "You'll have no more trouble with gangs."

14

JAR OF FLIES

Strabo hated the laundry facility.

When he'd first been shipped to Cog Hive Seven eighteen standard months earlier, laundry had been his work detail. He'd sweated for hours among the giant washers and dryers, toiling alongside malfunctioning droids and inmates through mountains of gore-soaked uniforms and sheets. Assigned to him seemingly at random, the sweat, the stink, and the backbreaking monotony of it had been worse than death.

But it hadn't lasted long. Soon enough he'd risen through the ranks of the Gravity Massive—strangling the former leader and moving effortlessly into his place—and as a result, he hadn't had to come back down here in almost a year.

Even so, from the moment he'd led the rest of the Gravity Massive inside, the stinging astringency of the cramped chamber was all too familiar to his nose, like a horrible kind of homecoming. The machines were quiet now, shut down for the night, but the faintly howling silence was somehow even more haunting.

"Don't see the point," he growled. "Coming down here in the middle of the night like this." He looked over his shoulder at the Gravity Massive member standing behind him. "You sure this was the message?"

"That's what it said." The inmate known as Izhsmash was a Nelvaanian, long-snouted and sharp-toothed, and Strabo's second in command. "Word came straight from Halcon."

"Captain of the guards call us all the way down here, for what? Something they can't tell us topside?" Strabo shook his head. "The whole thing stinks."

His lieutenant didn't answer. The Nelvaanian was a data pirate, shipped here to Cog Hive Seven on charges of information sabotage. He was not a fighter or a killer by nature, but his combination of loyalty and freaky tech skills had made him indispensable to Strabo and the Gravity Massive—or at least as indispensable as one could be in an environment where any two inmates might be called on, at any moment, to slaughter each other.

Now, Strabo knew, was not the time to raise that point. An hour earlier, Izhsmash had informed him that he'd received, via custodial droid, a covert message from CO Halcon, the captain of the guards here in Cog Hive Seven, telling them to bring the entire GM crew, thirteen in all, down into the laundry facility for some sort of clandestine summit between gang and guard. Strabo had been running the crew long enough to know that he ignored such a summons at his peril. Halcon probably wouldn't detonate the charges in his heart over such a minor act of disobedience, but the guard could make his life miserable in a thousand other ways, everything from cutting his rations to putting him in full lockdown until he was climbing the walls.

So here they were, the Gravity Massive en masse, making their way among the chemical vats and tubes pumping liters of industrial detergents, solvents, along with the liquid cryogens necessary to cool the superconductor power load running to the massive washers and dryers.

"How long we supposed to wait here anyway?" Strabo grumbled, casting his gaze alongside the washers and dryers, their gaping, seventy-centimeter bores standing open and motionless in the gloom. "Did Halcon even say what he wanted with us?"

"No."

"Not even a clue?"

"He told me to come down." Izhsmash shrugged. "That's all."

"Son of a vogger knows he can't touch us, right?" Strabo said. "On account of—"

Suddenly he stopped talking. He'd just detected the none too stealthy *tap-tap-tap* of steel-toed boots approaching in the half darkness from the far side of the alcove. There was only one point of entrance to the facility, which meant—

They're already here waiting for us.

"Halcon," Strabo bellowed out, his strident voice only slightly dampened by the claustrophobic confines of the room. "We're here. You want to tell us what's so important this time of night?"

There was a solid *whump* as the hatchway sealed shut behind them, and by the time he realized what was happening, Strabo had already seen who was in front of them.

Not guards.

Bone Kings.

And in front of them, Vas Nailhead himself, his angry bald scalp bulging toward the Gravity Massive like a pustulant sore.

Under the circumstances, Nailhead appeared as surprised as Strabo felt. "What the . . . ?" he was saying, striding forward, already close enough that Strabo could count all sixteen Kings clustered up behind him. *"You?"*

"Nailhead." Strabo glared back at him, the name twisting from his lips like a curse. In his peripheral vision he was aware of Izhsmash and the rest of the Massive troops grimly preparing themselves for battle, pulling out short-handled wire scourges, rope darts, and flying claws from inside their uniforms. These chain weapons, fashioned from scavenged materials, sharpened and honed in secret, were the preferred pain-inflicting tools of the Massive and were always kept close at hand. "What are you doing here? Looking for a rematch?"

"If that's what you want," Nailhead said, and his eyes flicked over Strabo's shoulder to Izhsmash.

"Got a message to bring the Kings down here," the Nelvaanian said. "Halcon sent it to me through a utility droid."

"Us too," Nailhead said.

"What?" Strabo squinted at him. "That can't—"

The rest of the sentence was lost behind a sibilant whoosh from the tall containment vats along the wall. Both gangs spun around to stare at the source of the sound, and when he recognized what it was, Strabo felt his blood run cold. Thick clouds of freezing cold vapor were pouring out of the tanks, rising around them, sucking the oxygen out of the air.

Cryogens, he thought, his mind flashing back to the warnings he'd received about the liquid nitrogen and helium detergents stored inside the tanks, how any sort of leak or breach would literally suck the oxygen from the lungs of anyone unlucky enough to be trapped inside.

Exhaust fans in the ceiling. The toggle switch overhead—

It was already too late. Strabo felt his trachea clamp down to a pinhole, choking on what should have been air but instead tore into the delicate inner lining of his throat like a swarm of wasps. His lungs crumpled like empty leather sacks inside his chest, the strength draining from his body all at once as the floor swung up to hit him in the face like a huge blunt fist. His eyes and nose were on fire, his lungs trembling on the verge of revolt. He could no more climb up to activate the exhaust fans than he could draw in another unobstructed breath.

From somewhere in front of him, there came a loose and thready shriek. Strabo hoisted his head up and looked out through tear-soaked eyes. Nailhead and the Bone Kings were crumpling, clutching their chests, hacking and wheezing, falling to the floor in piles among members of the Gravity Massive. In less than thirty seconds, the cryo leak had accomplished what no measure of diplomacy ever could, uniting both gangs in a desperate fraternity of oxygen debt. Strabo saw his own people collapsing next to the Kings, side by side, brought low in their final moments, as indistinguishable as flies in a killing jar.

By the moons of Rennokk, we're all going to die here, he thought wildly. A thumping, primordial self-defense mechanism kicked in, more powerful than anything on the conscious level, superseding all other instincts.

Get out. Get out. Get out now—

Stumbling backward, elbowing his way violently through the ranks of his own people, Strabo groped his way in the direction of the exit, only to find it sealed. Something rammed his arm, and he realized there was someone next to him, a large, frantic shape.

It was Nailhead. The bearded man had fought his way over, too, and was jerking even more desperately on the manual release lever, pounding on it, trying to get out. His once-imposing face was a hairy, sweat-slick moon of terror.

From just above the hatchway, Strabo felt something take hold of his arm.

He looked up.

The Zabrak, the one called Jagannath, was glaring down at both of them, his nose and mouth protected by some kind of jury-rigged respirator. Strabo just stared at him, uncertain if what he saw was real or a side effect of the cryogens. He didn't have more than a moment to ponder the possibilities before the Zabrak tossed him aside, striding among the center of the alcove to where the open cryogen vats were spraying out great gunmetal-colored clouds more intensely than ever.

Switch them off! Strabo wanted to shout, though at this point his voice was a pale memory. *You've got to—*

But Jagannath was already in motion. Using the rungs imbedded directly in the wall, he drew himself up and climbed effortlessly to the top of the tank, reached across, and closed two sets of valves. He toggled another switch, and Strabo watched in wonder as the blades of the overhead fans began swinging to life, sucking the cryogens out, venting fresh oxygen into the sealed room.

After a moment, the air began to clear. The fans spun on. Strabo watched them swirling round and round as slowly—terribly slowly—the burning knots inside his own lungs began to loosen and disappear.

The Zabrak switched off the fans again.

Silence fell.

"Hear me."

Strabo wiped his eyes, coughed and spat, and finally looked up. Around him, on either side, Kings and Massive members alike were gaping up at the Zabrak with identical expressions of desperate, half-conscious wonder.

"What the kark do you want?" Nailhead managed, but his voice was just a raspy, hollowed-out ghost of its former self.

Jagannath ignored him. "What happened here, this cryo leak, was no accident. The captain of the guards, Halcon, did this. I overheard him planning it. That's why he called you all down here."

Nobody said anything. It might have been the suddenness of what had just transpired, but neither gang raised the first murmur of dissent.

"He wants to wipe out the gangs," the Zabrak said. "All of you. You've become more trouble than you're worth. Warden Blirr wouldn't have let him get away with it all at once—some of you still have upcoming matches to fulfill—so Halcon was going to make it look like an accident."

Silence.

"I didn't have to save you," Jagannath told them. "I could just as easily have let you die down here. And *every one of you*—" His yellow eyes moved across both gangs, taking in their blotchy, pale faces. "You all saw how your so-called leaders behaved just now—turning their backs on you to save themselves. Clawing like dogs at the door to get out. They couldn't have cared less."

A collective snarl came out of the crowd. Strabo flung up his hands in an instinctive posture of self-defense. Members of the Gravity Massive and Bone Kings turned to glare at him and Nailhead, the pain and panic in their eyes already changing from accusatory suspicion to outrage rage.

"He's right!" someone shouted. "I saw it too!"

"They led us here!"

"It was them!"

"Hold it!" Strabo took a step back and bumped into Nailhead, who already had his back to the wall. The other inmates jammed in toward them, even closer. Izhsmash's lips had drawn back in a snarl to reveal sharpened canines and incisors. Strabo felt a half dozen hands coming from a half dozen different directions, groping to take hold of him, ready to rip him apart.

"The time of gangs *is* coming to an end here," Jagannath's voice said from up above. "Halcon won't rest until he's destroyed you all."

"He can't do that!" Strabo swung at the gang members, Kings and Gravity Massive alike. "We're protected! Because of what we do, the way we serve Radique—"

His voice broke off. All the inmates who'd been about to attack him just a split second earlier took a step back, creating an open space around him, as if they'd just found out Strabo was infected with some horrifically contagious disease. Even Nailhead moved away from him.

Jagannath stared down at him.

"What about Radique?"

Strabo lowered his head.

"How do the gangs work for him? What do they do?"

Strabo looked at Izhsmash, but the Nelvaanian refused to meet his gaze. None of them would. It was over for him. Strabo realized that he'd gone from their leader to a complete outcast in the time it took to mention that single name.

"Tell me," Jagannath said, casting one more glance across the two gangs before directing his gaze back at Strabo. The unspoken message was clear enough: *Your reign here is over. Only I can protect you now.*

Strabo opened his mouth and snapped it shut again. When he finally managed to summon his voice, the words came out involuntarily, as if jerked from his lips by an invisible hook.

"The parts," he said. "The weapons components."

"What about them?"

"They—they come smuggled in on the supply ships. We each get one piece, small enough to tuck into our uniform and hide in our cell. Nobody knows what anybody else gets. Nobody knows how they fit together. Nobody knows where they go and how they get there."

"How does Radique get them from you?"

"No one knows. They just disappear."

Jagannath glared at him. "Disappear?"

"It's all I know," Strabo said. "And he pays us the same way. With the *khipus*." He pulled up his pantleg to reveal the string of knots tied around his ankle. "They're coded to a hidden account, a form of payment that the guards can't access."

The Zabrak turned to survey the rest of the room. "I know that you all work for Radique in some capacity. Which means that you already serve a common purpose. Now you'll all serve one leader." He straightened up. "Me."

"Never!" Off to his left, Strabo saw Nailhead lunge forward with his fists clenched, eyes blazing, and realized that he himself had also stepped up to confront this indignity head-on, as some animal part of him refused to bow before the newly appointed leader.

The Zabrak reacted faster than either he or Nailhead could. Seizing Nailhead from behind, the one called Jagannath hooked his fingers into the flesh-eater's nostrils and yanked his head straight back to expose his throat before driving his fist into the cartilage of Nailhead's windpipe, dropping him to the floor in a wheezing, debilitated heap. Strabo saw the Zabrak pivot, shooting his foot straight up so that it hit Strabo in the solar plexus, leaving him doubled over and sucking air.

Darkness was closing in. Strabo fought to shake it off. Jagannath's voice seemed to be coming from very far away, but there was a cold ferocity to it that would not be ignored.

"You work for me now," the Zabrak said. "You can each maintain your loyalty to your crews, but as of now, I'm putting myself in charge at the top. I will mediate between you and the guards." He turned to Nailhead, staring straight into the flesh-eater's eyes. "Also, from this point on there will be no more harassment of the inmate known as Zero, is that understood? That goes for both gangs."

Nobody said anything. Strabo stared at his feet. For the moment, at least, he couldn't bring himself to look at the other members of the gang he used to run.

When he looked up again, the Zabrak was gone.

15

LIMERGE

"Rise up, my apprentice."

At the sound of that voice, Maul's pulse quickened. He rose to his feet and stared at the holographic image of his Master.

The one called Zero had been as good as his word. Less than two hours after Maul had dealt with the gangs, he'd received a coded message to come here to a remote corner of the prison morgue, to one of the empty chambers designed to hold inmates' corpses for disposal.

It had been waiting here for him.

The transmitter, fully assembled and functional.

And now—

The image of Sidious stood before him, the Sith Lord's yellow eyes blazing deep within the cowl of his cloak. His zeyd-cloth robes swept around him, the coarse fabric rustling audibly as Sidious raised his hand. In the background, small details of the top of LiMerge Tower's interior were clearly visible, and Maul was momentarily taken aback by the vivid resolution of the image. Scavenged or not, Zero's technology was of impressively high quality.

"Master," he said aloud, or tried to, but the words stuck in his throat.

"You look well, my apprentice," Sidious said. "I have been monitoring your progress among the inhabitants of Cog Hive Seven with great interest."

"Yes, Master."

"I observe that regardless of the circumstances," Sidious continued, "throughout these bouts with other inmates, you have taken great care not to reveal your true powers as a Sith." Was there a twinge of sarcasm in his voice? "That much is quite abundantly evident."

"You are referring to the most recent bout." Maul hesitated. "The wampa—"

"Proved to be something of a challenge, yes, so I saw." Sidious intoned. "Perhaps you found yourself wishing that you might be permitted to draw unreservedly on the power of the Dark Side? Or to be allowed the use of your saber staff?"

Sensing a trap, Maul demurred. "My strength comes from within."

"Does it indeed?" Sidious gave him a long, unreadable look. "I wonder."

"Master—"

"Pride and self-regard are not accolades to be earned only once. The power of the Sith must prove itself stronger with every test. Resting on your accomplishments now will only inhibit your ability to fully exploit the resources of anger and discipline that lie within you."

"Yes, Master."

"Protecting your identity and the true purpose of your mission will be meaningless if you die before you achieve it." Sidious paused, gazing at him piercingly. "Do my words sting? Perhaps you find my assessment unfair?"

"No."

The Sith Lord drew back. "I expect much from you, Darth Maul, only because I alone grasp your true potential for greatness in the dark side."

"Thank you, Master. My only wish—"

"Enough." Sidious's face went abruptly cold. "Your restraint, training, and discipline will only take you so far. What progress have you made in locating Iram Radique?"

"I have intensified my search. I've brought the prison gangs to heel and have made inroads in discovering the methods of their service to Radique." Maul met his Master's gaze. "It will not be long now." He paused, then pressed on. "Perhaps if you were able to confide in me the true purpose of our plans—"

Sidious raised one hand, cutting the words off. "You have been provided with all the information you require to complete your mission. For now, all you need to know is that we are continuing with our work to destabilize the Outer Rim, fueling insurgency and separatism."

The Sith Lord drew in a breath and released it, holding Maul's gaze with what might have been sympathy.

"Your reputation of loyalty to our cause is firmly established. I am not oblivious to the fact that you have been disappointed by your role in our plans up till now—that you may have craved a more pivotal role in the Eriadu operation, for example."

Maul tried to suppress his sense of surprise and failed. How had Sidious known of that? After his Master had used security droids to covertly orchestrate the assassination of six Directorate members at the Eriadu Trade Summit and attempted to kill Chancellor Valorum, Maul had been unable to understand why Sidious hadn't involved him personally in the operation. He assumed that he'd hidden his disappointment well, buried it deep inside him where even he had been able to overlook it. Yet his Master had seen through him.

"Suffice it to say that what you are achieving now with Iram Radique will far surpass any smaller errand that I could have given you."

"Yes, Master."

"Good, then. Rise and go forth. Take what is rightfully ours. The dark side is with you."

Maul tried to respond, but the vision in front of him, of his Master and the debris-cluttered floor of the LiMerge Building, was already starting to fade.

Stepping away from the holovid unit, Darth Sidious opened his eyes and crossed the floor of the LiMerge Tower to the turbolift, his mind already teeming with a collision of thoughts.

As with any mission involving Maul, the situation that Sidious was creating on Cog Hive Seven was not entirely stable. The Sith Lord harbored no delusions about his apprentice's ambition or pride, or how closely those elements were linked to the anger that was constantly sweltering inside his apprentice, fermenting as Maul's power continued to intensify. Locked in unswerving allegiance to their cause, the Zabrak's heart was a reactor of pure, distilled rage.

And that rage will serve him well.

Yes. When Sidious reflected back on the years of training that Maul had endured, proving himself repeatedly against the worst that the galaxy had to offer, he felt an unmistakable pride in his apprentice's strength and fortitude. By definition, Cog Hive Seven was an environment that no one survived, yet Maul had already established himself as a dominant presence without relying on the Force. Despite what he'd said to Maul, Sidious felt an increasing respect for what his apprentice continued to achieve. In the fullness of time, such abilities would continue to serve him better than he could possibly imagine.

By the time he left the building and walked out to hail a sky-cab to the Senate District, the Sith Lord's concerns had abated. The hour was yet early, and his schedule for the day, as Palpatine, was already full.

The air-taxi darted down toward him, whirring to a halt, and as the door opened, he realized with a start that the cab wasn't empty. Hego Damask was waiting for him inside.

"Darth Sidious," Damask said, gesturing to the empty seat beside him. "Will you join me?"

Palpatine flicked his eyes toward the air-taxi's cockpit, but Damask gave him a reassuring nod.

"I've rendered the surveillance equipment inoperative," the Muun said, "so that we may speak freely. As equals."

"Of course." Without hesitating, Darth Sidious slipped inside next to the Muun, his expression revealing just the right tincture of pleasant surprise. "It's always good to see you under any circumstances."

"Yes." Behind the transpirator mask, Darth Plagueis offered what might have been a faint smile. "I know we had plans to meet later in Monument Plaza for our usual stroll, but something's come up and I had to alter my schedule at the last minute. I thought it best that we meet now." He turned to Sidious and cast a passing glance back at the LiMerge Building. "I take it that you've been in touch with the Zabrak?"

"As a matter of fact, I just—"

"I recall you mentioning that you've dispatched him to Cog Hive Seven to find this elusive weapons dealer?"

"Iram Radique, yes." Sidious was careful to sound as casual as possible, although inside he was already puzzled. Darth Plagueis knew only the broadest generalities about Darth Sidious's ongoing work to destabilize the Outer Rim planets and orchestrate the Galactic Civil War. He rarely asked specific questions about where the weapons were coming from, or how exactly Sidious intended to use them to facilitate the Grand Plan.

"This Radique," Plagueis continued in the same conversational tone as he gazed out the window at the approaching Avenue of the Core Founders, "is rumored to be one of the most powerful arms dealers in the galaxy?"

"Radique is as dangerous as he is unpredictable." Sidious was aware of an unwelcome warmth beginning to climb upward through the back of his neck, enveloping his cheeks and forehead. "Which is why I sent Maul to assassinate him."

"I see."

Sidious leaned slightly forward in an attempt to catch Plagueis's eye. "I've been meaning to inform you. My mission there—"

"Is something I have absolute confidence in your ability to execute." Plagueis placed a hand on Sidious's shoulder. "I must commend you on your foresight and commitment to our ultimate purpose, Darth Sidious. As you might have guessed, with the increasing demands of my own . . . private pursuits on Sojourn, I find it profoundly liberating that I do not need to monitor the particular means with which you uphold our united goal."

"Yes, of course." Sidious regarded him speculatively. What exactly was Plagueis telling him? Did the Muun harbor his own dark suspicions about what Sidious had hoped to achieve in sending Maul to Cog Hive Seven? Or was Plagueis simply probing him for more detail?

"Well." Plagueis had already settled back again with a nearly inaudible sigh. "I suppose this is good-bye for now."

The air-taxi docked, and Sidious realized that he'd arrived at the Senate Rotunda. The cab's hatch released with a faint sigh, and as he began to step out, he felt Plagueis's hand take hold of his wrist.

"There is one other thing," he said, with that same tone of cordial detachment. "I thought you should know that all your talk of Cog Hive Seven piqued my interest."

"Indeed?" Sidious felt something tighten inside his throat. "How so?"

"I've spoken to a contact at the IBC and asked them to dispatch a financial consultant there under the auspices of a routine quarterly audit—a certain Vesto Slipher. He'll be reporting directly to me." Behind the mask, Plagueis's smile was pure diplomatic graciousness. "Perhaps I can help you ferret out this elusive arms dealer after all."

Sidious felt a faint knot tightening in his throat. "That's—extremely thoughtful of you."

"I know we are together on this," Plagueis said, "as equals."

Plagueis withdrew his hand. He was still gazing out at Sidious when the air-taxi's hatch closed between them and it lifted away from the Senate Plaza, leaving Sidious standing there alone.

16

NIGHTSIDE

The debris pile was made up of burned-out droid parts, condenser coils, and twisted rebar, all of it forcibly compressed into a perfect cube. Artagan had scavenged together a dozen such blocks down here a year ago while wandering through an unfinished wing off Maintenance Sublevel 3, the one that the inmates called Nightside.

Originally designated as Cog Hive Seven's garbage dump, Nightside was now a desolate industrial cave, its shadows bulking with unused scrap balers, shearing machines, and metal shredders. The stink of carbon composite and various ferroalloys hung permanently in the air. Prisoners came down here from time to time, scrounging through leftover debris, ever since the rumor began circulating that somebody once found a Baragwin shield disruptor in a pile of heavy smelting scrap. The story was probably apocryphal, but it drew them anyway.

None of which explained why Artagan Truax had brought his son here today.

"Very good." Artagan glanced at the block of debris and then turned back to Eogan. "This one now."

"That?" The boy gave it a sidelong glance. "It's too much! And my arms are already burned out from those dead lifts!"

"Excuses won't save you." Artagan gazed at his son sternly. "Do you wish to survive this place or not?"

Eogan nodded and shut his eyes. He was stripped to the waist, his bare torso pale and nearly hairless. He'd spent the last few hours chasing prison rats across elevated girders, attacking them with both hands tied behind his back. They were large, disgusting things, but they moved fast, and pursuing them required absolute focus and determination.

Afterward he'd practiced punching, kicking, swinging, ducking, lifting, pulling, Artagan coaching his son through the various holds, locks, and attacks that might one day make all the difference in a bout.

There were no rules here in Cog Hive Seven, no such thing as mercy, no quarter asked or given. After the morning workout, sweat gleamed from Eogan's upper lip and forehead, plastering the reddish brown hair against his brow in strands and clumps. "Now?"

"Whenever you're ready."

Reclining backward, Eogan tilted his head back and reached for the makeshift crossbar that his father had jimmied up beneath the pallet. Artagan waited while his son tested the bar to make sure the load was balanced, and he watched his son's features tense up in anticipation of the lift.

"Get under it," Artagan said.

"How many?"

"Start with one."

The boy shut his eyes and pushed. Muscles leapt out across his shoulders, chest, and abdomen, biceps straining, arms extending until he held the debris pile at arm's length off the floor. He started to lower it, but Artagan spoke.

"Hold it on my count."

Eogan didn't argue. The load trembled. The boy's jaw clenched, fighting gravity and fatigue every passing second. Throughout it all, Artagan stood over him without expression, watching the weakness drain from his son's body, feeling the familiar mingling of deep pride and dismay that came with the realization of how hard the boy was working, and ultimately how little it mattered.

Eogan grunted. "Father—"

"Five more seconds," Artagan said. "You can do it."

The boy tucked his chin. By now his face had gone a dark, plummy shade of scarlet, all the way up to his hairline. Veins stood out in his temples. A slight, involuntary whimper escaped his throat, and Artagan heard the load beginning to rattle as the boy's arms trembled harder than ever, threatening collapse.

"I can't—"

"Two more seconds," Artagan told him. "One . . ." He nodded. "That's enough."

The load dropped with a crash, and Eogan let out a gasp of relief, sitting up slowly, rubbing his shoulders, and trembling with the lactic acid buildup in his muscles. Artagan tossed him the towel and waited while the boy mopped his face and glanced back at the cube before finally lifting his gaze to look up at Artagan. His face was pale now, drained but clearly pleased.

"How much?" Eogan asked.

"A hundred and twenty."

"I've never lifted that much before!"

"You asked for a true test," Artagan said. "I gave you one." Reaching down to ruffle his son's sweaty hair, he felt a tenderness that he rarely allowed himself to acknowledge, the deep love whose only counterweight was the deep knowledge that all too soon it would be taken away.

He withdrew his hand.

"Now," he said, "the Fifty-Two Fists."

Eogan's eyes widened. "Father . . ."

"Now."

Reluctantly the boy assumed the position of readiness, neck straight, body rigid, arms upraised, a veil of doomed hopelessness already descending over his face. Comprising a blizzard of lightning-fast attacks over a period of less than five seconds, the attack known as Fifty-Two Fists required total commitment to absolute destruction of the opponent. Done properly, it could kill a man three times Eogan's size and weight. But the slightest tremor of intent left its unlucky practitioner wide open to all manner of retribution.

"Now," Artagan said.

The boy launched himself at his father, arms scissoring in a blur of punches. At first the results appeared promising. But all too quickly, Artagan saw a hole, lunged forward, and threw his son to the floor.

Eogan lay supine, gasping for air, eyes shining, cheeks and forehead blazing. Only now did the anger come, belated, impotent.

"Are you going to cry, then?" Artagan didn't bother hiding the disappointment on his face. "You know the rule."

"Yes, Father." The boy jerked his head up and down fiercely, fighting back tears. From the beginning, the rule had been simple: for every tear, a drop of blood.

"Then get up," Artagan said, extending his hand. "And we'll try again."

"Yes, Father."

"And all for what?" a new voice jeered from the far end of the shop, ringing off the flat metal surfaces that surrounded them. "One match? Two if he's lucky?"

Father and son turned to look at the guard stepping out from behind a massive briquette press hunkered in the far corner. Making his way toward them, CO Voystock approached the debris block and gave it an appreciative kick before turning his full attention to Artagan and Eogan.

"You're wasting your time, kid," the guard said wryly. "You know that, right?"

"I'm training."

"For what, a one-way trip down the cremation shaft?"

"That's—" Eogan's face contorted, becoming bitter. "What would you know about strength and discipline?"

"Strength and discipline, huh?" Still grinning, Voystock tucked his thumbs into his belt and rocked back on his heels. "I like that. Remind me to have it engraved on your dad's corpse as an inspiration to others."

"My father could tear a man like you to pieces without breaking a sweat."

A little bit of the guard's smile faded. "Forget it, junior. I don't fight the elderly."

"He held the Blasko Title for three straight seasons, did you know that?" Eogan took a step toward him. "Without that switch on your hip, you wouldn't last five seconds against him."

"Don't push it, boy. Remember who you're talking to."

"I'm almost ready. Tell him, Father."

"Right." Voystock laughed, but there was no humor in it, only the brittle exasperation of a man whose patience was being sorely tried. "Kid, you wouldn't last five seconds in a fight. Even your old man knows it." Reaching up, he ran one hand over his stubbled jawline. "Why do you think he's paying me to help you two bottom-feeders bust out of here?"

"What are you talking about?"

"You don't believe me? Ask your dad. What do you think I'm doing down here, breathing in all this metal dust for my health?"

The boy fell silent. His eyes shifted from Voystock to his father, and then he said, in a very quiet voice: "Is it true?"

"Eogan—"

"Is it true?"

"Son," Artagan said, "we'll both die here if we—"

"You said I was strong enough! You said that I was ready to fight!"

Artagan closed his eyes. This was going to be harder than he'd expected, he realized, and infinitely more painful. He drew his hands out of his pockets so that Eogan could see how badly they trembled. "Son, it's over for us here."

"Don't say that. It's not true!"

"You're already stronger and faster than I am," Artagan continued, "but you're not a killer." He steadied his hand and placed it on the boy's bare shoulder, felt the tension that had gathered there, twisted into knots of postadolescent indignation. "There's deep steel in you, yes, but there is also great mercy. Kindness." He drew in a deep, resigned breath. "This is no place for a boy like you."

Boy. That single word seemed to lie more crushingly upon Eogan than any of the weights he'd had to lift. "Then why did you bring me here?" he asked.

Artagan looked away. It was the one question he couldn't answer. "It was . . . a mistake."

"A *mistake?*"

"I miscalculated. Relied on salvation from a man who could not provide it." He moved past his son, shifting toward Voystock. "Can you get us into medbay?"

Voystock gazed at him for a long moment. "When?"

"Right now."

"What's the rush?"

"I would prefer not to linger here any longer here than we absolutely have to." Artagan realized that he was clenching his fists and forced himself to open them. His fingernails had cut tiny red half-moons into the lines of his palms. "Yes or no?"

The guard sighed and nodded. "Yeah," he said, and checked the chrono strapped to his wrist. "I can disrupt the primary and auxiliary feed to the medbay. When the power doesn't come back on the grid, maintenance will have to run a black start. It will take fifteen minutes to bootstrap the main server arrays back online."

"But if you disrupt all the power, then how—"

Voystock held up one hand to stop him. "At that point, our standard protocol is to reroute all power through the GH-7 so they can patch surveillance through the droid's photoreceptors—that's when you'll make your move."

"All right."

"You realize they'll see your faces. You'll have to do something about that."

"It's not a problem," Artagan said.

"You've got fifteen minutes. If the droid hasn't deactivated the electrostatic charges in your hearts by then, there's nothing else I can do."

"I understand."

"I mean it." Voystock locked eyes with him. "You're on your own. We're not friends, which means you and your boy are a couple of hard targets just like any other runaway. I don't know how you're going to get out of medbay and I don't care. Anybody asks me if I've seen you, I tell them everything."

"Then let's go."

"Father, no!" Eogan wheeled around, and now all his renewed anger and disbelief were focused where Artagan had been expecting it all along—directly on him. "He's setting us up, can't you see that? He's just going to steal every credit you have, drain the accounts, and send us right back into the cells again! He'll betray us the first chance he gets!"

"Eogan, he's our one hope of getting out. And we have to go now."

"I can learn the Fifty-Two Fists! I just need more time!"

Artagan took hold of his son, clasping him in a sweaty embrace. The boy squirmed, pushing back, fighting to resist. He *was* stronger than Artagan now, and under any other circumstances he would have broken the hold, but his arms were tired, the muscles spent from lifting.

At last he collapsed into Artagan's arms, glaring up at his father in impotent fury.

"That's why you worked me so hard," he said tonelessly. "So I couldn't stop you."

"Stop *us*," Artagan corrected, and flicked his gaze at Voystock, narrowing his eyes. "Are you ready?"

Voystock nodded. "Just waiting on you. Let's go."

17

GHOST VOLTAGE

An hour after he'd stashed the transmitter and left the prison morgue, Maul was circulating silently among Cog Hive Seven's genpop. He'd dispatched another message through a maintenance droid—the same one he'd used to summon the gangs down to the prison laundry—and was waiting to hear back from the inmate he'd contacted.

In the meantime, he stood and watched the crowds of prisoners moving about their business. There was, as always, a kind of heightened sensitivity that came whenever he'd spent any significant time with his Master—an increased awareness of things both hidden and exposed, the crackling prescience of latent energy fields that he'd come to think of as ghost voltage. Even here, among the dregs of the galaxy, Maul found it revelatory and exhilarating.

He was crossing the gallery outside the mess hall when he spotted the inmate called Izhsmash through a crowd of inmates. The Nelvaanian's expression did not change, but the recognition in his eyes told Maul that he'd received the message Maul had sent earlier.

Without a word, Maul pivoted, heading down the corrugated durasteel ramp through the narrow passageway that led into the maintenance tunnels below. Bare electrical fixtures threw their flat, declamatory glare across the floor beneath his feet, outlining his silhouette as crisply as a shape cut from the blackness of the universe itself. Twenty meters down, he stopped and ducked deeper into the shadows, listening for approaching footfalls.

After a moment, Izhsmash spoke, his voice hushed. "I came alone," he said. "What do you want?"

Maul turned and stepped into view. "Information."

"You can threaten me all you want. I won't talk about Ra—" Catching himself, he stopped. "I won't talk about that individual."

"That's not why I asked you here," Maul said. "In any case, I doubt you know anything about Iram Radique that I haven't already found out."

Izhsmash frowned. "Then why . . . ?"

"Strabo told me why you were sentenced to this place," Maul said. "You're a renegade programmer. A data thief. Word is that you wrote the original cryptoviral code for that attack on the Phage Network."

"That's never been—"

Maul held up his hand. "I need you to hack into the prison database. Get me information about all the inmates and their criminal history. I need a complete list."

"It's going to take time."

"I know something about slicing into systems myself," Maul said, his mind cycling back to what felt like a lifetime ago, when the one known as Trezza had taught him computer saboteur skills during part of his time on Orsis. "But right now I don't want the exposure. Let me know when it's finished."

The Nelvaanian cocked his head. "Anything else?"

"I'll let you know."

Izhsmash nodded and turned to go, and all at once the lights above them flickered and dimmed. Maul glanced at him, immediately aware of the inmate's reaction.

"What was that?" he asked.

"Some kind of brownout. Felt like a power outage."

"It's uncommon here?"

"Very." Izhsmash shook his head. "There's too many backups and auxiliary relays. The last time it happened . . ." He glanced over his shoulder, then back at Maul. "It was an escape attempt."

"What happened?"

"It was about a year ago. A couple of the cons got wise and tried to override the prison's main power grid from the medbay and reprogram the surgical droid to disarm the charges so they could get out."

"Did it work?"

Izhsmash shook his head. "They died in the medbay."

"The guards caught them?"

"It wasn't the guards."

"Who then?"

Izhsmash licked his lips. His eyes fell to the floor, then rose to meet Maul's, and his voice was just the ghost of a whisper. "Radique."

"Why?"

"He never lets anyone leave. Any inmate who's ever worked for him in any capacity, who might know anything about him, who might be able to provide his enemies with the slightest hint of his whereabouts. That's why he's based his operation in a prison where nobody survives. If they try to escape—"

Maul felt something quicken within him. In some deeply intuitive way that defied all logical explanation, he already knew that he'd found what he was looking for, the next step toward his mission here. Whether this was the dark side at work, as Sidious had promised, or something as random as pure chance, it scarcely mattered.

Before Izhsmash had finished speaking, Maul was already moving back up the ramp and across the gallery toward what awaited him on the far side of the prison's main level.

Toward medbay.

18

BLACK START

"Warden," Dragomir Chlorus said, "you still don't seem to understand the gravity of your situation."

"Really?" Sadiki Blirr sank back with a silent groan, rotating her fingertips against her throbbing temples, where the first vestiges of a killer migraine were slowly making themselves known. This conversation with the gaming commissioner had been one of the longest in recent memory, and there was still no end in sight. "Then you'd better run through it again. After all, I've already got an IBC representative onsite auditing my whole operation, but I suppose I'm just too dense to figure out what that means."

Chlorus sighed. "It's not the IBC that you need to worry about. The Desilijic Clan has taken an interest in your operation. And it's been going on for quite some time."

"The Hutts?" Sadiki gave a weary laugh. "I expect I would notice if I had a problem with them, don't you think?"

Chlorus's face remained grim. "Well, they've certainly noticed *you*. And they haven't taken fondly to the way that Cog Hive Seven has eaten away at their revenues."

"That's preposterous," she said. "Their gambling operations are more lucrative than ever."

"I'm not just speaking of gambling, Sadiki."

She peered up at him warily. "What else do you think we do around here, moisture farming?"

"You understand this is strictly off the record." The commissioner leaned in closer, lowering his voice. "I'm sure you've heard the rumors about Iram Radique. The weapons dealer said to run his operation from somewhere within Cog Hive Seven."

"Oh no." Sadiki's migraine jumped from nascent to fully formed in one breathtaking instant. "Not that old wheeze again."

"Yes, you've told me, Radique isn't in your prison, if he even exists at all. But the Hutts aren't so sure. In fact, they've apparently decided to see for themselves."

"What do you mean, see for themselves?"

"I simply mean that—"

The signal froze. In the background Sadiki heard a steady, low-frequency tone begin to pulse as a panel of red and yellow alarm lights sprang up along the top of the console. She straightened. "Look, Dragomir, I've got a situation here. I have to go. We'll talk again."

"Sadiki, wait—"

Cutting the call short, she jumped on the comm and tapped into central control for the prison's main power station.

"Control, do you copy?" she asked. "This is Warden Blirr. I need a status report for Section 1212."

"Copy that, warden," the guard's voice drawled back with a maddening lack of concern. "Looks like a minor malfunction down in medbay."

Sadiki hit the acknowledge button on the warning alarms, silencing them. "Minor malfunction? From my side it looks like the whole level's gone down."

"Stand by for confirmation." The readout along the comlink's display identified him as CO Madden. "Yeah, roger that, Warden. Looks like it's just a transient fault. We're resetting it now."

Sadiki brought up the surveillance screens for the medbay, but the monitors were solid blue across every frequency. "Where's my backup power?"

"Must've gone down with the primary."

"So you're telling me we've got nothing in there right now?"

"Negative. Ah, I mean, affirmative. That's—" Now Madden actually sounded a little nervous, which Sadiki would have found gratifying if he hadn't been expected to perform competently under these circumstances. "No worries. We're patching all surveillance through to the GH-7 surgical droid onsite. Should have audiovisual back up in just a second."

"Who's in medbay now?"

"Stand by." There was the chirp of an electronic tablet being nudged to life. "No organic life-forms. Currently it looks like it's just the GH-7. And . . ." A pause. "Hold it."

"What is it?"

"Thermal sensors are picking something up."

"Who is it?" Sadiki felt her migraine spilling over, sending sharp pains down the back of her neck.

"Might just be a faulty reading," Madden said. "Stand by."

His voice cut out. With a grimace, Sadiki turned and tapped in a series of commands, bringing up a current list of admissions to the prison's medbay. According to the current census, it should've been empty in there.

She hit the comm again, harder than she intended.

"Madden? Do you copy?"

A blast of static and then Madden came back, sounding faint: "Copy."

"Where's my surveillance?"

"Still recalibrating off the main grid." There was a hurried clicking noise of many different switches being thrown to no effect, and the guard muttered something that she couldn't hear. "External network's not coming back up for some reason. We're going to have to do a black start, bootstrap it back up. It'll take fifteen minutes, then we should be good."

"What about those other life-forms in medbay?" Sadiki asked. "How many are there?"

"I've got a squad heading down there now—that must be what we're seeing. I'll let you know the second we're back up."

Sadiki sat back and forced herself to be patient. Waiting around for information wasn't exactly her specialty, and in the past—working in casinos and managing large-scale offworld resort operations—her inability to suffer fools had served her well. But all too often, when power fell off the grid in Cog Hive Seven, there was nothing to do but wait.

The truth was, she was as much to blame as anyone.

Even before the sheer mathematical elegance of the algorithm had brought it to life, her brother's original designs for Cog Hive Seven had been beautiful, a seamless installation of utilitarian art. Redundant power backups and secondary electrical relays were all supposed to have been installed as part of Cog Hive Seven's initial construction—along with the metal shop, the factory floor, and a half dozen other independently sealed sublevels. But there had been construction delays, bureaucratic wheels to be greased, permits to be secured, and impatient investors demanding to see quarterly profit-and-loss statements. And in the end, they'd cut a few corners.

A lot of them, actually.

As much as Sadiki couldn't tolerate weak-minded excuses among underlings, she loathed them most vociferously in herself. The truth behind what had really happened here came down to far more than just a few loose ends. The truth was that when Dakarai's algorithm had started paying out and the money had come pouring in, she'd more or less completely abandoned any further construction inside the prison.

Given a choice, she knew that the IBC would have extended her time and credits enough to finish the space station properly according to the original specs. But it was Sadiki herself who had pushed it prematurely into its fully operational status, knowing full well that Cog Hive Seven's wiring, surveillance feeds, and power grids were substandard and, in some cases, virtually nonexistent. And it was Sadiki who had allowed herself to become overconfident about the implanted cardiac electrostatic charges inside the inmates' hearts, telling herself that as preventative measures went, it was more than enough of a deterrent.

But there had been other compensations. Some of them very lucrative indeed.

"Warden?" Madden's voice came back through.

"I'm here."

"We've got visual in the medbay coming on now. It's all low-light through the GH-7's photoreceptors, but—"

"Just patch me through," Sadiki snapped, and turned to the screens in front of her.

There was a sharp hiss, and a turgid upswell of white noise droned across the monitors. As it cleared, she found herself looking down through the surgical droid's floating perspective, drifting into the medbay, its walls and ceiling a green-tinted field of indistinct image-intensified blobs. Unfamiliar voices crackled through the droid's auditory sensor.

"Father," one of the voices was saying, "you know we can't trust him. Why would you—"

"He's the only one who can help us," a man's voice cut in. "We need him."

"But what if it's a trap?"

"Better listen to your old man, kid," a third voice growled. "I'm the only chance you've got."

Sadiki sat bolt upright in her seat. She recognized that voice.

Voystock.

She slapped the comm again, actually cracking the stud with the palm of her hand. "Madden, there's a *guard* in there!"

"Copy that, Warden, we just—"

"He's helping them escape, you idiot! Where are your people?"

"Say again?"

"The officers on duty, Madden. *Where are your men?*"

"I don't—" Madden's voice blipped out, then came back again. "Whoever's in the medbay has it sealed down from inside." Now he sounded like he was trying very hard not to start stuttering, but he wasn't doing a very good job. "I don't know how it happened, we were just—"

"Get in there now!"

"You want us to blast it open?"

"Whatever it takes."

"But—"

Sadiki cut him off and turned back to the screens, her headache utterly forgotten, superseded now by the pounding of her heart and the realization that she'd actually broken a sweat. Time itself seemed to have crystallized around her. On-screen, through the droid's photoreceptors, she could make out the forms of two inmates, an older man and a boy not more than sixteen, both clearly visible as they leaned in. CO Voystock stood in the background, making an adjustment to one of the control modules. The GH-7's manipulator was extending something—it looked like a hypodermic needle—toward the boy's chest.

In the distance she could hear the voices of guards outside the medbay, shouting commands and trying to get through the blast-doors.

And implacably, above it all, the mocking voice of the IBC's finest, Vesto Slipher, echoing in her head: *You've never had an escape?*

Of all the times for the IBC to be conducting an impromptu audit, Sadiki thought, and fought the urge to drive her fist into the console in frustration. She tapped in a command and brought up the holofeed of the datacenter, hoping to find Dakarai, but her brother wasn't there. Where was he?

Outside the medbay, the sound of blasters filled the audio track, distorting through the droid's aural pickups.

And for the first time, Sadiki Blirr realized that she was in real trouble.

19

IN MY TIME OF DYING

The power in the medbay was already out, and a cloak of darkness prevailed over its unfamiliar interior, save for the ambient glow of the diagnostic equipment, which cast a spectral blue glow on the figures moving through it, single file.

"Hold it," Voystock whispered, raising his hand without looking back. "That's far enough."

Artagan glanced at him. He and Eogan were halfway across the medbay, creeping their way forward in almost total blackness. "How long can you keep the main power out?"

"Leave that to me," the guard said. "I'll bring the droid around and take care of the programming to deactivate the charges."

Something shifted in the middle distance, and Artagan stiffened, glancing around. "Is there someone else in here with us?"

"No." Voystock shook his head. "I sealed the medbay up behind us. You saw me do it."

"I heard something."

"Shut up and stay put," the guard said. "Don't move. And don't touch anything." He ducked his head and vanished.

"Father," Eogan murmured a moment later, "you know we can't trust him. Why would you—"

"He's the only one who can help us. We need him."

"What if it's a trap?" the boy whispered, his voice going higher with urgency.

"Better listen to your old man, kid," said Voystock. "I'm the only chance you've got."

As if on cue, Artagan sensed something sailing past him in the blackness. Grabbing his son's arm, he ducked and felt it graze his shoulder. As the thing turreted around, he saw the GH-7's photoreceptors blink to life in the darkness, two perfect blue discs hovering before them.

Artagan listened and heard it again, the sound of someone else in the medbay with them, closer now.

"Voystock?" he hissed, turning in the direction of the sound. "Is that you?"

No one answered. In front of them, barely visible, Artagan saw the droid moving closer, its manipulator extending a long hypodermic needle.

"Father?" the boy asked.

"It's all right," Artagan said. "It will only hurt for a second. Then the charges will be deactivated. Go ahead."

"But—" Eogan started to say something and the needle plunged through his prison uniform and directly into his upper thorax. The boy let out a sharp squawk of pain, but his words were lost beneath the sudden volley of blasterfire from outside the medbay. Artagan heard voices, guards shouting at one another, and the shooting started again.

"What—?" Glancing around, Artagan Truax saw the GH-7 withdraw the needle from his son's chest, pivot in the air, and go flying backward. "What is this? What's going on?"

Five meters away, Voystock stood up, rising to his full height. "What's it sound like?" He turned around and faced the two inmates. Outside, the blasters had stopped firing again and Artagan heard a muffled voice barking orders, demanding whoever was inside to open up in there.

"You promised we'd have fifteen minutes," Artagan said. "I gave you the *khipu*! I gave you everything I had!"

"What, this?" Voystock held up the string with the knots in it and threw it in Artagan's direction. "Come on. You really think Radique would let you out of here that easily? After what you know about him?"

"Father?" Eogan stared at his father. "What's he talking about?"

"What, he never told you?" Voystock asked. He was grinning now. "Go ahead, old man. Tell your son why you're *really* here. Tell him how you brought him to this place."

"You don't know what you're talking about," Eogan said.

"Kid, I've heard just about enough from you." Without taking his eyes off Artagan, Voystock jerked his right arm back and drove his elbow into the boy's face. Eogan's head snapped sideways and he went flying into a tray of sterilized medical instruments, vascular clamps, and orthopedic drills, knocking them to the floor with a resonating crash of surgical steel. He lay there motionless.

"Eogan!" Artagan shouted, leaping up, then rounding on Voystock with a savage glare. "You'll pay for that."

"Easy, old man," Voystock said, his hand sliding down to the detonator console on his belt. "Nobody's paying for anything just now. That whelp of yours just signed his death warrant, and by the gods, you're going to watch him redeem it."

Artagan lunged at Voystock and fell on him, ripping away the guard's belt, fighting with a ferocity that was ultimately pointless. Within a span of seconds, Voystock had rolled free and hammered Artagan twice in the stomach and once across the bridge of the nose before smashing his skull with the butt of his blaster, over and over.

"Maybe next time . . ." *Wham!* ". . . you'll listen . . ." *WHAM!* ". . . when somebody tries to teach you . . ." *THUMP!* ". . . some karking respect!"

Voystock's hand went down to the detonator console, but it was gone.

Artagan groaned. With monumental effort, he managed to lift his head. His face and scalp were bleeding profusely from a half dozen different lacerations, but beneath it all something vital and defiant still shone in his eyes.

"Looking . . . for this . . . ?" Artagan was breathing heavily, barely moving air. In his right hand he held the dropbox that he'd ripped from the guard's belt. He no longer looked steady on his feet, but his entire countenance was blazing with a kind of desperate willfulness, a stark and uncompromising refusal to go down. "Come on and take it."

"I don't need that thing anyway," Voystock snarled, smearing blood from his own nose and raising the blaster. "Not when I've got this."

"But Radique said—"

"Radique's only instruction was not to let you escape." Voystock pointed the blaster at Artagan's leg. "He didn't say anything about not killing you."

And he pulled the trigger.

Artagan screamed. In the muzzle flash, he saw his own right leg explode in a gaudy bouquet of blood and gristle, leaving a ragged stump of gleaming bone exposed just below the knee. Curling back, he tried to scramble away and went sprawling backward across the floor.

"Hurts, doesn't it?" Voystock stepped closer. "You'll never walk again. You'll never fight. You're a cripple now. You'll live in excruciating pain for the rest of your miserable life." He raised the blaster, pointing it directly at the inmate's head. "Maybe if you beg for mercy, I'll spare you, grant you a quick death."

The old man stared up at the blaster, his face momentarily evacuated of all expression. Then he smiled.

It was a warrior's smile, full of pain and brokenness, and beneath it all a kind of cold-eyed clarity found among soldiers and killers whose entire lives had been spent plying their trade in the marketplace of mortal suffering. Beneath the blood, the old scars stood out clearly across his forehead.

When he spoke, his voice was calm and steady.

"On my home planet," Artagan said, "it is no small thing to make up a man's dying bed. It may only take a few seconds, and it may be nothing but the ground where he falls, but it is not a matter to be taken lightly. Are you sure that you are worthy of that honor, CO Voystock?"

"Honor?" Voystock snorted. "Old man, who do you think you are?"

"I am Artagan Truax." His words had become low and hoarse but remained unwavering. Beneath his lids, the whites of his eyes were turning red, filling up with scarlet from internal hemorrhaging. "I have killed men in eleven systems. I have fought well and withstood much and have not given quarter. I will not be broken by the likes of you today, nor will my son. *And I will not beg for mercy.*"

Voystock shook his head, finger tightening on the trigger. "Then you can—"

The words broke off. There was a sharp vertebral crack as the guard's head swiveled around backward 180 degrees.

Artagan Truax looked up and saw the Zabrak standing over the guard's dead body, holding him by the jaw and skull base. The one called Jagannath released his grip and Voystock sagged to the medbay floor in a boneless, lifeless heap.

"Jagannath," Artagan managed.

The red-skinned inmate was looking down at him with no pity in his yellow eyes.

"Talk," he said.

20

OPEN SECRETS

For a long moment the old man just stared up at him. His face had gone completely white except for his eyes, which had become bloody orbs. His breathing was hoarse and labored. He was shaking violently. Yet, for the time being, he still appeared to be lucid.

"What did you do for Iram Radique?" Maul asked. "Why won't he let you leave?"

The old inmate's lips moved, but the words they formed were too faint to hear. Blasters began firing again outside the sealed hatchway of the medbay. Leaning forward, Maul managed to catch his words.

"Eogan . . . ?"

"Your son is here," Maul said, glancing over to where the boy lay sprawled unconscious among a pile of surgical instruments. Then he looked back at the old man, taking in the sight of his maimed leg and the ever broadening lake of blood that surrounded him. "But you're not going to be in any position to watch over him any longer. Not like this."

The old inmate's face tightened. Already he seemed to grasp the severity of the situation.

"I can protect him," Maul said. "If you tell me what I need to know." He leaned in again. "What did you do for Iram Radique?"

The old man nodded. When he spoke again, his voice was husky, a forced whisper. "Saved his life."

"Radique's?"

Another nod.

"When was this?"

"Twenty years ago," the old man said. "On Lakteen Depot. Near the Giju Run."

"Where is he?" Maul asked. "Where can I find him? Is he here inside Cog Hive Seven right now?"

Artagan's mouth trembled. "He's—"

Outside, the shouts of the guards got louder. Now the blasters outside were very close. Metal fragments were ricocheting off the inner walls, pinging and scraping into the medbay. Maul knew they'd have it open within moments.

He turned, rising, and saw the older inmate's gore-streaked face gaping at him, just inches away. He reached out and grabbed Maul's wrist. Somehow, beaten almost to death and missing a leg, the old man had still managed to marshal his strength.

"Where is he now?" Maul asked.

The old man gaped at him, forcing the words out through sheer determination.

"Eogan," he said. "Eogan knows. *Everything*."

Before Maul could ask again, there was a sharp click followed by a humming noise as power came back on. Overhead fluorescents shuddered through the medbay around them, their intensity revealing the true ruin of the old man's face.

"Hold it right there!" a guard's voice shouted. The doors slid open as guards burst into the room, blasters at the ready, flanking it on either side.

Maul heard guards' boots thumping toward him as they knocked him to his knees, grabbed his arms, and pinned them behind his back. He started to stand up and felt the unmistakable hot metal ring of a recently discharged blaster barrel pressing against the back of his skull.

"Don't move, maggot," the guard behind him said. "We've got orders to take you directly to the warden." The hot steel nudged harder against his skin. "But that doesn't mean you might not have a nasty accident along the way."

Maul growled. Only then did he turn and glance back at the old man, who lay in a heap less than a meter away.

Eogan knows. Everything.

"Let's go," the guard said. *"Now."*

Maul turned his gaze from the old man and rose slowly to his feet to follow the guards out through the hatchway into the open corridor beyond.

21

SPINDLE

They brought Maul up in the crowded service lift, two guards flanking him on either side with another at his back, jamming the barrel of his blaster against his spine. Gazing up into the reflective surface of the lift's interior, he recognized the face of Smight, the young recruit who had first screened him when he'd arrived.

"What are you looking at?" Smight asked him.

Maul's lower lip drew back enough to reveal his sharpened canines. "Touch me with that toy of yours again," he said, his voice utterly expressionless, "and you'll find out."

Smight's face constricted, but he didn't poke Maul with the blaster again.

When the lift came to a halt, the COs ushered him into the gleaming office whose sleek and elegant interior couldn't have been more dissimilar from the rest of the prison. Stepping through the doorway, Maul saw the dark-haired woman with cold blue eyes standing just inside behind the desk. Her gaze was steady enough, but the smile on her face looked as if it had been glued into place by a pair of none too steady hands.

"Inmate 11240," she said. "I'm Warden Sadiki Blirr. You'll forgive me if I don't shake your hand."

Maul said nothing.

"We've had some unforeseen developments down in medbay this afternoon." She nodded at the monitors behind her. "Our surveillance of that time period is incomplete, and I'm hoping you'll be able to help me fill in the gaps."

Maul didn't respond.

"You heard the warden," one of the guards said, not Smight this time but a heavyset man with thick black eyebrows. "Tell her what you did to Voystock."

"He had an accident," Maul said.

"You're a karking liar," the guard snapped, reaching for his blaster.

"Actually," Sadiki said, waving him off, not taking her eyes from Maul, "I'm not even remotely concerned with what happened to Officer Voystock—or who was ultimately responsible for him getting exactly what was coming to him. By all accounts, he was as lazy as he was stupid, and he died in the process of aiding and abetting an ultimately unsuccessful escape attempt. None of which is particularly unusual around here, except that he went about it with remarkable clumsiness and incompetence." She gave a slight shrug. "Whatever fate befell him, I'm sure he deserved it. He will not be missed."

Now her smile was different, absolutely confident, even radiant, and Maul realized that his initial assessment of the warden had been wrong—the nervousness he'd perceived had been nothing more than an affectation, meant to throw him off his game. In a strange way, he almost admired it.

"What I am extremely interested in," Sadiki continued, reaching behind her desk and taking out a tablet so that Maul could see it, "are these electroencephalograph readings. Perhaps you recognize them?"

Maul glanced at the screen, watching the easy waveforms oscillating across it, rhythmic sine waves of deep sedation.

"This is a recording of your brain activity from your initial med screen upon arrival at the Hive," the warden said. "And here you'll see something very peculiar." She tapped a switch and the waveform jumped, lurching into an erratic, spiking landscape of sharp peaks and dips. "What's happening there?"

Maul met her gaze with absolute indifference. "I have no idea."

"Really." Something subtle twitched at the corner of the warden's lips. "See now, that's really interesting, because you've got my medical droid completely stumped. If you look here"—she pointed at the screen—"there are certain very specialized aspects of your cortex activating that the droid has never seen on any level of REM sleep. Apparently this particular waveform is called an omicron spindle. My droid says it's only seen it in certain very proficient telepaths. Which makes you very special indeed."

Maul's face remained cold and expressionless. Sadiki reached out and touched his face, tracing her fingernails down over the curve of his jaw. Leaning in, she dropped her voice to a whisper.

"You've got a secret, friend. And here's the crux of it. I don't think you're in my prison by accident—and I don't think you're here to fight."

"Then maybe you should let me go," Maul said.

"Oh," she said with a smile, "I could never do that. Not now that you've become such a favorite in the galactic gambling community. You've become quite a star, Jagannath. That is what they're calling you, isn't it? The Tooth?"

Maul stared at her narrowly. At length his attention was drawn to the desk that occupied the far side of the office. Underneath it, something was glowing very faintly, casting an almost imperceptible green light across the tan carpet. He looked up at Sadiki, who still held the tablet in her hand.

"Let me see that."

"This?" She hesitated a moment, then handed it to him. "Suit yourself."

Maul took the tablet and regarded the flat display screen for a moment, where the waveforms of his brain's electrical activity twitched and spiked. He shook his head. "This means nothing to me," he said, and with a flick of the wrist tossed it across the office so that it hit the floor under the desk.

Sadiki gazed at him serenely. She didn't seem at all bothered by this small outburst; if anything, it seemed to validate her own suspicions about who he was. "You're quite an exceptional specimen, aren't you? Exquisitely trained, practically custom built to survive in almost any environment—fierce, quick, resourceful, and adaptable against any imaginable obstacle or opponent. A precision instrument of savagery."

She paused, her voice softening slightly. "In a way, you really are the perfect inmate for Cog Hive Seven. You *are* the one we've been waiting for."

Maul's eyes darted under the desk, where the warden's tablet had landed. The display screen reflected upward to reveal what he'd thought might be there—a tiny streamlined piece of electronics emitting a faint green light from the underside of the desk. He gazed back at Sadiki. "Are we finished?"

"Not quite." She gestured at the guards. "Leave us."

Smight appeared uncertain. "Are you sure—"

"*Now.*" Sadiki gestured them out with an impatient jerk of her head, shutting the hatchway behind them and sealing it. When she turned back to face Maul, her expression had changed yet again, becoming focused and intense.

"You weren't supposed to survive your match with the wampa," she said. "You've deduced that for yourself, I suppose. In fact, I'd be willing to bet there are a great many things that you know but that you're not sharing with me. Like why you're searching for Iram Radique."

Maul's expression was unchanged. "Is that a question?"

"You may think that your true purpose here can be kept secret, but rest assured"—her face twisted, becoming angular and harsh—"there is nothing that goes on inside these walls that I won't find out about. You *will* inform me what you've already discovered about Radique's whereabouts here, and who sent you here to find him." She waited. "Was it the Desilijic Clan? The Hutts?"

Maul said nothing.

"Very well." She smiled, but there was no joy or pleasure in it. "Have it your way. And in the meantime—" Sadiki's lips drew back slightly further, showing just the lower rim of her teeth. "Rest assured that I'm going to keep matching you. Eventually I know you'll tell me everything."

Maul didn't move. "That all depends."

"On what?"

"On who else is listening."

She blinked at him, not comprehending. "Meaning what?"

Maul nodded back at the desk. "That device hidden under your desk is a miniature microphone. I'm guessing that you didn't place it there yourself—which means you probably had no idea that it was there."

"What . . . ?" Sadiki turned away from him and went to the desk, bent down to look underneath it, yanked the device loose, and then stared back at Maul. The expression of shock and dismay in her eyes was profoundly gratifying.

"So," Maul said. "I assume we're done here?"

22

BLUE WITCH

In his errands for the IBC, handling millions of credits for clients whose financial privacy was vital, Vesto Slipher traveled with the usual arsenal of security and surveillance disruptors. Most were standard electromagnetic emitters, ion-pulse shredders, and white noise generators— gray-market gear designed to foil any unwanted wiretaps or recording devices that might compromise his clients' confidentiality. He also traveled with surveillance gear of his own, including the bug that he'd placed under Warden Blirr's desk.

These days he scarcely gave any of these instruments a second thought as he installed them around whatever workspace he'd been given. Their deployment was, for him, as unremarkable as unpacking his overnight bag.

But this time he'd brought along something special, a gift from the Banking Clan's lab techs.

"We're still beta-testing it," the tech on Muunilinst had told Slipher before he'd departed, handing him a featureless blue tube about the size and width of his index finger. "We call it the blue witch."

"Poetic," the Muun said dryly.

The tech shrugged. "It creates a void on the most sophisticated security holo cams. Like a lens flare, except transparent, and it follows you around the room. Works on all electronics, audio and video. Completely undetectable. Careful, though." He'd tapped a button on the bottom and the thing blinked instantly to life. "She runs hot."

Slipher had inspected the device and shook his head, handing it back. "I've got my own equipment."

"Uh-uh." The tech crossed his arms. "He wants you to take it."

"He does?"

"I spoke to him personally. He wants to be assured that you've taken every precaution."

And so Slipher had brought the thing along with him. Now, sitting in his guest quarters off an unfinished upper level of Cog Hive Seven, he switched on the blue witch and waited for his holo-unit to activate. A high-frequency whine shivered through the air, and within a few seconds he found himself face-to-face with the Muun who had sent him here, arguably the most intimidating presence that he'd ever encountered.

"Magister Damask," Slipher said, bowing slightly.

"Slipher." Hego Damask was wearing a long-sleeved robe and a transpirator mask. In the background, the holofeed captured just the faintest hint of whatever world he was currently occupying, an elaborate fortress on a jungle moon of some sort. Slipher thought he could make out the cry of exotic birds in the distance. "You've taken all the necessary precautions for this transmission?"

"Yes, Magister."

"And what have you learned?"

Slipher felt a thin blade of anxiety slide upward from his stomach to press against his chest cavity. Though he'd only spoken twice with Hego Damask before departing for Cog Hive Seven, he'd intuitively grasped that when it came to relaying bad news, it made no sense to waste time. "Distressingly little, I'm afraid."

"Really." Damask's tone was impossible to read. "That is disappointing. Have you made contact with Maul?"

"Not directly, no. But the device that I planted in her office allowed me to listen in on a conversation between him and the warden. He denies knowing anything about Radique—denies, in fact, that he's even been dispatched here to find him."

Damask's eyes narrowed. "So he doesn't know that I sent you?"

"No, Magister. I was under the impression that you wanted your name kept out of it." Slipher waited, feeling a thin film of perspiration gathering over his skin. "Was I mistaken?"

For a long time Damask said nothing. "Perhaps Maul's true mission here is more secret than I was led to believe."

"If we knew who his control was—" Slipher began.

"I *know* who his control is," Damask barked. "That is not the issue."

Slipher nodded hesitantly. "Sir, if I may . . ."

"What is it?"

"Is it possible that Iram Radique isn't on Cog Hive Seven? Or anywhere, for that matter?" With no way of knowing how this hypothesis might be perceived, he drew in a breath and pressed on. "Surely you've heard the speculation that the man himself doesn't truly exist—that he's, well, a sort of ghost."

"A ghost?"

"A construct, fabricated by a cabal of arms dealers, a false front created to intimidate the competition. I mean, the fact is that no one has ever actually seen Radique and lived to speak of it. Perhaps Maul is discovering that for himself as well." Slipher's voice cracked, and he stopped long enough to swallow and steady himself. "Or someone has gotten to him."

Again, Damask did not respond right away, choosing to simply gaze back at Slipher over the bridge of his breathing mask. Then he reached out of view of the holo. For a moment Slipher feared he was going to cut off the transmission, but instead a wash of data sprang up, superimposed over the visual transmission—bright columns of digits and various ports of call rising over Damask's face.

"Eighteen standard months ago," Damask said, "a vigo from the Black Sun Syndicate docked an unlicensed shuttle out of Gateway. The destination was Cog Hive Seven. That particular cargo was a load of stolen Tarascii explosives that had gone missing from a BlasTech heavy-ordnance satellite the previous year. Six months later the same shuttle docked again. This time it was carrying a load of baradium."

"May I ask where you acquired this—"

"It doesn't matter," Damask said brusquely. "You could have easily uncovered it yourself if you had lived up to your reputation as an analyst."

"Magister, those specific ingredients . . ." Slipher stared at the holo, struggling to absorb what was being said along with the columns of data. The conclusion was unavoidable. "You think someone's actually manufacturing thermal detonators here on Cog Hive Seven?"

"Or worse."

"I can't imagine—"

"Our intelligence indicates the most recent shipment to arrive was less than a month ago. Orbital detection identified the payload as weapons-grade depleted uranium."

For the first time, Vesto Slipher realized that he had nothing to say. Not that it mattered. Damask seemed to have grown tired of listening to him.

"Iram Radique is *not* a ghost," Damask said. "Nor is he a construct, a false front, or a figment of communal galactic imagination. *He is real.* Given the facts at hand, there can be no doubt that he is alive and well and operating somewhere inside Cog Hive Seven. And depending on whatever high-grade ordnance he may be manufacturing next, I have reason to believe that Maul's mission may represent a greater threat to galactic stability and my own personal safety than even he is aware of."

"So you're asking me to—"

"I'm asking you to stop hiding your inadequacy under the pretense of idiotic speculation," Damask snapped, "and do your job. Get the information before Maul does. Deliver it to me and me alone."

"Yes, Magister."

"In the meantime," Damask said, "you may find it helpful to remember that until you have satisfied your assignment, you can consider yourself a permanent resident of the prison. Is that clear?"

"Absolutely, sir. And may I add, if I have disappointed you in any way—"

But it was too late. The holo was cut short, taking Damask's face and the data-flow with it. Slipher was talking to dead air.

23

FACTORY FLOOR

Maul sat in his cell, poised on the bench. The hatch stood open in front of him. The rest of genpop was out wandering the gallery, killing time, waiting for the alarms to signal the next fight. But for the moment he preferred solitude, or what passed for it. His recovery was not complete. He needed time and silence to rebuild his strength.

Leaning forward, he placed his right hand between his knees and lifted himself up off the bench with one arm, holding there for a count of fifty before lowering himself and switching to the other arm. He repeated this exercise ten times for each arm, back and forth. Then using both arms he lifted himself straight up into the air, extending his legs, body held erect until every muscle trembled with the strain. There was nothing particularly pleasant about the deep core burn, but it was familiar and provided an outlet for the anger that had continued to grow and fester in him since he'd returned from the warden's office.

He lowered himself back to the bench and exhaled, shaking off the sweat from his head. Even with the hatchway open, he felt a faint sense of claustrophobia. The cell felt minutely smaller. Perhaps it was. Retractable walls and ceiling panels would certainly be programmed for such subtle adjustments, and at this point, he'd almost expected Sadiki to be tampering with his sense of perception in whatever way she could. He'd frustrated her attempts to interrogate him, but that wasn't much comfort. What he'd really longed to do was rip her head off with his bare hands, but that wouldn't solve his problem, either.

I'm going to keep matching you.

He'd expected nothing less. She would keep fighting him until she killed him or he told her why he was seeking Radique. If the wiretap device hidden beneath her desk was any indication, she wasn't the only one trying to gain that information.

His thoughts migrated to Artagan Truax and his son. Both would be under heavy guard because of their escape attempt, rendering them currently inaccessible. But Maul knew that if he bided his time, the opportunity would present itself. He remembered the old man's whispered words.

Eogan knows. Everything.

Yes. And if he did—

Something moved outside the cell.

Instantly on his feet, Maul was moving to the open hatchway in less than a second. But what he found waiting for him was not an inmate at all.

The clawbird perched across the concourse gazed down at him with black and lightless eyes—the same bird he'd spotted in the tunnels.

It had something in its mouth.

A scrap of bone.

"What are you doing here?" Maul asked it.

At once, the thing let out a sharp, plaintive caw, then spread its wings and took flight.

Without making any conscious decision to do so, Maul went after it.

Running down the long corridor, bolting past the occasional inmate loitering outside the cells, he cut through great swaths of open space, never letting the bird out of his sight. The walls blurred by. Leaping a waist-level barrier, vaulting over a pile of debris at the far end of the walkway, he knocked two prisoners aside without slowing down.

The clawbird flew faster. It darted upward along the ceiling, cut left, and disappeared through a ventilation shaft.

Propelling his body upward, Maul flung himself after it, plummeting down a ten-meter drop, and hit the ground running, his eyes instantly adjusting to the darkness, chasing it through a half-visible maze of utility droids and subcorridors branching off in a half dozen directions. He couldn't see the bird any longer, but he could still hear it clearly up ahead, its wings pounding hard through the gray spaces, betraying its position.

Sprinting, jumping across an unfinished platform, he landed on the other side and cut across the catwalk that adjoined it to a web of cables that affixed it to the far wall. Maul grabbed the cables, pulled himself hand over hand to his destination, and swung himself up and through yet another hatchway, into the wide-open space that awaited him there.

The bird had landed on an insulated electrical conduit and was staring down at him from a thick warren of debris—wires, threads, bits of circuitry, and trash—that he realized must be the thing's nest. For a moment it just stared down at him with what might have been begrudging admiration. The small bit of bone was still clasped in its beak.

Maul glared back at it.

What are you doing here, bird?

He looked around at the space where the chase had led him, a region he'd heard described as the factory floor. According to prison lore, it was another unfinished level somewhere beneath the haunted reaches of the metal shop, and for a moment he simply peered into the arched ribs of the ceiling's support struts, then down onto the abandoned steel prairie of the durasteel plating.

The word *factory* seemed to have been applied in its loosest imaginable interpretation. Whatever was supposed to have been manufactured here had gotten no further than the machinery that had been installed to build it. Conveyer belts and pallet racks stood empty around him. Up above, smoked-glass lenses gleamed down. More surveillance. Omnipresent eyes.

Maul moved past all of it with barely a glance. The cold vacuum of space felt very near, pressing against the outer shell of the space station with its own hissing intensity, and he felt artificial gravity intensifying, a by-product of poorly calibrated field generators that nobody had bothered to install properly in the first place. Like much of Cog Hive Seven, this place had a slapdash inconsistency, as if the whole thing had been put together in the dark. Of all the technology, only the cameras, silent and omnipresent, seemed to function according to spec. Guards were watching. Guards were *always* watching.

He took several more steps and stopped short.

The structure in front of him—he supposed you had to call it a sculpture—was built entirely out of bones. It stood as tall as he was, a gangling conflation of ribs, skulls and phalanges, human and nonhuman alike, all wired together into some utterly new composition.

It wasn't the only one of its kind. Looking around, he saw that this part of the factory floor was a veritable forest of bone sculptures, some suspended from the ceiling, others perched on the walls. As indifferent as he was to aesthetics, Maul found the assemblages themselves strangely compelling. Whatever else was happening in the bowels of Cog Hive Seven, someone or something was down here creating a new race of horrors that the galaxy itself had never dreamed of in its blackest nightmares. It spoke to some part of him that he'd never known to exist. For an instant he thought of the clawbird with the bone in its beak, and he understood now why he'd followed it here. It had led him to the one who'd made all of these things.

That was when he heard it—the unmistakable servo whir of mechanized belt treads moving up from behind.

He spun around to see a small maintenance droid advancing blithely toward him, carrying more bones with it. When the droid saw Maul, it stopped and squawked at him in some form of machine language.

"What are you doing here?" Maul asked it.

The droid didn't move. Then, with a panicked chirp, it reversed its treads and tried to get away, but Maul lunged for it and hoisted it up, arresting its escape.

"Easy, Jagannath," a voice said. "There's no need to terrorize my droid, now is there?"

Maul set the thing aside and looked around to face the diminutive inmate standing behind him, beaming serenely up at him. It was the Chadra-Fan he'd met in the mess hall, the only one who hadn't reacted to the explosion in the kitchen.

"Coyle?"

"Lost your way among the great unwashed, did you, brother?" Brushing the droid off, Coyle patted it on its head and sent the thing on its way. "What are you doing all the way down here, we wonder?"

"I followed the clawbird," Maul said.

"Bird?" Coyle blinked at him. "Now that's a riddle worth pondering, isn't it? Why did the prisoner chase the bird?" Then, without waiting for Maul's answer, he knelt down and began gathering the bones that the droid had dropped, humming quietly to himself as he did so. "Mind giving me a hand with these, brother? Got a work in progress around here somewhere, doesn't we?"

Maul looked at the bone sculptures. "All these are yours?"

"Hobby of mine, isn't it?" Coyle gave the armload of bones a fretful glance. "These aren't going to be enough. I was supposed to meet a couple of the Kings here—they were bringing me another shipment." He swung one arm, encompassing the sculptures. "I build things, you see. And around a place like this, bones are some of the most common construction materials. Catch my meaning, do you?"

He gestured across the vacant darkness to the other side of the conveyer belt by the opposite wall, and Maul looked up. The Chadra-Fan's newest sculpture was a towering convocation of femurs, ribs, and vertebrae with sleek, skeletal wings and a face built completely out of skulls. It rose into the uppermost shadows of the factory floor, at least eight meters high.

But there was an aspect of it that Maul hadn't noticed before. Viewed from a certain angle, the bones crisscrossed to form a pattern. Like a mathematical equation or some foreign alphabet, a code that defied immediate interpretation.

He cocked his head, stepping closer. There was something *inside* the sculpture, something he couldn't quite see from here.

"What does it mean?"

"Mean? Mean?" Coyle chuckled again. "It means you still haven't answered *my* riddle, brother."

"What question?"

"Why does the prisoner follow the bird?" The Chadra-Fan peered up at his own sculpture for a moment, then, without waiting for Maul's answer, tucked a pile of slender bones under one arm and scurried up a ladder to the top of a maintenance gantry alongside the sculpture.

Maul glared up at him. "What else do you build down here?"

"Oh, all sorts of wonderful things."

"Weapons?"

"Ah, that's another riddle, isn't it?" Coyle gazed down at him, and this time his rodent-like face bore no trace of expression. "Anything can be a weapon," he said quietly, "isn't that so?" Then another glint of a smile as he ran his fingers along the underside of the gantry arm and held them up for Maul to see the faint reddish-black residue. "'Slimy to touch, greasy to feel, but mix me with blood and I'll eat through steel.'" His eyes twinkled. "Do you take my meaning, brother?"

"Enough riddles." Maul felt the last of his patience draining away. He grabbed the Chadra-Fan by the shoulder, drawing him close. "I know that I'm getting closer to Iram Radique. I need to talk to him soon. My employer has business to transact."

"Your employer?" a cool voice spoke up from behind him. "And what employer might that be?"

Maul released Coyle and spun around. The Twi'lek was standing less than a meter away, his gaze fixed on Maul's. His approach had been absolutely silent, as if he'd been borne forth on a current of dark smoke.

"Zero," he said.

"Jagannath." The Twi'lek nodded at him in acknowledgment, then turned his attention to the unfinished bone sculpture next to the maintenance gantry. "Ah." He touched it with what appeared to be genuine admiration. "This is coming along very well, Coyle. You've made great strides."

"I thank you," Coyle said. "I'm still not finished, though. I need more bones."

"No shortage of those. What is it that we say?" The Twi'lek considered. "'The worm turns . . .'"

Coyle smiled, finishing the saying: "'And there are always more bones.'"

"Worm?" Maul asked.

"Ah," Coyle said, turning back to Maul. "That's the next question, isn't it?" He smiled, but this time there was very little warmth in it, as he spoke in that same sing-song rhyme: " 'The nightmare had a nightmare of its own, deep inside the darkness, fully grown.' "

Maul turned to Zero for an explanation. "What is he talking about?"

"My friend here speaks of the Syrox," Zero said, "the Wolf Worm of Cog Hive Seven. The one that moves in the ductwork of the prison, where it lives and grows fat on the blood from the matches. A nightmare within our nightmare, if you like. You may have already encountered its offspring, Jagannath—and you no doubt will again. But the thing itself, well . . ." He stopped and shuddered with revulsion. "At night sometimes, in the lowest maintenance shafts, if you put your ear to the wall . . ."

"Horror stories don't interest me," Maul said.

"Being one yourself," Coyle piped up, "I would think they might, wouldn't it?"

Ignoring the Chadra-Fan, Maul kept his attention focused on Zero. "I met the man you told me about," he said. "The one who came here looking for Iram Radique. The one who saved his life. His name is Artagan Truax."

"Truax . . ." The Twi'lek's expression was impossible to read. "Is that right?"

"Radique exists," Maul said. "And I know he's in here somewhere. The gangs serve him . . . or someone who works for him. They smuggle the weapons parts in on the supply shipments. There's a chain of command, and Radique uses it protect his identity." He waited for Zero to deny any of this, but the Twi'lek just regarded him thoughtfully. When he spoke again, his voice was low and careful.

"Assuming that you are one step closer to finding the truth," Zero murmured, "you'll need to look much harder than that."

"Who's above the gangs?" Maul asked. "Who's the go-between?"

Zero gazed at him. "You know, Coyle is right. Cog Hive Seven *is* a nightmare. And yet . . ." The Twi'lek regarded him silently for a moment. "You have already witnessed courage within these walls as well, have you not? And perhaps even selflessness?"

Maul felt his forehead growing hot with anger. "I see only weakness. And weakness is its own punishment, just as strength is its own reward."

"Is it so simple, then?" the Twi'lek inquired, but the remark didn't seem to have anything to do with what Maul had said. "And meanwhile, you remain unswerving in your mission."

"Yes."

"The search for Iram Radique."

"Yes," Maul said again. And in that moment he glimpsed another possibility, one that hadn't consciously occurred to him before now. What if all of this—even these oblique riddles, this maddening uncertainty, the questions that themselves seemed pointless and incidental—might all be part of some larger test from Sidious, a means of evaluating his capabilities as a Sith Lord before he allowed Maul to participate fully in the Grand Plan?

He narrowed his eyes at the Twi'lek.

"I need to know everything."

"In that case, Jagannath, I invite you to look upon the answer to your own riddle. Do you remember it?" He gestured up at the bone sculptures.

"Why does the prisoner chase the bird?" And now Maul saw what was moving inside it, flapping its black wings in the shadows. "I don't—"

"Because it's a rook," Zero said.

Maul turned back around to look at him. But the Twi'lek had already turned and started to walk away from Maul, descending into the darkness.

24
WISHLIST

"Boy. Wake up."

Maul watched as Eogan opened his eyes and stared directly up at the red, tattooed face peering down at him. When Eogan tried to sit up, Maul held his shoulders down, pinning him flat to his bunk, leaning down to speak into his ear.

"Where's your father?"

"He's still in medbay," the boy said. "His leg—"

Maul shook his head. "I just checked. He's not there. Where was he taken?"

"Taken?" The bewilderment in Eogan's face erupted into panic. His face looked haggard and terrified, his cheek still bruised and swollen from where Voystock's elbow had struck it, and then realization began to seep through his features. "Why would anyone—"

"Your father knew Radique," Maul said.

"Who?"

"Iram Radique. Your father saved his life and followed him here to Cog Hive Seven. That's why he brought you here. In medbay he told me that you have information about where I can find him. He said you know everything that he knows."

"That's not . . ." Eogan shook his head. "I don't know anything about that, I swear."

Maul resisted the urge to shake him just to see what might come loose. It had not been a good night. Since leaving the factory floor and his highly unsatisfactory meeting with Zero and Coyle, he'd prowled the holding cells restlessly, making his way to medbay, only to find it deserted. The old man's cell was empty, too. Maul had questioned the gang members, but no one knew anything of Artagan Truax's whereabouts. Having spoken Radique's name aloud, the old man seemed to have vanished completely, swallowed whole by the system that imprisoned him.

"Look, you have to believe me," Eogan said. "If I knew anything, I'd tell you." He gaped up at Maul beseechingly. "I've never even heard of this guy Radique."

Maul looked down at him. Maddening as it was, everything the boy said rang true. His ignorance on the topic of Radique and his father's connection to the arms dealer sounded absolutely authentic.

There was only one part of the story that didn't make sense.

"If you don't have any connection with Radique," Maul said, "then why are you still alive? Why didn't the guards terminate you and your father after you tried to escape?"

To this, the boy had no answer.

Maul left him there in his bunk and went back out to the concourse, up the long hallway to the silence that lay beyond.

"Jagannath?" Izhsmash's voice whispered. "It's me."

Maul paused and glanced down to where the other inmate was crouched back against the wall outside the prison laundry facility. Even here amid the leftover reek of detergent, he'd smelled the Nelvaanian before he'd seen him, the dampish, feral odor of the inmate's fur already familiar to his nostrils.

"Brought you something," Izhsmash said, digging into the hip pocket of his uniform and slipping a tightly folded rectangle of flimsiplast into Maul's palm. "Just downloaded it off a utility server. Not the easiest thing to get, either, on account of—"

"Is it complete?"

"Uh-huh." There was no mistaking the trace of pride in the Nelvaanian's voice. "That's everybody, far as I can tell."

Maul scanned the list of inmates—two hundred and eighteen names in all, with numbers, cell assignments, and criminal histories in reverse chronological order, some of them going back several years. His own name was the most recent addition: a single name, Jagannath, and a list of trumped-up mercenary charges and crimes that Sidious had provided for him before he'd dispatched Maul on this mission.

Out of the corner of his eye, he was aware of Izhsmash beginning to edge away into the shadows.

"Wait."

The Nelvaanian stopped.

"Who's this?" Maul pointed to a name midway down the list, one that had leapt out at him instantly, echoing the last word he'd heard spoken from Zero, down on the factory floor.

"Rook?" Izhsmash looked up at him, eyes widening ever so slightly.

"Who is he?"

The Nelvaanian shook his head. "Don't know. Never heard of him before."

"He's here in Cog Hive Seven. What species is he?"

"No idea." Izhsmash shrugged. "Look, there're lots of inmates on this list I've never met," he said. He was already beginning to back away again, casting longing glances at the hallway. "Now, if there's nothing else you need—"

"There is." Maul's hand fell to the other inmate's shoulder, stopping him. "I need you to hack back into the system again—get into the algorithm itself. Fix the next match so I'm fighting Rook."

"What?" Izhsmash shot him a look of pure incredulity. "Do you have any idea how difficult that's going to be? Especially after I've hacked it once already?" He shook his head. "After what happened in medbay, the guards will be looking for anything out of the ordinary."

"You've done well," Maul said, nodding at the list of inmates. "You've already proven yourself more valuable to my cause than the one who was leading you. Strabo will learn his place beneath you," Maul said. "If he has not already."

"I'll need time."

"You'll have till the next match. By my count that gives you three hours."

"But—"

"I'll create a diversion," Maul said. "I suggest you take advantage of it."

"How will I know when the time is right?"

"I'll be in contact with you."

He took the list and walked away.

25

SKULL GAME

There was no meal being served at the moment, but Maul found Coyle in the mess hall anyway, on his hands and knees. The Chadra-Fan was humming to himself jauntily as he burrowed through the refuse bins in the corner, digging for scraps and tossing them onto a spare tray that he'd scavenged from the kitchen. Maul waited until Coyle stopped, straightened up, and turned around, his whiskers dripping with something thick and pasty.

"Jagannath," the Chadra-Fan said, beaming, as convivial as ever. "Ready to fight again, are you?" He rubbed his hands together. "We're all expecting to see you victorious, and very soon."

Maul didn't answer. His response, when it came, was to reach out and dump a small handful of bones onto Coyle's tray. The Chadra-Fan frowned at them, momentarily flummoxed, then looked back up at Maul, blinking quickly.

"What are these?"

"For you," Maul said. "To use in your work."

"Is that so?" Coyle picked one of the bones up and examined it thoughtfully. "Yes, I might have use for it, yes, indeed, I might. I thank you, Jagannath. You have my gratitude, yes, you do, although it makes me wonder—"

"I've been looking into your background," Maul said. "Why you were sent here to Cog Hive Seven in the first place."

Coyle's eyebrows twitched. "Oh yes?"

"You weren't always a sculptor. Before you came here, you made . . . other things." He waited. "Counterfeit currency, to be exact. Credits on demand."

The rodent's face became the very picture of serene innocence. "Did I?"

"If I were to ask you to ply your trade again for me," Maul said, "I could supply you with any number of bones for your sculptures in exchange."

"How much are we talking about, exactly?"

"Three hundred thousand credits."

"And what would you be wanting it for?"

"I need to buy something."

"Well." Coyle rubbed his hands together and bobbed his head from side to side thoughtfully. "Well, well, well. I would need materials, of course. A means of fabrication, a craftsman's best friends are his tools. And the end product—"

"Make a list," Maul said. "Give it to Zero. He'll get what you need."

"And for me?"

Maul stopped and turned back. "What do you want?"

"My newest work," Coyle said. "I believe you've seen it. It could benefit from a certain type of skull. A larger one—saurian, perhaps?" His tongue flicked out and moistened his lips. "I hear there's a Deathspine varactyl locked up in one of the lower cellblocks . . ."

"A varactyl?"

"Intriguing creatures, have you seen them, brother? Fifteen meters long." The Chadra-Fan grinned. "You see, it's a fascinating thing, the way the sinuses in their armor-plated skulls are designed to funnel and amplify sound, to create a certain specific type of noise when the air passes through—"

Maul nodded. "It's done."

26
OLD MAN

Artagan Truax awoke to the sound of voices in the darkness, two of them, conferring in hushed tones from a place he couldn't see. At first he wasn't even sure they were real.

The floor beneath him was cold and hard. He didn't know how long he'd been lying here—the pain in his leg, or what remained of it, was playing tricks with time, stretching it out while it sucked him in and out of consciousness. He was shaking and trembling, spasms that only made the agony more intense. His forehead was blazing with fever.

Through cracked lips, he forced the words: "Where am I?"

He wasn't sure if he'd actually spoken aloud, although he must have, because the two inmates stopped their conversation and peered down at him. Neither of them was human, he saw—one was an Aqualish, the other a Twi'lek, the one that the other prisoners called Zero.

"You shouldn't push yourself, Artagan," the Aqualish said. Its words came out as a series of barks, but Artagan—who'd spent more than enough time among such species, fighting for credits—mentally translated the words into Basic. "You need rest. You're badly hurt, and you really can't afford to make it worse than it already is."

Artagan tried to move, and felt the pain explode back through the hastily bandaged stump of his leg. The entire lower half of his body felt like it was on fire.

"Water," he croaked. "Need . . . a drink."

"When you were in medbay," the Aqualish continued, "you said some things to that Zabrak that you probably shouldn't have." He paused. "Information about Mr. Radique. Certain details that you really shouldn't have shared. We can agree on that, can't we?"

"R-Radique?" Artagan just stared up at him, stranded somewhere between shock and disbelief.

"Those guards wanted to kill you and your son on the spot for your escape attempt," the Aqualish continued, and glanced over at Zero. "Now, it's true that Mr. Radique was able to protect you from being terminated . . ."

Artagan said nothing.

"But his protection won't last forever," the Twi'lek said. "We need to know what you told the Zabrak, Artagan. Details. And please be as specific as possible."

"I just told him—"

"Yes?"

The old man opened his mouth and closed it again. "Where's . . . my son?"

The Aqualish and the Twi'lek exchanged a glance.

"Yes, your son," the Aqualish said. "Perhaps he might be able to help us with our questions."

"No." The old man shook his head. "Leave him alone. Leave him out of it!"

From somewhere inside the prison, the alarms began to sound.

27

VARACTYL

Izhsmash removed the little panel from the back of the force-feedback climate control valve using a slender metal shim and a pair of tweezers.

"Lovely," he muttered. "The wiring's on a trip switch stepped down all the way back to the primary alarms." Leaning in, he separated the wires. "Hand me the keypad."

Strabo thrust it over in disgruntled silence. Ever since the regrettable incident in the prison laundry, his status within the Gravity Massive had plummeted from leader to toady. Meanwhile, within that same stretch of time, without a word being spoken, Izhsmash had somehow risen to the level of de facto captain of the Massives. The reversal was humiliating. Yet there was little to be done—the rest of the crew somehow seemed to sense that Jagannath had appointed Izhsmash as their new captain, and that was the end of it.

Now he and the Nelvaanian were standing on a two-meter-wide expanse of latticework in one of the countless sublevels of the prison. Steam pipes and four-hundred-degree thermal vents bracketed the concourse on either side like heavy cylindrical pillars. From the other side of the wall that formed a seemingly abandoned stretch of holding cells, something screamed and thumped, emitting a short, loud hooting call. Whatever was in there, it sounded huge. And angry.

He shot a glance at Izhsmash. "You're sure this is the spot?"

"This is where Jagannath told me to hack in." The Nelvaanian picked at the wiring, threading the keypad into place. "No idea how he's going to keep from tripping the alarms, though. Personally, I think we're all dead." He glared at Strabo. "Hold that light steady, will you?"

Strabo almost shot back a retort but held his tongue. He was only here because he too had received a message from Jagannath telling him that his presence was necessary for this operation. Apparently his sole reason for existence now was taking orders from others.

"What if—" he began. But that was as far as he got before the hatchway to his immediate right exploded off its hinges.

Strabo leapt back with a cry of surprise. What he saw defied all expectation—an orange-skinned Deathspine varactyl, four meters high, came bursting forth into the concourse, its tail thrashing and whipping the air. The bird-lizard was shrieking and hooting wildly, slamming its body against the far wall, and immediately Strabo understood why. The Zabrak, Jagannath himself, was sitting astride its back, clutching its beaked face with both hands, jerking it right and left.

Jagannath? Strabo's mind whirred. *How did he get in there in the first place?* Then he saw it, just a glimpse through the open hatchway—the ceiling of the varactyl's cell, with the open panel that had been dislodged from above.

Directly in front of him, the bird-lizard bucked and swung itself 180 degrees around, braying all the louder as it tried to throw Jagannath from his perch. Its hind leg came forward, hooking one clawlike foot into the Zabrak's torso and slashing his skin. But the red-skinned inmate hung on with a kind of brute-force determination that Strabo had never seen before in any species. He was suddenly grateful that he'd decided not to defy Jagannath's orders to come here—and glad that he'd never had to face the Zabrak in a bout.

By now the entire prison was responding to the disruption. Guards' boots were pounding way up the hall. From the walls, alarms wailed and keened. Looking off to the right, in the midst of everything, Strabo saw Izhsmash working furiously over the keypad that he'd patched into the prison's surveillance system, swiftly tapping in digits with a focused intensity that was completely at odds with the mayhem around him.

What's he doing? Why is he—

A blur of activity snapped Strabo's attention forward again. Jagannath had managed to grip the varactyl by its crest and wrenched its armor-plated skull hard to the right, slamming it directly into one of the steam pipes along the far wall.

The creature shrieked again—a wailing mournful cry that turned out to be its swan song. The steam pipe burst apart, shooting a thick, scalding blast of focused heat directly into the thing's face, boiling its flesh and scalding its eyeballs in their sockets. The effect was immediate. Strabo's nostrils stung with the stench of burned feathers and flash-fried skin as the varactyl's flesh peeled back to expose the thickly plated vault of its cranium. Its body collapsed with the Zabrak still astride it.

Voices murmured behind him, and he glanced back over his shoulder. Curious inmates had joined the guards who were crowding up the hall now, drawn by the noise and activity.

"What happened?" somebody asked.

"Lizard broke loose," Izhsmash muttered. He'd already finished whatever he'd set out to do with the wiring, yanking the keypad loose and shoving through the open panel, then closing it up just in time. "Jagannath stopped it."

"Yeah, I guess he did."

In front of him, Jagannath had taken hold of the varactyl's boiled skull. With a final jerk, he snapped it completely free from its neck and yanked it upward. The scorched gray rag of the thing's tongue tumbled free and dangled from its mandible like a limp rag of surrender.

Silence fell through the hallway. Dismounting, the Zabrak hoisted its massive skull up over his head, the inmates and even some of the guards taking a step back as he carried the grisly trophy forward down the length of the concourse. At the end, he turned and kept walking.

"Where's he going with that thing?" one of the guards asked aloud.

Strabo heard another guard answer, under his breath, "*You* want to ask him?"

"Beautiful, isn't it?" Coyle peered admiringly at the skull in front of him. "Didn't take you long to procure, did it?"

Maul said nothing. He'd carried the bird-lizard's skull down the factory floor and dropped it unceremoniously at the Chadra-Fan's feet, and what he felt now, more than anything, was exhausted. Staying on top of the thing long enough to kill it had required more strength than he'd expected, and at some point during the fray its powerful claws had dug a deep gash into his right flank. Blood was oozing slowly but steadily from the wound.

Yet it would all be worth it if things went as planned.

"Are you all right, Jagannath?"

"I'm fine," Maul said shortly. "Just make sure you're ready with your end of the deal."

"I've already spoken to Zero about the necessary supplies."

Maul nodded. "I'll be back soon."

"You should rest, my friend. You think they'll be matching you again soon?"

"Very soon," Maul said. "If all goes as planned."

"Meaning what exactly?"

Maul didn't respond, just turned to walk away.

"Jagannath, wait."

Maul looked back. Reaching out, Coyle slipped something into his palm, a small, sealed packet. Maul glanced down and saw that it was full of finely crushed powder.

"What's this?"

"White metaxas root," the Chadra-Fan said. "It's flavorless and odorless, but a few granules will kill almost anything that ingests it."

Maul tossed it aside. "I don't need this."

"Suit yourself, but it might come in handy."

Maul left the packet where it fell. All he needed right now was rest. If he could spend even a few moments recuperating in his cell and fashion some kind of makeshift dressing for the wound, he knew he'd be all right. And if Izhsmash had been able to take advantage of the distraction he'd created to hack back into the prison's algorithm again—

And that was when the second set of alarms—the clarion call that meant the beginning of the next bout—began to shatter the world with sound.

28

SUBMERGED

By the time Maul had made his way back from the factory floor to the main gallery, the rest of the prison population was already on their way to lockdown. Alarms howled louder here, the clock ticking down. Holding his side where the varactyl had slashed him, he shoved his way through the foul-smelling herds of inmates, cutting a path down the corridor that led to his own cell. Stepping inside, he found a guard standing there.

"Hey, Tooth," the guard said. "Welcome back."

It was Smight, the young CO who had kept jamming the barrel of his blaster against Maul's spine on the way up to the warden's office.

But he looked different now—there was something twitchy going on in the corners of his mouth, some twisted species of chemically enhanced depravity that Maul had not seen on the young CO's face before now. His eyes gleamed dully in the recessed lights. Maul wondered if the guard was on something, if he'd speed-jacked some glitterstim before coming here, to nerve himself up for whatever his purpose was.

"They're matching you again, you know," Smight was saying, cracking his knuckles as he spoke. He shot a glance at the chrono on his wrist. "In about two minutes."

"Then you better get out of my cell," Maul said.

"In a rush, huh? Got someplace you need to be?" The guard sniggered and cast his eyes at the open wound on Maul's flank. "Maybe you shouldn't have been tussling with that varactyl, huh? Match hasn't even started and you're already bleeding."

Maul said nothing.

"Which reminds me," Smight added. "Warden sent me up here with something special, just for you." Reaching to his belt, he withdrew a pair of zip-tie restraints, Nylasteel, like the ones they'd used on the wampa. "Take a seat."

Maul sat on the bench and Smight slapped the zip-ties around his ankles, jerking them tight to the steel posts that anchored it to the floor. When he finished, he gave Maul one last, wild look.

"What's the matter? You got nothing to crack wise about?"

"You should be more careful what you put in your body," Maul said.

"What?"

"Spice. It will kill you. If I don't do it first."

Smight's face seemed to narrow with hostility. "Have a good fight," he said, and stepped out, as the hatch sealed behind him.

Maul didn't move. The alarms outside had stopped. There was a long, anticipatory silence, and then a sudden metallic creaking sound that seemed to come from everywhere at once as the prison itself began the process of reconfiguration.

Now he would find out if Izhsmash had been able to accomplish what he'd asked. The zip-ties would make it more difficult, but not impossible. There was nothing to do but wait.

The cell lurched into motion. It turned and swung around to the right, jerked upward once again, and tumbled head to foot 180 degrees, leaving him dangling upside down by the handgrips and the zip-ties on his ankles. Other cells were moving around his; he could hear the noise of their passing. At length, his rotated back down to its original position and stopped, the wall and ceiling panels adjusting themselves, tightening around him.

Maul listened for sounds on the other side of the wall. The list of inmates had not told him what type of species Rook was. What would it be this time? A growl? A snarl? A human voice?

He heard nothing. He looked at the walls around him. The cell didn't feel any smaller. But something had changed, the entire room tightening around him in some almost imperceptible way.

Seconds later, the cell began to fill with water.

It came spraying down from a pipe in the ceiling, an ice-cold gush of stinking gray liquid that drenched him instantly as it clattered across the metal floor and began pooling around his feet and ankles. From where he sat, Maul looked up at the pipe with annoyance but no real sense of surprise.

Rising to his full height, he jerked on the zip-ties that fastened him to the bench, already knowing that they wouldn't yield. He grabbed the bench and yanked. The steel posts weren't going anywhere, either, nor had he expected them to. For the moment, this seemed to be where he was fighting from.

The water had risen past his knees and was coming up to his waist. The entire ceiling seemed to be pouring down on him, and the acoustics of the room had begun to change, obliterating the echoes and leaving only a steady, discordant roar. It was happening so fast that it felt less like the water was coming down and more like he was sinking into it.

He could feel the sheer weight of liquid tonnage itself pressing in around him, rising to engulf his chest and shoulders, and then creeping up higher around his neck. Tipping back his head, he exhaled and watched his breath plume out in a visible cloud. The temperature in the cell had dropped twenty degrees in two minutes. He felt both his hearts quickening, pumping blood to his extremities, readying himself for whatever came next.

Where was Rook? Was he coming? Or had Izhsmash failed to hack the algorithm as he'd requested?

He gave another glance at what remained of his surroundings. The cell had grown darker, as if the lights themselves had been swallowed up by the flood.

Drawing in deep breaths, saturating his lungs with as much oxygen as he could, Maul plunged his head under the surface, acclimating his vision to the turbid murkiness below. At first he saw nothing. Lights shone faintly from the submerged walls, hazy in the depths. He could see nothing else down there.

Not yet.

He burst to the surface again, as high as the restraints would allow him to rise. The water was almost above his head, leaving only a narrow, cramped layer of stale oxygen above the surface. He went down again, and when he lifted his head, the water level had risen to the ceiling. There was a centimeter or two of air at the very top.

Maul sucked at it, feeling it disappear against his lips.

Across the cell, he felt the low, grinding reverberation of a hatch sliding open underwater. He pulled himself down but saw nothing.

An instant later, below the surface, something brushed against his leg. Squinting into the depths, Maul made out a pair of bulbous, glassy black eyes staring back at him.

An instant later, it struck.

29

SPECTATORS

Sadiki was in her office, watching the live holo of the underwater match, when her brother burst in behind her.

"Good," she said, "you're just in time. It's starting now. Take a seat."

Dakarai didn't move. He stood over her, his pale face mottled with high splotches of red in his cheeks and forehead. In his silence, his indignation was all the more apparent. It seemed to ripple off his skin in nearly visible waves.

"What's wrong?"

But of course she already knew. They had been through all this before. In the final weeks before Cog Hive Seven became fully operational—when Dakarai had realized how much of his original design was going to have to be jettisoned in order for them to move forward—he'd become sulky and remote, withdrawing even more thoroughly from her, disappearing for days at a time. His silence had taken on an almost palpable weight. Only by promising him absolute autonomy when it came to the algorithm and the bouts had Sadiki been able to placate him.

And now she had violated that rule as well.

"I can see that you're upset." Sadiki rose to her feet with a sigh. "Forgive me. I know this particular match isn't what your algorithm called for. But Dakarai, you have to trust me on this. The Zabrak is becoming a real problem for us. He needs to be broken. And this fight—"

He thrust a thin sheaf of flimsiplast in her face. Sadiki took it from him and glanced down at it. It was a printout of the algorithm's actual match, which was supposed to have pitted two completely different inmates against one another.

"I *know*," Sadiki said. "But I'm telling you—"

"Warden."

Sadiki turned and glanced at the holoscreen that had gone active above her head. Gaming Commissioner Dragomir Chlorus's face glared down at her, inflamed with fury.

"Commissioner," Sadiki said. "I'm beginning to think your position doesn't keep you busy enough."

"Sadiki, what do you think you're doing?"

"Matching my reigning champion. As you can see—"

"The bout that you posted indicates a completely different set of opponents. The odds that you gave on this fight have nothing to do with the Zabrak or the Aqualish. Which means that you either deliberately chose to defy the Gaming Commission regulations . . ." He paused. "Or you've been hacked."

"Hacked?" Sadiki chuckled. "Commissioner, I assure you—"

"Do you see a third explanation?"

"Please." She glanced at Dakarai, as if he might somehow, in defiance of everything she knew about him, speak up on her behalf. "If you'll just allow me to investigate—"

"It's too late for that. You've overstepped your bounds for the last time." There was a portentous silence as Chlorus summoned the full weight of his authority. "The Galactic Gaming Commission is shutting you down."

"What?"

"You heard me."

"You . . ." Sadiki's face didn't change, but her neck flushed red, the color rising slowly to her hairline. "You really don't want to start down that road with me, Dragomir."

"If you're implying that I don't have the authority," Chlorus said, "then you're sadly mistaken. If you think I'm bluffing, then you're wrong about that, too. And if I were you, I would keep all your inmates in lockdown until this is sorted out."

"Now you're telling me how to run my prison?"

Chlorus glared at her. "You should be thanking me. You have far bigger problems. And if you'd made the slightest effort to listen to me earlier, none of this would have reached the crisis point."

"I'm telling you, the Hutts haven't shown the faintest interest in—"

"The Desilijic Clan has *already* infiltrated your prison," the Commissioner said.

"Excuse me?"

"According to intelligence that I've just received, they've had their foot soldiers inside Cog Hive Seven for months in an ongoing effort to ferret out Radique. It's uncertain how many exactly, but the data that've come across my desk so far seem to indicate that their presence within the prison is significant."

"You're the gaming commissioner," Sadiki said. "How is this your business?"

"Let's just say you need someone to watch over you." Chlorus sighed. "I know your tendency to get in over your head."

Sadiki allowed herself a slow, restorative breath. In all the years she'd been here, this was as close as Chlorus had come to acknowledging the brief relationship that they had enjoyed during her early days managing the sabacc tables at the Outlander Casino and Resort on Coruscant. She'd been very young at the time, new to her position, easily swayed and even seduced by his authority. What happened between them had ended badly, with misgivings on both sides. But now was not the time or place to exhume that particular corpse and find out whether there was any life left in it.

She forced a smile. It felt like work.

"Dragomir, that's very kind. Under normal circumstances I'd be flattered, but—"

"Stop. Just—stop." Chlorus paused, and when he spoke again, he sounded more concerned than she'd ever heard him. "Sadiki, I've heard all your excuses and prevarications, but at this point, if you do know anything at all about the whereabouts of this man Radique, I recommend that you share it with the Hutts straightaway. Otherwise you may have a mutiny on your hands that even you cannot control."

"Mutiny? You mean a riot?" Sadiki glanced over her shoulder at Dakarai, but her brother remained expressionless, his face maddeningly unreadable. She turned back to the holoscreen. "All our inmates carry electrostatic charges implanted in their hearts. I can terminate any of them with the touch of a button. If any of them were foot soldiers sent in here by the Hutts—"

"Sadiki, I'm not talking about inmates," Chlorus said. "I'm talking about guards."

She just stared at him. "I beg your pardon?"

"How many guards does Cog Hive Seven employ at any given time?" Chlorus asked.

"Between seventy and eighty. But we screen each one carefully, with a full background check and identity verification—"

"All of which the Desilijic Clan could have easily forged in order to get their people inside," the Commissioner said. His voice was grave. "Be vigilant, Sadiki. I'll speak to you again soon."

Sadiki turned back to look at Dakarai again. But her brother was no longer looking at the commissioner.

He was watching the match.

30

TANK

Maul's lungs were screaming.

He'd already lost track of how long he'd been underwater. Time had twisted back upon itself and lost all meaning. Both his hearts were thudding faster, pounding through his entire body in an attempt to circulate any remaining air. Blackness crowded in around the edges of his vision, threatening to bury his consciousness beneath an avalanche of oxygen debt.

When the other inmate had first swum at him, he had slammed Maul in the diaphragm, driving out the breath he'd inhaled just before going down for the last time. Maul swirled around, pulling himself down by the zip-ties that fastened his ankles, coiling down alongside the submerged bench.

What he saw was an Aqualish swimming back toward him, cutting smoothly through the water—the one Maul hoped was Rook. He sprang up and plunged his fingers into the other inmate's bulbous eyes. The Aqualish recoiled and disappeared—only to come at him again from behind with a violent strike to the back of his skull.

Maul sucked in a mouthful of contaminated water and gagged, expelling it in an involuntary contraction. Around him in the near-darkness, nothing stirred. A thin sediment of silt and filth seemed to have settled across the bottom. His gaze settled on the blurry glow of lights from the other side of the cell, and he became aware of how little time he had left.

He looked down at the bench to which his ankles were still fastened.

The pressure seemed to be squeezing his chest like an enormous fist. If he weren't bound here, if he just had one more breath of air—

Stop it. It was his Master's voice, unmistakable in its scorn. *Your inadequacy is worse than disgraceful. It's nauseating.*

Maul steeled himself. The cold words sobered him. If he was destined to die here, even under these humiliating circumstances—if such was the fate that the dark side had selected for him—then it would not be with the whimpering of his own weakness in his ears.

Yanking himself down to the very floor of the cell, he flattened his body beneath the bench, groping in darkness until his numb fingertips located the rounded shape of one of the bolts holding the steel plating together. There were several such bolts, but this one felt like the loosest. Raising an elbow, he drove it down against the bolt, then lifted it up and hit the metal again until the screw loosened enough that he was able to twist it loose and pluck it free.

Putting his mouth to the newly exposed hole, he sucked in fresh air and blew out bubbles through his nose before drawing in another deep breath, letting the oxygen replenish his bloodstream. The results were immediate. The blackness around his vision began to fade. Yet he made himself wait here beneath the bench for another moment, until he saw the vague shape of the Aqualish swimming just above him.

Maul shot up through the water as far as the ankle restraints would allow and seized the other inmate by its tusks, snapping one of them off. The Aqualish trumpeted out a nasal shriek of surprise and pain, and Maul hammered him in the abdomen. When his opponent bent forward, he pounded Rook's skull into the cell wall. Blood seeped from the Aqualish's head as he rounded on Maul, cutting back through the water.

Gone again.

Maul squinted, scanning the depths. Where had the other inmate taken himself? Had the hatchway been left open so that Rook could come and go, attacking him at his leisure?

He pulled himself back down under the bench, pressed his lips to the hole in the floor, and was about to inhale another breath when he felt something thick and slippery and hideously alive squirt up inside his mouth. Recoiling, Maul spat it out and saw a thin white worm floating up past his face, wiggling defiantly, its tiny mandibles working fiercely to grip hold of something. He narrowed his eyes and looked back down at the hole. More of the things were beginning to push their way up into the cell through the hole, pulsing up from below in a steady stream.

Maul turned away. Was there any manner of foulness that this place did not specialize in? How much longer—

Wham!

White-hot pressure exploded against the back of his skull, leaving him dizzy and disoriented. In his peripheral vision, he was narrowly aware of the Aqualish coming back around, his body rippling effortlessly toward him, cocking back its fist again to deliver another blow. Maul fought to anchor his thoughts. With his supply of air shut down, he knew he had to finish this now.

Slimy to touch, greasy to feel, but mix me with blood and I'll eat through steel.

He stuck one hand down under the bench, scraping his fingers against the thick accumulation of sticky reddish-brown gunk that had made a home for itself in the seams between the metal plates. Cupping the stuff in one palm, kneading it together, he held still and waited. He had one chance to get this right. He knew he would not have to wait long.

The opponent made his move. As he darted toward Maul, Maul grabbed him by the tufts of hair on either side of his face and shoved the handful of toxic girder mold into the open laceration in the Aqualish's scalp, grinding it as deeply into the wound as he could.

The results were even more gratifying than he'd hoped. The Aqualish recoiled and began to scream, bubbles flooding out of him as he clutched at his head with both hands. The wound was already sizzling and bubbling, flecks of tissue drifting away.

Maul seized his head and locked his arm around the Aqualish's neck. Grabbing another handful of girder mold from under the bench, Maul reached down and smeared it into the zip-ties that bound him here. Then he pulled the Aqualish down so that the blood from his wound churned through the water to interact with the mold. The resulting catalyst attacked the Nylasteel instantly, cutting through it. All at once Maul's legs were suddenly, shockingly free.

Kicking loose, turning around in the water, Maul dragged the other inmate down headfirst toward the submerged floor of the cell and held him there, watching the steel plating dissolving beneath it. A ragged hole had already begun to open, widening while he watched, water siphoning down through it. Within seconds it would be sufficient for what he required.

He and the Aqualish were sucked down together, pushed through on the current, Maul holding tight to his neck. A moment later they spilled out into an open drainage shaft. The pipe opened below them, and Maul threw the Aqualish up onto a platform overhead and sprang up alongside him into the open air. He whooped in a deep breath of air, filling his lungs, and turned to fix the other inmate with his gaze.

"Are you Rook?"

The Aqualish nodded and barked out a froggy, croaking "Yes."

"You know what this is?" Maul asked, still holding on to a handful of the girder mold that he'd brought from the cell. "And what it can do to you when it interacts with your blood?"

The Aqualish faced him. His face was horribly disfigured from the acid, his eyes badly wounded from the puncture attack, but beneath the physical trauma there was no mistaking the disbelief in his expression.

"This—this can't be happening. I'm not supposed to be matched, *ever*. He said I was never going to have to fight."

"You're going to die," Maul told him. "Right now. Slowly. I'll burn the rest of your face off. Unless you tell me everything."

"I don't know what you're—"

"About Iram Radique."

The one called Rook made a poor show of not understanding, but it didn't last long. Maul held the mold up to the bleeding head wound, in close enough proximity that the inmate's flesh actually began, faintly, to sizzle. The Aqualish tried to jerk back, but Maul held him fast. When he spoke, the words came out in a scream.

"What do you want to know?"

"How do I get to him?"

"You can't! Nobody can! Even I don't speak to him directly!"

"You're lying."

"I'm not, I swear!"

"Then you're worthless to me," Maul said, and prepared to smear the rest of the mold over Rook's face.

"Wait—wait! I can tell you this," the Aqualish panted, his gills flapping as he tried vainly to salvage what remained of his composure. "The weapons—they arrive in different pieces."

"I already know that," Maul said. "What happens after the gang members smuggle them in? Where do they go? How does Radique retrieve the pieces from them without being seen?"

"The birds," Rook said. "They collect the different components. Bring them to the shop. If you follow the clawbirds, you'll find Radique."

"When does the next shipment arrive?"

"There's a supply ship docking tomorrow during the first watch, but that's—that's truly all I know."

"Is there anyone else between you and Radique? Another link in the chain?"

Gaping at him, his wounded eyes darting back to the handful of mold packed into Maul's fist, the Aqualish murmured some oath in its own native language. "Please, I cooperated. I told you everything."

"Answer me," Maul said. "Who else is there?"

Rook's three-fingered right hand swept out, smearing something on the wet surface of the pipe. Maul looked at it. It was a circle.

"What does that mean?" he growled.

The Aqualish made a wet, shuddering noise. "It's all I know. Don't kill me. Don't—"

"You were dead when you were matched with me," Maul said. "But I will give my word to you. It will be quick."

He took hold of Rook's head with both hands and cracked the thing's neck in a single, instantaneous jerk. The Aqualish shuddered and fell motionless, slipping backward and toppling from view.

31

CLARITY

Midnight.

The morgue.

Maul had found his way down here after the last fight. No one had tried to engage him along the way. Something had changed in the handful of hours since he'd killed Rook—a fundamental shift in the polarity of genpop itself. Now the other inmates, including the gang members and even the guards, stayed away from him completely. Not so much out of fear or respect as self-preservation, the way a herd of nonsentient life-forms will keep their distance from one carrying a lethal infection. It was as if they sensed what Maul had done and how he'd marked himself for death.

Not that he cared. If it got him closer to Radique, nothing else mattered.

Now he knelt before the image on the holoprojector, lowering his head before the face of his Master.

"My Lord, I have continued to endeavor—"

"Enough." Sidious cut him off midsentence, his tone barbed with thorns of irritation. "Why do you continue to try my patience, my apprentice? Why do you persist in humiliating yourself while making me wait for answers that you should have provided days ago?"

Maul narrowed his eyes in an attempt to see more clearly. Through the makeshift holoprojector, Sidious was staring down at him from what felt like miles above, distant yet formidable, a weight that he could not lift. The question, apparently, was not rhetorical.

"I am trying, Master. The path is difficult."

"You dare to make excuses?" Sidious's voice roared in his head. "After the years I have spent training you? Honing your skills, preparing you for every eventuality, training you in the ways of survival, endurance, and attack? How long have you begged for an opportunity to play some role in the Grand Plan?"

"And I am grateful," Maul told him. "My loyalty to you is beyond question, pledged with my very life's blood—"

"Declarations of loyalty are worthless without victory." Cruelty dripped from Sidious's words. "Abstractions do not interest me at this point. Time is short. Do you understand?"

"Yes, my Master."

"I wonder if you do. Or if the time has come for me to find another apprentice more deserving of the honor."

Maul stiffened and rose. "No!"

"Then prove that you are worthy. Stop wasting my time with empty pledges of fidelity and complete the mission that you have been charged with."

"Master, if I were only allowed to call upon the power of the dark side—"

The thought snapped off, unfinished. Maul felt an invisible hand clamp down over his throat, gripping the cartilage and cutting off the airway. Stumbling, he dropped back to his knees, to the coldness of the morgue floor.

"You have been given everything you need and more. You enjoy untold physical advantages that these inferior combatants could only dream of. And you know very well the consequences of revealing your true abilities in the dark side, especially at this late stage. Many are watching. You are not the only one inside Cog Hive Seven searching for Radique."

"Yes, my Master."

"Do not make me wait any longer. Find him now and make the appropriate arrangements."

Maul managed a single, strangled nod of compliance, and at once the pressure disappeared. As suddenly as it had materialized, the holoprojector image flickered out, and the incorporeal vision of Sidious was gone, devoured by the void from which it had sprung.

Maul fell to the floor and dropped his head, pressing his brow down against cold steel. Never had he experienced such urgency from the Dark Lord, such profound and overwhelming sense of purpose, driven by . . . what? Was there something else worrying his Master, some danger to Lord Sidious himself that he had not shared with Maul? The idea made him uneasy, as it always did.

He kept his head down, awaiting answers that would not come. He stayed that way for a long time as the tension gathered in his core muscles, clenching his fists, tightening his jaw, drawing everything rigid. Red rage was already beginning to boil up from inside him. And, as always, he welcomed it, even as he drew clean breaths of air into his lungs. In the moments when everything else betrayed him, the rage was there, a lone companion.

He lifted himself up and stood erect. His chest burned, his muscles ached, his head throbbed, and there was a low rattle in his lungs.

Master. I dedicate myself to you.

The hatchway slid open. Maul stepped through, and that was where they were waiting for him, just inside the open concourse. Caught utterly off guard, he scarcely had time to comprehend what was happening.

What—?

A huge black and red explosion went off in front of his eyeballs, and he knew no more.

32

WHITEOUT

Maul awoke to blinding lights, a blazing firestorm of incandescence that seared his eyes, obscuring whatever stood just behind them. He tried to move and discovered that he couldn't. His arms and legs were lashed and stretched spread-eagle, and he hung suspended in midair, above . . . what? It was impossible to say.

What had they shot him with? Some kind of stun weapon, powerful enough to knock him completely unconscious. Whoever was responsible was clearly prepared to evade the surveillance cameras as well—it would explain the painfully intense lights, bright enough to mask whatever they were planning on doing to him.

At length he heard a sound coming from off to his left, someone laboring to breathe. Incoherent words. Croaking noises. The rasping harshness of respiratory distress. Maul was still listening to it, trying to process the details of his circumstances, when he picked up the creak of approaching footsteps.

"Where's the old man?" a voice asked.

"In the corner," a second, more familiar voice answered. "Next to the baler."

"Has he said anything significant?"

"He's delirious." The familiar voice was calm but not dispassionate, colored with an overtone of what might actually have been sympathy. "He contracted blood poisoning after he lost his leg. The infection's already spreading to his brain." From directly in front of him, the one who had spoken most recently leaned in close enough that Maul could make out his features. "Hello, Jagannath."

Maul squinted up at the face of the Twi'lek above him. "Zero?"

Zero gazed at him. "You've caused quite a stir around here," he said. "You really shouldn't have killed Rook. Mr. Radique was paying handsomely to keep him safe from being matched."

"So you do know him."

"Sending the Nelvaanian to hack into the algorithm was your first mistake." The Twi'lek's expression was slightly puzzled now, as if he couldn't quite figure out what had driven Maul to such a grave misstep. "There have already been repercussions, you realize. Severe repercussions."

Reaching down, he hoisted a limp corpse and lifted it close enough that Maul could see it.

It was Izhsmash. The Nelvaanian's broken jaw hung slack on its hinges. His mouth and eye sockets were stuffed with scraps of broken circuit board and twisted wire—a message for whoever found the body.

There was a faint, throat-clearing noise somewhere off to the left. Maul jerked his head up, struggling to pull himself free from the thick web of cables that lashed his arms and legs to walls that he couldn't see.

"Is he here with you?" Maul asked. "Is Radique here?"

Zero ignored the question. "The guards and inmates will find your body next to the Nelvaanian's," he said with that same puzzled empathy. "They'll know what happened. Such warnings must be sent from time to time. It is his will." Leaning in close enough that he could lower his voice, he spoke almost apologetically: "No one threatens Mr. Radique, Jagannath. You understand, don't you? It's just business."

"I have business with him," Maul said. "Tell Radique—"

"Good-bye, Jagannath," the other voice said. It was the first time that Maul had heard it. "It's a pity you have to end your time in Cog Hive Seven as a cautionary tale. You were an intriguing specimen while you lasted."

"*Wait.*" Maul lifted his head again and caught sight of the figure next to Zero—it was a Weequay, one he'd never seen before. Or had he? The craggy, sun-baked face was raked back in a speculative frown, his high

STAR WARS: MAUL: LOCKDOWN   161

forehead crowned with a topknot, and Maul remembered the inmate that he'd seen on his first day here.

The clawbird was perched on his shoulder.

"Repercussions, Jagannath."

Without another word, the Weequay glanced at Zero, and the two of them turned and left the room.

There was a jolting, mechanized clamor of heavy machinery being throttled reluctantly to life. Force-feedback servos chugged and became a steady pulsating drone. Maul thought of the factory floor.

Before he could comprehend what that meant exactly, he felt the cables around his wrists and ankles beginning to draw tight, pulling him in four different directions.

As suddenly as they'd appeared, the blinding lights went out, burying him in utter darkness.

Maul jerked and yanked at his restraints, but the cables around his arms and legs only pulled tighter, stretching the sockets of his shoulders, cranking tension into hips and knees. He fought to pull himself free, but the restraints held fast. Something popped in his right wrist. Every joint began to burn. They were going to rip him to pieces.

From above him, above the hum of the machinery, he heard a brisk flapping of wings.

In the darkness, the wheezing noises began again. Labored words.

"Going . . . to kill us both," a voice rasped.

Now Maul recognized the voice. The old man was in here with him, Eogan's father—the one who'd lost his leg to Voystock's blaster. He searched his memory for the old man's name, and it came to him almost at once.

"Artagan?"

"Never should have . . . saved his life," the old man's voice said. "Should have stayed with the Bando Gora. Too late now, I suppose."

Twisting his entire body as far as the cables would allow, Maul turned his head in the direction of the old man's voice. By now the tension in his extremities had transcended pain, catapulting him into an entirely new realm of consciousness. Again he thought, almost instinctively, of using the Force, of calling upon strength and ability whose magnitude could almost certainly save him from death. Surely such things had been placed at his disposal for a reason, a larger purpose, hadn't they?

From the hinterlands of conscious thought, he heard his Master's voice ringing out in his mind.

There are aspects of who we are, Sidious had once told him, *that can only be revealed to us in the deepest pit of intolerable suffering, in those moments when all else is torn away—when we stand at the very brink of eternity itself and stare death in the face.*

Maul didn't breathe. Sweat poured from his face. Still facing Artagan, he managed to catch the old man's eye. "What did you say?"

"Bando Gora," Artagan muttered. "All hail the skull . . ."

"You were in the Bando Gora?"

". . . were going to kill Radique." Somewhere in the darkness, the old man mumbled something else, an incoherent slur of consonants, then he became lucid again. "I betrayed them, saved Radique from them. They've been hunting me down . . . ever since."

For a moment Maul didn't speak. Beneath the pain and the rattling of the machine that was about to rip him to pieces, a new revelation had already begun taking shape in his mind. "That's why you brought your son here to Cog Hive Seven."

The old man grunted in assent. "Radique swore . . . he'd protect me . . ."

Maul felt himself measuring what the old man said against whatever he knew to be true. The realization—a piece of the puzzle abruptly snapping into place—brought a sudden upsurge of determination.

Summoning up all that remained of his strength, he wrenched his right arm as hard as he could away from the cable, dislocating his shoulder from its socket with an audible pop. A loopy, over-elasticized numbness spilled through the joint on a wave of pins and needles, threatening to render his entire arm useless, but the move brought just enough slack to the cable so that the binding slipped free around his right wrist.

Jerking his arm loose, he reached across with a hand that was already rapidly going numb, fumbling with his left wrist. It seemed to take forever, but at last the left hand came free as well. Only after he'd gotten his ankles loose did he slam his upper torso against the floor, knocking the right shoulder back into place.

There.

He rose and crossed the room, his eyes fully acclimated to the darkness now. This was the factory floor, as he'd expected—the bulky machinery, Coyle's bone sculptures hulking in the background like an inevitable reminder of where they were all destined to end up. If Zero had brought him here, along with the Weequay—

"The Weequay," he said aloud. A half dozen steps later, he'd reached the spot where the old man lay on the floor, hideously diminished by his wounds, burning with fever. Maul could feel the heat radiating up from him like a blast furnace, could smell the sickness on him. "The one that was here with Zero. That's him, isn't it? That's Iram Radique."

A foggy groan that might have been acknowledgment came from the old man. "Radique . . . ," he managed.

"I need to find him. What was his connection to the Gora?"

"Can't . . . tell . . . you."

"Why not?"

". . . only tell Eogan . . ."

Maul reached down and lifted Artagan Truax up, hoisting him over his shoulder.

". . . you doing?" the old man asked. "Where you taking me . . . ?"

"Out of here," Maul said. "We've got things to discuss."

33

RECONFIG

"Warden?" ThreeDee said. "They're ready for you."

Finishing her coffee, Sadiki rose from behind her desk and directed her attention to the bank of holoscreens overhead. The monitor on the far right displayed the guards' ready room, where a group of Cog Hive Seven's off-duty COs, nine in all, were gathered around a long table. Some of the men stood silently or leaned against the wall; others sat upright nursing tumblers of Rancor Aid, casting anxious glances at the hatchway. Even out of uniform, the men had a visible tension that seemed to radiate from them in waves.

"Warden?" the droid prompted.

"I heard you," Sadiki said distractedly, not taking her eyes from the screen. She'd called the meeting two hours earlier, switching out the second-shift duty roster at the last minute to ensure adequate coverage throughout the gallery and the cells. "Do me a favor and raise the temperature in there by five degrees."

"May I ask why?"

"I'd like them to see them sweat a bit." She turned back to the droid. "Have you reached my brother yet?"

"Master Blirr is not in his quarters, nor is he in the datacenter," ThreeDee answered. "In all honesty, I have no idea where he might have gone."

"Keep trying." She glanced at the chrono. "We're only two hours away from the next match. I'd like his input on the combatants."

"Combatants?" ThreeDee swiveled around to face her. "Respectfully, Warden, weren't we specifically ordered by Gaming Commissioner Chlorus to suspend all bouts, pending—"

"Dakarai's algorithm has already made its selection," Sadiki cut in, "and the last time I checked, current betting activity for this next match was already in the millions of credits. Apparently the galaxy's casinos and high-stakes gamblers have already forgiven us for what happened."

"But the Gaming Commission—"

"They can fine me." Sadiki raised her coffee cup and drained it. "As Dragomir himself said, I've got more important things to worry about." An errant realization occurred to her, and she smiled. "And so does he, I think."

"They could shut us down completely!"

"I doubt that very much," a voice said from behind her, and Sadiki turned to see Vesto Slipher striding into her office.

"Slipher," she said, not bothering to hide her surprise. "How did you get in here?"

"As you know, the IBC enjoys yellow-card access to the security codes within most of its subsidiaries," the Muun said mildly, raising one eyebrow. "Surely that's not a point of contention."

"Not at all. I just assumed you were leaving us." She put on a smile. "I'm pleased to see you've changed your mind."

Slipher pursed his lips with distaste. "If it were up to me," he said, "I would have left already. But my employer has asked me to stay on for a day or two while we get these . . . complications with the Gaming Commission sorted out."

"I appreciate their concern."

"Believe me," Slipher said, "it's not my idea. I don't understand it myself, and I'd hardly choose to remain in this cesspool a moment longer than necessary." The Muun nodded at her desk. "But you seem to have gotten Commissioner Chlorus into quite an uproar. The IBC is simply protecting their investment in Cog Hive Seven."

"Of course." Sadiki looked across the bank of holoscreens, taking in the full sweep of Cog Hive Seven, a view that she never found boring. The mess hall, the metal shop, the factory floor, all components of some infinite sociological experiment in galactic natural selection. Although she hadn't ventured down among the inmates themselves since the prison had opened, she recognized almost all their faces and, in some cases, knew their daily routines better than they themselves did.

"Now," she said, "if you'll excuse me, I've got a meeting with the guards."

"So I see." Slipher looked at the screen, where he could see the guards loitering in the ready room. "Staffing problems?"

"Simple housekeeping issues, really." Sadiki tapped a command into the keypad at her desk, initiating remote access to the prison's datacenter. Glancing over her shoulder, Slipher watched the monitors as the digitized three-dimensional ray-tracing of Cog Hive Seven took shape, complex arrays of intersecting green and red lines rearranging themselves outside the officers' ready room. Seconds later, there was a distant, lurching groan from beyond the walls of her office.

"You're reconfiguring the prison now?" the Muun asked. "But the next bout isn't scheduled to start for two hours."

"Simply changing some details around," Sadiki said. "It's one of the benefits of our station's modular structure. There's really nothing that can't be rearranged."

"I see."

"I'm going down to the ready room." She turned to the droid. "Keep an eye out for my brother."

"Of course," ThreeDee chirped.

"On second thought . . ." She paused to consider. "Perhaps you'd better join me after all. Just to be safe."

"As you prefer."

Without another glance at the screens or the Muun, Sadiki left the office and went down to meet the men.

34

HOOLIGANS

When the back panel of his cell slid open, Vas Nailhead assumed that he was dreaming.

Unlike most of the inmates here, Nailhead spent a good deal of his time alone in his cell. After a lifetime in various prisons around the galaxy, he had no real interest in mingling with the rest of the inmates. As purported head of the Bone Kings, he still continued his reign of terror—but with the Zabrak, Jagannath, in charge of both gangs now, Nailhead's title had become largely symbolic.

Nothing excited him anymore. He still ate flesh, but he didn't enjoy it like he used to. These days he spent most of his day brooding over fan mail and endorsement offers or lapsing in and out of shallow, unsatisfying sleep. More and more, he found himself thinking of his home planet, his family, the offspring he'd left behind. His fellow Bone Kings still swore an oath of loyalty to him, but secretly Nailhead wished that the algorithm would pit him against one of them, just to change things up.

He dreamed of leaving here, but like every inmate, he knew the only way out was through the floorboards.

He dreamed of the worm.

This time, when the prison had started shifting around him with the familiar rumble and clang of reconfiguration, Nailhead simply assumed that he'd drowsed through the clarion call and that the next fight was about to begin. It had happened from time to time. He lifted his head and glanced around, wondering not quite idly if he might be selected for a match, perhaps against Jagannath himself in a battle that—if Nailhead won—might restore some of the excitement and glory to his life. But as consciousness cycled back to him, he realized that the door of his cell was still open, and there was none of the usual clamor of inmates returning to lockdown.

So what was happening?

That was when the panel slid open behind him.

"Nailhead," a voice said.

Vas Nailhead stared at the Noghri stepping into his cell. It was Strabo, his sworn enemy, who until very recently had been head of the Gravity Massive. Yet here he was standing in front of Nailhead with a glint of bemused disbelief, as if Strabo himself couldn't quite believe he'd come here.

"What's this about?" Nailhead growled.

Strabo said nothing. And then Nailhead saw them, the other inmates, gathered behind the Noghri—a ragtag mixture of Bone Kings and Gravity Massive members standing side by side. The Massives were armed with their cable darts and melee weapons. The Kings were all carrying bones, sharpened and studded with metal tips and scraps, specialized modifications that they'd added.

"Somebody let us out," Strabo said.

"What?"

"Reconfigured our cells. Opened up a back passageway for us."

"Why?"

"Who knows?" Strabo shrugged. "All I know is, things used to be different around here. Maybe not great, but at least they made sense, you know what I mean? Before that red-skinned freak came in and changed everything . . ."

"Uh-huh." Nailhead found himself nodding. "Back when we were in charge," he ruminated, and glanced up at Strabo. "So you think . . . ?"

"Maybe this individual—whoever it is—opened the walls for us. Maybe because they want a certain situation taken care of."

"You got a plan?"

"I've got a weapon." Strabo nodded at the open hatchway from which he and the others had just emerged. "What if we follow the passageway? See where it takes us."

"Yeah?"

"There's worse ways to spend a few hours," Strabo said, and, reaching out, he tossed a sharpened femur bone to Nailhead, who plucked it handily from the air, though he still had no idea what was going on. "So what do you say? Care for a walkabout?"

"Yeah." Standing up, placing his hands on his hips, and stretching his back, Nailhead grinned back at him. "I guess maybe I do."

Side by side, the two gang leaders headed back through the hatchway with the others following behind them, into the walls of the prison.

35
READY ROOM

The fat CO's name was Hootkins, and Smight could already smell him starting to sweat.

"Well?" he asked. "What's the deal?"

Hootkins didn't say anything, just slammed the half-liter tumbler of Rancor Aid that he'd been nursing and pressed one meaty hand to the wall behind him. Smight felt himself twitching with impatience. It *was* getting unpleasantly hot in the ready room among all these bodies pressed in around him—and what had the warden summoned them all together for, anyway?

He waited, bouncing on his heels, as Hootkins glanced at the guard standing to his right, a pumped-up glandular catastrophe named Logovik. Smight knew almost all the names of the guys on his shift, Stubens, Merrill, Glant, but he was still learning the rest of the roster. Not that it mattered much—none of these old-timers would give him the time of day.

Not yet.

When the warden had summoned them all to the ready room on short notice, no uniforms or weapons necessary, Smight had snorted another half gram of glitterstim from his private stash before hitting the deck. He'd already discovered that the stim gave him confidence and a telepathic boost that made everything feel heightened and somehow more vibrant at the same time, as if—*zing!*—an invisible saber had been drawn from its scabbard, straight up his nose. Not to mention the courage that it gave him for certain unauthorized aspects of the job—going face-to-face with that red-skinned inmate, 11240, in his cell, for example, or the mission they'd just undertaken down on the factory floor. It had made him feel like the king of the galaxy.

The truth was, Smight *loved* the spice. Smuggling his stash into Cog Hive Seven had been a lot easier than he'd expected, and he'd even managed to sell a little to a couple of the other COs. Making friends had always come easy to him that way. Too bad he hadn't had a chance to offer some to Hootkins. Who knew, he thought—maybe the porky loser could use some as a diet aid.

"So," Smight asked, drumming his fingertips against the table in front of him, "what's the problem?" One of the side effects of the stim was that it made you restless, ready to move ahead while everything else dragged behind. "You guys don't actually think—"

"Shut up," Hootkins snapped without bothering to glance at him. Now the fat man had one ear pressed to the wall of the ready room. Listening for a long moment, he turned back to Logovik. "Yeah," he said, "it's on. It's not big, but it's happening."

"What's on?" Smight asked. "What's happening?"

"Warden's reconfiguring."

"What, now?" Smight checked his chrono. "But we don't have another fight scheduled till—"

The main hatchway of the ready room whirred open and Warden Blirr stepped inside, followed in short order by her administrative droid. She stopped there, looked coolly across their faces, and smiled.

"Good afternoon, gentlemen. I want to thank you for coming on such short notice."

The guards straightened up. Logovik muttered a grunt of acknowledgment, and a few others offered unenthusiastic greetings in response. Among the men, Sadiki Blirr wasn't particularly popular. Apparently some of the guys actually found her attractive, but Smight was indifferent to that aspect of her. Fact was, the spice had more or less switched off that part of his mind, at least for the moment, and he was grateful. In a place like this, he decided, the fewer the distractions, the better.

"I'm sure you're all wondering why you're here," Sadiki said, "so I won't waste your time." She turned and faced the droid. "ThreeDee, is my call patched through?"

"Yes, Warden."

"Okay, go ahead." She gestured to the group of guards gathered on the far side of the room. "If you men wouldn't mind stepping to either side, I have a feeling that we're going to need all the space we can get."

As they shuffled out of the way, leaving an entire corner clear, the droid's holoprojector flickered to life.

For a moment Smight wasn't sure whether what he was seeing was real or a side effect of the stim. Eight meters in front of him, the mountainous shape of his employer had already come into focus to fill the entire corner of the ready room. Smight gaped as Jabba Desilijic Tiure shifted his enormous tail, gazing out at the audience that awaited him.

"Hello, Jabba," Sadiki said. "I appreciate you making time in your busy schedule for me."

"Sadiki Blirr." The crime lord's mouth opened just enough for him to run his tongue along his upper lip with a lascivious sneer. "You know, if you ever get tired of running that prison, I would be happy to make you one of my slave girls."

"Such a generous offer." She remained absolutely composed, even congenial, before him. "Unfortunately, I'll have to decline for now."

"To what do I owe the honor?"

"Ah, well." Sadiki gestured at the guards who had come to abrupt attention behind her, including Smight himself. "I believe I have some of your people here."

36

WHAT THE FEVER SAID

Eogan had been doing pull-ups on the uppermost bar of his cell when the walls began to move. His initial, panicked thought was that he was about to be matched, that death had come for him even sooner than he'd feared.

Please, no. I'm not ready. Not yet. Not ever.

When the reconfiguration stopped and nothing happened, Eogan felt a wild surge of relief, followed immediately by a sense of shame so overpowering that it drove him to the floor of the cell, where he lay motionless, hating himself for his cowardice. What would his father have thought of him, head down, praying to whatever gods might be listening that he would not have to fight, not now, not ever?

"Eogan?"

He jerked his head up at the sound of the haggard voice and looked around to see Jagannath standing there. The Zabrak was holding something in his arms like a bundle of laundry. It took a moment for Eogan to realize that the bundle was a man and that the man was, in fact, his father.

"Father?" His gaze flew up to the Zabrak, hot and accusatory. "What did you do to him?"

"I did nothing, boy," Jagannath said. "I found him like this."

"Eogan." Artagan Truax gazed at his son through dazed and bleary eyes. His skin had gone the color of old flimsiplast, the flesh so pale so that the blue tracery of his veins was clearly visible in his cheeks and on the bridge of his nose. Eogan regarded the swollen stump where the old man's leg had been, sensed the fever radiating out of his father's face and the foul smell of infected tissue, and knew what it all meant before the Zabrak could say the words.

"He's dying."

Jagannath nodded. "He contracted blood poisoning from the wound." Lowering Artagan Truax to the bunk, he said, "He won't talk to me. You need to question him. About Iram Radique and the Bando Gora."

Eogan shook his head. "I don't know what that—"

"Listen to me, boy. There's no time for excuses. I saw Iram Radique. I need to know anything else your father can tell us about Radique's relationship with the Bando Gora. They are the ones who are going to take possession of Radique's most destructive weapon, a proscribed nuclear device. This is my mission."

"But I've never heard of the Bando—"

"It's a death cult. Your father told me that he used to fight alongside them, that they tried to kill Iram Radique and he saved Radique's life."

"My father would never join a cult," Eogan said. "He doesn't know what he's—"

"*Gora!*" the old man shrieked, his face twisting into a mask of terror. His hands flew up to hook and claw the air. "All hail the skull beneath the hood! *Flay the skin and drink the blood!*"

Eogan took a startled step back. "I've never heard him talk like this before."

"I need to know what he knows," Jagannath said. "I have urgent business to transact between them and Iram Radique. If he can tell you anything about how to contact them—"

"*No!*" All at once the old man lunged upright, seizing his son by the shoulder and pulling him close. Sudden clarity had descended over his face, and his pupils sharpened, fixating on Eogan. "Iram Radique will never do business with the Gora. *Never.*"

"Ask him how to reach the Gora," the Zabrak said to Eogan. "Ask him how we can contact them. Get him to talk."

"I—I'll do what I can," Eogan said. "But there's another match coming. What if I have to fight?"

The Zabrak glared at him. "You'll die."

Eogan opened his mouth and closed it again. There seemed to be no reasonable response to the words, and he didn't attempt one.

"Everything here," the Zabrak said, "everything you see around you, is a test. Make no mistake. If you lack the strength or ability to survive, the Hive will break you." He stepped closer to Eogan. "At his core, your father was strong enough to survive and protect you, but you don't have his heart. Even the way he is now, in this wasted state, you'll never be half the man that he is." He jerked his head at the old man groaning and muttering to himself on the bunk. "Now make yourself useful and get him to talk."

Eogan said nothing. His jaw trembled. "Father, it's me. It's Eogan." Glancing back up at the Zabrak, he said gently, "We need to know about Iram Radique."

The old man's eyes fluttered and closed. All strength fled from him and his mouth fell open, his face going slack. For a terrible instant Eogan thought he'd died. Then he saw the chest rise and fall, a shallow and halting breath, but a breath just the same, followed by a few brief, barely coherent words.

"What was that?" Jagannath stared at Eogan. "What did he say?"

"He said 'Zero.'"

"*Zero?* What about him?"

Eogan frowned up at the Zabrak.

"He said . . ." The boy glanced down at his father, then back up at Jagannath, blinking in confusion. "He answers to another name."

37

BESTIARY

Smight began to inch backward and realized that he was already pressed up against a wall. He wasn't sure exactly when his heart had started pounding, but now it felt ready to explode. Rivulets of sweat trickled from between his shoulder blades and crept down the center of his spine, plastering his damp shirt against his skin, and he forced himself to take a low, shuddering breath.

Stay cool. They won't see anything that you don't show them. Hoping to disappear between the guards on either side of him, he realized there was nowhere else to go. *Just breathe.*

"So, Jabba," Sadiki was saying from the front of the group, "I keep hearing rumors of you sending foot soldiers into my prison to work as guards. I'm hoping you can clear that up for me." Waving her hand toward the nine guards in the ready room, she said, "Do any of these men look familiar?"

Smight didn't breathe. None of the guards around him moved. On the holovid, the Hutt reclined, his slitted eyes moving languidly back and forth, taking in the room. At length he let out a slow, guttural laugh, the mocking *ho-ho-ho* that Smight had come to identify with a particularly unpleasant frozen sensation through his bowels. He had only heard that laugh once before, and it had been one time too many.

"You *are* wasting my time, Warden," Jabba said, answering in the guttural Huttese that Smight's ear translated effortlessly into Basic. "I recognize none of these swine."

"Are you certain?" Sadiki asked. "Because I'll be happy to return any of your own men to you unharmed in the spirit of maintaining peace with the Desilijic Clan." A slight frown line formed over her forehead. "The ones that you don't claim, well . . ." She glanced at ThreeDee. "Let's just say they're slightly more disposable."

"Kill them all and toss their carcasses to swamp slugs," Jabba said. "It is all the same to me."

"I see. Well, perhaps I should ask the men."

She pushed a button on the wall. Smight heard a faint whirring sound to his right and glanced over his shoulder. Across the ready room, directly opposite the holoprojection of Jabba, an oblong panel slid open to expose a recessed area that had not been there just a moment before—a result, he guessed, of this last reconfiguration. From this angle, Smight could not see inside it, but he had the sudden realization that whatever was back there had already started to move out.

"Gentlemen," Sadiki said, "I'm sure you all know Mr. Nailhead and Mr. Strabo."

A thin blade of silence sliced through the ready room. Then Nailhead and Strabo stepped into view, and Smight heard the other guards drawing back with sharp curses and sounds of disbelief, cramming into whatever space they could find, reaching instinctively for weapons and dropboxes that weren't there.

"Wait a second," Hootkins called out, somewhere off to Smight's left, the fat guard's suety voice now high-pitched with fear and panic. "Warden, what is this? *What are you doing?*"

Smight, for his part, could not move. He felt his whole body go strangely weightless. All at once his legs seemed to have disappeared; the same paralysis seized his chest, and he realized that he was physically incapable of drawing breath.

Sadiki just smiled. "It's a simple question," she said, stepping forward to fill the space between the Bone Kings and the guards. "Any of you working for Desilijic Clan please step forward." She gazed at the guards. "No one? Are you sure?"

"Me!" Lodovik shouted from off to Smight's left, and jumped forward, practically knocking down the men on either side of him. "Jabba sent us here to track down Iram Radique!"

"Ah," Sadiki said. "And what were your orders exactly?"

"Jabba told us to find out everything we could. To ferret him out and drive him into the open."

"Is there anyone else in this room that you would care to identify?"

"Crete! He's part of it!" Logovik shouted, pointing at a tall, gray-haired guard on the other side of the room. All at once he couldn't seem to get the names out fast enough. "And Galway! Tyson! Olyphant! McCane! Over there, Webberly! And"—his hand swung toward Smight—"that new guy, the rookie, I don't know his name, Jabba sent him in, too. He forged the background check for all of us and told us we had to—"

"Scum." From the holo, Jabba's lazy smile had disappeared, overwhelmed by a vicious sneer of disgust. "You just signed your death warrant."

If Logovik even heard the Hutt, he ignored him. His eyes flashed desperately from the Bone Kings back to Sadiki. "That's it, that's all of us! Can I go now?"

Sadiki gazed at him pityingly. "I'm sorry, Officer . . . Logovik, is it?" She gave a slow, sad shake of her head. "But I'm afraid your employer is right about one thing. I couldn't possibly let you go now. And gentlemen . . ." She glanced back at Strabo, Nailhead, and the amalgamation of gang members, Bone Kings and Massives alike, that they'd led here. "Whatever happens next, you and your gang would do well to remember that the only dropbox in the room is strapped to my hip."

"Wait!" Logovik managed. All the remaining color had drained out of his face, leaving it sickly and pale. "But—"

"Best of luck, gentlemen. And I thank you for your candor."

Sadiki stepped back, clearing the way for the Bone Kings.

For an instant there was silence, and within that split second, Smight heard it: a low, snarling chuckle.

It was Nailhead.

Then it happened.

It might've been the glitterstim, but Smight experienced the events of the next few seconds in what felt like sickening slow motion.

As one, the gang members burst forward across the ready room with a deafening howl, overturning chairs and leaping across the table, attacking the guards in a solid wave. Smight was knocked to the side and the table landed on top of him, temporarily blocking him from view, although he could still catch a glimpse over the top of it with agonizing clarity.

In the space between seconds, the entire room had already exploded in a mass of activity, swinging bones, flashing teeth, and crashing fists. All around him, the guards tried to scatter, but there was nowhere to go. The gang members' angle of attack had blocked the only possible path to the chamber's main entryway, and they piled on top of the guards, overwhelming them easily.

Pressed between the overturned table and the wall, Smight dropped to his knees and then to his stomach, as if there might be some way that he could crawl across the floor and find his way out without being detected. He already felt his grasp on reality skidding, slipping perilously away. All around him, guys he'd come to know on a first-name basis were screaming, squirming in every direction, scrambling for a way out.

From this angle, he could see Hootkins trying to jump over him, the fat man shoving belly first, fighting desperately to plow a path between two of the Bone Kings, making a last-ditch run for the exit. His face was a blur of terror. After two steps, Hootkins stumbled and lost his balance, and two of the Kings grabbed him and slammed him to the floor, impaling him with sharpened ribs that they'd lashed to their wrists like claws and ripping him to pieces.

Good-bye, Hootkins.

Smight kept staring. He seemed unable to look away. Right in front of him, a threesome of Massives and Bone Kings had gone to work on two other guards, Crete and a bald, broad-shouldered guy who might have been Webberly—from here it was impossible to say. Another one of the gang members had McCane up against a wall, tearing open McCane's shirt and using a broken skull to scoop out his thoracic cavity, while Nailhead and his lieutenant, an animal named Massif, were holding on to the hands and feet of Olyphant, literally ripping him in two, bathing in his blood.

Good-bye, Olyphant.

Smight felt a kind of queer, fatalistic certainty take hold of him. If he stayed here another thirty seconds, the gang members would run out of guards to destroy and would find him. He couldn't stay here.

He sat up.

Crash! The chair hit the wall just above his head, splintering to pieces. Logovik, the guard who had ratted them all out, the one who had brought all of this down on them, swung an arm down and picked up one of the chair fragments, jerking it up over his head like a makeshift weapon. Seeing him here spiked a sudden upsurge of anger into Smight's brain, and in stark defiance of the fear he felt in his own chest, he grabbed Logovik by the ankle.

"Happy?" he shouted. "You did this to us!"

"You got what you deserve, maggot." Logovik swung his elbow back, hammering Smight in the side of the face, and Smight's eyes exploded in a supernova of bright white stars. When his vision cleared, he heard the unmistakable sound of Vas Nailhead unleashing a war howl, the inmate raising the sharpened femur gripped in his hands and bringing it down on Logovik's skull with a brittle, pulpy crunch.

Good-bye, Logovik.

Logovik fell, but before he could even hit the floor, Nailhead seized him by the throat, swinging him back upward, and went to take a great, ravenous bite of the man's face. Smight turned away. He didn't feel bold anymore. Now he felt like he was going to be sick. A foot connected with his chest, driving the air out of him, imbedding the nausea more deeply in his guts. He was going to die here along with all the rest of them.

He writhed, squirming, and then he saw it.

The open panel from which the Bone Kings had emerged.

It was still open.

Chaos still gripped the ready room, which seemed absurdly cramped for the outburst of activity within it, but the one-sided assault was already losing momentum. On both sides, Nailhead, Strabo and their minions were merrily eviscerating the final remaining guards, years of compressed rage exploding out of them in seconds as they shredded the men and left their bodies impaled against the walls.

Amid it all, Warden Blirr looked on serenely. After another moment, she turned and walked out with her droid behind her, the hatch sealing shut.

Smight didn't have much time.

Still on his hands and knees, he scampered forward as fast as he could between the bodies and under the broken remains of the table. Ducking his head low, he leapt through the open passageway into darkness.

38

ANTIDOTE

From twenty meters back, Maul watched Zero emerge through the line in the mess hall. He waited while the Twi'lek sat down, picked up his fork, and began, thoughtfully and deliberately, to eat.

Three bites. Four. Five.

Maul sat down across from him.

"Hello, Zero."

The Twi'lek's fork fell from his hand with a clatter. His jaw fell open to reveal the half-chewed mouthful of food he'd been in the process of swallowing. It wasn't a pretty sight.

"Jagannath," he whispered. "You're supposed to be—"

"Dead?" Maul glared at him. "I can understand your confusion. When you left me on the factory floor, I was on the verge of being pulled to pieces. Yet here I am."

The Twi'lek managed to swallow, but he still couldn't speak. His eyes darted right and left, the muscles of his throat twitching visibly beneath his skin, as if he were struggling fruitlessly to digest the physical evidence of Maul's presence here.

"You—you don't understand," he said. "You can't be here. *He* thinks you're dead."

Zero started to stand up, and Maul's hand moved faster than the eye could see, grabbing Zero's fork and slamming it down so that it impaled the Twi'lek's sleeve, pinning his arm to the table.

At the next table, three big inmates rose to their feet and started toward Maul.

Without taking his gaze from the Twi'lek, Maul spoke, just loud enough for Zero to hear. "Tell them to sit back down."

Zero looked up at his bodyguards. "It's all right," he said in a thin voice. "Go sit down."

The inmates returned haltingly to their meals.

"It's an interesting thing," Maul said softly. "Whom we serve and why. At first you told me that Iram Radique doesn't exist. The next thing I know, you're working for him."

"You have no idea—"

"I took the old man with me when I walked out of the factory floor," Maul continued. "He's not doing well. That blood infection's going to kill him. But he did tell me something interesting before he became completely delirious. He told me that you answered to a different name."

Zero's face showed no expression. "Which is?"

"That's what you're going to tell me."

"Jagannath, please." The Twi'lek's voice was low and urgent. "You must listen to me. I've been in this place from the beginning. There's a reason I've survived this long."

"Right before I killed Rook," Maul said, "I asked him if there was someone else—someone above him, who worked directly with Radique. He drew something with his finger. At the time I thought it was just a circle. But it wasn't." He leaned in closer, until his face was almost touching the Twi'lek's. "It was a zero."

"Rook?" The Twi'lek shook his head. "Rook was just—"

"A decoy," Maul said, and nodded, his voice holding no inflection whatsoever. "I see that now. Handing him over was your way of taking my attention from where it should have been the whole time." He glanced at Zero's tray, where the Twi'lek's special meal sat half eaten. "You know, I noticed that you always enjoy a better quality of food than the other inmates. One of the benefits of being the one who can smuggle things into the prison, I assume. Unfortunately, it also makes you far more vulnerable."

"To what?"

"I slipped a crushed gram of white metaxas root into the vat just before you came through the line today," Maul said, in that same dispassionate voice. "Coyle tried to give it to me earlier. Fortunately, he still had it when I came back and asked for it again. I'm told that it's odorless and flavorless, but fast-acting." He glanced down at the half-finished meal. "And you've already eaten enough to kill you."

Zero stared down at the tray in dawning horror, and then shoved it away from him, as if mere physical proximity might be enough to stop what had already begun. "Wh-why . . . ?"

"There is an antidote," Maul said, opening his hand to show Zero a small clear vial of gray powder. "Something I lifted from medbay. If I give it to you in the next thirty seconds, you'll survive."

"I already told you—"

"I've seen Radique's face," Maul said. "Now I need to make arrangements with him. I'm willing to pay three hundred thousand credits for a proscribed nuclear device—I have the money here. I will make contact with the buyers personally and arrange for their arrival to take possession of the weapon."

"He . . ." Zero's hands had begun trembling. He gazed at them in terrified wonder, then back up at Maul. "He'll never agree to the deal."

"Why not?"

"He knows the Bando Gora. They tried to kill him once already. They are sworn enemies. He's made a blood oath never to do business with them."

"Then you'll have to change his mind, won't you?"

"You—*fool*—" Zero's entire body had begun to shake. When he spoke again, his voice was trembling, the words spilling from his lips in halting bursts. "You have no idea—what you've done—"

His head fell to the table with a crash.

With a grimace of irritation, Maul hoisted Zero's face out of his food, inspected his eyes, and let his head drop again.

He left him like that and walked out of the mess hall.

39

CRAWL

Smight ran.

By the time the screaming in the ready room finally trailed away to silence, he was on his feet, barreling full-tilt down the maintenance shaft, sprinting headlong through the near-darkness. He didn't know where he was going or what he would do when he got there, but right now that wasn't as important as putting as much distance as possible between himself and the gang members who had pursued him.

His skull was pounding; his lungs blazed. Rounding a corner, unable to go another step without resting, he sagged against the cold wall and sucked in a deep, ragged breath. The glitterstim had worn off completely now, and he felt wrung out and edgy, shaking so hard that he could scarcely stand up, his knees threatening to betray him at any second.

Look at the facts.

Fact #1: He was an unarmed guard trapped inside a prison full of homicidal monsters, any of whom would relish the opportunity to kill him.

Fact #2: He couldn't go back to Jabba for help, even if there was some way of contacting him.

Conclusion: He was a walking dead man.

Smight fought the almost irresistible urge to weep, to scream, to collapse. None of those things would help him now. A tiny voice inside him whispered that if maybe he could sneak back to his quarters and score a little bit more of the stim that he kept tucked away among his personal items, it might help clarify things, but even that seemed hopeless. Coming down from the spice's euphoria only made him more aware of how much he'd depended on it up till now. He didn't know where he was or where he was going.

He felt his gorge rising with disgust. Self-pity wrapped itself around him like a damp, familiar cloak. Having failed in his mission for Jabba, he'd validated everything about himself that he'd secretly suspected to be true—cowardice, inadequacy, incompetence. What, then, was the point of going forward?

Then, in the tunnel ahead of him, something moved.

Smight listened. There was a muscular enormity to it, a great slithering massiveness like nothing he'd run across inside these walls. He could actually hear the sticky, clicking snap of its mouthparts.

The Wolf Worm.

He'd heard the stories of the Syrox—they all had. A thing that lived inside the pipes and ducts of the prison, that fed and grew sleek and fat on the blood of the matches. Some of the other guards even swore they'd seen it, although there was never any hard evidence of its existence.

That was when he heard something else. Not out loud. In his mind. Voices—

—*helphelp*—

—the words—

—*murderkillyoustrangleyouall*—

—emanating through his brain.

—*outletusoutletusFEED*—

Smight inclined his head more closely toward the wall, captivated in spite of himself. He *wasn't* imagining it. The voices emanating through his brainpan were a tangle of horrors, a braided skein of a thousand different tongues, human and nonhuman, all shrieking and begging and snarling and roaring for mercy, deliverance, revenge.

Smight was not a particularly intelligent man by nature, but he knew enough to trust his perception, even when it flew in the face of what he thought to be true. And his perception on this matter was crystal clear.

The Syrox was not only real, it was *sentient*.

Its mind was a threnody of violence and pain, stitched together from every inmate whose body the thing had devoured during its time squirming through the guts of the prison. Their collective minds, though dead, were somehow still living inside it.

Glancing up, he caught just a glimpse of something so thunderously huge and fat that it filled the entire passageway, gleaming and pale and blind-eyed, surging toward him with its mouthparts peeling open like the petals of some hideous albino flower. Smight glimpsed pink and a dozen rings of teeth. The smell that came pouring out from inside it was wretched beyond description, the stink of a mass grave.

His heart sprang up to the pit of his throat and clung there, cowering.

He turned and fled.

Fear made him weightless, boiling him down to his most essential reflexes. The overall effect made the stim seem weak by comparison. Strength that he'd never imagined exploded through his legs, pumping him in the opposite direction, adrenaline pounding hard through every synapse.

He could hear the thing squeezing through the corridor behind him, surging forward faster now, closing the distance with every passing second. He kept his head down and doubled his pace, navigating the twists and turns purely by instinct, the gray walls flying by in a blur. Off in the distance, the thunderous approach of the thing disappeared beneath the steady pounding of his heart, its rhythms optimized for bare-bones survival.

He ran harder. He could run forever if he had to.

Swinging around the corner, he slammed headlong into something solid but not as hard as a wall. It knocked him flat, and he looked up to see Vas Nailhead squinting down at him. The inmate, like the Bone Kings gathered behind him, was drenched from head to foot in blood.

"Well, well." Nailhead stood there with Strabo alongside him, the

Bone Kings and Massive clustering closer. "I guess there's no end to what you'll run into down here, is there?"

Smight didn't move. Couldn't breathe.

"What's the matter, *maggot?*" Nailhead wiped his mouth with his wrist, smearing the scarlet streak of gore sideways across his beard. "No blaster you can point at me? No dropbox you can punch my numbers into?" He grabbed Smight and yanked him to his feet. "What's wrong, *bro,* you got nothing you want to say to me?"

"Well," Smight managed, in a voice that didn't sound remotely like his own. He could hear it coming again, the noise getting louder as it moved up the passageway. "There is one thing . . ."

"Yeah? What's that?"

He pointed up the corridor. "You better watch out."

Nailhead tilted back his head. Behind him, Strabo was also staring. As their expressions changed, Smight himself became aware of something—the presence returning, huge and warm and terribly eager.

And then the screaming started.

40
NOBODY'S HERO

Maul elbowed his way deeper into the crowd outside the mess hall. He'd left Zero in the mess hall, slumped over in his food, having gained nothing from their last exchange. As he'd stood to go, the three inmates who'd approached them earlier had grabbed the Twi'lek and carried him off, no doubt rushing him to medbay. Maul doubted they would make it in time, but he supposed it was possible, if they hurried.

Right now he had more pressing business to take care of.

He found the boy in the cell, sitting next to his father's body. The old man lay motionless on the bunk, breathing shallowly. His skin was mottled with a sallow, blotchy cast.

"Jagannath?" Eogan asked. "What—"

"Pick him up," Maul said. "We need to move."

"Where?"

"Follow me."

Gently Eogan leaned down and gathered his father's body in his arms.

The morgue was as silent as Maul remembered it. They stepped through the hatchway single file, the boy shifting his father's weight to his shoulder in order to get through the entrance.

"What are we doing here?" Eogan asked uneasily.

Maul didn't look back. "Lay him down there," he said, nodding to indicate one of the empty tables extending from the wall.

"You still haven't told me what—"

"Has he said anything else about the Bando Gora?" Maul asked. "Anything at all?"

"No, I told you, he's—he can't talk. The infection, it . . ." The boy swallowed, unable to complete the thought. "He needs medicine."

Maul said nothing, reaching down beneath the lowermost console to retrieve the holotransmitter from where he'd stashed it, pressing in the code to activate its primary drives. Then he turned to face Artagan Truax.

"Old man."

The eyelids lifted slightly, regarding him dully. Cracked lips moved but made no sound.

"I need you to enter the hailing frequency for the Bando Gora," Maul said.

Artagan Truax managed to shake his head. "Don't remember . . . anything."

"You're going to have to remember," Maul said. "Or I'm going to kill your son."

Eogan turned to stare at him. The old man tried to sit up.

"The frequency," Maul said. "Put it in."

After what seemed like forever, Artagan Truax began to type. His fingers clicked shakily across the key controls, stabbing in coordinates in uneven bursts. Finishing, he sagged backward into silence.

"Is that it?"

The old man said nothing. Maul was still watching him when he became aware of the boy's eyes, fixed on the passageway outside.

"Do you hear that?" he asked. "It's the clarion call."

Maul listened. Eogan was right.

"Leave me," he said. "Now."

The boy glanced at his father. "Where should I—"

"It doesn't matter. Take him away. Back to your cell," Maul said. "Just go."

When Eogan had lifted his father in his arms and carried him off,

Maul switched out the hailing frequency for the holotransmitter and activated the device again. He knelt before it, his head lowered, waiting.

Within seconds Darth Sidious appeared in front of him. This time he didn't bother with the formalities.

"You have news?"

"I do, my Master," Maul said.

"What is it?"

"Iram Radique," Maul said. "I found him."

Moments later, Maul was back down on the factory floor, making his way through the bone statues, searching the shadows for the one who could help him advance to the next stage of his search.

His Master's response to the news of Iram Radique's identity had not been what he'd hoped. Sidious had listened impatiently while Maul told him about the Weequay, and how he'd narrowly escaped being pulled to pieces without betraying his abilities as a Force user.

In the end, his Master had simply nodded, as if all of this should have happened far more expediently than it had, and demanded that Maul contact him when the deal was finished. He'd said nothing about the Bando Gora or the difficulty of brokering an arrangement between the cult and Radique. That detail had been left for Maul to arrange—hence, his return to the factory floor, where he'd nearly died.

He stepped forward, listening carefully until he recognized the sound of the Chadra-Fan's humming in the darkness.

"Ah, Jagannath." Coyle turned, already smiling up at Maul expectantly. "You have come for what is yours, yes?"

"Is it ready?"

"Just finished." Still humming, the other inmate turned and walked away, leading him around a pile of loosely assembled bones, then digging through debris both mechanical and organic until he found a flat metal case, holding it up for Maul's inspection. "Three hundred thousand credits." A glimmer of pride lit the Chadra-Fan's eye. "Authentic enough to fool the most discriminating inspection. Do you approve?"

Maul looked down at the stacks and rows of bundled currency, then picked one up from the top and held it to the light. The craftsmanship, while thorough, probably wouldn't hold up to close scrutiny—but it would open the doors that he needed to go through to arrange the final details with Radique.

At this point it would have to suffice.

Amid the press of reeking bodies that filled the corridor, Maul pushed his way along with the metal case at his side. A bulky Bone King bumped shoulders with him, too close to be accidental. Without turning or even breaking stride, he drove his fist into the King's solar plexus, leaving him doubled over on the floor, gasping for air.

He stopped in his tracks.

His gaze had fallen on an inmate standing absolutely motionless amid the flow of bodies around him. For a moment the entire world went still. All sound dropped away.

It was him.

The one he'd seen standing side by side with Zero on the factory floor.

Radique.

The Weequay was gazing back at him through the crowds of inmates, the clawbird perched on his shoulder. Maul watched as he pulled a scrap of greasy-looking bantha suet from the pocket of his uniform and held it up unhurriedly for the bird to snatch from his fingers. In the blink of an eye, the food disappeared, and the Weequay dug out another chunk. The bird gobbled it even faster than before, its head bobbing in an eager attempt to get the morsel down its throat.

With the metal case that Coyle had given him still at his hip, Maul shoved his way through the crowd, knocking over other inmates. But when he got to where the Weequay had been standing, the other was gone.

Maul turned and looked in every direction. The corridors were clearing now as the last stragglers returned to their cells for matching. The clarion blared on.

You're so close now. You can't stop.

Maul turned and almost ran headfirst into the guard standing there.

"You heard the clarion." The guard glared at him. "Why aren't you in your cell?"

"I'm on my way now," Maul said.

"Hold it, maggot." The guard glared at the metal case in Maul's hand. "What's that?"

"I salvaged it from the pile in Nightside."

"What's inside?"

"Nothing."

"Nothing?" The guard yanked the case from Maul's hands and popped it open, lifting the lid and tipping it upside down.

A loose pile of bones fell out, clattering to the floor. Kicking them aside, the guard tossed the case and glared at Maul. "Get to your cell now."

41

THE MAIN MONKEY BUSINESS

Good things were happening.

Sadiki sat with her boots propped up on her desk, sipping coffee and smiling. She and ThreeDee had finished watching the slaughter of the guards from the comfort of her office, where she wouldn't have to worry about getting blood on her suit. As pure spectacle, it didn't disappoint. Too bad she hadn't had time to auction the holovid broadcast rights—or, even better, take bets on the outcome. Not that anyone in their right mind would have bet on a group of unarmed prison guards against Strabo and Nailhead and their followers. She had no doubt there would be repercussions to what she'd done—one didn't trifle with Jabba the Hutt without getting some pushback in one form or another—but at the moment she was feeling relatively . . . what?

"Invulnerable," she said aloud, and the droid perked up.

"Excuse me?"

"Bulletproof. That's where we are right now." Sadiki took another sip of coffee. "It's a good position to be in, ThreeDee."

"Yes, Warden. However, I can't help but wonder—"

"Shush." Sadiki held up her hand. "You're spoiling the moment. How long till the next fight?"

"It's starting any minute now. The algorithm—"

She checked the screens in front of her, took her feet off her desk, and stared downward at the display. "Wait a second," she said, looking up at the droid. "Where's Dakarai?"

"I don't know."

"This isn't right. There's got to be some mistake." She watched as the algorithm selected its two combatants. "Find my brother. Find him *now*."

"I'm sure I don't know where he is."

Sadiki cursed. "Where's the override?"

ThreeDee made a quick chirping sound, and its breastplate dialed open to extrude a slender adapter, plugging it into the console next to Sadiki's desk. "Accessing algorithm override," it said, and there was a long pause. "I can't override the system. I'm afraid the combatants have already been locked in."

"My brother can fix it," Sadiki said.

"I'm afraid that's simply not possible."

"Why?"

"Because he's the one who locked them in."

Sadiki frowned at the display. "Dakarai's in the system somewhere. He's accessed it remotely somehow. It doesn't make sense; why would he do that?"

The droid swiveled its head to regard her, its photoreceptors pulsating busily.

"Respectfully, Warden, when was the last time you saw Master Dakarai?"

Sadiki didn't answer. She was still looking at the screens.

Dakarai, she thought, *what are you doing?*

42

BLEED THE FREAK

Maul made it back just seconds before the reconfiguration began. He'd just stepped through the hatchway when it sealed shut behind him, the floor and walls already starting to shift. As the now-familiar clamor of gears and clockwork filled the air, he turned his gaze upward to where he knew the warden and the rest of the galactic gambling community would be watching. His involvement in the next bout seemed to be a foregone conclusion.

What would it be this time? Fire? Ice? The sarlacc from the Great Pit of Carkoon?

The cell reeled and swung as the architecture of the prison fell into its newest alignment. Maul held fast to the handgrips of the bench, riding it out. At this point it really didn't matter what they pitted him against. Now that he'd seen Radique face-to-face—

The cell came to a halt.

Maul cocked his head, listening for whatever opponent the algorithm had selected for him. Whatever it was, he would kill it as quickly as possible and get on with his business at hand.

The wall of the cell came open.

Maul looked into it, muscles tensing for the attack—

And felt all his resolve go swirling away in a sudden rush of bewilderment.

The Weequay stepped out to face him.

*　*　*

For a moment he couldn't speak. The Weequay was walking toward him with the clawbird resting on his shoulder. Maul stared, his senses heightened by the intensity of his shock, as the bird lifted one of its talons, shifting its position, to reveal the knots of *khipus* tied around its feet.

"You were supposed to die already, Jagannath," the Weequay said. "Torn to pieces on the factory floor. I should have finished you myself."

He was still coming. Maul was struck again by the ineluctable suspicion that everything that had happened to him since the moment of his arrival here—from the ongoing matches to the riddles to the machines that had nearly ripped him to pieces—had all been part of some larger trial or examination overseen by Sidious, and that perhaps now he had arrived at the greatest test of all.

"Wait," Maul said. "I won't kill you."

"You're right about that."

Maul reached up and yanked open his collar to reveal the bundles of credits that he'd stuffed inside his uniform before leaving Nightside. He held them up. "Three hundred thousand credits. They're yours."

The Weequay didn't answer. Instead, he raised his arm, and the bird took flight, arrowing across the cell like a shadow cut loose from the object that cast it, streaking straight for Maul's face, talons extended. Ducking, Maul swung one fist to knock it aside, but the bird dove down under his arm at the last second and came up screaming, claws fastened to his face, pecking furiously at his eyes.

Maul grabbed the bird blindly, ripped it from where it had fastened itself to his face, and tried to fling it to the floor, where he could stomp it to death, but it squirmed free and took flight, still cawing and shrieking across the cell in a trail of feathers. He raised his head and wiped his eyes. His vision was a curtain of blood beyond which the Weequay arose, the vaguest of shapes, though nearer than ever.

"I know exactly what you are," Radique's voice said, very close. "And I know who sent you here." He was raising something over his head—some kind of melee weapon, some dagger or pike whose specifics

Maul couldn't immediately discern—already intent on delivering the deathblow. "Now I will give you what you deserve."

A supernova of pain exploded through Maul's right flank, and his right arm went numb even as he lifted it in an attempt at self-defense.

But the paralysis went far deeper than that. For the first time since he'd arrived at Cog Hive Seven, Maul had no idea how to proceed. Killing Radique now would mean the end of his mission—total failure in the eyes of his Master and the Sith.

Yet anything less would cost him his life.

"You serve the Bando Gora," the Weequay's voice was saying, from somewhere behind the scarlet veil.

"No," Maul said. "That's not—"

From behind him, the pounding of wings.

Maul reacted on instinct, swinging his left arm back to pluck the clawbird out of the air. His right arm remained useless—whatever the Weequay had done to him with the melee weapon seemed to have severed his control of it, at least temporarily. Gripping one of the bird's wings with his left hand, Maul bit down on the other wing and clamped it between his teeth, spreading them apart to their fullest span.

Keep it disoriented. Work it into a frenzy until it cannot tell friend from enemy. It's the only way.

The bird fought him with everything it had, twisting and writhing, pecking frantically, screaming in his grasp. Its talons raked his face, carving deep furrows across his cheekbones. But Maul did not let it go.

He swung it through the air, slashing it across the Weequay's face in a definitive stroke, simultaneously breaking its back while raking the thing's claws over the Weequay's eyes. The bird fell to the floor, a broken thing, its wings protruding at awkward, irrational angles.

Maul wiped the blood from his face. At last his vision had begun to clear. Stepping back, he raised his left hand in one final attempt to communicate with the Weequay.

"Hear me," he said. "I'm not here representing the Bando Gora. I need to buy a weapon from you. I need—"

Radique attacked him again, a quick, brutal series of blows to neck and face. They came almost too fast to register, a fierce storm of blows, and Maul was aware of the floor shifting beneath him, dropping him to his knees. When the Weequay's pike smashed into his skull again, Maul realized that right here and now, in the midst of his crisis, Radique was going to beat him to death.

It was going to end here.

Master. The uncertainty of it loomed over him, clouding his thoughts. *What should I do? How can I—?*

Wham! Another blow, the most vicious one yet, split the thought in half, and Maul dropped to his stomach. He knew that failure would cost him everything, that he would never be able to return to Sidious and the Grand Plan, and yet—

Maul's thoughts cycled back to his early childhood, further back than he'd ever dared reflect, to his earliest training, the endless, hostile torture that he'd endured on Mygeeto. As painful as it had been, there was knowledge there, a realization that in the end, the galaxy was a cold and uncaring place that would never protect him. And if he was going to survive, it would only be because he would never give up.

Never.

Give.

Up.

Not then.

Not now.

Never.

Something broke open inside him, a vein of pure instinct that ran even deeper than his commitment to the mission. On his feet at once, he grabbed the Weequay by his seclusion braids, jerked the other's head back, and thrust his own head forward, driving the horns of his skull against the inmate's throat.

Radique's windpipe burst open, splintering beneath the attack. His body fell limp, and Maul released the braids, letting him drop to the floor.

Maul stepped back from the corpse.

He stood there for what felt like a long time.

It was over.

Master, I had no choice.

But there was only silence.

43

KALDANI SPIRES

"I suppose this means you may congratulate your apprentice," Darth Plagueis observed, "on a job well done."

He had just turned his attention from the holovid screen to gaze out the window of his penthouse at the top of Kaldani Spires, down on the unsuspecting crowds thronging Monument Square, far below.

On the opposite side of the room, Sidious stood simmering with his fists clenched, the muscles of his jaw tight with anger. He could not discern Plagueis's expression reflected in the glass, nor could he guess his Master's thoughts from his tone of voice. All around them, Plagueis's lavishly appointed penthouse had fallen absolutely silent, a reverential stillness prevailing over the richly brocaded carpeting, resonating from the elaborate furnishings, tapestries, and artifacts that adorned the rooms and corridors. Sidious could hear the pounding of his own outraged pulse.

They had just finished the holo of Maul's most recent bout—the first one that they'd watched together, although Sidious had been monitoring each of his apprentice's fights carefully from the time Maul had first arrived on Cog Hive Seven. Today, without warning or precedent, Plagueis had summoned him here so that they could watch the fight together.

It was as if he'd known what would happen.

"His mission *was* to assassinate Radique without relying on the Force," Plagueis mused, as he turned back to face Sidious. "Was it not?"

As was so often the case, the elongated, grayish blue face behind the transpirator mask was neither smiling nor frowning. Instead Damask wore the distant, abstracted expression of a profoundly advanced intellect lost deep in his own counsel. "Which means that he's finished there, yes? Ready to be extracted?"

Sidious managed a single nod. Deep within him, the rage grew more intense, and he still did not trust his own voice.

"And yet," Plagueis said, regarding him thoughtfully, "you seem . . . less than pleased."

With the deliberate effort of a man releasing a clenched fist, Sidious made a conscious effort at composure. *He's testing me. Examining my motives.* And again, the question cycled back through his head: *How much does he know?*

"Of course I'm pleased," Sidious said, careful to maintain unbroken eye contact with Plagueis as he spoke each word. There could be no indication of treachery here, no hint of the true purpose behind the mission. "Maul has done exactly as I requested."

"Not that I'm questioning you, of course," Plagueis said. "As I've said before, your business with the Zabrak, especially when it comes to this sort of thing, is exactly that—*your* business." He paused just long enough for Sidious to wonder if all of this was, in fact, just a passing remark, the equivalent of an idle thought that passed through a consciousness as heightened as Plagueis's. "I do wonder, however, about what might happen if Maul revealed his true identity as a Sith Lord while still imprisoned in this place. The implications for our plan might prove . . . substantial."

"Impossible," Sidious said. "Maul's loyalty to us is above reproach. He would gladly lay down his life before compromising the secrecy of his mission."

"Of course." Plagueis shook his head. "I just wish to remind you that there are still aspects of this operation that may not be completely under your control. Or mine." For a moment his expression was sympathetic, indulgent in a way that, as a younger man, Sidious had once enjoyed but now—if he was honest—found placatory, almost patronizing. "It is a painful yet necessary reminder, Darth Sidious. Beings such as ourselves, ones who enjoy the promise of nearly unlimited power, live with the paradoxical risk of forgetting that there are some elements of the galaxy that we cannot control."

"Are you suggesting that the mission was a miscalculation from the beginning?"

"Such speculation is meaningless now." Plagueis waited again, and Sidious sensed him closing in on his final point. "No, I suppose my true purpose, looking back on what has already happened, is to question why you felt it necessary to go to such elaborate lengths, taking inordinate chances that might potentially leave our plans vulnerable, in order to find this arms dealer."

Sidious said nothing.

"Unless there is something else that you had intended him for," Plagueis finished.

"As I said," Sidious began, "the assassination of Iram Radique was necessary in order to further our ultimate goals with the Grand Plan . . ." He paused, deliberately leaving the explanation unfinished long enough to observe whether Damask might be interested in hearing more of the cover story, which had been carefully fabricated to hold up to the most intense scrutiny, if necessary. At no point in the operation could the Muun be allowed to speculate that Sidious had truly sent Maul to Cog Hive Seven in order to purchase the nuclear device that the Bando Gora would ultimately use against Plagueis. Such a possibility, even now, was inconceivable.

But Plagueis had already waved aside the explanation, and then, as quickly as it had appeared, the casual tone was gone. Gazing back at the holoscreen where they had watched the contest, his mood darkened. "He is a prideful one, the Zabrak, is he not? As excellent as he is in combat, it must be incredibly difficult for him to show restraint in not using the Force."

"He has had experience in such restraint," Sidious reminded him, although he knew where the discussion was leading now, and saw little purpose in defending Maul at this point.

"I do not doubt it. It would be a great shame, however, if, instead of merely killing the arms dealer, Maul inadvertently revealed more about his identity . . . and the identity of those who sent him." Plagueis was staring at him directly now. "In fact, I would venture to say that such an unfortunate turn of events would prove to be extremely humbling for its original architects."

Humbling. The word plunged to the pit of Sidious's stomach and lay there like a rock. "I will take measures to personally ensure that such a thing never happens," he said stiffly.

Plagueis didn't say anything for a long time. When he spoke again, the voice in which he answered was low but firm.

"Contact the Zabrak," he said. "Inform him that he is to destroy Cog Hive Seven immediately, eradicating all evidence of our plans there." He paused. "If you wish, you may allow him to think that he will have the opportunity to escape."

Sidious drew in a breath and held it. The muscles of his diaphragm felt uncannily unsprung. Over the past few minutes, the tension that had gathered within the penthouse had left him feeling suffocated, as if the oxygen content within these walls had been slowly but steadily drained.

"Is there anything else, then?"

"Nothing pressing," Plagueis said. "I do enjoy our conversations, Darth Sidious. There is no one else with whom I know I can be completely and totally candid. Let us not wait so long until the next meeting."

"Certainly not." Sidious nodded and, making his good-byes, found his way out, hearing the hatch seal and lock itself behind him.

Humbling.

The word was still there, twisting in his guts like poison.

By the time he reached the turbolifts leading down through the tower to the main lobby, he was breathing normally again, and the shaking within his chest was almost completely gone.

44

SHOP

Smight crawled out of the conduit and fell on the floor.

He didn't remember how he'd gotten there, how long he'd been fumbling along in the dark, trying to find his way through a steadily narrowing capillary bed of ventilation shafts and pipelines that fed the prison its continuous ration of power and water and heat. His brain had long ago stopped recording outside stimuli. All his more sophisticated sensory and analytical skills had reduced themselves down to a nearly primordial state.

He'd seen too much.

It had started with the worm. Watching the enormous white thing in the tunnel eat the Bone Kings had been bad enough. If Smight lived to be a hundred, he knew he'd never forget the way that Strabo and Nailhead and the others had disappeared, sucked upward from the floor of the tunnel directly into the hideous, Y-shaped mouthparts as they wrapped themselves around the inmates. But it was the sound that would stay with him most—the suppurating, slurping noise that the thing had made, not quite loud enough to cover the high, keening peals of their screams. And the wet slap and clomping sounds of the jaws as they snapped shut.

It made him sick to think about it.

The thing had devoured them wholesale, leaving Smight—sprawled low on the floor of the shaft where he'd fallen—just enough time to scramble backward, while the white worm finished consuming its prey.

He was afraid that if he ran, it would sense him; if he made too much noise, it would hear.

And so he'd crawled.

Silently.

Agonizingly.

Slowly.

He'd crawled.

The rattling tattoo of his heart, the pounding in his skull, had made it impossible to say whether the thing was still pursuing him or whether it had stayed where it was to digest the feast, and at this point Smight had discovered that he didn't much care. If it got him, then it got him; if it didn't, he'd spend the rest of his life having nightmares that it had. Neither prospect was particularly tempting.

Now, having finally stumbled and fallen through an errant hatchway leading from the tunnel where he'd spent an unknown stretch of time, he lay motionless against the cold smoothness of some unfinished stretch of floor, his hands and knees aching from the long, endless trek.

For a long time he didn't dare to open his eyes, certain that when he did, the worm would be there waiting for him, coiled above him, its gasping sucker poised ready to strike. After a moment he became aware of bright lights shining through his eyelids and the acerbic stench of unfamiliar chemicals. Ultimately, curiosity got the best of him.

He opened his eyes.

What . . . ?

The spotless, brightly lit space that surrounded him was like no other area of the prison that he'd seen before. It was part warehouse, part laboratory. Long tables held scientific equipment whose names Smight didn't know—glass crucibles, slender tubes, and exotic-looking flasks, strangely elegant in shape and size, lined up alongside a miniature cityscape of mixing and spinning machines, instruments for heating and cooling.

Along the far wall, stacks of shipping crates, all different sizes, stood in neat rows with various destinations and manifests stenciled on their sides.

Not sure where he was going or why, Smight paced among the boxes and circled back to the lab equipment. None of it made any sense, nor did he expect it to. He'd long ago come to terms with his own limitations when it came to matters of science and intellect.

But beyond it, on the far side of the lab, he saw something more familiar. The entire second half of the room was a different kind of workstation, equipped with state-of-the-art grinding and boring tools, fabricating machines, metal shears, drills, and precision calibration devices.

Smight stared at them. He'd had an uncle who'd worked in the yards at BlasTech, and he knew these things.

They were weapon-making tools.

The realization of what he'd stumbled across dawned in his mind like the warmth of a new sun rising, and for a moment he couldn't quite believe the magnitude of what was happening.

It's here. This is it. I actually found it.

He stepped back, taking in the entire space around him—the lab, the packaged crates—in light of this new revelation.

Radique's operation. It's here.

When Jabba had dispatched him to help infiltrate Iram Radique's operation inside Cog Hive Seven, Smight had gone in with a certain degree of incredulity. Like everyone, he'd heard the stories of the enigmatic arms dealer operating under any number of aliases, and like most thinking people, he'd already decided there was a good deal of folklore mixed in with the truth. Why would any self-respecting gunrunner, especially one as successful as Radique, ever choose to hide out inside a prison, particularly one in which he'd have to fight other inmates as a condition of his stay?

Yet Smight had taken the job—of course he had. As an opportunity to work his way up in the Desilijic Clan, the assignment had been impossible to turn down. Falsified ID and background papers in hand, he had arrived onsite to confer with the other foot soldiers that Jabba already had working undercover as guards, gathering information from the inmates and reporting back whatever he found. The stim had helped to take the edge off, and the matches had made it interesting, but he'd never really expected—

This.

The crates. He needed to check them. Smight crossed hurriedly to the nearest steel box, popped open the steel fasteners, and leaned forward to peer inside, sucking in a breath of whistled appreciation at what he found there.

Like most of Jabba's hired hands, he prided himself in knowing about weapons. Consequently, although he might not have actually fired a J8Q-128 Finbat missile before, he recognized it immediately from its listing in Gundark's Gear Catalogue. The Finbat was a portable, shoulder-fired concussion warhead, precision-tooled to penetrate the armor plating of military-grade vehicles.

Reaching down, Smight lifted the launch tube from its packaging, hoisting it up to his shoulder, feeling the heft and power of the thing as he lowered his head toward the sight. His finger gripped the trigger. The weapon's silent promise of death spoke directly to the remnants of panic and fear still rattling around inside him from his encounter with the worm. One blast from the Finbat would annihilate anything in a five-hundred-meter radius, including the worm. For one completely irrational moment Smight almost considered bringing it back into the tunnel to go after the creature himself, although of course such an idea was madness—detonating a concussion missile inside a space station was suicide. But he would've loved to splatter that thing's guts all over the ventilation shaft.

He set the Finbat aside and went on to the next crate, exploring its contents, already wondering how he was going to tell Jabba about what he'd found, and how he could use it to maximize his position here. Just moments earlier he'd assumed he was a dead man—if, by some miracle, he managed to get out of here alive, Jabba would track him down and treat him like any other loose end, chopping him off.

But now—

He imagined the conversation, how he would tell his boss he'd discovered the very heart of what he'd been sent to find. How best to execute such a plan?

While thinking it over, Smight did a quick inventory of the crates. Among many other items, he found a proton missile launcher, a pulse cannon, an entire box of Mandalorian assault rifles, flechette launchers, and something that he was pretty sure was an LS-150 heavy accelerated charged particle repeater gun. There were several packages of explosives, including a crate of breaching grenades, anti-starfighter cluster bombs, and a carefully packaged selection of freshly manufactured thermal detonators. Upon further reflection, Smight realized that none of the weapons were technically up to factory spec—Radique had assembled them here, making subtle improvements in their precision and firing capability.

He reached the last crate and stopped.

Unlike the others, this one was locked. Although it was smaller than the others, it was also considerably heavier. There was no type of writing or information on it whatsoever. Even the most cursory inspection revealed that its shell was constructed of something far more formidable than durasteel.

Smight placed his hands against it.

The case was warm.

No, check that—the case was *hot*.

It also seemed to be humming.

Right away, even before he'd detected the vibrations inside it, Smight knew whatever was in the last crate was different, far more valuable and potentially dangerous than anything else down here—something special. Radique would never leave it here alone for very long, and he sensed that a man of Radique's intellect and experience wouldn't want to hold on to it any longer than he absolutely had to.

Which meant he would be back soon.

Good, a voice inside him whispered, and the idea rose into his mind unbidden.

That was how Augustine Smight, once just another lackey among thousands in Jabba's army, first realized that he was destined for greatness: by the ease with which he adapted to his situation and turned it to his advantage.

There wasn't much time. He went back around to the guns and artillery that he'd sorted through, handpicking the weapons that felt most comfortable in his grasp. In the end he settled for a DT-12 heavy blaster pistol like one that he'd first used when he'd learned to shoot, and—because he'd always wanted to try them—a pair of flechette gauntlets.

And so it was that he found himself strapping the holster to his belt and the gauntlets to his wrists, positioning himself against the last crate in the room, and engaging in the one activity that he'd never expected to do while he was here—smiling.

"I don't think those belong to you."

Startled, Smight stared at the figure standing in front of him. "What—" He swallowed and found his voice. "What are you doing here?"

He jerked the DT-12 upward, but it was already too late. A shattering blow struck him in the side of the head, just above his right ear, and he knew no more.

45

RED SABER DREAMS

Maul lay dreaming.

It wasn't common for him, and when he did dream, he was rarely aware of it at the time. His equivalent of REM sleep was not the sort that invited the typical neurological sorcery between conscious and unconscious thought. His warrior's brain had no use for it.

So the fact that he was dreaming now, heavily sedated and stretched out in medbay with tubes and wires running through his body as he recovered from his last fight, would have come as a surprise. The simplicity of the dream only underscored its verisimilitude, and for a short time he believed it was actually happening.

He was in another bout.

Standing in front of the hatchway in his cell, waiting for his opponent to show himself, he looked down and saw something sitting on the floor in front of him, an unremarkable black steel box no bigger than a mouse droid. Yet one glance told him that it held what he'd come here to find, the goal behind all his time spent slogging through the slime and filth of Cog Hive Seven.

He reached down for the box to open it, and a noise came from the other side of the wall—a grunt, the sound of something alive, preparing itself to come forth and do battle to the death. With that same irrefutable dream logic, Maul understood that this particular foe would be the most indomitable yet, far worse than the thing he'd fought upon first arriving, worse than the wampa or the Aqualish or the Weequay with his clawbird.

This would be the one that defeated him.

The hatch slid open and his enemy stepped out.

Maul stared at him.

And in the end, that part of the dream was not such a surprise after all.

"Open it," the other Maul said, staring past him, down at the black box. "It's yours. What are you waiting for?"

Maul stared back at himself, an identical reflection standing five meters away. Somehow, at least in the dream, the fact that he'd come here to fight himself made perfect sense—as if this moment, and not the arrangement with Iram Radique, had been the inevitable goal he'd been seeking the entire time he'd been here.

And all at once, Maul knew what was in the box.

"No," he said. "My Master forbids it."

"Your Master?" this other Maul snarled. The answer only seemed to enrage the doppelgänger. "Don't be a fool. It belongs to you. You'll need it if you're going to defeat me. Otherwise, you're as good as dead. *Take it!*"

"I can't. It will undermine the mission that I'm sworn to uphold." Maul's voice constricted. "I need to show restraint. I need to—"

"You're lost without it!"

Dream or no dream, Maul felt anger boiling up in his chest, taking hold of his lungs and the nerves in his spine. His jaw clenched.

"Perhaps," he told his other self, "before you make such statements, you'd better try me first."

"Really." The doppelgänger laughed. "It's too late for that. You've already been weighed and measured, and found wanting." He nodded back down at the floor. "See for yourself."

With a sudden sense of foreboding, Maul looked back at the box.

It was open.

It was empty.

Because the item that it contained was already in his hand.

His saber staff.

Staring at it, Maul felt a crushing wave of shame come thundering over him—the realization that, in opening the box and taking up the weapon of the Sith, he'd failed his Master. He had done the one thing he'd sworn not to do, and as such—

The other Maul lunged for him. On reflex, without a moment's hesitation, Maul flicked the activation stud on the saber. It sprang to life in his grasp, its two red blades shooting out on either side, and in spite of everything, Maul felt a surge of power explode through his being, swallowing him up and enveloping his very soul.

The certainty was upon him, the realization of his own true strength. This was what he was made for.

He swung the saber staff around in a graceful whirring arc, and in a single, sweeping motion he bisected the other Maul cleanly at the waist, the upper and lower halves coming apart bloodlessly, landing in pieces on the floor of the cell. Looking down at his own face, Maul saw his own dying face smiling back up at himself.

"Good," his voice said, and in an instant he realized his error.

He was the one on the floor, the fallen one.

Looking up at himself, the other, the victor.

But it wasn't his own face staring down at him anymore. It was a Muun, one he didn't immediately recognize, though an uncanny familiarity encompassed his presence, the nagging sense that he should have known him, had perhaps encountered him elsewhere, in a dream within a dream. An unfamiliar name came over him like a death rattle.

Plagueis.

Darkness closed in, and when he awoke in the medbay, bathed in sweat, his fingers were gripping the cot, curled around the emptiness of the cylindrical shape that was not there.

46

HANGAR

"Slipher, huh? How long you been with the IBC?"

Vesto Slipher glanced at the prison guard standing in front of him, stationed just outside Cog Hive Seven's main hangar bay. He didn't particularly want to get into a lengthy conversation with the man, whose ID badge read *Dawson,* but at the moment he seemed to have little choice. The guard was bored, starved for conversation. He was balding, with a wispy gray mustache that stood in marked contrast to overgrown eyebrows whose wiry, rebellious hairs seemed to enjoy a prehensile life all their own.

"I've been with the Banking Clan for a substantial period of time," Slipher said, choosing for the moment to indulge the guard. "Since the bank has held the loan on your operation here. Hence my inspection of the *entire* facility." And then, nodding at the hatchway that led to the loading bay: "Now, if you don't mind?"

"Hang on," Dawson said, swiping his badge and tapping in an access code. The hatch slid open. "You want to watch your step in there. Landing crew's prepping for a bunch of new meat showing up in the next hour or so, so you're probably gonna have to make it fast."

"Not a problem."

"Just give a holler when you're ready to come out," Dawson said, and as Slipher stepped past him, he took hold of the Muun's shoulder. "Oh, and hey."

Slipher stopped, a bit taken aback. "Yes?"

"You catch that last fight?" A broad grin spread over the guard's face. "Jagannath taking on that Weequay and his clawbird?"

"I missed it, sadly."

"Sadly is right," Dawson said. "Best match I've seen in a while. Won three hundred credits on that red-skinned rimmer." He beamed. "I tell you, this might not be the safest job in the world, but you get some nice perks along the way."

A thought occurred to Slipher. "You're a gambling man yourself, are you, Mr. Dawson?"

"Me?" The guard sniggered. "You kidding? Does a sarlacc live in a pit?"

"Perhaps a sporting man such as yourself could use a little extra money from time to time. I could make it worth your while."

Dawson regarded him suspiciously. "What are we talking about here?"

"Nothing that would get you into any trouble, of course. Simply keeping certain information to yourself and performing an errand for me later, if you have time."

"What kind of errand?"

"I'll let you know when the time is right," Slipher said, waving the question away. "How often do you receive supplies here? Weekly?"

"Usually, yeah. They offload them with the new inmates."

"And the binary load-lifter droids that do the work, they're all networked with the prison's main datacenter?"

"Well, yeah." Dawson pushed one hand up beneath his cap to scratch his head. "I mean, we've got a couple of refurbished CLL-8s that the docking crew needs to access directly, but everything else gets run by remote from upstairs." He squinted at Slipher. "Why?"

"Just trying to get a better gasp on how things run day to day," Slipher said, and stepped through the hatch. "Thank you, Officer. You've been very helpful. I'll be in touch."

"Yeah, uh-huh."

The cargo bay yawned out before him, a cavern made of steel.

Moving through it, Slipher sidestepped the chief gantry officer and various members of the ground crew scurrying around to prepare for the incoming arrival, his breath emanating visibly from his mouth in a foggy cloud. The air in here had become significantly colder, with a pervasive chill that seemed to rise up from the steel floors. Buttoning his tunic around his neck, Slipher kept moving. Workers on either side glanced up in his direction, but none of them questioned his presence. He supposed that word had already spread among them that an IBC consultant was making an onsite audit, and such interference was nearly always met with a combination of indifference and anxiety.

It took him almost five minutes to walk across the bay. The big binary load-lifters that Dawson had mentioned stood idly on the far side, two of them lined up against the far wall, three meters high, awaiting instructions. Neither of them looked like newer models, although Slipher himself had only limited experience with such units.

He stopped in front of the less battered-looking droid, gazing up at its single photoreceptor.

"Are you equipped with a standard analytic drive?"

The load-lifter made a grunting noise in assent.

"I'm expecting a special package with today's shipment," Slipher said. "It will be addressed to me directly—Vesto Slipher. Its contents are highly confidential and shall not be subject to any of the routine screening and security processes. I will require immediate notification when it arrives. Do you understand?"

Another digitized grunt from the load-lifter.

"You will keep this information to yourself and not report it to your dock supervisor," Vesto said. "This command is authorized by IBC yellow card security variant 377055. Is that understood?"

The droid straightened up immediately. Something clicked inside its circuitry and its photoreceptor brightened noticeably. The automated voice from the thing's articulator drive sounded rusty but coherent.

"Affirmative."

"Good," Slipher said. "I'll expect to hear from you soon."

47

AIRBORNE

Maul awoke to a prevailing sense of doom.

Rising on the slow dark tide of consciousness, he felt remembrance of what he'd done settling over him like another form of gravity, heavier and more oppressive than the prison itself. For a moment he just lay there staring up at the medbay's ceiling, its austere rectangles outlined by the recessed lighting of sleeping diagnostic equipment.

Why was he still alive?

The meaning of the dream was clear enough. He'd failed his Master, failed his mission. Ultimately he'd been betrayed, not by some foreign enemy, but by his own survival instincts. But what else could he have done? Dying here would have accomplished nothing.

Still, he could not shake the feeling that this had been a test and he had failed.

There was nothing left for him now.

Thoughts began to organize themselves in his brain. He would need to get back to the transmitter in the morgue and contact his Master, to explain his position—if Sidious would even speak to him. In all likelihood the chain reaction of plausible deniability had already been initiated. His Master could very well have decided to leave him here to rot, or—

All at once, Maul heard a noise above his head, a brisk whirring sound that he guessed was the surgical droid. The thing would be here to change out his IV tubing, to check the readings of the instruments wired to his skull and chest.

Looking over, he saw something completely different: a clawbird perched on the end of the table, staring at him.

Maul scowled at it. *I killed you, bird. Ripped you to pieces. Left you broken on the cell floor next to your master. What are you still doing here?*

While he was looking at the thing, trying to work out the details of its miraculous resurrection, a second bird swept down and landed next to it, and then a third.

Sitting up, Maul looked around.

The room was filled with birds.

With a faint croak, the first bird hopped from the end of the table to Maul's leg, and then up to his shoulder, where it settled itself. He turned his head to gaze at it. At the knotted *khipus* wound around its legs.

Of course.

Their former master would have needed more than one bird to pick up the different weapons parts and drop off the payment. And now that Maul had killed him—

He was their new master.

Yanking the monitor wires and tubing away from his body, Maul tossed it all to the floor and swung his legs around. Standing up, he discovered new strength that he hadn't known was there.

All around him, clawbirds seemed to sense this renewed purpose. They'd already begun to flap their wings, rising into the air, preparing to take flight.

Maul nodded.

"Let's go."

Following the birds was easier this time.

They flew just ahead of him in a black and rustling cloud, leading him through the main concourse, where the other inmates drew back in obeisance, stepping away, some of them even lowering their heads as if recognizing some newly coronated ruler.

Maul pursued them downward through a labyrinth of passageways.

When the path became narrow, the flock flattened itself out, and when it opened again, they spread again to fill the available space. They went on like that for what felt like a very long time, deeper down than he'd imagined the prison ever went, although it was difficult to gauge distances and depths in a world that was constantly changing.

A stillness came over the world, a sense that he was venturing where few had gone.

At last Maul stood before a closed door.

The hatchway opened.

"Jagannath," a voice said from inside. "Welcome to the inner circle."

48

WATCH THE THRONE

The customized Ubrikkian space yacht dropped out of hyperspace, flanked by a complement of six Z-95 Headhunters, all of them materializing at once into the void immediately outside the short-range detection systems of Cog Hive Seven.

For a moment, nothing seemed to move. The *Minstrel*-class yacht, christened *Star Jewel*, appeared to hang suspended almost lazily in space, as if evaluating its options. Opulent to the point of obscenity, the *Jewel* was as lethal as it was extravagant. Its optimized CL-14 hyperdrive motivator had made the journey from Hutt space through the Triellus trade route almost too swiftly for the purposes of its owner, who had expressed emphatic interest along the way in building an even greater appetite in the kell dragons he'd kept chained in his throne room. When they'd left Nal Hutta, the dragons were already hungry. By the time the hyperdrives settled into silence, the creatures were literally drooling on the throne room floor.

Now, seated before the great transparisteel dome in all his vast, draconian majesty, Jabba Desilijic Tiure turned from his beloved dragons to gaze outward into the vast expanse of nothingness, none of which belonged to him, although he felt right at home here. It hadn't been too terribly long ago—really just a few short centuries—since he'd relocated his base of operations to the B'omarr Monastery on Tatooine, and he was still young enough that such unexpected jaunts across the galaxy appealed to the daring side of his nature.

Everything had gone as expected. There was no sign of the target that had brought them here, not yet, although there was no rush. The *Jewel*'s crew, the usual entourage of slave girls, carnivorous pets, and cutthroat enforcers (Trandoshans, Gran, and Gamorreans), made the final preparations for their own dark business here—an opportunity that Jabba, having come so far, had no intention of letting slip away.

"Ramp down the turbolasers." He activated the comlink to the *Jewel*'s bridge, where his pilot and second-in-command, Scuppa, had sequestered himself for the duration of the trip. "Power all systems down to silence. I want no detectable heat signature from the ion engines until my signal."

The order had the expected results: seconds later, Scuppa himself appeared in the throne room, expressing himself with characteristic bluntness. "I don't like this."

"Scuppa, my boy, come closer and join the party." Beckoning the pilot toward himself and the rabble surrounding him, Jabba grinned. "Surely you don't think you're better than us?"

"I never said—"

"Good. Squeamishness is for the weak." Jabba waved him over, taking perverse delight in the pilot's reluctance. It wasn't that Scuppa had any qualms about mingling with the exotic concubines, hired muscle, or low-level hangers-on that were currently amusing themselves taunting the kell dragons; he simply wasn't comfortable being away from the ship's navigational system when they were this far off the trade route. After all, one never knew what trouble one might run into in the Outer Rim. "We won't have to wait long now."

"It's a mistake to power down the turbolasers," Scuppa said. "If the prison barge gets the drop on us . . ."

"They won't." Jabba reached down for the bowl beneath his hookah and drew out a Klatooine paddy frog, dropping the unfortunate creature live and squirming into his mouth. "I've already dispatched the *Star Jewel*'s guard to locate them before they find us."

"Another bad idea." Scuppa's lower lip reshaped itself into an even more displeased moue. "With the Headhunters gone, we're already more exposed than ever."

"Relax, Scuppa. It's almost time. Sit down, enjoy the show."

He gestured to the open area directly below his throne. The pilot remained standing in the open hatchway while two of Jabba's bodyguards—a psychopathic Gamorrean war criminal and a dwarf Oskan blood eater—thrashed in mortal combat across the floor in front of where Jabba himself was seated, just outside the reach of the kell dragons. Within a few seconds, the blood eater had slashed open the Gamorrean's face and latched on to him to feed. Already Jabba felt himself growing bored, restless in the way that all too often characterized the final moments before he allowed himself the full gratification of settling the business at hand.

Today that business was revenge.

Over the past three years, the credits that he'd lost to Iram Radique's arms sales had metastasized from a minor annoyance to an intolerable insult. Even so, Jabba had been prepared to absorb a certain degree of indignity, at least temporarily—in his almost six hundred years of experience as a crime lord, he'd discovered that men like Radique rarely lasted long enough to bother with. Even when they took ingenious measures to protect themselves, like disappearing into the woodwork of Cog Hive Seven, as Radique had, it was simply a matter of time before they backed the wrong army, allied themselves with the wrong crime syndicate, sold guns to the wrong separatists. After a meteoric rise in reputation, they invariably disappeared without a trace, never to be spoken of again. Jabba, in his great leniency and mercy, had decided that he would stand by and allow Radique to fall victim to his own success. For the time being, he would continue to send his men into the prison as guards to discover the arms dealer's identity, but nothing more.

But things had changed on Cog Hive Seven.

As of yesterday, they had changed very quickly indeed.

Of course, Jabba hadn't been personally attached to any of the lackeys he'd sent into the prison undercover—but to stand by and allow his own people to be slaughtered, ripped apart, and devoured by the inmates of the prison, while the prison's female warden stood by grinning like a monkey lizard, was an affront to the very pillars of his authority.

Watching his foot soldiers being destroyed, Jabba had made up his mind that if he couldn't put Iram Radique out of business, then he would simply destroy Cog Hive Seven completely. Ultimately it would prove both simpler and far more gratifying. And he'd realized immediately how to do it.

An alarm sounded on the control panel beside his throne, the signal of an incoming transmission from the pilot of one of the Headhunters.

"Transport ship in sight," the pilot reported back. "We're closing in on her now."

Jabba saw Scuppa straighten up in anticipation, while down below the throne, the blood eater finished its meal to the scattered applause of the others. The Gamorreans and Trandoshans were as eager as he was to get on with their true business at hand.

"Get to the armory," Jabba told them. "Suit up." He turned to Scuppa. "You should be relieved, my friend. I'm going to let you reactivate your turbolasers."

Within minutes, the prison transport barge *Purge* had drifted into attack range, although Jabba had ordered Scuppa to ignore any request from the *Purge*'s captain to identify himself. Failure to respond to the prison barge's hailing frequency had resulted in the anticipated result—the barge had brought its own weapons systems online, under the assumption that the *Star Jewel* was a pirate vessel, or worse.

"I'm speaking to the captain of the unidentified space yacht." The voice of the *Purge*'s captain through the intercom sounded strained with impatience. "You are in a designated approach corridor for prison transport to Cog Hive Seven. Identify yourself at once or you will be fired on."

Scuppa's voice, equally anxious, crackled through the *Jewel*'s commlink. "Jabba, how much longer—"

"Easy, friend." Jabba waited, a smile writhing over his lips, saturating his entire face with the pleasure of impending attack. Silently counting off the seconds, he peered out the dome, yellow eyes gleaming with excitement as he gazed out on the *Purge*. Down below, the Trandoshans and Gamorreans had gone to the armory to suit up and prepare the weapons.

The throne room was almost empty.

Except for the dragons.

49

CABAL

Maul's first impression of the weapons shop was that it was more of a surgeon's operating room than a workspace—a long, brightly illuminated theater of apparent sterility whose every surface seemed polished and clean. At the moment, however, he was more preoccupied with the identity of the one who'd beckoned him inside.

"Come in," the Muun said, still standing inside the open hatchway. "I just got here myself." He smiled thinly. "We've both certainly earned a look around, to say the least."

Maul regarded him coldly. Whatever else he might have been, the individual standing in front of him clearly wasn't a prisoner of the Hive. His uniform was IBC standard fiduciary garb, the green tunic and trousers exactly what one would expect of a galactic financial executive. The Banking Clan's presence here in an illegal weapons operation in the middle of a prison raised more questions than it answered.

"I'm Vesto Slipher," the Muun said, and then, as if reading Maul's thoughts, he added: "Believe it or not, my purposes here aren't entirely at odds with yours—not as much as you might think. But please, step inside."

Maul entered the chamber and looked around, his mind quickly absorbing and processing a dozen different details simultaneously.

The shop was swarming with activity. Inmates he'd never seen before, human and nonhuman alike, stood in rows before the assembly tables, sorting components from different crates, passing them back and forth among themselves, putting them together by sense of touch. Maul stood observing them for a long moment, trying to process what it was that bothered him about them. They functioned in nearly total silence, but there was something peculiar about them that he couldn't quite put his finger on—until one of them raised his face in Maul's direction.

And then he saw.

They had no eyes.

Their empty eye sockets were caves of blindness, raw and dark and hollow. After a moment, the inmate who'd been facing Maul turned back down to the partially assembled weapon in front of him and returned to his work.

"Radique removes the eyes," Slipher said conversationally. "Apparently it's a prerequisite to working down here. Another safeguard, I suppose—a means of preserving absolute secrecy."

Maul said nothing. He was remembering his very first day in the mess hall, the blind inmates that he'd noticed sitting off by themselves, groping with their food and utensils. That was how they lived. Now, except for the soft click and snap of assembled parts, the only sound was the faint rustle of the clawbirds, who had settled into the far corner of the room, into a kind of makeshift nesting area.

What are they still doing here if Radique is dead? Don't they know?

A flicker of motion caught his attention from the far end of the shop. There was someone in the corner, his wrists and ankles bound—a guard that Maul recognized. The one called Smight. He'd been gagged, but his eyes were huge, gleaming with a mixture of anger, fear, and confusion.

"Ah, yes," Slipher said, noticing that Maul was looking at the guard. "Apparently we're not the only ones who found ourselves down here. I'm quite sure Mr. Radique would not like the idea of an intruder ransacking his arsenal, would you? Particularly someone as unsavory as Mr. Smight here."

"Radique is dead," Maul said. "I killed him."

"Dead?" Slipher glanced at him for a moment, then laughed. "That's funny," he said. "You know, for a moment I almost believed you."

"It's true."

"Oh no, Iram Radique is very much alive, I assure you. The Weequay that you killed in that last bout was a proxy. Radique has a dozen of them in circulation at any time to ensure his own safety."

"How do you know?" Maul asked.

Instead of answering, the Muun turned to look at the rows of blind inmates as they painstakingly assembled the components on the tables in front of them. "Do you know what they're building?"

"Weapons."

"Not just weapons," Slipher said. "Lightsabers."

Maul felt something go tight in his chest. *What?*

"Synthetic lightsabers—Radique's newest innovation. A radical departure from anything that's been accomplished up to this point. Apparently it works on a synth-crystal—" The Muun walked over to the end of a long counter and picked up a sleek red gem, holding it up admiringly to catch the light. "They're baked in a geological compressor. Can you imagine the power inside just one of these?"

"Ah." A voice spoke from behind him: "But power is in the eye of the beholder, is it not?"

Maul knew who it was even before he turned around and looked down. Coyle was standing there, peering up at him. "What are you doing here?"

"I called him down," Zero said as he stepped through the hatchway and sealed it shut behind him. "After I sent a message summoning Mr. Slipher. I felt like it was time we all met face-to-face."

Maul stared at him. "The poison—" he began, and then he remembered the one who had first told him about it. Coyle smiled and gave him a slight, apologetic shrug as if to say, *What is life but a riddle that none of us can answer?*

"You really think you could've slipped anything remotely dangerous into my food without my being alerted about it first?" Zero asked. "Jagannath, you continue to surprise me."

Maul looked at their faces, from Zero to Coyle to Slipher, and then back to Zero again.

"You've found your way to Radique's inner circle," Zero told him. "The backbone cabal, if you like. The clawbirds recognized it when they brought you here . . ."

Zero reached down into the crate behind him, drawing a blaster rifle from inside it and pointing it at Maul's chest.

"Unfortunately, this is where it ends for you. You've seen too much. Mr. Radique would never allow you to leave."

Maul looked back at the rows of eyeless inmates, hunched before the workstations, silently assembling the weapons. A possibility had taken shape in his mind without his realizing it, but he saw it now, clearly.

"They're not functioning properly, are they?" he asked.

Zero hesitated. "What?"

"Radique's synthetic lightsabers. The crystals aren't working like he thought they would."

"How did you—" Slipher began, but Zero silenced him with a look.

"We're having no such problems." Tucking the blaster rifle under his arm, Zero walked over to the workspace, reached into the packing crate, and pulled out a long cylindrical shaft, holding it up for inspection.

"Then you won't mind a demonstration," Maul said. "Go ahead." He took a step forward, tipping back his head to expose his throat. "Use it on me."

For a long moment Zero didn't move or speak. Then, with the lightsaber still in one hand and the blaster in the other, the Twi'lek turned to look across the workspace to where the guard, Smight, was still glaring at them with a gag in his mouth, his hands and ankles bound.

"Bring him over here," he said.

Coyle walked over to Smight and, with strength that belied his size, he picked up the guard and slung him over his shoulder like a sack of laundry, carrying him over to Zero.

"Cut him loose," Zero said, and when the Chadra-Fan hesitated: "Go ahead. He's not going anywhere."

Shrugging, Coyle plucked a sharpened question-mark-shaped object from his back pocket—some claw or tooth from some lesser species, no doubt scavenged for one of his sculptures—and hooked it through the plastic restraints on the guard's wrists, snapping them free. Zero turned to Smight.

"Take this," Zero said, handing the lightsaber to the guard and nodding at Maul, "and kill the Zabrak."

Smight stared at the lightsaber. The gag was still over his mouth, but Maul could see all kinds of things going on in the guard's face: anger, humiliation, uncertainty, and ultimately a kind of murderous resolve.

He flicked the switch.

A narrow red beam shot out from the lightsaber's hilt. The beam was thinner than any that Maul had seen before, and instead of humming, it crackled and hissed unsteadily from base to tip. Weird oscillating skeins of plasma writhed up and down the length of the beam like hundreds of semitransparent serpents. On the whole it looked even more unstable than the man holding it.

"Go ahead," Zero said.

A terrible kind of righteousness came over Smight's face, as if—in grasping this weapon, even in its most bastardized state—he'd arrived at a moment of supreme, almost sacred self-actualization. He lifted it up over his head, preparing to bring it down on Maul's exposed throat.

He was still swinging it down when the blade arced sideways, looping back on itself. Maul saw it slash around like the tail of a scorpion, something alive and venomous, hooking through Smight's face and carving it cleanly in half, then jerking sideways. The guard didn't have time to scream. His right arm hit the floor, the red blade still flicking and leaping erratically from his limp fingers, chopping what remained of Smight's body to pieces before it finally crackled and died out in a spreading lake of dark arterial blood.

They all took a step back from what remained of the corpse. Coyle mumbled something under his breath. Zero was staring at the malfunctioning lightsaber, his face unreadable. Slipher looked as if he was going to be sick.

"Well." Maul nodded at the synthetic lightsaber. "Mr. Radique won't be pleased with that."

With a grunt, Zero brandished the blaster rifle he'd picked up earlier. "Forget that. We don't need it to kill you."

"I could help you with your problem," Maul said.

Slipher was watching him very closely now, alternating glances between him and Zero. "How?"

"When I was a mercenary, I assassinated a Jedi once," Maul said. "It gave me the opportunity to study his lightsaber closely, to disassemble it. I was able to reverse-engineer the components themselves, to study its design. I could fix what's wrong with these."

"You're lying," Zero said. His finger tightened on the blaster's trigger. "You'll say whatever you have to in order to save your skin, and now you're—"

"Stop."

The voice on the intercom was not one that Maul had heard before. It rang out through the shop, clear and deep and resonant, filling all available space. At the sound of it, every one of the blind inmates at the long counters stopped what they were doing and turned their faces upward, as if they could somehow see who was addressing them.

Zero too was looking up at the recessed speakers in the ceiling of the room, though he still kept the blaster trained on Maul. "Mr. Radique . . ."

"Let the Zabrak speak."

Maul bent down and picked up the blood-soaked lightsaber from the disfigured corpse that had once been CO Smight. Working quickly, without speaking a word, he snapped open the latch on the hilt and tipped it forward, allowing the various microcomponents to slide out into his hand. It took less than ten seconds for him to sort through them, plucking out the synth-crystal and holding it up for inspection.

"This is worthless." Maul dropped the crystal to the floor and crushed it under his heel. "Your process is flawed. It's too unstable. It's possible that your geological compressor isn't generating sufficient heat and pressure to fully fabricate the proper crystalline structure. All these lightsabers are going to do is kill their users." He lifted his head upward in the direction of the voice. "I can make them function properly."

There was silence in the room. It seemed to go on for a very long time.

"But I need something from you in return," Maul said. "You know what it is."

The silence came again, longer this time. Unbearable.

Maul waited.

An eternity.

And another.

"Kill him," the voice said.

And Zero pulled the trigger.

50

BEHIND THE MASK

The Twi'lek's finger was still tightening on the blaster's trigger when Maul threw the disassembled lightsaber at him.

The pieces struck Zero flush in the face, more of a distraction than anything else, but it bought Maul enough time to lunge at him, knocking the Twi'lek to the floor. The blast he was firing went wild, caroming off the ceiling and ricocheting to the floor.

Maul took hold of Zero's throat, already knowing that killing him was pointless, that there was no way out of here even if he slaughtered all of them, that—in finding what he'd been sent to find—he'd only signed his own death warrant. It was too late now. Even Zero seemed to realize that. On the floor beneath Maul, he was shaking his head, laughing at him bitterly.

"You idiot," the Twi'lek said, spitting blood. "You think this is going to solve anything?"

Maul didn't answer. He drove his fist into Zero's chin, and to his great surprise, he felt the inmate's entire face shiver and go sideways, his flesh appearing to split open and then peel back with a gelatinous suddenness so unexpected that Maul stopped his attack and stared down at him.

The Twi'lek mask was dangling halfway off the newly exposed face of the man underneath him. Maul stared at him, stunned. He knew this face, or one very like it. It was the warden of Cog Hive Seven, Sadiki Blirr—but in a masculine form.

He says that you answer to another name.

"Dakarai?" Vesto Slipher said. The Muun sounded even more shocked than Maul felt. "What . . . ?"

Dakarai Blirr rose to his feet and tore the rest of the mask away from his face, flinging it away, where it landed on the floor in a misshapen heap. He looked completely indifferent to Slipher, and to Maul, for that matter—his full attention was focused on the ceiling.

"I can explain," Dakarai said quickly, and Maul realized two things simultaneously. First, Dakarai was talking to the voice that had given him the instruction to kill—the voice of Iram Radique.

And second, Dakarai was very scared, for reasons Maul could not determine.

"I needed the disguise to move among the inmates," the man said, "in order to program the algorithm. It allowed me to serve you as well as my sister. Neither of you needed to know . . . neither of you *could* know. It was really the perfect solution. I could meet with you as Zero, and—"

"Finish him, Coyle," the voice said.

"Wait!" Dakarai said. "You don't have to do this! You can just—"

The Chadra-Fan acted without hesitation. Picking up the blaster rifle that Dakarai had been holding just seconds earlier, Coyle pointed it at him and fired, discharging a single shot. The point-blank impact flung Dakarai's body backward across the shop, and he landed in a lifeless heap beneath one of the assembly tables.

"Mr. Slipher," the voice on the intercom said, as if nothing had happened. "You may proceed as planned." There was a pause. "Take the Zabrak with you."

Vesto Slipher managed a queasy nod. "Yes, Mr. Radique." Without bothering to look back at Maul, he started out the door.

Maul followed.

51
TO THE HOLD

The trip took only a few minutes, although to Maul's mind it seemed to go on much longer. He stood beside Vesto Slipher in the turbolift, both of them staring straight ahead, neither one speaking. Too many things had happened too close together, and Maul needed time to process them all.

The revelation of Zero's actual identity had clearly been a surprise to everyone—including Radique himself. Yet in a way it made perfect sense. As Inmate Zero, Dakarai had been able to help the arms dealer coordinate the arriving weapons shipments while monitoring the inmate populace and programming Cog Hive Seven's matching algorithm. Keeping secrets from Radique and his sister must have felt like the perfect double life. His mistake had been thinking he could mislead everyone indefinitely.

And Radique himself . . .

Maul couldn't stop thinking about that voice, its unfathomable strength and power. His thoughts flashed back to the way that, when it spoke, every one of the blind prisoners—rows of convicts who'd willingly given their eyes to serve him here—had turned their faces upward toward it, as if toward deliverance itself.

It made him wonder if this man really was a man at all, or something else altogether.

* * *

The turbolift continued its steady ascent.

"What's in the cargo bay?" Maul asked finally.

Slipher kept his eyes straight ahead. "Mr. Radique is having a new geological compressor delivered with today's shipment." His voice still sounded unsteady. "I've arranged to have it received via binary lifter and held for me there."

"So he knew there was something wrong with his lightsabers?"

"I'm assuming he did. He seems to know everything else. Well . . ." The Muun considered. "Almost everything."

"How long have you worked for Radique?"

"*Worked* for him?" Slipher gave a dry chuckle. It came out eerie and humorless, like the nervous tic of a condemned man. "Technically I still don't. I came to Cog Hive Seven as an employee of the IBC, and I'm here representing other interests as well." He tugged at his collar and swallowed audibly. "You might say that I was unexpectedly recruited by Mr. Radique during my tenure here. My understanding is that's how it works."

"How what works?"

"His whole empire. One often finds oneself serving his purposes without realizing it."

Maul grunted. The interior lights of the turbolift flickered off for a span of several seconds, and the faint illumination of the object in Slipher's hand—the thing he'd called the blue witch—emanated up over their faces in an eerie blue glow.

Maul peered at it incuriously. According to the banker, the device masked them from all electronic surveillance inside Cog Hive Seven. They'd been using it in Radique's weapons shop, though for how long he didn't know. Certainly such a device would come in handy in a place where all the walls had surveillance cameras mounted within them.

"We both find ourselves in the same regrettable situation," the Muun said. "We are dutiful servants dispatched into this floating landfill, forbidden to leave until we provide our masters with the information they seek." He gave a melancholy sigh. "I might as well be wearing an inmate number myself."

"You know nothing of my mission."

Slipher gave him a glance, cocking an eyebrow. "I know you're here on behalf of the Bando Gora," he said, "in an effort to procure some unthinkably destructive weapon and put it in their hands." He cast Maul a sidelong glance. "Does that summarize it properly?"

Maul said nothing. For a moment he entertained the notion of simply killing this self-pitying plutocrat right here in the lift, snatching the blue witch, and finding the load-lifter droid himself. What could Slipher's presence here possibly bring to their arrangement now, except the ever-present possibility of betrayal?

"Money stands at the nexus of all things," the Muun said. "Those who moderate its ebb and flow inevitably find themselves at the confluence of the galaxy's deepest secrets. Even the most confidential information arrives almost as an afterthought."

"Do you ever stop talking?"

Slipher sniffed, seeming only moderately offended. "I was merely explaining how I ended up in this position."

Maul kept his arms at his sides, but his fists were already clenched. Visions of leaving Slipher here in the turbolift with a broken neck were growing steadily more vivid in his mind.

"Your position here is hopeless, you know," Slipher told him. "Even if you were successful in bringing them here, Radique will never do business with the Bando Gora."

"We'll see," Maul said.

"And of course you know that Komari Vosa is in charge of the Gora now." He tilted his chin slightly, raising the witch in his hand. "You are familiar with Vosa's background, are you not?"

"More underworld scum. The galaxy's thick with it."

"Not quite. Vosa is the high priestess of the cult. I'm told that she maintains a fortified citadel on Kohlma and uses narcotics and advanced mind control to manipulate an entire army of operatives and assassins to do her bidding." And then, almost as an afterthought: "And of course she's still extremely lethal with a lightsaber."

Maul shot the Muun a look of thinly veiled shock. "What?"

"Oh yes, she's a former Jedi," Slipher said casually. "Surely, given your background, I'm not telling you anything that you don't already know."

At first Maul said nothing. At his sides, his hands had already balled into fists, squeezing tightly until they began to tremble. "What else do you know of her?"

"Who, Vosa?" The Muun feigned innocence. "Oh, very little, I'm afraid. Her nearly psychopathic levels of aggression apparently prevented her from becoming a true Jedi Knight. Nonetheless, she joined a Jedi task force to stop the Bando Gora's activities on Baltizaar." His expression darkened. "Unfortunately, the mission proved a catastrophe. The cult abducted Vosa and dragged her off to the burial moon of Kohlma. What happened next . . ." The Muun shuddered theatrically. "Well, by all accounts, they tortured her to the very brink of madness—the point where she embraced the dark side of the Force, slaughtered those who had kidnapped her, and became the true leader of the Bando Gora." Slipher glanced back at Maul. "She started out as a Jedi, however. Is that significant?"

Maul said nothing.

At last the lift came to a halt.

If they're waiting to take us, Maul thought, *this is where it will happen.*

But as the doors slid open on Cog Hive Seven's hangar bay, there were no guards waiting there to take him into custody, no armed corrections officers lying in ambush. The only activity in the bay came from a small detail of tactical landing technicians who were too busy wrestling with a pile of pallets and skids on the opposite side to take much notice of them.

"Relax," Slipher said. "The landing techs aren't armed. And they don't carry dropboxes, so they can't trigger the charges in your heart."

"I wasn't concerned." Maul stepped out into the bay. The space was huge, erratically strewn with packing debris and empty shipping crates waiting to be returned on the next flight out. Across the open space, he saw the binary load-lifter that Slipher had spoken of, although the immediate mission seemed far from his thoughts.

She's a former Jedi.

Had it not occurred to his Master to tell him of this? Or had its withholding been part of the larger challenge that he'd come here to face?

The realization that his mission on Cog Hive Seven would culminate in confrontation with a Jedi, albeit one whose powers had been corrupted into a life of organized crime and cult-based lunacy, plunged a dagger of bitterness deep into Maul's brain. It would not be Vesto Slipher that Komari Vosa would be facing when she and the Bando Gora arrived here, Maul decided. Certainly his own Master intended for Maul himself to dispatch the Jedi scum personally.

Was *that* the true test?

Still seething, he slipped quickly across the hangar bay, moving through the shadows, leaving the Muun behind.

"What are you doing?" Slipher hissed as he hurried to keep pace. "You need to stay with me."

"It's been too long since I've killed something," Maul said. "Be careful, or it might be you."

"Don't be a fool. Our mission here requires both stealth and my active participation, and you know it."

Maul silenced him with a glare—but not just a glare. For the slightest of moments, he allowed himself to reach out with the Force. The Muun faltered in his steps, mouth opening just wide enough to emit a glottal clicking cough, taken aback by the invisible vise grip of pressure taking hold around his neck and chest, choking as he labored to draw breath.

Maul found the sharp expression of shock and fear on the banker's face only mildly gratifying, given these extenuating circumstances. He kept Slipher there for a split second, prolonging the sight of the Muun's eyes bulging in their sockets. Then, leaning forward, he spoke in a whisper.

"Komari Vosa," he said quietly, "is not the only one with the skills you mentioned. You would do well to remember that."

"Wh-what?" Slipher's face tightened in an ecstasy of disbelief. *"You . . . ?"*

Maul squeezed harder. Perhaps it was the explicit mention of the Jedi, or simply his own inability to hold back any longer, but suddenly all he wanted was to snap the neck of this insect and finish what he'd started. Only then did he realize the sheer magnitude of his transgression—a betrayal of his purpose here, the one thing that he'd sworn not to do.

Releasing Slipher, pushing him away, he pivoted and approached the larger of the binary load-lifters, stepping around behind the droid to avoid being seen by the hangar's crew members, then cast a glance back at the Muun. "Is this the one?"

"Y-yes." Slipher reached up and touched his throat, still badly shaken. He kept his distance, eyeing Maul as one might regard a vicious animal whose true nature had suddenly become abundantly evident. "I have to give my authorization first."

"Then do it. We've wasted enough time."

Slipher turned to face the droid's photoreceptors, looking deeply grateful to have something else upon which to focus his attention. "IBC yellow card security variant 377055," he said. "Voice-verify consultant Vesto Slipher."

"Verifying," the droid echoed back, joints creaking with a series of soft hydraulic noises as it straightened up. "Command prompt?"

"Access analytical upgrade subroutine 1188. I'm here to pick up a package."

"Accessing." Another muffled hissing noise. "Input data format?"

The CLL unit muttered something in binary that came out sounding like a series of mismatched tones ending with a defeated electronic gurgle. Then its photoreceptors went dim and it dropped both of its flat spatulate arms to the floor with a sharp metallic clang that rang out through the hangar like blasterfire.

"You!" On the far side of the hangar, Maul saw the crew of cargo technicians turning from the empty stack of packaging cartons to stare across the open space at them. "Identify yourselves. What are you doing down here?"

"Don't come any closer," Slipher called back. "He's going to kill me!"

The crew members froze and drew back. Glancing quickly at Maul, the Muun threw his hands into the air.

"My name is Vesto Slipher. I'm a field support analyst for the IBC."
He cast a fearful glance at Maul. "This prisoner, Inmate 11240, abducted me from my quarters and brought me down here as a hostage.
He's trying to escape on the freight barge when it arrives. Alert the
warden." Then, casting his eyes at Maul once more, the banker couldn't
seem to repress a small smile. "I suppose you ought to have killed me
when you had a chance."

"Who says it's too late now?" Maul asked.

"Tell me how to fix the lightsabers," Slipher murmured, "and I'll do
whatever I can with Warden Blirr to see that you walk away from all of
this. Otherwise there is nothing that I can do to guarantee your safety."

Maul felt the space around him closing up like a trap. "Where's the
geological compressor?"

"It must not have arrived yet." Raising his voice again, Slipher called
out to the men across the bay. "You men, stop wasting time! Hurry,
before he—"

"Shut up." Reaching outward, Maul snatched the blue witch from
the Muun's grasp, then turned to the gathered crew members, who
were staring at him from across the bay. Slipher's moronic outburst
hadn't left him much to work with, but it was enough.

"Don't come any closer," Maul said. "Stay right where you are."

"Inmate 11240," one of them shouted back, "what's that in your
hand?"

"It's a plasma detonator." Maul held up the blue witch just high
enough that they could see it, raising his voice to be heard across the
hangar. "High-grade industrial munitions."

"Doesn't look like any detonator I've ever seen."

"Take another step and you'll see all you need of it," Maul said.
"Who wants to be first?"

"Don't be a fool," Slipher murmured. "You can't—"

Maul shoved him away, in the direction of the other men. "You've
done enough."

"You're cutting me loose?" The Muun reared back, incredulous.
"That's insane. They'll kill you in seconds!"

"I'll take my chances." Jamming the blue witch in his pocket, where its glow could be seen through the fabric of the uniform, Maul turned back to the load-lifter that stood behind them. Taking hold of the thing's manipulator arm, he swung himself upward onto its main control console.

"Inmate 11240, what are you doing?"

Maul ignored them, focusing his attention on the load-lifter. The thing's processor cowling was a single metal plate, and he pried it open, popped the bolts, and yanked it off to expose its central processor. Thanks to Trezza's instruction back on Orsis, he'd had some experience slicing into the basic motivator drives of labor droids. They all were built relatively the same.

"Inmate 11240—"

"Stay back." Working instinctively, he found the thing's upgraded cognitive drive and isolated the wiring that he needed to reprogram it manually. It wouldn't cause the load-lifter to do anything more than malfunction, but right now a malfunction was all he needed.

The droid lurched forward, jerking its right leg up, manipulator arms raised above its head. The load-lifter's great gyro-stabilized joints slammed past Slipher as it stormed headlong across the open landing deck, instantly colliding with a stack of shipping cartons.

Crates fell. Pallets crashed. Maul had already jumped back down, landing on the floor in a tuck and roll, as one of the load-lifter's enormous flat manipulators swung in a huge arc, upending a ten-meter-high stack of pallets and skids in front of it. The empty skids tumbled, crashed, and splintered in every direction.

Then it pivoted and started off in the direction of the loading crew. The men scattered, most of them heading for cover while the deck supervisor ran for the communications center overlooking the cargo hold. Across the hold, blue strobes began swirling on both sides, splashing the walls with light, as the load-lifter pivoted and began scooping up what it had knocked over, only to dump the pallets on the opposite side of where it stood.

"Fool," Slipher's voice sneered behind him, and Maul glanced back over his shoulder to see that the Muun had already gotten to his feet. "Did you actually believe you could abandon me here?" He thrust out his hand. "Give me back the blue witch."

Maul said nothing, but it didn't matter. The banker was talking again, caught up in his own outrage and oblivious to the load-lifter advancing behind him.

"My intellect is vastly superior to yours in every imaginable capacity," Slipher sneered. "Even if there was any chance that you could—"

Those were his last words. All at once, from less than a meter behind him, the load-lifter's flat manipulator arm came arcing upward. It caught Slipher at neck level at a perfect forty-five-degree angle, severing his head neatly in one easy slice and sending it spiraling through the air. The entire action was almost silent. For a split second, his decapitated body seemed to hang there on its own, and then it crumpled to the floor of the hangar bay as the load-lifter's right foot came down on top of the body, crushing it beneath the full tonnage of its weight.

It was an unceremonious death for Vesto Slipher, arguably one of the IBC's brightest young minds, dispatched without fanfare by a machine as brainless as he was brilliant. And in the end, no one in the known galaxy seemed particularly to notice.

Maul, for his part, didn't even bother looking back. Through the chaos, on the far side of the bay, he saw the lift that he and Slipher had come from. He could make it from where he was in less than five seconds as long as none of the loading crew had blasters, which he doubted.

He ran.

52
PURGE

"I don't like it."

The prison barge *Purge*'s newly appointed navigator and second-in-command, Bissley Kloth, was at the bridge, still engaged in the process of hailing the gaudily arrayed space yacht that had positioned itself directly in front of him, when the entire console erupted in a storm of proximity alarms.

Kloth snapped them off briskly, taking control of the situation with a quiet confidence that belied his age. At twenty-two, he was still a young man, but he'd already been working aboard the *Purge* for five years, since he was old enough to hire on for a full share. Hauling convicts and local scum out to various detainment stations and galactic penal colonies including Cog Hive Seven wasn't the easiest way to earn a living. Yet he'd quickly gotten used to it—most of it, anyway—including the occasional unwanted encounter with tramp vessels adrift in the Outer Rim. And although the *Purge* was really no more than a garbage barge retrofitted with holding cells and a makeshift medbay, Kloth had a vision of one day transforming it into a floating prison of its own, one in which he might even someday be in charge. He would be *Warden* Kloth.

Today the *Purge* was carrying forty-six inmates, human and nonhuman alike.

"Mr. Kloth." That was the *Purge*'s captain, Wyatt Styrene, limping across the bridge toward him, his pale blue eyes alight with reckless enthusiasm. A former smuggler himself, Styrene knew these uncharted systems as well as anyone Kloth had ever met, and he'd never run from a fight. "What's the word?"

"Proximity alarms from that space yacht." Kloth nodded, indicating the luxury ship that had still not responded to their call. "I've got it under control. It's not—"

A sudden volley of explosions slammed into the *Purge*, rocking them hard enough that Kloth had to grab the console in front of him and hang on. Checking the screens before him, he saw for the first time what he'd somehow overlooked until it was too late—an attack swarm of Z-95 Headhunters closing in from below them, firing on their underside in a steady volley of concussion missiles. The alarms screamed.

"Where did they come from?" Kloth shouted, unaware for the moment that he was asking the question aloud. Of course the Headhunters had been the ones that had triggered the proximity alarms he'd foolishly attributed to the space yacht in front of them—a ruse that he couldn't believe he'd fallen for, although Styrene's expression seemed untroubled. In fact, Kloth could've sworn the old pirate had a wry grin on his face.

"They want to tussle, we'll give 'em a tussle." Without glancing back at Kloth, he powered up the full retinue of the *Purge*'s weapons suite. "Go secure our cargo, Mr. Kloth."

"Captain?"

"Go on, I've got the bridge. Besides—" He gestured toward the hatch. "It's almost feeding time for them, innit?"

Kloth strode quickly back through the *Purge*, nodding at the guards on either side as he opened the hatchway leading to the vessel's main hold.

"Everything secure down here?"

"Locked down," the guard shouted back. "What's going on topside?"

"Not sure," Kloth said, making a split-second decision to keep the arrival of the Headhunters to himself for now, for the sake of maintaining some semblance of order. "Captain's at the bridge now. It's under control."

"Tell that to them," the guard said, pointing down into the hold, where the *Purge* had been outfitted with its containment cells.

Kloth could already hear the convicts down below, some of them screeching, shouting, or demanding answers in the near-darkness. Typically the inmates they brought out to Cog Hive Seven had lapsed into a silent stupor of boredom by this point in the voyage, but the blasterfire had stirred them up, and Kloth heard them calling out to find out if the ship was under attack.

"I'm going down to check the main cargo hold," Kloth told the guard. "Who else is down there?"

"Carrier and Hayes."

Two good men, Kloth thought, or at least battle-tested. He nodded, already ducking forward. "Tell the captain that if I'm not back up in five minutes—"

Thwam!

Something broadsided the vessel from amidships, heavier than a turbolaser, almost like they'd been struck by an asteroid, or another ship. Kloth was already halfway down the gangway amid the holding cells when it struck, and the impact pitched him back into the console wall behind him. It was followed by an unfamiliar high-pitched grinding noise from somewhere below, like an oscillating blade shearing through steel.

The guard beside him hoisted his blaster, checking the cartridge, his face drawn tight with nerves. "What the kark is that?"

"It feels like—" Kloth began, and the words snapped off in his throat.

It feels like we're being boarded.

Seconds later, from down below, he heard it.

The voices of the prisoners had fallen absolutely silent.

53

IS THERE A GHOST

"What in the name of . . ." From behind her desk, Sadiki Blirr was watching the holoscreens that showed the events down in the cargo hold, the CLL load-lifter pivoting on its gyros and thundering into the wall. "Status report. What's going on down there?"

Next to her, ThreeDee didn't respond. The droid had been trying in vain to communicate with the CLL unit for the last five minutes, and its silence was not reassuring.

"My apologies, Warden." ThreeDee withdrew its adapter from the wall console. "I'm afraid the load-lifter's motivator has been manually compromised somehow. I cannot access it from here."

"What do you mean, manually compromised?"

"Someone rewired it onsite."

"That's absurd." Cursing aloud, Sadiki looked at the screen. The crushed remains of the decapitated and trampled Vesto Slipher were sprawled across the floor, almost unrecognizable. She had no idea what the Muun had been doing down there, nor did she particularly care. The sight of his corpse elicited nothing more profound in her than a headache. But it was one more headache that she was going to have to deal with, at the worst possible time. She glanced at the chrono display.

"What's the ETA on that incoming prison barge?"

"The *Purge* is due to arrive within thirty minutes," ThreeDee told her.

"You've confirmed that?"

"Captain Styrene made contact when the vessel first came out of hyperspace. I haven't heard from them since then."

Thirty minutes. Sadiki stood with her hands gripping either side of the desk and remained there, perfectly motionless for the moment, allowing herself to take stock of the situation. By themselves, a malfunctioning droid and the untimely death of an IBC representative weren't catastrophic, but given what was at stake, she sensed the hand of something far more dangerous behind it.

And why had Dakarai disappeared? Where was her brother when she needed his counsel the most?

"Warden," ThreeDee said, "I have Gaming Commissioner Chlorus on the line. Shall I have him leave a message?"

"Yes." She stopped and reconsidered. "No. Wait. Put him through."

Chlorus's face appeared on the screen directly in front of her. He didn't wait for her salutation. "Sadiki, what is going on over there?"

"Commissioner." She smiled, finding it surprisingly easy to do. "You're looking well."

Chlorus held up his hand to stop her. "You're operating in direct violation of the commission's orders to shut down your gambling operation. Now I'm getting reports of ongoing hostility between inmates and guards."

"I wasn't aware that penal reform fell under the aegis of the Gaming Commission," she said.

"Don't do this, Sadiki. Don't put me in this position."

"On the contrary, Commissioner." Sadiki's voice changed, darkening ever so slightly, her eyes never leaving his image on the screen. "It's you who put me into this position. Long ago."

"I fail to see—"

"I didn't want to bring this up, but you've left me no choice." She tapped a series of commands into the holo console, and a new series of images superimposed themselves over the display on the monitor. "Do you recognize this place?"

For a moment Chlorus didn't answer. "Of course. It's the Outlander Casino and Resort on Coruscant."

"Where we first met," Sadiki said as the next series of images came up. "Remember this?"

Now Chlorus's entire face went blank with shock as he stared at the surveillance photos. "Where did you get these—"

"It doesn't matter. What matters is what the board members would have to say about a respected commissioner finding himself with a young, highly impressionable casino manager in what you'll have to admit is a very compromising position." She leaned forward slightly. "Can you see the images clearly? I can increase the bandwidth if you prefer. There are some very good shots of—"

"Those photos prove nothing!"

"You're right," Sadiki said. "Perhaps I should just forward them to the commission and let them draw their own conclusions." She waited for a moment. "Unless you have another suggestion?"

"Enough." Chlorus's shoulders sagged. "What is it that you want?"

"Ah." Sadiki nodded. "Now we're making progress. Here's how it's going to work. As soon as we finish this conversation, you're going to reverse your ruling against my operation, reinstating Cog Hive Seven's rights and privileges as a gaming facility under the commission's regulations, making it fully operational, effective immediately."

"I couldn't possibly—"

"And," she cut in, "I want you to contact your friend Lars Winnick at the IBC and come up with a plausible explanation for the unexpected disappearance of one of their field agents."

"*What?*"

"His name is Vesto Slipher. I'll send the specifics along directly. How you manage it does not concern me, as long as I'm not subjected to any more of these degrading spot audits."

"Sadiki . . ." Chlorus reached up to clutch at the collar of his tunic, struggling to loosen it. "You grossly overestimate my scope of influence in these matters."

"And you, Dragomir, grossly underestimate the amount of damage that these surveillance photos could inflict on your career," she said. "You've done great things for the commission and the relationship between gambling communities. You've driven galactic revenue to new heights. A man like you might be senator one day . . . and after that, who knows?" She let the words sink in, knowing they would saturate his colossal ego. "Do you really want to throw all that away over some cheap tryst with a casino manager?"

Chlorus gazed at her. A faintly gleaming mustache of sweat had broken out across his upper lip, and his eyes looked raw, rimmed with red. Finally he shook his head. "I forgot how obstinate you become when you want something."

"Don't forget again," Sadiki told him, and before he could answer, she pressed the button to break off the transmission. She heard Three-Dee approaching her with a refill for her coffee.

"Well done," the droid observed. "If I may say so."

"Child's play." She held out the cup, allowing him to fill it. "Where's Inmate 11240?"

ThreeDee turned to her, not understanding. "Excuse me?"

"Clear the monitors. Show me all the tunnels and lifts leading away from the cargo bay. Roll the feed back five minutes. Do it now."

The holoscreens flickered and changed, displaying a dozen different walkways, every possible exit from the cargo bay.

Sadiki took her time, examining each screen individually, using the time to consider what had just happened. She hadn't wanted to confront Chlorus with the surveillance photos, not because she didn't want to humiliate him—the man's reputation, like his towering vanity and none-too-secret political ambitions, could not have mattered to her less—but because the photos represented the last and most potent form of leverage that she had over the Gaming Commission. Every predatory instinct within her had wanted to hold on to the images until they could be exploited for maximum value. Now they were out there, and—

She froze, her thoughts breaking off as she caught sight of something on one of the screens, an odd bluish blur in the corner of one of the turbolifts. From here it looked like nothing more than a visual aberration, like a ripple of slightly discolored heat from an exhaust vent. Except that there were no such vents in the lift, and—

The ripple shifted noticeably.

Sadiki leaned closer, staring at the image.

There *was* something inside the lift.

Something that didn't want to be seen.

She hit the alarm.

54

HOT BOX

The lift stopped, and Maul knew he'd been caught.

He glanced down at the blue witch in his hand and then dropped it with disgust, letting it hit the floor with a clink. It rolled to the corner and lay there spluttering feebly for a moment before finally dying out. It served him right for trusting the Muun's gadget for an instant longer than he had to. He never should've taken the lift back up from the cargo bay. Now he was trapped in here. For an instant he imagined Slipher's severed head lying in the corner, laughing at him.

No matter. Such thoughts were useless to him now. He glanced up at the ceiling, a meter above his head, and then the walls around him, instinctively taking stock of any possible way out. Suddenly the lift itself felt very small, more like a cage—or a coffin.

Bracing his hands on one smooth wall and his legs on the other, he lifted himself upward and began to climb his way to the ceiling. It was a slow process, but there was a maintenance hatch up there, in all likelihood bolted shut from the outside. He didn't know if he'd be able to get it open without losing his grip on the walls, and even if he did—

"Very impressive," a woman's voice said from the speaker inside the lift, a voice that Maul recognized immediately as belonging to Sadiki Blirr. "Of course, at this point I should have expected nothing less from Cog Hive Seven's most celebrated inmate."

Ignoring her, Maul crawled another meter upward, keeping his arms, legs, and shoulders rigid to hold himself in position. At this angle, the only way to get the hatch open would be to slam his head against it.

"There's no sense trying to get out that way," the warden's voice said. "The lift is industrial grade, durasteel-reinforced from the outside. We use it to transport our more imposing inmates, like that wampa you fought. It's got some very interesting features, from my perspective at least." Something clicked and began to hum inside the walls. "Even if you managed to escape, there's nothing inside the shaft to hold on to. Which means you'll die in there, either slowly or quickly, depending on how ambitious you are."

Maul said nothing.

"Still determined to injure yourself?" she chuckled. "Here, let me help you."

The lift jerked upward, then plunged. Maul slammed face-first into the ceiling as it dropped straight down. It halted and he hit the floor hard. Sprawled on his back with the walls spinning around him, he reflexively shot out his arms and legs again to stabilize himself for the next move. But the lift began to rise smoothly upward again, as if nothing had disturbed its passage.

"I'd like to make you a proposition," Sadiki's voice purred. "As you may have guessed, we don't get many inmates like you here. In fact, you're arguably one of a kind. So in the spirit of entrepreneurial enterprise, I'd like to do the only thing that makes any sense."

Maul glared at the speaker. "Kill yourself and save the universe the trouble?"

"Not quite." She laughed. "I'd like to offer you a job."

"My answer is no."

"You haven't heard my terms."

"It doesn't matter." His expression remained unchanged. "I prefer death."

"At least do yourself the courtesy of admitting you're curious," she said. "You seem almost supernaturally adept at isolating and exploiting the weaknesses of your opponents under the most adverse of circumstances. So . . ." She paused long enough for Maul to wonder if he was supposed to be hanging on her every word. "This is what I propose. You come to work here in the executive level of Cog Hive Seven, where you will report directly to me. There are certain aspects of our operation here that you might find very illuminating."

"What aspects?" Maul asked.

"Before I get into the details, I would expect an oath of absolute loyalty," Sadiki told him. "Of course, you'll enjoy complete autonomy, stay here in a luxury suite, and receive a generous salary that reflects exactly how valuable you truly are to this operation. Who knows?" Something eased into her voice, a note of bemusement that Maul could actually hear, though he couldn't see her face. "You may even discover what you've been searching for all along. What do you say?"

"You're forgetting one thing," Maul said, bracing himself against the wall opposite the speaker.

"What's that?"

"This place where you live . . ."

"Yes?"

"It's still a prison."

Pumping one leg straight out, he drove his heel into the speaker and smashed it to pieces, strangling the warden's voice off into a fuzzy, digitized warble, and then silence. The speaker itself popped loose from its housing, dangling down on a tangle of multicolored wiring.

Seconds later, the lift stopped again.

He'd expected nothing less. Having not received the answer she wanted, the warden was going to make him hurt. Apparently she wasn't ready to trigger the charges implanted in his hearts, but she wasn't going to let him get away, either.

Working quickly, Maul yanked the dislodged speaker plating from its wires, paused just long enough to inspect the beveled edge and decided that it would have to suffice, and began the slow, creeping process back up toward the hatchway at the top of the lift.

Halfway up, he noticed it.

Around him, the durasteel walls were starting to get hot.

55

INBOUND FLIGHT

CO Dawson was onsite when the prison barge *Purge* docked outside the Hive's loading bay, but he didn't actually see the action—not all of it, anyway. Later on he would testify before a galactic board of inquiry that the only reason he'd survived was that he hadn't stuck around to watch it all go down. That wasn't quite the truth, but it was close enough—and by that time, there wasn't anybody else left to contradict him.

He was on deck with a dozen other guards and the prison's loading and landing crew as the *Purge* settled creakingly into its docking berth just outside the space station. Like most of the freighters and transport ships that arrived here, the barge was far too big to land inside the hangar, so that docking became a ritualized mating ceremony of pressurized coupling adaptors and a long extendable gangway whose port extended down into the cargo hold itself.

When the port finally opened, Dawson and the other guards straightened up, each of them gripping go-sticks and stun pikes, awaiting the signal from Doyle, the chief gantry officer on duty, that typically indicated the off-loading of new prisoners and supplies. Standard loading and unloading protocol was that the *Purge*'s own guards would step off first, with inmates to follow.

Dawson and the others stood staring expectantly at the open port.

But the port remained empty.

"Come on." After a moment, Dawson glanced at the guard next to him in annoyance. "What's this about?" he muttered. "I was supposed to be off-shift twenty minutes ago. Now we've got to stay here waiting for—"

He broke off midsentence. Two nervous-looking guards had just stepped out of the port, each of them struggling to hold up one end of an ungainly, heavy-looking shipping crate. They were followed by four more guards, escorting a group of nine prisoners—at least they were wearing prison uniforms, although CO Dawson thought these creatures were even more imposing than what he was used to. Trandoshans, Gamorreans, Gran—species that he'd tangled with before, certainly, but never all together like this. And then he realized why they looked so dangerous.

They were all smiling.

Grinning, actually.

"Scrummy-looking buggers, aren't they?" Dawson growled, tightening his grip on his static pike, already thumbing the power button and wishing they'd been armed with blasters. He didn't like the feel of things, and was already aware of an unpleasant tension gathering in his lungs, making him feel as though his uniform was buttoned too tightly across his chest and throat. Lately there had been a paranoid air of skullduggery inside the prison itself, rumors that the Hutts or other crime syndicates had been sending their own people in as inmates or even guards to undermine operations here. Dawson didn't believe it, but the possibility still made him uneasy.

He glanced back at the other guard, Greer. "Let's knock some of the snark off their faces, shall we?"

"The matches'll do that soon enough," Greer murmured back. "But I'm not sure I'm willing to wait that long."

"Me either."

They stepped forward, pikes at the ready. The guards carrying the shipping crate had stopped ten meters in front of them and put it down with a noticeable expression of relief. Eyeing the inmates, Dawson and the others came forward to receive them.

"Gentlemen, welcome," Sadiki Blirr spoke up from behind them, and Dawson glanced back over his shoulder to see the warden standing there, along with her droid. Dawson took his hand off the butt of his static pike and forced himself to calm down. It was highly unorthodox for management to come down personally to supervise the offloading of new inmates, and he wondered if there was something special about this entire operation after all.

Warden Blirr eyed the inmates and the guards who'd escorted them. "Where's your captain?"

"Still aboard the vessel."

"Captain Styrene usually comes down to greet me himself," she said, and turned to the new inmates. "How many are there?"

"Just these nine."

"Only nine?" Sadiki glanced at the droid for verification. "We were supposed to receive thirty-two inmates."

"Just nine," the guard answered back stiffly, and Dawson noticed the man's eyes flicking anxiously back toward the docking module, as if he couldn't wait to get back aboard—or anywhere, for that matter, as long as it wasn't here.

Frowning, Sadiki approached the shipping crate. "What about the freight? Is this all of it?"

"Everything on our manifest."

"I highly doubt that."

"See for yourself."

"Thank you," Sadiki said. "I will."

As she walked over to inspect the crate, Dawson saw the whole thing shift slightly to the right. Whatever was in there was large enough to make the entire crate move. He was already opening his mouth to shout out a warning when the lid burst open.

"*Warden*—" Dawson started, but that was all he had time for.

The Trandoshan who'd been hiding inside the crate had a WESTAR-M5 blaster rifle in both hands. By the time Warden Blirr dropped to the floor—her reflexes, Dawson realized, had just saved her life—the 'Shan was already firing point-blank into the group of guards directly in front of him. Blaster bolts streaked flickering ribbons of death into the unsuspecting front line of Cog Hive Seven's COs, and everything around him started happening with dreamlike clarity. Dawson saw Greer, the guard two meters away from him, go rag-dolling backward across the floor of the hangar with a sizzling hole in his chest, leaving nothing more behind him than a stinking cloud of burned flesh and fabric.

Blinking, Dawson recoiled and hit the floor. He could hear the warden's administrative droid clucking out panicked noises in the distance. Somewhere off to his right, Warden Blirr herself had disappeared completely from sight—hit or not, he couldn't tell, nor at this moment did he particularly care. The thought that kept circling through his mind— *This can't be happening, whatever it is. I was supposed to be off the clock twenty fracking minutes ago*—did nothing to help him get a grip on himself.

In front of him and all around, things were happening almost too quickly to track. The two guards who had carried the crate out of the *Purge* were running, actually flat-out *sprinting,* back up the gangway for cover, while the prisoners they'd brought down had already thrown off their manacles and leg restraints—which Dawson realized, with a dawning sense of horror, had never been fastened to begin with. Cold sweat broke out over his forehead, making his scalp feel too tight for his skull. The whole thing had been a setup, and they'd walked right into it.

Grinning wider than ever, the "prisoners" charged forward. The Trandoshan inside the crate was pulling out blasters, rifles, and sidearms and tossing them out to his confederates, who seized them eagerly and joined in the one-sided firefight.

Dawson turned to flee.

The hangar around him was already full of smoke and the sheared-metal stench of spent blaster rounds. The remaining guards and loading personnel were taking cover on both sides of him, but the hangar had been cleared to accommodate the incoming prisoners and supplies and there was nothing to hide behind. He thought if he could get to the turbolift, he might stand a chance of—

Bang!

An explosion from inside the *Purge*'s berthing port jerked his head around, and he looked back just in time to see the bodies of the two guards who'd just run in come flying back out, their corpses sprawling limply across the floor of the hangar.

There was something coming out of the smoke.

Something big.

Staring, Dawson realized that he was looking at some kind of giant floating holovid projector hauled forward by a pair of kell dragons, grayish black quadrupedal lizards, straining frenziedly at their leashes. The image on the holovid was a bloated, leering figure that he recognized only from secondhand footage and word of mouth, though he knew immediately who it was.

Jabba the Hutt.

All at once Dawson knew the rumors were true.

But at that point, of course, it was entirely too late.

56

12 X 18

Braced at the top of the turbolift, Maul used his free hand to jimmy the edge of the speaker's faceplate into the locked ceiling hatch, prying it open. The edge was too big for the gap, and his hand kept slipping.

He closed his eyes, summoning the power of the dark side, searching the hatch, probing it for structural weakness. It didn't budge. Blinking back sweat, he rededicated himself to the task at hand. It was growing feverishly hot inside the lift, where Warden Blirr had no doubt intended to roast him alive, or until she broke down whatever rebellious aspect she saw in him, and turned him into . . . what? Her mascot, her house pet, or something even more servile?

The notion revolted him, and he jammed the metal strip in deeper between the locked hatch and its housing, wiggling it back and forth. Boiling with impatience, he released a concentrated energy field against the hatch, battering it, but it still wouldn't budge.

Maul cursed, the anger rising up inside him from wherever it lived and toiled endlessly. Tightening his grip on the makeshift tool, he started working again on the hatch, forcing himself to take his time, fighting to ignore the suffocating heat, the baked air that filled his lungs, as if he were drawing breath directly from a blast furnace.

He fixed his gaze straight up. The hatch itself, an unremarkable twelve-by-eighteen-centimeter rectangle, had become his entire world. Twelve by eighteen, and in the end it represented the difference between completing his mission and perishing in shame and obscurity.

Slipher—Radique—the khipus—

He clenched his teeth, the heat very close to him now, pressing in from all sides, clinging to him like a second skin. By now the walls had become scalding steel plates, burning the palm of his hand and the fingers holding him in place. The inside of his mouth felt cool by comparison. A drop of sweat hit the floor and he realized that he could actually hear it sizzle. If the temperature kept going up like this, he guessed that he might have another minute or two before he blacked out from heat prostration, and then—

He kept working. There was an odd, meaty smell rising up around him, and when his blistered palm shifted slightly on the wall, he realized that it was his own flesh beginning to roast.

Master. I will not fail.

He breathed in, breathed out. An odd, narcotic dizziness had started to take hold of him, and he reached down deep into whatever remained of his consciousness, forcing himself to focus. He needed to find Eogan Truax. If he could just—

All at once, the hatch popped open.

Cool air rushed down from above in a blessed, invigorating cloud, and Maul dropped the steel plate to the floor and scrambled up through the hatchway, into the near-darkness.

He was standing on top of the lift, gazing up the endless expanse of the shaft. The sweat had already dried on his skin. Giving himself a moment, he narrowed his eyes, stretching out with his feelings while his eyes acclimated to the lightless space. The details began to resolve themselves around him. In front of him was a series of steel rungs imbedded directly into the wall at half-meter intervals, an easy jump from here.

He sprang forward, caught the first rung, and began to climb.

Boy, I'm coming for you.

57

KILLING BOX

Everything was going fine until the kell dragons broke loose.

When the shooting had started, Sadiki hadn't wasted any time on incredulity. In her experience, it was what she'd always thought of as the "idiot beat"—that shocked, stubborn moment when the human brain refused to accept the obvious, even when it was happening right in front of your face—that got you killed. Her instincts took over. Crawling across the floor on her knees and elbows, keeping her head down, she'd found immediate cover behind one of the unused load-lifter droids while the initial volley of blasterfire had overtaken the cargo hold. That had been the worst of it.

"Bo shuda, Warden Blirr," Jabba's voice called out through the holoprojector's recessed speakers. *"Ohta mi marvalec fiz plesodoro."*

Translating the words effortlessly, Sadiki understood the message perfectly in Basic. *Hello, Warden Blirr. Let me see your beautiful face.*

She'd peered out from behind the droid and seen his image hovering there, a full stereo projection, larger than life, borne forward on a repulsor platform drawn by the two enormous kell dragons. Of course Jabba would never risk coming down here himself. She could only assume that he was safely ensconced on his space yacht, far enough away to remain unharmed, not so distant that he'd miss out on any of the fun.

As imposing as he was, the arrival of the Hutt, in person or virtually, hadn't really been much of a surprise. By this point Sadiki had already figured out most of what was happening and why, and when her ears stopped ringing from the firefight, she'd come around from behind the load-lifter, stepping fully into view.

"Jabba," she said, hands up, stepping closer, picking her way among the bodies of fallen guards and deck crew members. The survivors, apparently, had already retreated from the hangar. "Welcome to the Hive. I take it that I've done something to provoke your ire?"

The Trandoshans and Gamorreans swung around to point their blasters at her, but Jabba's holo gestured at them to lower their weapons. The platform where the image projector sat shuddered visibly, with the dragons yanking hungrily on their leashes.

"Warden Blirr," Jabba answered, continuing in Huttese, "I thought we were friends."

"Hmm." Fearlessness, she realized, or at least the appearance of it, would be the key to surviving the next five minutes. She glanced at the smoking carcasses of her own people littered across the floor and shrugged. "Apparently not. To what do I owe the pleasure of this visit?"

"You executed my foot soldiers."

"Then I guess we're even."

"As if that weren't bad enough," Jabba continued on blithely, "you allowed them to be eaten by this inmate scum that you pit against one another for sport."

"A nice touch, don't you think?"

"You know me well." He chuckled and shook his head. "Under normal circumstances I would applaud such butchery, but you don't seem to grasp the basic elements of respect."

"Respect?" Sadiki cocked her eyebrow. "So you're here to school me on the fine art of diplomacy?"

"Among other things."

"Sorry, Jabba, but it won't wash," she said, taking another step forward, hands still up where he could see them. "And besides, you told me explicitly that those weren't your men. I gave you every opportunity to take them back, and you denied knowing every one."

"Sadiki, Sadiki . . ." The Hutt narrowed his eyes. "We're both businesspeople. Let's stop wasting each other's time."

"By all means." She'd ventured close enough now that she could see into the crate where the Trandoshan was standing, a snarl twisted over his face, the WESTAR rifle still gripped in his claws. At her feet, the body of one of the guards was twitching, his static pike still clutched loosely in one hand, as the last of his life drained from him. "Just tell me what you want."

Jabba peered at her from beneath wrinkled eyelids. "What I want?"

"This is how this works, isn't it? You send in a handful of hired muscle and I get all intimidated and fork over whatever it takes to make them go away. So what do you want?"

"How about your pretty head?" Jabba told her. "Mounted on my palace wall, where I can admire it for all eternity."

Sadiki smiled coldly. "I'm afraid that's not on the table for negotiation."

"How disappointing. Then how about a quick meal while I'm here?"

She glanced at the holovid, perplexed. "A meal?"

"Yes." Jabba cast his eyes down at the creatures leashed to the front of his platform. "For my little pets."

At once, both dragons sprang forward and came barreling toward her, lunging over the bodies of the fallen, while Jabba's entourage stepped back to give them all the room they needed to finish her off.

Sadiki figured she was close enough by now, and she was right. In a quick jackknifing motion she grabbed the static pike from the limp grasp of the guard on the floor, turned, and thrust it into the neck of the Trandoshan, jamming the electrically charged tip into his reptilian skin and delivering a massive, heart-stopping shock. As the 'Shan jerked and shuddered with the current pulsing through him, she grabbed the WESTAR from his hands, wheeled around, and fired a series of blasts directly into the face of the first kell dragon.

The dragon caught the high-energy particle beam straight between the eyes at less than a meter away, the impact pulverizing its bony calvarium and frying its lizard brain in its skull, but not entirely stopping it. Skidding sideways on its claws, captive of its own momentum, the thing floundered headlong into the crate where the Trandoshan had collapsed and slammed into it, still twitching. Its scaly body landed in a bulky heap at Sadiki's feet.

Don't forget the other one.

She pivoted, finger on the trigger. The second dragon circled around behind her with a guttural hiss. Tensing, she pointed the WESTAR at it and squeezed off a round, but she was too late. In a flash the thing was on her, knocking her flat. Squirming beneath it, Sadiki drew up her legs, fought to pull herself away—

—and that was when she felt its jaws clamp down around her right calf, teeth ripping through her leather boot, deep into the flesh and muscle, grinding down toward bone.

She screamed. Agony like nothing she'd ever experienced came spilling out to engulf the entire lower half of her body, swelling in a bright balloon of pain that threatened to overtake reality itself. She arched her back, her fingers groping blindly for the WESTAR, drumming the floor of the hangar, but the blaster rifle was gone, lost where she could never find it.

Crack! Something in her lower leg came loose with a brittle snap, and her vision doubled, then tripled, as tears of pain spilled up from her eyes.

"Easy, sweet one," Jabba's voice growled at the dragon, "take your time." Faintly, from somewhere far beyond the pain, Sadiki heard him laughing, that hollow, orotund *ho ho ho* that nearly everyone who heard it associated with impending death. "You see, Warden, I like to starve my precious dragons, to build their appetite." Squirming on the holovid, tail twisting with delight, the Hutt sat back and splayed his fingers over the great sac of his bloated stomach. "But I also train them to eat slowly, to keep you alive as long as possible. So she works her way slowly upward, a little at a time."

Writhing upward, blinking back tears, Sadiki stared down with a mixture of horror and disbelief at the stump where her right foot had been. It was gone—torn off completely. The splintered nubs of tibia and fibula protruded visibly from the tattered pantleg. From directly above it, the kell dragon leered up at her, face and teeth smeared bright red, its eyes alive with unslaked appetite. As the lizard nudged its way closer, snuffling eagerly, Sadiki could smell the thing's breath seething from its nostrils, a noxious jungle stench of stomach bile and rancid meat mixed with the fresher coppery smell of her own blood.

Anger cut a white streak across the cloud of impending shock, and she knew what she had to do.

"ThreeDee?" She twisted backward, her eyes flicked across the hangar until she found what she was looking for: the administrative droid, standing along the far wall. *"ThreeDee?"*

"Yes, Warden?" The administrative droid looked back at her from the wall of the hangar.

"Initiate reconfiguration series 121, immediately."

"Yes, Warden."

"Jabba," Sadiki shouted, forcing her voice to remain steady. From where she lay with the kell dragon standing over her, she was unable to make eye contact with the Hutt, but she knew he was there. "Jabba, can you hear me?"

"Of course I can," he said. "Do you think I would miss the sound of you begging for your life?"

Sadiki managed to shake her head. "Call it off," she said, through gritted teeth. "This is your only chance. The rest of your men, now, tell them to stand down."

"Or?"

"Your people will *all* die here. I swear it."

"You swear it?" Jabba sat back and roared with laughter, his massive bulk shaking with the force of it. "You are in no position—"

She closed her eyes as the entire hangar began to shudder around her with a deep metallic tremor, the clockwork of Cog Hive Seven going through what would be its final reconfiguration. To Sadiki, the tremor was reassuringly familiar, the stirring of a great hydraulic giant whose sole purpose now was to save her life. Dismissing the sight of the dragon, pushing past the shock of blood loss and the trauma, she reached back with both hands as far as she could. There was a long metal tube welded to the wall at her back, and she seized hold of it as the floor panels below dropped suddenly open below her.

With a shriek, the dragon plunged into the shaft, gone.

Jabba's yellow eyes widened. In front of him, the Trandoshans and Gamorreans backed away while the great walls began collapsing around them, the ceiling buckling, the entire hangar folding up from the top down while newly revealed gaps and shafts yawned open on either side of the *Purge*'s docking port. On his hovering repulsor platform, the Hutt's expression had already changed from shock to startled outrage.

"Presumptuous wench!" Spittle flew from Jabba's lips, and his entire face seemed to swell and bulge with contempt. "I will have you brought before me. I will devour your flesh! *I will wallow in your blood!*" His slitted yellow eyes gleamed and rolled back at the Gamorrean nearest the *Purge*'s port. "Signal Scuppa! Turn them loose! *Turn them all loose!*"

The holovid disappeared.

All around them, indifferent to events within it, the cargo bay continued to reconfigure. The shaft that had opened up to swallow the kell dragon now stood five meters wide, too far for any of Jabba's henchmen to jump across, but Sadiki had a feeling that it wouldn't stop them for long.

"Warden," a voice said behind her, and she glanced up to see Three-Dee standing over her, gripping her arm. "I've got you. Let me help." Leaning forward, the droid's breastplate opened to extrude a slender manipulation tool with a hypodermic gripped in its articulated pincers.

"Where . . . did that come from?"

"You had it installed in me personally during the initial upgrade. Three years ago."

"I don't remember that at all."

"It doesn't matter." The needle slid into her arm, and an instant later, Sadiki felt the pain beginning to ebb. It was still there, but whatever the droid had injected into her had created a feeling of welcome detachment, as if she were observing it from a great distance. "We need to get you out of here right away."

"I'll be fine."

"Eventually, yes. Right now you need immediate treatment."

She stopped arguing, allowing the droid to lift her up so that she could lean on it. ThreeDee's arms were surprisingly strong, and she was grateful for their stability, because the narcotic was working fast, already taking away whatever remained of her equilibrium. Limping, she started back toward the turbolift.

"This way," ThreeDee said. "I've already communicated with the GH-7. He's waiting for you in medbay."

Sadiki blinked, trying to see clearly. In front of her, the lift was open and waiting. There was a rumbling behind her, a thunder that had nothing to do with the reconfiguration.

She glanced back toward Jabba's side of the hangar.

Behind her, on the far side of the five-meter gap, newly released prisoners—the thirty or so inmates that she'd initially expected—were spilling out of the *Purge*'s berthing port, shrieking and howling at their unexpected freedom. Like Jabba's entourage, they couldn't get across the opening in the hangar floor, not yet. But it didn't stop them from grabbing up blaster rifles and sidearms from the weapon crate on their side and opening fire in every direction.

In the few seconds they'd been out, Sadiki saw that five of the inmates had already yanked loose the long berthing platform from the *Purge*'s port and were dragging it over to bridge the open space. It wouldn't take more than a few minutes, she realized with a kind of dazed certainty, before they'd be scattering throughout the cargo bay and then upward into all levels of the prison.

And unlike the current inmates, none of them had electrostatic charges implanted in their hearts yet.

You're losing control here. It's all slipping away.

"No," she muttered aloud. "Not yet. Not like this."

But a profound heaviness had already settled over her, weighing her down. She was losing consciousness as well. Fading fast. Watching the prisoners pushing the gangway across the open gap, she felt her final thoughts rising back faintly like an echoing voice from the bottom of a deep and hollow well.

How many more guards do I have left? Thirty? Forty at the most?

The droid's grip tightened on her arm. "I have already activated all emergency alarms." ThreeDee was urging, lifting her now, carrying her forward. "Armed guards and support crews are on their way down now. They will stabilize the situation. Come along."

"We have to get down . . . ," Sadiki heard herself saying, "down below . . . to check on . . ."

"Yes. Later."

She nodded foggily, the very final dregs of consciousness draining away. The last thing she saw before her eyes sank shut was the binary load-lifter that she'd been hiding behind earlier, making its way across the floor, toward the gap in the floor. With one great step, it breached the open shaft and made its way to the weapons crate. It reached down inside, oblivious to everything that was going on around it, and pulled out a medium-sized black box from the very bottom of the crate. Sadiki watched all of this with glazed fascination.

A final dazed question swirled through her mind.

What's it doing in there?

Then blackness.

58

THE DARK BACKWARD

Maul was a hundred meters up the lift shaft, groping his way upward through unrelenting blackness, when the Hive started changing shape around him.

Another reconfiguration? Now?

He'd never been this deep inside the prison when the process had occurred. From here everything seemed to be happening faster, on a cataclysmic scale. It was like being trapped inside the works of the galaxy's biggest and most deadly clock. Gaps opened in the walls, and the walls themselves broke apart and began to rotate and realign. Steel scaffolding swung and clanged on its hinges. Within seconds the entire infrastructure was buckling and oscillating in a thousand independently governed directions, flinging whole levels of itself at him, articulated vent shafts and automated platforms pivoting and swinging around him with mechanical abandon—as if this entire world, no longer content with simple reconfiguration, was determined to tear itself apart. From the left, a thick bundle of electrical conduits erupted out of a newly formed gap in the opposite walls. Maul ducked as the pipeline sailed by his scalp, slamming into the wall that had just risen off to his left. Another panel swung open to his right and extruded a meshwork of strut channels that swiveled through a shaft on the opposite side.

He held on tight to the rungs he'd been climbing. The shaft wall that he'd been scaling just moments before jolted stammeringly into motion, clanking and scraping, rising at an angle and then turning on itself, twisting until it was perpendicular to its original orientation, and he was hanging from the rungs, his body dangling straight down above an open abyss whose depths he couldn't gauge.

It seemed that Warden Sadiki had lost patience and decided to conduct the next bout without him.

Maul stared straight down. An updraft of air rose from the void. Far below, hundreds of meters down, a series of levels dilated open like the valves and chambers of some colossal mechanical heart at the bottom of the shaft, and for an instant, he thought he glimpsed it—the throbbing turbines at the very center of the prison, the great gnashing driveshaft upon which all the clockwork turned.

At last, with a final clattering slam, the prison fell still again.

Maul hung there, waiting.

The silence came next.

It was suddenly very cold in the updraft, and he was aware that his shoulders were aching, that he couldn't hang on here forever. But he no longer had the slightest sense of direction—only that Cog Hive Seven's artificially generated gravitational field was already sucking him irrevocably down toward the void, where the gears at the heart of this place would no doubt grind him to a paste.

He reached out with his feelings, trying to get a sense of where he needed to go, the nearest exit, even the nearest wall.

Something brushed against the back of his neck, soft and sticky.

Looking up, he saw that the open spaces around him were webbed with a filmy, gossamer substance, dangling in threads. At one point the strands might have been nests, but when the prison had reconfigured itself, they'd been torn apart, and now they rippled in the currents of air rising from below.

Maul narrowed his eyes. The webworks twitched and seethed, bundles of tiny living things, their white bodies squirming in the silken strands. They looked like—

All at once, the rungs in his hands began to vibrate.

Maul gripped them tighter, feeling the entire surface shaking over his head. Unlike the mechanized uproar that he'd just experienced, this was a singular, living presence, slithering its way through the steel panel that had once been a wall, the one from which he was currently dangling. Its weight caused the support armature itself to sag and buckle below it.

The Syrox. The Wolf Worm of Cog Hive Seven.

The clamor must have roused it, brought it here, where it would have to be reckoned with.

It was already very close. Maul realized that the Hive's most recent reconfiguration had probably thrust him directly into its nesting grounds, where it spawned its sucklings, such as they were. Had the Warden done this on purpose? Was this to be his next fight after all?

Accidental or on purpose, it hardly mattered. He could feel the thing itself passing through the tunnel directly above him in an oozing, peristaltic wave.

Maul squinted straight ahead into the darkness, focusing until he could make out the vague shape of what he hoped was another wall, fifteen meters in front of him. Clutching the rungs overhead, he began to work his way hand over hand to the far wall. He had no sense of what he'd find there exactly, only that he couldn't linger directly underneath the weight of this thing above him, which felt like it might tear through the passageway overhead and come spilling down on top of him at any second.

Above him, the repulsive weight of the worm slithered along at the exact same pace, as if it sensed his proximity. Maul knew where it was because of the way the groaning steel protested louder than ever, bolts and rivets popping free now, whole panels bulging and snapping out of place.

What do you want?

The thing paused again, searching.

Stretching out with his feelings, Maul heard a tangle of voices exploding in his mind, hundreds of them stitched together in an irrational patchwork of agony and confusion.

Inmates.

All the ones that the worm had devoured since its arrival here. Shrieks. Mad, inarticulate laughter. Oaths of vengeance never to be exacted. Pleas for mercy never to be granted. It was as if the door to an asylum had been flung open inside his skull, allowing a wave of incoherent screams, individual cries, and desperate fragmented phrases into his mind.

—swear I will—

—kill you and rip your karking face off it—

—hurts me it's eating my—

—skin when it burns you can't—

—save me this place is like—

—blackness, it's a pit, I can't—

—run anymore there's no end to this pain when it's—

—bleeding me dry I can't feel my hands and I'm—

—blind my eyes are rotting in my—

—skull what's that thing in my—

—brains we shall eat—

—WE SHALL EAT—

Maul reached the far wall and swung himself forward. In the darkness, his feet found a narrow toehold at the edge of a scaffolding perhaps three centimeters wide, but sufficient to steady his weight.

Pressing his back to the wall, arms outstretched for balance, he stood there for a long ten-count as the worm above him slithered slowly out of range, hauling its albino bulk along behind him with the unhurried determination of a thing that knew its ultimate role here, and saw no need to rush.

He let out a breath and took a closer look at where he was standing. The scaffolding where he stood wrapped itself around an oblong recessed platform that had recently been formed by three intersecting walls, each one on hinges. He pressed his weight tentatively against them. None of them looked particularly solid.

Enough of this.

Kicking the panel in the middle, he watched as it swung open to reveal a low, arched doorway through which a faint orangish yellow glow emanated, hazy in the cold metallic dust.

He swung himself inside it and hit the floor running.

59

SYROX

The worm knew about darkness.

Blind from birth, void of consciousness in any traditional sense of the word, it did not know that it was also called the Syrox. Nor did it have any sense of how far it had traveled from home. On its native planet, Monsolar, where its species had been revered for thousands of years, it had been worshipped as a god and dreaded like the plague, its silken bag-tents clustering in the high branches and filling the nightmares of the local tribes.

For generations the elders and priests had spoken in hushed and reverent tones of the swollen, pale Wolf Worm that lived in the remote jungles. Their culture was embroidered with the graven images and death songs of a thing whose hive mind was informed by all the spirits of those it had devoured, their souls trapped for an eternity of undying torment, while fueling its unending hunger.

The worm knew about hunger.

Given the dread that it evoked among those who knew it best, its origins were ignominious in comparison. Each year, its newly hatched pupae swarmed in their countless trillions within the silken treetop bag-tents. Growing, they soon fell from the nests into Monsolar's unfiltered rivers, streams and swamps, destined to colonize the stomachs and intestinal tracts of anyone foolish enough to drink the unfiltered water. Gestation time could be slow, sometimes years, as the worm grew stronger in the bowels of its host.

It was in the small intestine of an otherwise forgotten inmate and Monsolarian named Waleed Nagma that the Wolf Worm had first arrived at the Hive, three years ago. Nagma had died unremarkably, seconds into his very first fight, but the Syrox larvae inside his gut—only a few millimeters long at the time—had survived. It had, in fact, already absorbed Nagma's consciousness in the few seconds immediately following his body's death, so he became the first of what would eventually become hundreds of tenants trapped inside the Wolf Worm's mind.

Soon there would be more. So many more.

As the Wolf Worm found a home here, fattening its body on the blood of dead inmates, its mind had become a chamber of horrors, a prison within the prison where all the sentient and nonsentient beings that it had eaten were doomed to measure out an eternity by the yardstick of endless torment. It had spawned countless larvae of its own, and they had continued to breed down here, hungering and growing larger, but none had ever approached the size of the Wolf Worm itself.

Now, still as sightless as it had been on the day it had hatched, the worm was aware of its own existence only as a vast and endlessly renewing collection system of screams and agony. It thought of itself—in the rare moments that it thought at all—in the collective sense, not as "I" but as "we," not as "mine" but as "ours." Sleepless and restless, it knew nothing but the unending torment of those whose blood had fortified its continuous, slithering tour of these reconfiguring shafts and tunnels.

And hunger.

Always hunger.

60

CLOSING TIME

"Eogan."

The boy looked at his father, sprawled on the bunk of his cell. It was the first time the old man had spoken since the boy had carried him back from the morgue. His voice, though weak, was surprisingly clear.

"He's coming."

"Who is?"

"Radique." With what seemed like tremendous effort, Artagan Truax lifted himself up onto his elbows and faced his son. "Coming . . . to . . . kill me."

"But I thought you saved his life."

"Doesn't matter." The old man shook his head. "Since I helped the Zabrak summon the Bando Gora here . . ."

"But—"

"Quiet, boy." Artagan's voice grew firm, edged with a vestige of its former strength. "There's something else . . . I need to tell you. Something I've never said before."

Eogan waited.

"Before you were born . . . your mother and I were . . . both part of the Bando Gora. Thought they held the secrets of the galaxy. It was the wrong road, but . . . we didn't know it at the time. Even when . . ." Artagan took in a shuddering breath. "Even after she died. I stayed with them. You were just a baby. There was no way out."

There was silence in the cell.

"The day came, sixteen years ago . . . I heard them plotting to kill Radique. To ambush him, hijack his weapons shipment. Radique was powerful, even then. I saw my chance for both of us. I thought if I broke with the Gora at that moment . . . saved Radique's life . . . earned his trust . . . then at least you'd have an advocate, somebody to watch over you . . ."

Artagan broke off into a coughing fit, then gradually regained his voice.

"At first the plan worked. When the shooting started, I had a ship ready. We got away with Radique. He left us at the first spaceport—promised he'd be in touch. To repay his debt. But . . ." Artagan drew in a sharp, painful breath and released it. "I didn't hear from him for years. We traveled . . . you and me. Holding fights for money. I knew it couldn't last forever. Kept waiting to hear back. Finally, years later, a message arrived. It was him. Told me that he could help us. Here . . ."

"So you brought me back," Eogan said. "To this place."

The old man nodded. "When we first got here, I sought him out. And I found him—or he found me. Within the first month, he made contact. Offered me a job helping him build weapons here. He offered me protection. For myself, and for you. All I had to give him . . . were my eyes." Artagan shook his head. "*I couldn't do it*. Couldn't be blinded for him. So he disappeared again. Until now. When I sent for . . . the Bando Gora. And now. He's coming . . . to finish me."

Eogan stood up.

"I won't let him."

"Doesn't matter. I'm . . . already dead anyway."

"Not like this," Eogan said, taking his father's hand and squeezing it.

"Sorry, boy," a voice said behind him. "But it's going to be *exactly* like that."

Eogan turned around. A half dozen inmates—humans and non-humans alike—were standing there blocking the entryway. It took less than a second for Eogan to register that none of them had eyes. How had they found their way up here?

Then he saw the birds. One of them opened its beak and let out a shrill, croaking caw.

The birds had led them here.

"Mr. Radique sent us," the blind man said. He was clutching two long shafts of sharpened steel in both hands, long and gleaming like a pair of homemade machetes. All the others were similarly armed. "To deal with the old man for summoning the Bando Gora to the Hive." He shook his head. "Our actions have consequences, don't they? Just as all rivers lead to the sea, their paths may differ, but the end result is never in doubt."

"No." Eogan stepped toward them. "You can't—"

The blind man loosed a keening shriek and flung himself at Eogan, both arms spinning. Eogan ducked and lunged for the man's knees, and felt a wave of muscle slam into his cheekbone, driving him to the floor. His thoughts sucked down a star-shot funnel of half-conscious agony.

Feet were trampling him, stomping him down. From somewhere on the other side of the cell, his father was trying to talk, struggling to make himself heard. Eogan put up his hand. It was hopeless.

"Father, no!"

Lifting his head, Eogan saw them surrounding his father, swinging the blades down onto him, flinging up great gaudy fans of blood as they hacked away at what remained of his body. They attacked like animals, as if their lack of sight had somehow blinded them to any sort of human mercy.

In the midst of it all, the Zabrak's words comparing him to his father echoed through Eogan's mind: *You don't have his heart . . . you'll never be half the man he is.*

Eogan shook his head.

Not anymore.

Something changed inside him, something deep and final. Without even being aware that he was doing so, he leapt forward and felt his body—his muscles and his adrenaline and the very blood in his veins—flying into motion, launching into a series of lightning-fast strikes.

Every part of him was in motion at once, fists and feet swinging out, delivering a blizzard of punches and kicks that seemed to connect with the six blind men simultaneously in a blur of speed and shattering bone. They were falling at either side of him now, their blades clattering to the cell floor, and Eogan knew that up until this moment, if he'd ever attempted such an assault, he almost certainly would have died. It was nothing like what he'd imagined—as if he'd given up his body and had been brought back to life by something profoundly faster and more powerful than himself, resurrected for a singular moment of triumph.

When it was over, he dropped his fists to his sides and stood gasping amid a pile of bodies, his arms soaked in blood to the elbows.

A voice from the middle of the pile: "Eogan?"

"Father." He came forward and yanked one of Radique's men to the side. The old man's body was there, horribly chopped and hacked, but somehow still clinging to the last scraps of consciousness.

Artagan held up one bloody hand. He was smiling.

"The Fifty-Two Fists," he managed.

Eogan felt the walls of his throat swelling. He couldn't speak.

"I'm so proud of you."

The boy dropped to his knees and embraced him. Even now, there was thunder in the old man's chest, the battered heart pounding defiantly even as it came to the final moments of his life.

He held the old man like that until the thunder stopped.

Some uncertain amount of time later, he heard footsteps again, entering the open hatchway. Looking around, Eogan saw Jagannath standing there. The Zabrak was staring at the pile of bodies strewn throughout the cell, the makeshift weapons and slowly drying blood. At last the eyes of the red-skinned inmate came to meet Eogan's.

"You did all this?"

The boy said nothing.

"Your father—"

"Dead," Eogan said.

The Zabrak nodded, as if he'd expected nothing less. "Come on."

"Where are we going?"

"The cargo bay."

Eogan frowned. "The—"

"I have unfinished business there."

61

PRESSURE AND TIME

Even before the lift door opened on the hangar, Maul heard the blasters going off in a steady volley of explosions. Eogan stared at him, the whites of his eyes gleaming in the recessed lights. "What's going on out there?"

"A firefight," Maul said. He hadn't expected it, but at this point, nothing came as a surprise. "Keep your head down."

The lift opened and a blaster bolt exploded inside it, decimating the control panel behind his head. Eogan let out a startled shout. Ignoring the boy, Maul dropped into a defensive crouch and stared out at the hangar, giving himself five seconds to analyze everything that was going on in the cargo bay.

Two distinct groups were staging a pitched battle on either side of an open five-meter gap that divided the hangar floor in half. On the side nearest where they stood, a small group of Cog Hive Seven guards was exchanging fire with what appeared to be a much larger mob of prisoners, all of whom seemed to have more powerful weapons.

The prisoners were clearly winning.

Not only were they having a far better time of it—some of them, Maul noticed, were actually laughing as they fired on the guards—but they'd very nearly managed to manipulate a long docking gangway over so that it spanned the open chasm in the hangar floor, allowing them complete access to the entire hangar.

Maul wondered fleetingly why the guards didn't simply trigger the bombs implanted inside the inmates' hearts, and then realized that the men that he was seeing must have been the incoming prisoners.

A screaming guard ran across the floor. His face was literally on fire, his features melting even as he ran.

Things were falling apart on Cog Hive Seven.

"What do we do now?" Eogan shouted.

Maul ignored him. Great rafts of blaster smoke and burning metal hung in the air. The guards were running low on ammunition, and there didn't seem to be any backup coming. In the midst of all this, Maul saw the enormous holovid of a Hutt perched on a repulsor platform, rolling his eyes and chortling with delight.

Jabba.

He registered the crime lord's virtual presence here and in the same moment dismissed it as irrelevant. Whatever Jabba the Hutt was doing here in the middle of Cog Hive Seven—in person or by proxy—was a complete enigma, but it had nothing to do with his own mission.

Keeping his head down, Maul bolted across the hangar to the CLL binary load-lifter blundering heedlessly back and forth among the fray. Judging from the carbon scoring along its armored carapace, it hadn't been completely successful in avoiding stray blasterfire. Exposed wiring and circuitry dangled from the central processor, fuming with sparks and contrails of pale gray smoke.

"Droid!" he shouted.

The thing pivoted and regarded him dully through the yellow haze.

Maul cast his mind back to the last time he'd been here with Slipher, remembering what the banker had said. "IBC yellow card security variant 377055."

"Voice-verify?"

"Vesto Slipher," Maul told it. "There's a package arriving here. You're holding it for me. Where is it?"

The droid didn't budge. *"Voice-verify?"*

Rather than answering it, Maul swung himself up onto the back of the droid, casting a quick glance across the wires of the thing's processor. His experience hacking into systems was limited, but it was sufficient to identify the manual override on the load-lifter's primitive security system. Redirecting wires into the remaining circuits, he snapped them back into place.

The low, unwavering hum that followed seemed to take an eternity. Out of the corner of his eye, he saw Eogan racing toward him, dodging a hailstorm of shrapnel and landing next to the CLL unit. The boy glanced at the ongoing firefight, up at the droid, then finally back to Maul.

"What's it doing?"

"Giving me what I came for."

"We can't stay here." Eogan pointed across the hangar to where the gangway had finally bridged the gap. "They're already coming over." With a roar, armed prisoners started storming into the hangar as the last of the guards turned to flee. "They'll kill us!"

"They're indifferent to us," Maul snapped, not sure why he was bothering to answer. He hadn't expected the boy to survive this long, certainly not by following him across the hangar. Inmates were streaming past them on both sides, chasing the guards, heading for any still-functional turbolifts. Less than a meter away, he saw one of the corrections officers turn to glance back—just in time to catch a red bolt of energy directly in the throat, flinging him into the wall, a smoking corpse. The boy stared and made a noise like he was going to be sick.

"We have to get out of here!"

"Run if you want," Maul told him, "or stay and die. It makes no difference to me."

Eogan stared at him, opened his mouth, and shut it again. The thunderclap of the blasterfire had begun to recede. Maul turned back to the hangar, where the last of the prisoners were swarming their way toward the prison's upper levels.

"Mr. Slipher," the droid said, "here is your package."

Opening its housing, the thing reached inside itself and handed over a featureless black shipping crate.

Maul took it from him.

It was time to go.

62

READY APPLIANCE

"Warden, they've breached the hangar containment barriers."

Sadiki glanced up from the medbay support console to the guard whose name she couldn't recall at the moment. Stretching the mechanized ortho-prosthesis that the GH-7 had just finished stat-grafting onto her ankle, she winced with pain. The initial round of medication was already wearing off, but that was good—she could feel her mind clearing.

"How many are there?"

"Forty-two."

"Including Jabba's own bodyguards?"

The guard nodded. "All still heavily armed." The guard stole a furtive glance at her foot, then looked back up at her face. "We've sealed off the main level, closed the cellblocks, and put genpop into lockdown, but—"

"But what?"

"Well, that last reconfiguration sequence that you ordered . . ." The guard hesitated. "It opened up a whole wing of unfinished throughways, and some of those places aren't secure."

"No hatchways?"

"No hatchways, no airlocks. Some of the guys are saying they don't even have surveillance out that far."

"They're right," Sadiki said. Withholding the truth now wouldn't help any of them. "How many of our people are left?"

"I spoke to Captain Garvey five minutes ago. He's reporting heavy losses from the hangar—"

"How many?"

The guard swallowed. "Thirty-six guards that we know of, maybe more if they haven't had a chance to respond." His face became pale. "And we're running low on firepower."

"Where's my brother?"

"Nobody's seen him for several hours."

"Get a search party together." Sadiki rose to her feet. "Contact me as soon as you find him."

"Warden? Where are you going?"

"Get the escape pod ready," she said. "Tell him that I'll meet him there."

63

SOJOURN

"Your delivery has been received," 11-4D said.

Darth Plagueis turned to look back at the droid. "The replacement geological compressor?"

"That's right, Master."

Somewhere beneath the transpirator mask that covered his mouth, Plagueis permitted himself a smile. He and the droid were making their way through the cold stone research chambers where he'd spent whole months of his time, working with unwavering purpose among the various species that he kept caged up.

"Thank you, FourDee."

Plagueis focused his attention on the vat in front of him where the remains of the Bith Sith Lord, Darth Venamis, floated in a semitransparent bath of preserving fluid. Venamis's corpse was still animated and twitching spasmodically with the last dregs of life that Plagueis invested in it, only to snatch it away again. He had been working for almost twenty uninterrupted hours on this particular project with limited success, and the notification from his droid signified a welcome diversion.

"Did Slipher confirm its arrival?" he asked.

"Not exactly, Master," the droid replied.

"Why not?"

"Because it appears that Mr. Slipher is dead."

"Oh?" Plagueis pondered the news for a moment, before turning to face the droid. "Did Maul kill him?"

"No, Master. From what I was able to glean from surveillance uploads from the prison, Mr. Slipher was killed instantly when a CLL binary load-lifter decapitated him." The droid paused. "And then crushed him underfoot."

"A humble end for such a promising mind."

FourDee let out a small electronic gurgle. "I'm not sure that I take your meaning."

"It's unimportant," Plagueis replied, and scratched his chin in thought. "A droid, you say?"

"Yes. I'm sure it was accidental. It was the same droid, in fact, that you had tasked to deliver the package directly to the Zabrak."

"Ah." Plagueis beamed with pleasure. "So Maul has everything he needs to facilitate his mission, then. You're sure?"

"I've confirmed it through surveillance holofootage," 11-4D said, and then paused for a moment. "If I may inquire, what was the purpose of keeping this information from Master Sidious?"

"That is an excellent question, FourDee," Plagueis said. "I suppose you could say for the purpose of strengthening our relationship."

"Sir?"

"Between Lord Sidious and myself." Plagueis returned his attention to the Bith in the vat before him, although his thoughts were now far away from the resurrected Venamis. "The Zabrak's assassination mission inside the prison is of great interest to me. As you know, I have extended a great deal of latitude to Lord Sidious in the past."

Reaching out with the dark side, Plagueis watched in a distracted way as Venamis's lifeless face stirred in the viscous chemical soup, one eye opening and rolling up to gaze at him. Then he continued. "Especially now, as we approach the pivotal moment in our plans for Palpatine's impending chancellorship, I find his increasing tendency toward self-reliance to be disturbing. Of course the time will come when I will let him know that I was the one who provided Iram Radique with the fully functional geological compressor that he needed—and thus allowed Maul to complete his mission. But the moment of revelation is not yet ripe."

64

THE TOMBS

Alarms were going off everywhere.

Beaten unconscious and left for dead by Jabba's men in the alley adjacent to the *Purge*'s holding cells, Bissley Kloth finally opened his eyes and staggered to his feet, stirred by the shattering klaxons that were ringing out from somewhere in the ship's bridge. He drew a breath and summoned his resolve. His last memory had been of coming down to check on his thirty-nine passengers, who had fallen so ominously silent. Now he found himself staring down at the ragged semicircular hole that had been cut through the vessel's lower hull, leading to the interior of a completely unfamiliar and ornately designed space yacht.

Looking down into it, Kloth seized upon the full extent of what had happened with a dreadful clarity. The ship that had attached itself to the *Purge* was the same yacht that he'd spotted in the middle distance during their approach to Cog Hive Seven. They'd been boarded, which meant the passengers had come with the explicit purpose of facilitating a breakout of—

He swung around, pushing his way through the open hatch leading to the holding cells themselves.

They stood empty.

The prisoners were out.

No.

Kloth's burgeoning sense of dread only seemed to amplify the alarms in the *Purge*'s flight deck. Shaking off the last of his disorientation, he flung himself up the steps through the gangway and nearly tripped over the corpse of one of the crewmen sprawled in front of him in a pool of his own blood. The other guard lay facedown two meters farther up the corridor.

Kloth ran the rest of the way to the bridge and stopped in his tracks. Here the ship's interior reeked of blasterfire and overheated wires. In front of him, the *Purge*'s captain, Wyatt Styrene, sat harnessed into the swivel seat in front of the ship's command suite, his head bowed in apparent contemplation of their fate.

"Captain," Kloth said, grabbing Styrene's shoulder, and Styrene's head tilted back to reveal his slashed throat. It was only the harness itself that had kept him from tumbling out of his seat.

Kloth's reflexes took over. Hardly pausing to consider what he was doing, he unbuckled Styrene's body and dragged it away from the *Purge*'s controls. He seated himself in the pilot's chair and glanced at the screens in front of him, gazing at the prison's cargo bay, to which the prison barge was still attached.

What he saw on the monitors made his heart vault up into his throat. Although he could make out very little from this angle, it appeared as though the entire hangar was littered with dead prison guards, dozens of them. In the midst of it, somewhere in the foreground, a shape—Kloth thought it was a Hutt—sat atop a repulsor platform, gesturing at two Gamorreans as they gathered up weapons from the floor.

What was going on?

There was a sudden concussion from below, like an echo of what had happened earlier. Something else hit the *Purge*, slamming into it hard enough to shake it from its mooring, and in an instant, all the barge's controls and monitors went dead, plunging Kloth into blackness.

Reaching forward, his hands scrambled blindly for the controls, struggling to reactivate them, but it was pointless.

The *Purge* creaked around him. From down below the barge's hull came the brittle snapping noises of steel valves being ripped away, followed by an enormous whooshing pop as the vacuum-sealed suction-coupling mechanism broke completely open. Kloth's thoughts flashed to the space yacht that had affixed itself to their hull like a parasite, the pirates who had cut their way into the hold.

Then he knew.

Dropping to his hands and knees in the darkness, he fumbled his way out of the bridge and down toward the concourse below, moving more quickly now, going purely by memory and sense of touch. By the time he'd reached the corpses of the guards, he sensed that he was very close indeed.

Kloth stopped, adrenaline flooding through his body, trying to catch his breath. Slowly he rose to his feet. Sickly green auxiliary lights illuminated the ragged hole in the *Purge*'s lower level, but when Kloth looked down through the hole, he no longer saw the lavishly appointed interior of the space yacht.

It simply wasn't there anymore.

Something, or someone, had pried it away, leaving only the ragged hole.

But the hole wasn't empty.

Kloth stepped back, feeling a low, atavistic horror crawling its way from his belly up into the pit of his throat.

Something was coming up through the hole, dragging itself toward him, a figure like nothing he'd seen before, even among the inmates and wildly varying galactic scum he'd transported from every system imaginable.

Kloth stared at it for a moment, held rapt by a power he could neither identify nor resist. The thing's head was covered with a skull, with long, sharpened horns protruding out from either side. The hollow sockets where its eyes should have been shone with a primordial blue light.

That's madness, the color of madness—

Whether this was a mask or actually its face, Kloth had no intention of sticking around to find out, particularly as it became clear that the thing hadn't come alone.

The hole was full of floating blue eyes.

They were making their way up into the *Purge,* and now Kloth saw that he had nowhere to go—and that, in all the time he'd had since waking up on the floor outside the containment cells, he'd failed to secure a weapon for himself, and now it was too late.

The things moved toward him like an army of the dead, with terrible determination and strength. Kloth took a step back and stumbled over the body of a guard, failing to catch himself before toppling backward against something sharp and angular. When he looked up again, the skull-faced things had surrounded him.

"Where is he?" a female voice asked.

Kloth looked up at her. The woman in front of him had a shock of pure white hair that seemed to bristle straight upward from her forehead, which only accentuated the expression of dark intensity etched deeply across her face. She had weird, chemical-yellow eyes, the color of a dying, toxic sun. Under other circumstances, Kloth thought he might have found her striking, even beautiful, although right now he was sure—absolutely positive, in fact—that she could have murdered him without a qualm.

"Who?"

"The one I've come to meet."

"I don't . . . I don't know who that is," Kloth managed. "I don't know who *you* are." Staring at her, he fought a wild, irrational impulse to try to explain how all of this must have been some terrible mistake, and how this woman and her skull-faced army must have been in the wrong place entirely. "This is just a prison barge, I'm only the navigator, I don't know—"

Crack! The slap across his face knocked him back to reality.

"I am Komari Vosa," the female said, "and this is the Bando Gora. We've come to acquire a weapon."

65

AS BELOW, SO ABOVE

"Which way is it?" Eogan asked.

Maul didn't answer. For the past five minutes they'd been heading down a concourse that had looked familiar, but the reconfiguration had changed everything. For all he knew, it wasn't over, and the prison was going to continue rearranging itself until it ripped itself to pieces.

Maybe that's the whole idea.

He threw back his head and made a sharp cawing sound, a sound that he'd now heard frequently enough to be able to mimic with some accuracy.

"What are you—"

Maul held up his hand for silence, cocked his head, and listened. The sound came back to him, an imperfect echo of the shrill cry.

"Duck your head."

"What?" Eogan frowned. "Why—"

A sudden flurry of activity came bursting down the corridor. Maul crouched down as a great dark cloud of clawbirds swept through the length of the corridor in an almost solid wave, cawing and shrieking as they came.

He tucked the package under his arm and ran after the birds with the boy at his heels. The flock flew even faster as a collective unit, spiraling and diving downward through the newly reconfigured passageways of the lowermost levels, swirling like smoke through the chambers of some great mechanical nautilus.

Maul could see where they were going.

It was coming now, very near.

He saw the door ahead of him. Watched the birds funneling down through it.

Maul leapt through, the boy just behind him.

They landed back in a familiar place: the weapons shop where he'd stood not long before. Coyle was still there, his rodent nose twitching anxiously. The blaster that he'd used to kill Dakarai Blirr was still gripped tightly in his hands.

"Jagannath," the Chadra-Fan said, eyeing the package under Maul's arm. "We were beginning to worry you hadn't been successful in your quest, weren't we?" He glanced back over his shoulder, where a tall figure stood behind the counter.

The tall man stepped into the light.

"The outcome was never in doubt," he said, and gazed at Maul. "Greetings, Jagannath. I'm Iram Radique."

66

HUSH

In the end, Sadiki had no choice.

Yes, the escape pod was prepped and waiting for her. FourDee was already there, and perhaps Dakarai, too, if they'd found him. Communications were failing fast. Whole relay sections were going down. Radio transmissions had already been reduced to static.

As much as she needed to get out of here, Sadiki knew that she had to go back to her office one last time. There was a final detail that needed taking care of.

She stepped through the hatchway and paused long enough to look across the office. Even now, in the midst of everything that was happening, Sadiki felt a creator's wistful appreciation for the prison: the project that she and her brother had designed together, the algorithm into which Dakarai had breathed life, and the sheer elegance of the plan itself. It had been almost perfect. Only the persistent rumors of the existence of Iram Radique—that incorporeal galactic bogeyman whose base of operations was allegedly somewhere inside the prison—had marred the otherwise perfect machine of money and violence that was the Hive.

Not that it mattered now. The experiment had served its purpose. Soon everyone inside would be dead. Then she would head for the escape pod to depart with Dakarai, leaving Cog Hive Seven to tear itself to pieces. There would be other opportunities, other worlds.

Tapping in the command for inmate population control, Sadiki watched as a long list of digits scrolled across the screen in numeric order, each one representing an active prisoner here. There were a little over four hundred of them currently—the scum and filth of the galaxy, none of which she ever wanted to run into again.

She selected the entire list and clicked a single command: *Terminate.*

One by one, numbers began to disappear off the top of the list.

For a moment she sat there, watching them vanish. It would require some time to complete, she realized—she didn't want to overload the system at this critical juncture, and she would rather be sure that every single inmate was dead before she ventured down below again. Besides, the process wouldn't take too long. Perhaps only thirty minutes or so, until it reached the highest numbers.

She was rising to leave the datacenter when something inside the wall moved.

Stepping back, pushing her chair out of the way, Sadiki gazed up uncertainly at the wall in front of her, above the monitor displays. At this point her sensibilities were so keenly attuned to the screens and keyboards and numbers that the unexpected presence of something living, rustling, so close to her caused the small hairs on the back of her neck to prickle.

Her thoughts returned to the prison's most recent reconfiguration, initiated in her desperate last-ditch bid for self-preservation. It had been a drastic move, and if she had planned on spending any more time aboard Cog Hive Seven, it would have been catastrophic. Instead, she simply didn't care. Except—

Except that it had resulted in some unwelcome alterations in the prison's infrastructure. Subtle, nagging changes. For example, staring at the wall in front of her, Sadiki noticed a slight gap, perhaps two or three centimeters wide, where the pressure-treated plates hadn't joined together properly. It was a small thing, but—

Something was *moving* inside the gap.

Retreating swiftly from it, Sadiki walked across the chamber and reached into the wall cabinet on the opposite side, pulling out the KYD-21 blaster pistol that she'd stashed there and had never actually planned on using. This particular model, fabricated in hadrium alloy with a guardless trigger, was one of her personal favorites. It had heavy-duty stopping power despite its size, and its cool ridged handgrip felt good in her grasp.

Sadiki pointed it at the gap between the walls.

"Who's there?" she said aloud, suddenly disliking the sound of her own voice. The quivering of her diaphragm gave it a kind of quailing tremor that she'd always found so repellent in others.

A wild possibility flicked through her mind, and she took a step closer to the gap between the wall plates.

"Dakarai?" she said loudly. "Is that you?" Extending her arm, she tightened her finger on the trigger. "Jagannath? Have you found your way back up? You'll regret it, I guarantee that."

She listened but heard nothing. Closer now, cocking her head slightly, Sadiki leaned in toward the narrow opening and held her breath.

She waited.

All at once something huge and white exploded from the wall, unfathomably large and faster than she could see, lashing outward toward her face, striking straight for her eyes. It was so big that Sadiki's first impression was that the wall itself had somehow burst to life in front of her.

Then her vision disappeared in a liquid swarm of reddish black, and a jagged corkscrew of pain went curving down to the very base of her skull, twisting down her spine to encompass her entire body.

Sadiki screamed in pain and fell to her knees, then scrambled backward across the floor. Her finger squeezed the trigger, firing off shots at random, and behind the cloak of blindness, she heard metal screeching and twisting around her, as if something bigger than she'd ever seen was dragging itself out of the wall.

Then she knew what it was.

The Wolf Worm.

Clutching the blaster in her right hand, she wiped her left wrist across her eyes in an attempt to clear her vision, but she still couldn't see. If anything, the blindness had become more pervasive, overtaking whatever remained of her vision and stranding her in total blackness.

Backing her way into the far corner, extending the blaster outward in her trembling grasp, she held her breath and listened for the thing's approach, tracking its advance purely by sense of sound. She *could* hear it, the massive weight of the thing, the sticky squelching of its advance toward her across the floor of the datacenter.

Sadiki fired again, three times in quick succession, and tried to remember how many rounds she'd already squeezed off. The KYD held seventy-five shots, so there was no immediate threat of running out of ammo . . . but who knew how long this would be her only weapon?

Somewhere in the enervated darkness, the thing in front of her moved again. For an instant Sadiki almost considered making a blind run for the hatchway on the opposite side of the room—she thought she could find it from memory, but if she was wrong . . .

She listened, visualizing it.

And then all sound disappeared.

She squeezed the blaster's trigger again, felt it recoil slightly, but heard nothing. Her entire universe became one of pin-drop silence. It was as if she'd gone deaf as well as blind, all her most vital sensory organs abandoning her at the moment she needed them most.

And then Sadiki realized what was happening.

Somehow the sealed datacenter had put itself into silent mode.

"No!" she cried into the void, but the soundproof systems devoured her voice, swallowing it whole, along with every other sonic disturbance. She had no sense of where the thing was now, how close or far away, whether it was hovering just centimeters from her face, its maw open and ready to latch onto her.

Panic seized her, and she started firing randomly into the great expanse of darkness, swinging the weapon back and forth, strafing the space around her as if she could somehow shoot a hole through it, penetrating the thick layer of isolation that had left her utterly exposed here.

At last the blaster stopped recoiling, and she realized it was empty.

"No," Sadiki croaked again, but heard nothing. "No."

This wasn't happening. Couldn't be. Not now, after she'd come so far and worked so hard to build her empire. From the beginning, she'd taken every precaution, calculated every risk, considered every angle. For all of it to end up here, with her crouched in some remote corner, blind, deaf, and mute . . .

Tears formed in her sightless eyes, and her body started trembling, the imperfect balance of sanity tipping away from her in increments. Knees drawn up against her chest, arms extended, she gripped the useless weapon in both hands, as though if she held on to it tightly enough, it might yet save her.

She was still sitting like that when it fell upon her.

67

THE MAN COMES AROUND

Maul looked at Radique for a moment in silence. After searching for him for so long, the sight of him standing less than two meters away brought with it a distinct tremor of unreality, as if this too might be little more than a dream.

Radique was a tall near-human with blue skin, gleaming black hair, and glowing red eyes. He was dressed in black robes, with black gloves and boots fashioned from the same thick, well-polished reptile skin. His face was lean and cold, as if carved from a solid block of Vardium steel. Crimson eyes gazed back at Maul, and his lips twisted with a kind of quiet arrogance that spoke of a thousand enemies vanquished, a thousand attempts on his life survived.

The clawbirds had settled around behind him, gathered at his feet.

"I see you found my pets," Radique said. "Or they found you."

"You knew they would," Maul said. "You sent them for me."

"Perhaps I did."

"We have to go," Maul said. "The Bando Gora is already among us."

"The Gora." Radique's face tightened with the briefest flicker of pain. "You've made a grave mistake bringing those vermin here." He glanced at Eogan. "The boy's father paid for it with his life. Now it seems that your life too shall be forfeit because of them."

Maul didn't move.

"You don't believe me? Or you don't believe in the power that I wield?"

"Neither." Maul stepped forward. "I've simply been given no choice in the matter, and neither have you." He cast his gaze across the weapons shop. Of the assembly line of eyeless inmates that had been laboring over the different gun parts and components the last time he'd been here, fewer than half remained. The ones that were left sat rigid in front of partially assembled weapons, gripping the table with white knuckles. Were Radique's people deserting him, fleeing during these final moments? Or was there some deeper mutiny taking place?

"You're mistaken," Radique said.

Maul looked back at those red eyes. For a long moment neither of them spoke. Then all at once the entire prison gave a violent, galvanic shudder, hard enough to shift the racks and rows of crates strapped down against the back wall. Radique never lifted his gaze from Maul.

"It's all coming to an end," Maul said. "If we don't act now, we'll all die here."

"We'll die regardless." Radique pressed his finger into Maul's chest. "You still carry an explosive in your heart, Jagannath, don't forget. And your time is running out."

He nodded down to the floor beneath the workspace, and Maul looked down to see where the other prisoners had gone. They lay dead under the table, their eyeless sockets upraised into whatever version of oblivion had overtaken them.

"What happened?"

"If I had to speculate," Radique said, "I believe that Warden Sadiki has launched the Omega Initiative. It's a fail-safe mechanism designed to systematically trigger the electrostatic charges in the hearts of all the inmates here."

"Including you?"

"Well." Radique's smile was razor thin. "I've got what you might call a special dispensation."

"Wait," Eogan said. "So you mean—" He glanced at Maul, then back at Radique, his voice going higher in pitch. "How much time do we have?"

"That depends on your number. Lower ones go first. But you'll get your turn, I'm sure."

"Then we have no time to waste," Maul said. "Somewhere in your shop you've got a proscribed nuclear device. You're going to help me deliver it into the hands of the Bando Gora. That's all."

The room shook again, harder. On the floor, the piles of the eyeless dead shifted and twitched together like a deputation of spastics.

"Why would I defy a lifelong oath never to do business with a cult of criminal thugs who tried to kill me?" Radique asked.

Without answering, Maul pushed past him toward the table, where a half-packed crate of Radique's synthetic lightsabers sat open, forgotten by the inmate who'd been working on it. He reached in and took one of them out, popped open the hilt, and withdrew the crystal.

"Boy," he said, "open the package."

Eogan blinked and then dropped to his knees next to the parcel that they'd brought up from the loading bay. Peeling back the outer shell, he withdrew an oblong console, laying it out on the floor. The compressor unit itself was sleek and nearly featureless, with the exception of a small transparent dome on top.

"You recognize the new geological compressor," Maul said. "You were expecting its arrival—you sent Slipher to go retrieve it." Without waiting for Radique's response, he lifted the lid and dropped the synth-crystal inside.

He closed his eyes, placing both hands on the compressor, letting the power of the dark side move through him as the console warmed beneath his palms. He could feel the crystal changing inside it, its very atoms shifting, the lattice tightening and binding together into new molecules, becoming something utterly different beneath the applied pressure of the Force.

Opening the compressor, he removed the crystal and held it up. It looked different now—darker, heavier, its facets gleaming with a deeper shade of red.

Maul slipped it back into the lightsaber, reassembled the components, and held the weapon up, flicking the switch.

The beam sprang to life in his hand, filling the shop with the familiar oscillating hum that he would've recognized in his sleep. The blade was solid, straight, and true. Maul could feel the power of the thing vibrating through the bones of his forearm, a natural extension of his own innate strength.

Extending his arm to its full length, he waited while Radique examined it. The arms dealer's bluish face had changed color in the light of the beam.

"Remarkable," he whispered.

"I can show you how it's done," Maul said. "But first I need the nuclear device delivered. And I need the explosives disarmed inside my chest—the droid from medbay can do that."

"What makes you think—"

"There's no time to argue. Do we have a deal or not?"

Radique looked at him. The room gave another jerk, and Maul saw that several more of the workers had dropped to the floor on top of the bodies that were already there.

He held out his hand.

Switching off the lightsaber, Maul placed it in the other's waiting palm.

"The nuclear device is in that crate," Radique said, giving a side nod to the large box strapped to the wall in the far corner of the shop. He hadn't taken his red-eyed gaze from the lightsaber in his hand. "Over there. At the end."

"Come, boy." Maul nodded at the crate. "We don't have much time."

"Wait, what about the electrostatic charges in our hearts?" Eogan asked.

"We'll detour past the medbay," Maul said, keeping his eyes fixed on the red-eyed man. "Mr. Radique will have the droid ready for us."

"How do we know—"

"It's in his best interest. If I'm dead, I won't be able to show him what he needs to know about the lightsabers."

Without waiting for acknowledgment from Radique, Maul crossed over to the crate and unstrapped it. It was warm to the touch, and humming slightly from within.

"Now, boy."

Reluctantly Eogan picked up his end and they lifted, carrying it out of the shop. One of Radique's clawbirds flew in front of them, and they followed it down the concourse toward the upper levels of the prison.

Not long afterward, they started to come across the bodies.

68

MALEFACTORS

"Jabba," Vosa said, staring into the hologram. "Why am I not surprised to find you in the middle of this?"

The holovid of the Hutt perched above her, glaring down at her through baleful eyes. His henchmen—the remaining Gamorreans who hadn't followed the newly released prisoners on a looting spree through Cog Hive Seven—aimed their blasters at the Bando Gora standing behind her.

"Komari Vosa," the crime lord snarled in Huttese, his no-longer-amused gaze traveling across the group of skull-masked Gora soldiers. "What are you and your brain-dead army of minions doing here?"

"We were summoned here." Vosa gestured across the hangar. "I trust you'll let us pass?"

Jabba cursed, uttering a phlegmy oath in Huttese. "You trust wrong, insect! I will crush you like the foul infection that you are!"

"You'll try." Reaching down, Vosa withdrew the twin curved-hilt lightsabers that she wore at her hips, activating both blades simultaneously, filling the air around her with an electrifying vibrational hiss.

The effect—even on Jabba himself—was immediate and impressive. The holo flickered, and when it returned, he gestured to the Gamorreans flanking him, grunting out an order of execution. *"Dugway! Kee-puna!"*

The Gamorreans opened fire from either side, but Vosa moved faster than they could shoot, faster even than the naked eye could see. Adapting the Form One style of Soresu, she whirled her lightsabers in front of her, their blades absorbing and deflecting the blasts easily from all sides.

The outcome was never truly in doubt. Darting forward, she slashed the blaster directly from the hand of the nearest thug, piston-kicked him backward, and spun to bisect the Trandoshan behind her neatly at the waist. Throughout it all, the expression on her face—focused yet unhurried, almost relaxed—revealed virtually nothing about what was happening inside her mind, nor about the true purpose of her visit here.

Heads down, Bando Gora soldiers charged forward to overtake Jabba's entourage, their staffs blazing with greenish balls of fire that arced and exploded in the faces of the startled Gamorreans. Within seconds, they'd decimated the Hutt's hired muscle, leaving their bodies splayed limp on the floor of the hangar.

"Now," Vosa said, deactivating the lightsabers as she made her way toward the holovid, "since we've dispatched with the unpleasantries, I take it you'll allow me to complete my work here?"

"You fight well for a Jedi whore," Jabba told her, arms upraised in a gesture of mock surrender. "I see that you've lost none of your skills."

"*Jedi?*" Vosa frowned, a single wrinkle creasing her forehead, as if the word itself triggered its own private dose of pain. "That word is blasphemy to me."

"Is it?" Jabba chuckled, probing more deeply. "And what of your beloved Master Dooku? Surely as his former Padawan, there must be a lingering warmth in your heart for him still, after all that he did for you?"

"Dooku." Vosa's lips tightened, and all the easy confidence that she'd displayed just seconds earlier began to ebb away. The tightness that replaced it made her face appear angular, and her yellow eyes blazed. "You dare not speak that obscenity before me now or ever."

"Ah." Emboldened by her response, Jabba pushed on. "And yet I wonder. Have you considered that he may yet harbor feelings for you? That in time, he could possibly come and join you to lead your army of—"

"*Enough!*" The word burst from Vosa's lips, and in a fusillade of inarticulate pain and rage, she lunged forward, swinging both lightsabers outward at the holovid, the blades sweeping through his image.

The Hutt chuckled with appreciation. "You *do* contain great depths, Komari Vosa. Perhaps you would consider an alliance?"

"The Bando Gora allies with no one."

"You've associated with Gardulla Besadii in the past. Help me get rid of her, and perhaps I'll let you leave this prison alive."

Vosa shook her head. "Never."

"Foolish to the last." The Hutt nodded, unperturbed. "Make no mistake, scum. I will exterminate you in due time. Just not *this* time."

"Or ever."

"We'll see." Waving one hand at the berthing dock from which Vosa and her army had emerged, Jabba's holovid image settled back on the repulsor platform with a faint smirk. It was the indulgent expression of a singularly untrustworthy uncle whose favor was merely an indication of profound treachery to come. "My business here is through. Be on your way."

But Vosa was already gone, storming across the hangar, followed by her army, toward what awaited them on the upper levels. She moved quickly, as if there were something else pursuing her, something that she alone could see.

And so it was.

Ensconced in her private darkness, Vosa had always moved with a speed and purpose unmitigated by the weakness of human emotion. Back in the hangar, the holovid image of the Hutt had touched upon it briefly but agonizingly, with his flagrant evocation of the Order and the one whose name still caused her unspeakable pain.

Vosa hated herself for the way she'd responded. Her first and most enduring instinct—to bury that pain, sinking it so deeply into her unconscious mind that it could no longer touch her—had not worked as it should.

It wasn't supposed to hurt like this anymore.

Making her way up through the empty corridors of Cog Hive Seven, she felt cracks forming in her resolve.

Press on.

Yes. That was all that mattered. The Order was dead to her now, a crumbling artifact of her distant past. As was her former Master, her sworn enemy, whom she now thought of only as an abomination before everything that mattered . . . although the memory of his face and their times together still held powerful sway over her. When she thought of him, Vosa felt something moving inside her chest, a gravitational shift that took hold of her most basic emotions. Curse the Hutt for mentioning him, dredging those thoughts up now.

But it was too late to stop. With an uncharacteristic twinge of masochism, Vosa allowed herself to think on the name consciously, touching on it like the tip of the tongue to an infected tooth, just once—*Dooku*—and pushed it aside.

Glancing back at the captain who'd followed her with unfailing loyalty and the skull-masked fighters gathered behind her, Vosa reassured herself that this was right. She had a new alliance, new blood oaths, as leader of an unstoppable army of fighters who would willingly lay down their lives for her.

It was enough.

69

LOW NUMBERS

Getting the crate across the open area outside the mess hall took longer than Maul had anticipated.

They had to step over all the bodies.

The gallery was littered with them. Everywhere they looked, inmates of the Hive were sinking to the floor, faces gone slack and lifeless, landing unceremoniously on top of the dead prisoners who'd already succumbed to the electrostatic charges. The smell of death had begun to fill this place as the prison transformed itself into a vast, floating crypt. The clawbird that was leading them stopped occasionally to land on one of the bodies and pluck out an eye.

It wasn't entirely silent. Off in the distance, from the long corridors leading to the cells, Maul heard occasional shrieks and cries for help—the pleas of those who hadn't yet died, perhaps, or the primitive outcry of the new inmates that Jabba had released from the incoming barge, the ones without bombs inside their hearts. At one point, a spate of blasterfire rang out and ceased abruptly, followed by a wild, shrieking symphony of lunatic laughter.

Madness had triumphed in the final hours of Cog Hive Seven. Twenty meters in front of them, a group of prisoners—Maul realized that they were the last surviving members of the Bone Kings and Gravity Massive, brought together in the penultimate moments of their lives—came scurrying out of the mess hall carrying a tremendous steaming vat of stolen food. They walked past Maul and Eogan without so much as a sidelong glance. Nobody stopped them. The last remaining guards seemed to have gone into hiding.

Unless those were the screams Maul kept hearing. He wondered if the newly arrived inmates were holding the guards somewhere and torturing them slowly.

Or perhaps they'd met the worm.

As they approached the far side of the gallery, Eogan kept glancing down, trying to read the numbers on their uniforms, as if it could give him an idea of how far along the process was. Even Maul—despite his commitment to the task at hand—found himself wondering how much longer they had. There were to be no more matches to save him now.

"The medbay is just through here," he said. "It's not too late. The surgical droid can—"

Maul stopped walking—not out of uncertainty, but simply to stretch out with his feelings, to see if he could ascertain where the Bando Gora was at this precise moment. Somewhere in the outer reaches of his sensibilities, a pang of unease stung him, a twinge that he associated most closely with those moments at the top of the LiMerge Building, when he'd stared at the window of the Jedi Temple in the distance.

Vosa is here. Very close now.

He would finish his task for his Master, yes. But the possibility that he might drop dead from something as maddeningly trivial as an electrostatic discharge in his hearts before he could confront the filthy ex-Jedi who'd come here to face him was more than even Maul himself could bear.

In the end, that was what decided it.

"The medbay, then," he said with a nod, ignoring the expression of relief that flashed across the boy's face as he said it. "Quickly."

70

THE KILLING MOON

Wait.

Vosa held up her fist without glancing back at the Bando Gora warriors who stood behind her, and they came to a halt.

They'd made their way up from the hangar toward the prison's main holding level, encountering almost no resistance from the remaining residents of this place. Not that she'd expected any. These inmates seemed to be dying faster and faster around them—dropping to their knees without so much as a whimper. The corpses, the smell of them, reminded her of Bogden, the burial moon where so much had changed for her.

Of the handful of armed maniacs they'd confronted in the prison's utility corridors, only one or two had presented the slightest challenge to her soldiers. Using their staffs, the Gora had gutted them and ripped them to shreds, accomplishing Vosa's bidding with the mindless, unwavering obedience to which she herself had enslaved them. It had happened quickly: a streaking storm of violence, then stillness.

Watching them go about their dark and bloody work brought her no sense of pride, although it did appease some dark and atavistic hunger within her—a need to establish dominance over the situation and impose her will upon it. For her, stability and power would always be a matter of conquest, the relentless commitment to absolute mastery. After what had happened with the Jedi and her former Master, she would never allow herself to feel out of control again. It would be a form of suicide.

Now she stood motionless, her mind reaching out into the rippling currents of the Force until she became aware of its most pronounced disturbance.

Maul was here.

Closer than she'd hoped.

And after she had found him and taken possession of the weapon that she'd been summoned here to acquire, she would kill him.

Gladly.

This way, she instructed them, giving the order silently, a telekinetic command that sent them down a corridor. Her heart was beating faster now, driving her forward. And it might have been that sense of reckless urgency that allowed her to walk into what happened next.

Rounding the corner, she saw it—the thing to which her Force sensibilities had somehow been blinded.

On either side, her warriors froze in their tracks.

The creature in front of them was a colossal, gelid horror, its engorged presence filling the entire concourse in front of them. Vosa realized that it was some kind of roiling white worm, five meters high and perhaps three times as long, its hooked, leech-like mouth currently filled with the still-squirming bodies of the inmates it had just devoured.

The thing rounded on them, raising its hideous blind head with a sudden jerk that caused the severed lower half of the torso it had been eating to fall back out on the floor. When it lunged forward, mouthparts peeling back, the Gora attacked it with their staffs, strafing it with balls of energy that exploded off the worm's slick and pulsating skin without stopping it.

It recoiled, flattening itself against the floor, then shot forward again with speed that defied its great, dripping bulk. Before Vosa could command her soldiers to step back, the worm opened its mouth, sucking two of the warriors into its maw.

Vosa activated her lightsabers and dove at it. Slashing both blades across the thing's flesh, she carved deep lacerations into its underside. Pale yellow fluid came trickling out, sticky and viscous, and with it, Vosa realized that she could hear the voice—or voices—of the worm inside her head, a tangled litany of threats and pleas for mercy.

Jedi—Jedi is here—

Kill us, Jedi—

Set us free—

—rip your lungs from your chest—

—tear the scream from your lips—

Devour you whole—

Vosa sprang at it again, her blades coming to life in a blinding, gyroscopic storm of Jar'Kai technique that had served her so well in the past. Spinning both blades in the rising-whirlwind maneuver, she launched a frontal attack on the worm's underbelly. Its innards spilled out, layers of pulsating fat and vessel sluicing outward to fill the open corridor around her ankles. Throughout it all, Vosa didn't yield or even slow her attack; rather, she gave herself over to it completely, allowing the killing rage to transport her into a state of weightless abandon.

Badly wounded, the thing reared back again, as if what she'd done had introduced it to pain that it had never known before. It jerked sideways and went slithering quickly backward through an open hole in the wall behind it.

For a moment Vosa stood with both lightsabers still activated and her army behind her, all of them waiting for what might happen next. Had the thing run off somewhere to die? In that instant she allowed herself to think that the battle—this part of it, at least—might be over.

Then the ceiling moved above her.

Her soldiers, as one, lifted their heads and looked up.

When the ceiling blasted open, the worm came spilling down on top of them with a deafening crash, flattening the warriors in an avalanche of its flesh. At once Vosa knew she'd underestimated the thing's cunning, and now she understood what those tangled voices in her head had represented—the conflagration of inmate sensibilities, survival skills, and pure, vicious instinct that comprised its hive mind. The last of the Bando Gora warriors edged back, clutching their staffs, momentarily shaken and awaiting new orders.

Vosa waited, facing off against the thing herself. The worm lifted its head, its mandibles clicking and snapping audibly with a spastic, giddy eagerness. From this distance, Vosa could see that the cuts she'd inflicted on it had already begun to crust over and heal.

Then it opened its mouth, unhinging its jaws to the widest possible extent.

The result was hideous. In that moment, the thing actually seemed to become *all* mouth, until the entire front of its head was nothing more than an enormous, gaping black hole that—for an instant—loomed as wide as the corridor itself.

This time even the Bando Gora were not fast enough.

Sucking in, the worm inhaled them all in a great, slurping vacuum, clearing the space around Vosa in the space of a heartbeat.

Yet she stood her ground, lightsabers ready, reaching out to the thing, or whatever element of sentience it might have possessed.

"What are you?" she asked aloud, startled by the sound of her own voice, and although she'd hardly expected an answer, one was forthcoming, put forth in an outburst of varying tones and inflections.

We are—

—that which—

—you fear—

—most—

Vosa drew in a breath. A terrible coldness spread through her like nothing she'd felt since her early days on Bogden, when the Gora torturers had worked day and night to break her spirit, crush her body, and drive her to the brink of insanity, and ultimately beyond, into what she'd become now. The moment was excruciating. It was like looking in a mirror and seeing her two selves: who she had once been under Dooku and the Jedi Council, and what she'd become, her own pitiless face reflected back at her in the soulless, grasping mandibles of this blind and unstoppable predator.

We are you.

"No," she managed, but it was too late.

It came at her again in one quick lunge, and Vosa reacted without thought, using an instinctive burst of Force push to drive herself backward up the corridor, opening up a twenty-meter gap between herself and the thing. It was enough time and space to allow her to hit the floor in a dead run and not look back.

Looking back on those vertiginous moments, when time itself had become a blur and conscious thought was utterly lost to her, Vosa remembered little. She had never fled from another opponent like that before, which was perhaps why it felt so utterly disorienting.

It wasn't so much the worm that she was trying to outrun, but what the thing had promised her within itself—a final resting place where her identity would descend into the murk of murderers, crime lords, tyrants, and anonymous scum whose agonies would ultimately become as familiar to her as her own. In the end, she would be just another voice crying out from inside the great, swollen tube of the thing's being.

At last her steps slowed down and she regained control over herself.

Resolve came quickly. No one would ever be allowed to know what had happened here. There was no reason to speak of it.

Coming here had been a mistake.

She was preparing to leave, to find her way back down to the ship, when she heard screams coming from up the corridor—and, in the silence that followed, the voice of the one she'd been sent to meet.

Maul.

71

THE SUM OF ITS PARTS

The medical droid was nowhere to be found.

"Wait," Eogan was saying. He'd put down his end of the crate and was now pacing quickly through the medbay, searching for the GH-7, as if the droid might have gone into hiding somewhere. "You said that it could deactivate the charges. Where did it go?"

Maul said nothing. He'd assumed that Radique would meet them up here to use whatever inside influence he had to disarm the explosives in his chest—he knew from Radique's expression that he wanted Maul's insight on the lightsabers. Which meant the arms dealer needed to keep him alive, at least long enough to—

KRRRAACCK!

The walls shook hard enough that Maul had to steady himself against the hatchway. By now the entire prison was rocking steadily around them, the tremors coming with such violence and frequency that they never really seemed to stop. Gaps were opening in the joinery overhead, where exposed wires spat and fumed with sparks.

"Jagannath . . ."

Maul turned and looked over to where the boy had already stopped in his tracks, staring down at the scorched pile of processors and components scattered haphazardly across the floor. What was left looked so little like a droid that they'd stepped right over it before. The GH-7's head and manipulator arms had been blasted off completely, and the rest of its circuitry seemed to have caught fire and melted into slag.

"What happened to it?" Eogan asked, his tone splintering with near-panic. "We have to fix it!"

"That's impossible," the low voice said behind them.

Maul and Eogan turned to look at the hatchway through which they'd entered. Radique was standing there, blue skin gleaming, staring at them coldly. Maul watched as Radique spread his arms wide, allowing his clawbirds to land on him, a dozen or more perched from shoulder to wrist on either side. The feathered black bodies and piercing soulless eyes were a visual echo of his own. They made low, restless, hungry sounds.

"What happened to the surgical droid?" Eogan asked him.

"Blasted to pieces by hostile inmates would be my guess," Radique said. "Not that it matters now. You're Inmate 10009, aren't you?" Raising his face back up to meet Eogan's desperate expression, Radique shook his head. "I think your number is up."

"No!" the boy yelled, and swung out his fist at the weapons dealer, but the punch was wild, and Radique saw it coming with plenty of time to duck. The clawbirds on his arms took immediate flight, cawing and shrieking as they swept down on Eogan, going for his eyes. The boy swung his arms furiously, trying to ward them off, but there were too many of them. Over his shoulder Maul could hear the hungry, greedy noises they made as they pecked at the boy's face and hands. All around them the medbay shook harder, as if stirred to life by the attack.

Maul's arm shot out, grabbing Radique by his black tunic and jerking him close. "Call them off."

Then he felt it—the lightsaber activating in Radique's hand. Radique raised it up in front of him and swung it at Maul. Maul ducked, the blade humming over his head.

"One final match," Radique said, stepping forward. "I think Warden Blirr would have approved, don't you?" He paused to admire the blade in his hands. "You do amazing work, Jagannath, you know that? You must tell me your secret."

"Come closer," Maul said, "and I will."

Radique's lips quirked into a slight smile. "You'd like that, wouldn't you?"

Maul just looked at him, into the red eyes, measuring the distance between them.

"When it comes to weapons," Radique continued, "I am a proud man. But . . ." He turned the blade from right to left, inspecting it more closely from all angles. "I have no problem acknowledging the work of a fellow master's hand when I see it. Surely it's not just a matter of the geological compressor. So tell me, Jagannath. How is that you knew exactly what my synth-crystals required in order to become fully functional?"

Maul moved all at once. Gripping the bank of diagnostic equipment behind him, he leaned back and swung his right foot up, driving it hard into Radique's chest.

With a sudden grunt, Radique flew backward, crashing into the far wall, the lightsaber spinning out of his hand. Maul caught it in the air and swung it around just as the clawbirds came at him from all sides, dive-bombing his face and throat, their talons and beaks assaulting him.

He whirled, the red blade becoming a blur, cutting the birds down around him as they screamed and cawed and swooped. Within seconds the air was full of black feathers drifting downward. Maul kicked their bodies aside and brought the tip of the blade down to where Radique was sprawled on the floor, head to the side, exposing the throbbing vein in his neck.

"Jagannath," another voice managed, and from somewhere behind him, Maul heard a soft thud.

Keeping his blade close to Radique's throat, Maul glanced around where Eogan had fallen. The boy's once-smooth face was a crosshatched nightmare of cuts and scratches from the birds' attack, but that wasn't what had killed him. He lay motionless on the floor, not far from the disassembled droid that could have saved him.

It was over for the boy, Maul saw. Eogan's eyes were still open, but their whites were already beginning to glaze. His lips were slightly parted, as if he'd still been trying to say something, make some final pronouncement or plea, when the charges had finally gone off in his heart.

"Too bad." Radique shook his head. "Not that he didn't deserve it.

His father was a worthless waste of skin, and so was he." His raised his head back up to Maul. "Shall we continue our fight?"

Maul looked down at Eogan's body one last time. In the end, he felt no obligation to the boy himself; compassion and pity were as alien to him as they'd ever been. Yet Eogan had stood with him to the end, and something about his death needed to be set to rights.

He brought the lightsaber closer to Radique's throat. "This match is over."

Radique grinned. "Not yet."

Maul didn't see the blaster until it went off in Radique's hand. It was a pocket model, small enough that Radique must have been able to hide it in his sleeve. The shot caught Maul point-blank in the meat of his right shoulder, ripping through the muscle and knocking him backward into a wild sunburst pattern of his own blood.

"The lightsaber," Radique said. "Give it back to me. Now."

Maul tried to move his right arm, flexing his fingers. With the tissue and nerve damage in his shoulder, he was not at all sure that he could get the lightsaber out and cut Radique down before he fired again. At this distance, one shot was all he'd need.

"Suit yourself." Radique leveled the blaster at his face. "Then I'll take it off your corpse."

Maul saw his grip tighten on the weapon, the knuckle constricting visibly behind the trigger guard, and heard a sudden grunt as the boy sprang up from the floor and threw himself at Radique. The arms dealer hadn't seen him coming from that angle, and Eogan was fast enough to knock him flat, holding him to the floor while he groped for the blaster, twisting it around in his hand.

"No!" Radique snarled, trying to elbow him off and push him away without releasing the blaster. "No! *No!*"

The boy didn't bother wasting his breath, nor did he try to take the weapon from Radique. Jaw set, lips clamped tight, his bloody eyes fixed on the task at hand, Eogan simply kept twisting the blaster until Maul heard the bones in Radique's wrists crack, until the barrel was pointed straight back up at his face—

—and it went off in a single blinding flash.

Radique's head jerked sideways and disappeared in a cloud of blood and cranial matter that evacuated itself across the wall behind him. His corpse slumped sideways into a sagging pile, the boy pulling himself away from it, then drawing himself upward into a standing position, wiping his hands on his pants. He drew in a low, shuddering breath.

"So now . . ." He turned to Maul. "I guess we're even."

Maul glanced at the boy's chest, and Eogan shrugged. "In the medbay the first time, when my father and I tried to escape, the droid put a needle in my chest. It must have been enough to deactivate the charges."

"You knew?" Maul asked.

"I wanted to be sure." Eogan reached down and picked up the blaster from Radique's broken and stiffening fingers. "How's your shoulder?"

Maul said nothing, and the boy tilted his chin upward, glancing abruptly behind him. That was when Maul became aware, suddenly, of another presence standing in the door of the medbay, watching them. Her arrival had eluded him until this very second, but now he recognized it fully.

"Komari Vosa." The name twisted from his lips like a curse. "You have come."

72

STICK IT OUT

"Maul," Vosa said, stepping into the medbay with a glance at the arms dealer's body and the boy standing over it. "Am I interrupting something?"

Ignoring the question, Maul glanced at the curve-handled lightsabers that hung from her belt. "You wear your heritage on your hips."

"Not my heritage," she said. "My livelihood."

"My Master specifically ordained for us to meet," Maul said. A new species of tension was taking shape in his chest, filling his lungs and spreading outward into his extremities as the fullness of the dark side made itself manifest. "We have business, you and I."

Vosa stood her ground, feet planted, face attentive, body poised to strike. "The only business that we have is your imminent destruction."

Charging at her, he sprang up, swinging his lightsaber in a swooping hum to meet her in midleap. Vosa was ready for him, and their blades clashed together, her initial defensive pose absorbing the momentum of the attack and pushing him backward. From the corner of his eye, Maul saw Eogan raise Radique's blaster pistol, and before he could utter a word, Vosa stretched out her hand and knocked it from his grasp with a burst of Force push, slamming the boy to the floor.

"Stay out of this," she told him. "You'll—"

The room reverberated with a massive, crackling boom, followed by a series of low-level aftershocks. It was as if Cog Hive Seven, having lost interest in all the routine reconfigurations, was now determined to shake off entire layers of itself.

"Wait," Maul said. "I summoned you here to take possession of a weapon. Not to—"

But Vosa was moving again, whirling backward, spinning and evading, and no matter how he tried to defend against her, his blade met open air. The awareness of what she was doing, drawing on the Force and her own repulsive relationship with it, only made him more determined to end this battle decisively.

"You're weak," she goaded him, dropping back and making him come to her. "Your right arm is slowing you down. Even your weapon is betraying you."

Maul kept coming, relying more and more on his left arm, saving the right for when he'd need it most. But Vosa seemed to anticipate everything he was doing, dropping low and then springing up and outward into an open space along a row of diagnostic machinery in the corner of the medbay.

Maul's lower lip drew back to reveal his teeth. If defeating Vosa was what he needed to do in order to get the weapon in the hands of the Gora, so be it. Gripping the lightsaber's hilt, he squared his shoulders and swung again, thrusting his blade at her in a series of perfectly angled slashes. Vosa came back at him on the offense, both blades spinning.

"Jar'Kai," Maul snarled, deflecting her assault on reflex. "Predictable." He swung the lightsaber down, but at that moment the corridor shook again, jerking sideways, throwing them both off. Vosa recovered first, darting back, again too quick, and the speed with which she evaded his attack only inflamed the rage inside Maul's mind, stoking his wrath until it crystallized into a kind of malignant grace.

Now he gripped the lightsaber in both arms, forcing his damaged right arm into service and gripping the hilt of his saber with his full strength. It was time for Juyo, the Way of the Vornskr—the last of the Seven Forms. He seized upon it eagerly, allowing himself to be swept up in the chaotic frontal assault of thrusts, slashes, and jabs.

"Maul—" A tremor of new fear pulsed across Vosa's face, disrupting her composure, as if she'd finally recognized the true ferocity of his purpose.

Darting backward into a desperate evasive measure, Vosa whirled one of her blades behind her, hacking loose a massive shelf of surgical instruments from its place on the wall, and with a swing of the hand she used a Force push to fire them at him in a glinting storm of steel.

Maul ducked the flying instruments and bobbed back up with a silent snarl. In his mind, the duel was all but over—his opponent was now dragging out the inevitable moment of defeat in a series of small humiliations. By turning to such diversionary tactics, Vosa had all but admitted that she was no match for the erratic staccato blows that he was delivering, seemingly from everywhere, all at once.

Kill her. Kill her now. Then you may deliver the weapon to any of the Bando Gora who remain.

Pivoting easily, he swung out at her, the dark side streaming so powerfully from him now that it seemed to be pouring forth in great, explosive torrents. His blade was moving almost too fast to see, cutting great fan-shaped swaths in the air around him. All around them, the whole world seemed to be blowing itself to pieces.

Vosa went low, swinging out one leg in a last, fruitless attempt to catch him off balance, and he brought the lightsaber down in a great, hungry arc, holding off just long enough to savor the expression on her face.

"Now. Plead for your life."

"Sorry." She tilted her chin up at him, wiped the blood from her lip, and grinned. "You're going to have to try a lot harder than that."

Before he could respond, she rammed the top of her skull into his shoulder, head-butting the open wound. A rocket of white-hot fury sizzled inside Maul's forebrain, all but obliterating conscious thought. He let out a roar and prepared to finish her off.

That was when the floor erupted beneath them, the alloy plates bursting open to reveal something so vast and incomprehensible that Maul didn't recognize it until it tried to bite his leg off.

With a jolt of shock, he saw that the thing that had exploded upward had already taken his foot into the hideous suction cup of its mouth.

The worm.

Its appearance here provided Komari Vosa the last opportunity she needed to right herself and make her escape, leaping upward and then bounding off the wall console behind her.

Coward, a voice shouted from inside Maul's brain, *weakling, Jedi scum. It is exactly like your kind to flee at the first sign of—*

In that split second, the thought broke off as he realized that she wasn't running away.

She was coming at the worm.

73

THE WRECKERS

Lightsabers alive and oscillating in front of her, Vosa landed astride the thing, her feet finding their balance with preternatural ease, hacking downward through the upper part of its head.

Down below, Maul yanked himself from the worm's mouth, scrambling back to right himself. He heard a cry, and looked over his shoulder to see that the thing, in all its massive weight and appetite, had turned, writhing sidelong to pin Vosa beneath it.

The worm turns, and there are always more bones.

It was coiling the full extent of its hideous body in an attempt to simultaneously hold her down and devour her. On the far side of the medbay, Eogan was struggling to fire on it with the blaster that he'd taken from Radique's hands, but none of that was going to have any effect on what was happening to Komari Vosa.

The worm was going to eat her alive.

Maul met Vosa's eyes. Yet even now, he saw, in what was surely her final moment of life, there was no surrender in her response, no hint of fear in the way she fought it. Watching her, Maul felt a realization stirring beneath the rage to which he'd given himself over, an unfamiliar sense of connection, primitive and undeniable.

She was no Jedi.

She was no Sith.

She was something completely other, and the idea of giving this worm the privilege of ending her life now was not to be tolerated, not by Maul, not today.

He charged at it, the makeshift lightsaber swinging sideways in both hands as he thrust it directly into the thing's gaping maw, then planted his feet and spun the blade in a 360-degree arc. His right arm felt like it was on fire. His right shoulder was screaming at him. He ignored it, sweeping the saber around again, carving the very teeth from its mouth, slashing at the mandibles from the inside, then spinning it the other way until he'd chopped the mouthparts themselves to ribbons.

The effect was immediate. With a piercing scream that Maul heard both in his mind and in his ears, the worm spasmed and slashed its tail, rolling sideways, as if bewildered by the fact that—after everything that had happened—it had somehow been bested.

At last it fell still.

Maul staggered backward, dragging himself from the thing's maw, and saw Komari Vosa staring at him, hollow-eyed, from the other side of the medbay. She looked exhausted but triumphant.

"You did that." Reaching up, she shoved the blood-soaked hair from her brow and gave him a wicked grin. "You killed it."

Maul said nothing. His gaze traveled from the great dead bulk of the worm to where Eogan Truax was standing, and he remembered what he had forgotten.

"It doesn't matter."

She frowned at him. "Why?"

"There are electrostatic charges implanted in both of my hearts," Maul told her. "They're going to go off at any second."

"But—"

"I'm going to die in this place." He glanced at the crate on the far side of the medbay. "The material for the weapon is in there. Take it." Something tightened in the pit of his stomach, and he turned from her, walking toward the hatchway. "In giving it to you, I will be accomplishing the will of my Master."

"Wait," she said, moving toward him cautiously, hands raised. "What do you mean, an electrostatic charge?"

"There is nothing you can do."

"Maul, stop."

Something in her voice froze him in the doorway.

"I see now that I was wrong to attack you. When you stated that you wanted to deliver a weapon into our hands, I anticipated an ambush—some kind of trap." Her voice faltered slightly. "I am not used to extending such trust."

Maul said nothing.

"I am a Force user, you know," Vosa's voice said, and he could tell from the sound of her voice that she was drawing nearer to him. "Maybe there's something I could do after all."

74

DIASTOLE

When Vosa's hands reached out to touch his chest, Maul had to fight back an instinctive desire to lash out and knock her away.

"Don't move," she said, eyes closed. "If this is going to work, I need to see inside."

He forced himself to hold still, jaw clenched, arms rigid at his sides. He could feel his hearts pounding together in unison, cardiac muscle contracting, ventricles paddling their way through a sea of leftover adrenaline from their battle as they counted down the final helpless seconds of his life.

But now there was something else inside him, too, a subtle, probing presence that he identified as a telekinetic representation of Vosa herself winding its way through the chambers of his heart.

"What are you—" Eogan asked from behind her.

"Quiet." She waited, and glanced at Maul. "Hold your breath."

Through gritted teeth, Maul said: "Why?"

"Because everything moves when you breathe, and I've only got one shot at this." Raising one hand slightly, she spread her fingers and then brought them together as if taking hold of some invisible object. "Your hearts are always in motion. I've got less than a second when all four chambers are at rest."

Maul felt a bright shock of pain cut through his left chest. He fought the urge to react—it took every ounce of willpower that he had—and then it was gone.

Vosa opened her eyes and looked at him. "That's it."

"Whoa," Eogan said, sounding impressed. "How did you do that? You're sure you got them both?"

"No," Vosa said, "but if I'm wrong, we'll all know soon enough." She glanced at the crate on the floor of the medbay. "Come on, let's move this thing out of here before another one of us ends up dead."

The journey back to the hangar was largely uneventful. Carrying the crate between the three of them, with Eogan helping to compensate for Maul's steadily weakening right arm, they made good time. Only once did they come across any sign of life—a small-scale standoff in the prison's metal shop between a heavily armed group of new inmates and the last remaining guards. From what Maul could see, the guards were winning, but only because they knew the terrain. He watched without any particular interest as two of the corrections officers ambushed one of the inmates from behind and tossed him into one of the huge steel baling and shredding machines. The prisoner didn't have time to scream.

Beneath him, the floors of Cog Hive Seven gave a sudden galvanic lurch. The familiar clamor of clockwork began to reverberate through the walls.

"What was that?" Vosa asked from her end of the crate.

Maul and Eogan exchanged a single glance. Then Eogan nodded her onward. "It means we have to hurry."

By the time they got to the corridor outside the hangar, the walls were peeling apart, sliding sideways and slamming together in an ill-fated attempt to align themselves into new levels and layers. The slamming and scraping noises down here were close to deafening. Vosa kept throwing wild glances around her as they stepped over the gaps opening up in the floor around them. In every direction, the great metal landscape was racked by constant, erratic shuddering.

"Is this normal?" she shouted.

Eogan ducked as a massive sheet of steel flew past his head, spiraling in midair and imbedding itself in the opposite wall. "Nothing's normal here," the boy muttered. "The sooner we're out of here, the better."

Maul trained his eyes on the corridor ahead. As preoccupied as he was with getting the crate aboard the Bando Gora's ship, there was no mistaking the fact that this reconfiguration was different—that gears and sprockets of Cog Hive Seven were bent on ripping themselves to shreds. Whether this was some kind of automated self-destruct mode or simply the inevitable outcome of the matching algorithm run amok, he neither knew nor cared. They were running out of time.

Then he realized something else was happening as well.

The walls were closing in.

He spied the docking port and moved faster, forcing Eogan and Vosa into a near-run to keep pace.

"Going somewhere?" a voice behind them asked.

Maul's head snapped around to see the fully projected hologram of Jabba poised on his repulsor platform, leering back at them like the last lord of creation. Standing directly in front of the hologram, Maul could see a Trandoshan mercenary, a blaster rifle gripped in his hands. The mercenary leveled the weapon at them until the blaster's barrel became a perfect, staring O.

"I see you've made a friend," Jabba said, nodding at Vosa. "Sewage always sinks to meet the lowest level. Why am I not surprised?" He didn't wait for their reply. "What's in the crate?"

"None of your concern," Maul said. "We're leaving with it."

"Leaving?" The Hutt chortled and cast a glance at the walls of the hangar. "No, I think you'll be staying here. I like the idea of seeing you and your new companions being crushed to a pulp inside this metal coffin."

Vosa's hands went to her lightsabers. "Last chance, Jabba."

"Not this time, scum." With a grimace, the Hutt gestured, the repulsor platform pivoting around, and the Trandoshan opened fire.

Maul was already moving. Dropping his end of the crate, he leapt forward, activating his lightsaber midair, and executed a weightless Ataru-style spin, ducking the volley of blasterfire and swinging the blade in an arc at the Trandoshan's neck. The blow decapitated his opponent so swiftly that, for a moment, the mercenary's headless body remained erect at the edge of the floating platform before tumbling off, disappearing into a gap that had just opened below them.

Jabba's eyes rolled up to meet Maul's. The crime lord was saying something, but the words were blocked out by the bleating cacophony of mechanical noises, and it hardly mattered anyway. With an offhand swing of one arm, the Hutt indicated the docking berth.

Maul jumped back down to where Eogan and Vosa were waiting, and together they carried the crate up the gangway toward the port where Jabba's ship, the *Star Jewel,* was ready for departure.

75

500 REPUBLICA

The lights were dimmed for the evening, and Palpatine emerged from his shower, freshly toweled and draped in a Dramasian shimmersilk robe, to find Hego Damask seated in the dressing room, waiting for him.

"Master." The senator paused in his tracks, his slippered feet coming to rest on the richly brocaded rug. "Welcome." The unheralded appearance of the Muun here in his apartment, at this hour of the night, caught Palpatine off guard, even as he was forced to admit that Damask, as Lord Plagueis, had been in his unconscious thoughts for some time. "This is an unexpected pleasure."

Plagueis nodded. "There are times when those seem to be the only pleasures left," he replied cryptically, and then waved the thought away. "But never mind that. You must forgive me the melancholy ruminations, Lord Sidious, even as you forgive the uninvited visit."

"Any visit from you is welcome."

"Even now?" the Muun inquired. "Under these circumstances?"

Sidious gazed at him for a moment before nodding. "Ah," he said. "You refer to the recent developments on Cog Hive Seven. Yes. I've been informed."

"There *is* no Cog Hive Seven any longer, it seems," Plagueis replied ruminatively. "At this point all scanners report nothing but a loose metallic debris field somewhere in the Outer Rim."

"As requested."

"Indeed," the Muun agreed. "Apparently the entire space station ripped itself to shreds . . ." He paused, meeting Sidious's gaze. "Immediately after the departure of your apprentice. And he did complete his mission perfectly, did he not?"

"Yes," Sidious said with a nod.

"According to our initial bioscans, there were no survivors," Plagueis said, almost gently. "Including your primary target, Iram Radique."

Sidious stared at the Muun for a long, searching moment, wondering if there was something else beneath Plagueis's words, an entire substratum of meaning that he'd overlooked until now. Had Plagueis begun to guess at his true purpose in sending Maul to Cog Hive Seven? How would he react to the revelation of what had happened in those final moments, if he ever found out that the Bando Gora had been there and taken possession of the nuclear device whose procurement had been his ultimate goal there?

Yet Plagueis was apparently already moving on to other things.

"As you have already learned," he said, "the Force has a purpose and will for all things that even you and I have only now begun to discover. By exploiting its fullness, we stand to inherit untold power and glory." Plagueis paused. "Together."

Sidious said nothing for a long moment. Then he nodded. "Very well," he said, and then, with some difficulty, managed an indulgent smile. "Although I cannot help feeling that in some way, by risking the possibility of exposure, I have failed you as well."

"Have you?" Plagueis regarded him inscrutably. "It seems early to make such a sweeping condemnation." Then, with a slow exhalation of air that signaled the conversation was over, he rose to his feet. "It is late, Senator Palpatine, and I know that your hours of privacy and leisure are becoming increasingly limited, so I'll show myself out." His yellow eyes gleamed. "We'll speak again soon."

He left Sidious standing in his dressing room. It was a long time before the Sith Lord moved again, stepping away from the place where he'd been standing, and going to seal the hatch of the dressing room, closing himself inside.

76

AFTERIMAGE

In the cargo hold, Maul squatted in the corner, staring protectively at the crate in front of him. He could feel the lethal warmth and vitality of the weaponized uranium, and knew that its deliverance here into the hands of Komari Vosa meant that he had been successful. But it meant little to him.

Although he been released from Cog Hive Seven, the electrostatic charges deactivated and dislodged from his hearts, some part of him still felt caged.

He had not yet heard from his Master.

Rising to his feet, he paced the length of the hold, turned, and walked back again, his eyes never leaving the crate. Until such time as Darth Sidious came to him directly to commend him on the success of his mission, he remained restless and pensive.

The hull of the *Star Jewel* trembled slightly around him, its great engines gnashing their way from the Tharin sector through the Sisar Run on its way back to Hutt space, where Maul would part ways with Eogan, Komari Vosa, and the weapon itself.

From there, the future was uncertain. He was acutely aware of Sidious's instructions not to reveal himself as a Sith Lord or rely upon the Force.

Unless . . .

No. There could be no mistaking the message. Sidious had intended for him to unleash the full strength of the dark side, and the final moments in the prison—with the worm, with Vosa herself—had been another test, in which he only hoped he'd proven himself worthy.

So why hadn't Sidious come to him yet? And when would he hear from his Master again?

He began to pace the hold again, then stopped at the sound of the hatchway hissing open behind him.

"Maul."

Spinning, he dropped his hand to the hilt of his lightsaber, where it remained, even as he recognized the face of the woman emerging from the shadows.

"What do you want?"

At first Vosa didn't answer. It was impossible to say what she was looking at. From the angle of her head, Maul assumed that her attention was fixated on the crate he'd been guarding . . . although she might have been looking at him.

"Just checking on our cargo."

Maul didn't move. There seemed to be no appropriate reply to this comment, and he gave none.

"Jabba's chef is preparing dinner in the galley," Vosa said. "I'm fairly sure that he won't poison us . . . but we should let the boy eat first." Then, venturing a step nearer: "You *do* eat, don't you?"

Maul glared at her, held up one hand. "That's close enough."

"He worships you, you know. The boy. What he saw you do back there—"

"The galaxy will harden him soon enough," Maul said. "If it doesn't kill him first."

"Perhaps you should take him with you. As an apprentice."

Maul eyed her speculatively. "What would you know about apprentices?"

"Nothing," Vosa said in a quiet voice, and then gave a vague, noncommittal nod in the direction of the crate. "I don't need to know the details of your mission on Cog Hive Seven. I know that your mission there was in service to a sovereign purpose far beyond yourself."

"As was yours," Maul said. He'd expected her to deny it, to assert that the Bando Gora served only their own purposes, but Vosa actually nodded again.

"Perhaps that's so," she said. "Yet when I look at you, and the way that you and I fought that worm together, I can't help but wonder . . ."

"Don't," he growled.

"I only meant to say—" She faltered, weighing her words carefully. "We're neither of us the people that we once were. Who's to say where we might end up?"

Maul flicked his gaze in her direction, his yellow eyes meeting hers for a fraction of a second. What he felt there, that uncanny familiarity, felt more dangerous and potentially ensnaring than it had back on Cog Hive Seven, and he dismissed it at once.

"How long until we arrive?"

"You're impatient?"

Maul dismissed it. "Simply ready to put this business behind me."

"I see." Vosa smiled at his tone, as if she'd expected nothing less. "Not long now."

"Then leave me."

"Perhaps I'll see you up above?"

But Maul had already turned his back on her to stare down at the crate in the corner of the hold. It wasn't until he heard her leave and the hatch seal shut behind her that he took his eyes off the crate and turned to glance back at the door through which she'd already disappeared.

ABOUT THE AUTHOR

JOE SCHREIBER is the author of several novels, including *Star Wars: Red Harvest, Star Wars: Death Troopers, Chasing the Dead, Au Revoir, Crazy European Chick,* and *Perry's Killer Playlist.* He was born in Michigan but spent his formative years in Alaska, Wyoming, and Northern California. He lives in central Pennsylvania with his wife and two children.

Read on for an excerpt from

Honor Among Thieves

by James S. A. Corey
Published by Del Rey Books

From the Imperial Core to the outflung stars of the Rim, the galaxy teemed with life. Planets, moons, asteroid bases, and space stations peopled with a thousand different species, all of them busy with the great ambitions of the powerful and also with the mundane problems of getting through their days, the ambitions of the Emperor all the way down to where to eat the next meal. Or whether there would be a next meal. Each city and town and station and ship had its own histories and secrets, hopes and fears and half-articulated dreams.

But for every circle of light—every star, every planet, every beacon and outpost—there was vastly more darkness. The space between stars was and always would be unimaginably huge, and the mysteries that it hid would never be wholly discovered. One bad jump was all it took for a ship to be lost. Unless there was a way to reach out for help, to say *Here I am. Come find me,* an escape pod or a ship or a fleet could vanish into the places between places that even light took a lifetime to reach.

And so a rendezvous point could be the size of a solar system, and the rebel fleet could still hide there like a flake in a snowstorm. Hundreds of ships, from cobbled-together, plasma-scorched cruisers and thirdhand battleships to X- and Y-wings and everything in between. They flew through space together silently, drifting closer in or farther apart as the need arose. Repair droids crawled over the skins of the ships, welding back together the wounds of their last battles, sure in the knowledge that they were the needle in the Empire's haystack.

Their greatest danger wasn't the enemy, but inaction. And the ways a certain kind of man coped with it.

"I wasn't cheating," Han Solo said as Chewbacca bent to pass through the door in the bulkhead. "I was playing better than they were."

The Wookiee growled.

"That's how I was playing better. It's not against the rules. Besides, what are they going to buy with their money out here?"

A dozen fighter pilots marching past in dirty orange-and-white uniforms saluted them. Han nodded to each one as he passed. They were an ugly bunch: middle-aged men who should have been back home on a planet somewhere spending too much time at the neighborhood bar and weedy boys still looking forward to their first wispy mustaches. Warriors for freedom, and terrible sabacc players.

Chewbacca let out a long, low groan.

"You wouldn't," Han said.

Chewbacca's blue eyes met his, and the Wookiee's silence was more eloquent than anything he might have said aloud.

"Fine," Han retorted. "But it's coming out of your cut. I don't know when you went soft on me."

"Han!"

Luke Skywalker came jogging down a side corridor, his helmet under his arm. Two droids followed him: the squat, cylindrical R2-D2 rolling along, chirping and squealing; and the tall, golden C-3PO trotting along at the back, waving gold-chrome hands as if gesticulating in response to some unheard conversation. The kid's face was flushed and his hair was dark with sweat, but he was grinning as if he'd just won something.

"Hey," Han said. "Just get back from maneuvers?"

"Yep. These guys are great. You should have seen the tight spin and recover they showed us. I could have stayed out there for hours, but Leia called me back in for some kind of emergency meeting."

"Her Worshipfulness called the meeting?" Han asked as they turned down the main access corridor together. The smell of welding torches and coolant hung in the air. Everything about the Rebel Alliance smelled like a repair bay. "I thought she was off to her big conference on Ki-amurr."

"She was supposed to be. I guess she postponed leaving."

The little R2 droid squealed, and Han turned to it. "What's that, Artoo?"

C-3PO, catching up and giving a good impression of leaning forward to catch his breath even though he didn't have lungs, translated: "He's saying that she's postponed her departure twice. It's made a terrible shambles of the landing docks."

"Well, that's not good," Han said. "Anything that keeps her from sitting around a big table deciding the future of the galaxy . . . I mean, that's her favorite thing to do."

"You know that's not true," Luke said, making room in the passageway for a bronze-colored droid that looked as if it had barely crawled out of the trash heap. "I don't know why you don't like her more."

"I like her fine."

"You're always cutting her down, though. The Alliance needs good politicians and organizers."

"You can't have a government without a tax collector. Just because we'd both like it better if the Emperor wasn't in charge, it doesn't make me and her the same person."

Luke shook his head. The sweat was starting to dry, and his hair was getting some of its sandy color back.

"I think you two are more alike than you pretend."

Han laughed despite himself. "You're an optimist, kid."

When they reached the entrance to the command center, Luke sent the droids on, R2-D2 whistling and squeaking and C-3PO acting annoyed. The command center had taken a direct hit in the fighting at Yavin, and the reconstruction efforts still showed. New panels, blinding in their whiteness, covered most of one wall where the old ones had been shattered by the blast. Where the replacements ended, the old panels seemed even darker by contrast. The head-high displays marked the positions of the ships in the fleet and the fleet in the emptiness of the rendezvous point, the status of repair crews, the signals from the sensor arrays, and half a dozen other streams of information. None of the stations was staffed. The data spooled out into the air, ignored.

Leia stood at the front of the room, the bright repair work and grimy original walls seeming to come together in her. Her dress was black with embroidery of gold and bronze, her hair a soft spill gathered at the nape of her neck in a style that made her seem both more mature and more powerful than had the side buns she'd worn on the Death Star. From what Han had heard around the fleet, losing Alderaan had made her older and harder. And as much as he hated to admit it, she wore the tragedy well.

The man she was talking to—Colonel Harcen—had his back to them, but his voice carried just fine. "With respect, though, you have to see that not all allies are equal. Some of the factions that are going to be on Kiamurr, the Alliance would be better off without."

"I understand your concerns, Colonel," Leia said in a tone that didn't sound particularly understanding. "I think we can agree, though, that the Alliance isn't in a position to turn away whatever help we can get. The Battle of Yavin was a victory, but—"

Harcen raised a palm, interrupting her. He was an idiot, Han thought. "There are already some people who feel that we have become too lax in the sorts of people we're allowing into our ranks. In order to gain respect, we must be free of undesirable elements."

"I agree," Han said. Colonel Harcen jumped like a poked cat. "You've got to keep the scum out."

"Captain Solo," Harcen said. "I didn't see you there. I hope I gave no offense."

"No. Of course not," Han said, smiling insincerely. "I mean, you weren't talking about *me*, were you?"

"Everyone is very aware of the service you've done for the Alliance."

"Exactly. So there's no reason you'd have been talking about me."

Harcen flushed red and made a small, formal bow. "I was not talking about you, Captain Solo."

Han sat at one of the empty stations, stretching his arms out as if he were in a cantina with a group of old friends. It might have been an illusion, but he thought he saw a flicker of a smile on Leia's lips.

"Then there's no offense taken," he said.

Harcen turned to go, his shoulders back and his head held high. Chewbacca took a fraction of a second longer than strictly needed to step out of the man's way. Luke leaned against one of the displays, his weight warping it enough to send little sprays of false color through the lines and curves.

When Harcen was gone, Leia sighed. "Thank you all for coming on short notice. I'm sorry I had to pull you off the training exercises, Luke."

"It's all right."

"I was in a sabacc game," Han said.

"I'm *not* sorry I pulled you out of that."

"I was winning."

Chewbacca chuffed and crossed his arms. Leia's expression softened a degree. "I was supposed to leave ten standard hours ago," she said, "and I can't stay much longer. We've had some unexpected developments, and I need to get you up to speed."

"What's going on?" Luke asked.

"We aren't going to be able to use the preliminary base in Targarth system," she said. "We've had positive identification of Imperial probes."

The silence only lasted a breath, but it carried a full load of disappointment.

"Not *again*," Luke said.

"Again." Leia crossed her arms. "We're looking at alternatives, but until we get something, construction and dry-dock plans are all being put on hold."

"Vader's really going all-out to find you people," Han said. "What are your backup plans?"

"We're looking at Cerroban, Aestilan, and Hoth," Leia told him.

"That's the bottom of the barrel," Han said.

For a second, he thought she was going to fight, but instead she only looked defeated. He knew as well as she did that the secret rebel base was going to be critical. Without a base, some kinds of repair, manufacturing, and training work just couldn't be done, and the Empire knew that, too. But Cerroban was a waterless, airless lump of stone hardly better than the rendezvous point, and one that was pounded by asteroids on a regular basis. Aestilan had air and water, but rock worms had turned the planetary mantle so fragile that there were jokes about digging tunnels just by jumping up and down. And Hoth was an ice ball with an equatorial zone that only barely stayed warm enough to sustain human life, and then only when the sun was up.

Leia stepped to one of the displays, shifting the image with a flicker of her fingers. A map of the galaxy appeared, the immensity of a thousand million suns disguised by the fitting of it all onto the same screen.

"There is another possibility," she said. "The Seymarti system is near the major space lanes. There's some evidence that there was sentient life on it at some point, but our probes don't show anything now. It may be the place we're looking for."

"That's a terrible idea," Han said. "You don't want to do that."

"Why not?" Luke asked.

"Ships get lost in Seymarti," Han said. "A lot of ships. They make the jump to hyperspace, and they don't come back out."

"What happens to them?"

"No one knows. Something that close to the lanes without an Imperial garrison on it can be mighty appealing to someone who needs a convenient place to not get found, but everyone I know still steers clear of that place. *Nobody* goes there."

Luke patted his helmet with one thoughtful hand. "But if nobody goes there, how can a lot of ships get lost?"

Han scowled. "I'm just saying the place has a bad reputation."

"The science teams think there may be some kind of spatial anomaly that throws off sensor readings," Leia said. "If that's true, and we can find a way to navigate it ourselves, Seymarti may be our best hope for avoiding Imperial notice. As soon as Wedge Antilles is back from patrol, he's going to put together an escort force for the survey ships."

"I'd like to go with him," Luke said.

"We talked about that," Leia said. "Wedge thought it would be a good chance for you to get some practice. He's requested you as his second in command."

Luke's smile was so bright, Han could have read by it. "Absolutely," the kid said.

The communications panel beside Leia chimed. "Ma'am, we've kept the engines hot, but if we don't leave soon, we're going to have to recalibrate the jump. Do you want me to reschedule your meetings again?"

"No. I'll be right there," she said, and turned the connection off with an audible click.

Han leaned forward. "It's all right, I see how I fit in here," he said. "The weapons run from Minoth to Hendrix is off. That's not a big deal. I'll just bring the guns here instead. Unless you want the *Falcon* to go along with the kid here."

"Actually, that's not why I wanted to talk with you," Leia said. "Something else happened. Two years ago, we placed an agent at the edge of Imperial space. The intelligence we've gotten since then has been some of the most valuable we've seen, but the reports stopped seven months ago. We assumed the worst. And then yesterday, we got a retrieval code. From the Saavin system. Cioran."

"That's not the *edge* of Imperial space," Han said. "That's the middle of it."

Chewbacca growled and moaned.

"It's not what I would have picked, either," Leia said. "There was no information with it. No context, no report. We don't know what happened between the last contact and now. We just got the signal that we should send a ship."

"Oh," Han said with a slowly widening grin. "No, it's all right. I get it. I absolutely understand. You've got this important guy trapped in enemy territory, and you need to get him out. Only with the Empire already swarming like a hive of Bacian blood hornets, you can't risk using anyone but the best. That about right?"

"I wouldn't put it that way, but it's in the neighborhood of right, yes," Leia said. "The risks are high. I won't order anyone to take the assignment. We can make it worth your time if you're willing to do it."

"You don't have to order us, does she, Chewie? All you have to do is ask, and we're on the job."

Leia's gaze softened a little. "Will you do this, then? For the Alliance?"

Han went on as if she hadn't spoken. "Just say *please* and we'll get the *Millennium Falcon* warmed up, skin out of here, grab your guy, and be back before you know it. Nothing to it."

Leia's expression went stony. "Please."

Han scratched his eyebrow. "Can I have a little time to think about it?"

The Wookiee made a low but rising howl and lifted his arms impatiently.

"Thank you, Chewie," Leia said. "There's also a real possibility that the whole operation was compromised and the retrieval code is bait in a trap. When you make your approach, you'll need to be very careful."

"Always am," Han said, and Luke coughed. "What?" Han demanded.

"You're always careful?"

"I'm always careful enough."

"Your first objective is to make the connection and complete the retrieval," Leia said. "If you can't do that, find out as much as you can about what happened and whether any of our people are in danger. But if you smell a trap, get out. If we've lost her, we've lost her. We don't want to sacrifice anyone else."

" 'Her'?"

Leia touched the display controls again, and the image shifted. A green security warning flooded it, and she keyed in the override. A woman's face filled the screen. High cheekbones, dark eyes and hair, V-shaped chin, and a mouth that seemed on the verge of smiling. If Han had seen her in a city, he'd have looked twice, but not because she was suspicious. The data field beside the picture listed a life history too complex to take in at a glance. The name field read: SCARLET HARK.

"Don't get in over your head," Leia said.

ABOUT THE TYPE

This book was set in Galliard, a typeface designed by Matthew Carter for the Mergenthaler Linotype Company in 1978. Galliard is based on the sixteenth-century typefaces of Robert Granjon.